THE
UNDERGROUND

SARA FRANCIS

Book 3 of *The Terra Testimonies*

PUBLISHING

READ THE
WHOLE TRILOGY

The Isles
The Mainland
The Underground

I dedicate this book to my grandparents. My inspirations for Stanley Wyght and his love for family and country.

In memory of Pop Pop and Grandma Raciti. No matter where you are, I feel the warmth of your love. Thank you for your support in this life and in the next. I look forward to seeing you again.

To Grandpa and Grandma Koshofer. My fans, my advocates, and my inspiration. The stories you continue to share with me always fill me with joy, laughter, and awe. With my books, I hope to return the favor. I love you both.

WE ARE ORGANIZED CHAOS.
WE WILL FIX HUMANITY.

LIBERTY OR DEATH

TIMELINE OF IMPORTANT EVENTS
(following the ages of the Hodgins Triplets)

0
- Shane, Mark, and Aymie Hodgins are born
- Marcellus betrays the Order of Xenophon (OX) and Titans Nikita Patya and Walter Jarvis

1
- Nikita sends Masdit and Gerrior to kill Marcellus and the triplets. The triplets are separated.

7
- Carl Mallory creates the first Mutants: Jordan the Slowloris and Theo the Shrew

14
- Shane and Mark meet in New York City
- Aymie escapes captivity and is taken by Stanley Wyght to Wyght's Home for Young People (WHYP)
- Masdit and Gerrior abduct Mark who is rescued by Thyme and brought to WHYP

15
- The triplets are reunited at WHYP
- Sonny Wilcox joins the WHYP family to offer intel about the Order of Xenophon
- Mark erases the Order of Xenophon's virtual presence

16
- Joshua Wolfrum leaves for his mission as a spy within the Order of Xenophon
- Nikita and Walter attack WHYP, abducting hundreds of children

17
- Nikita Patya and Walter Jarvis found the Isles in secret

18
- Project Resist, Rescue, Protect, Retake (RRPR) is launched
- Mr. Nik rescues the Alexus children from death and brings them to the Isles
- Alison Alexus becomes the first Bionic

20
- RRPR faces off with Titan PH in Fargo
- Mark leaves for the Isles
- Mark and Aaron pass the Commencement Test
- Sami and her best friends are Spliced into Mutants by Carl Mallory

24
- Titan PH destroys RRPR's base in the Battle of North Dakota

25
- The Isles Meeting begins
- RRPR reunites at the Underground with Interpreter Director Virginia Michaelson
- Mark, the Isle Members, and RRPR fight against Mr. Nik and Wally in the Battle of the Isles

THE ACCIDENT'S CLIMAX

PROLOGUE

Shannon: i

Hello Terran,

If you're reading this, you're a survivor who has found and read/ heard our previous testimonies from the Isles and the Mainland. However, allow me—Royal Strategist Shannon Hollinger—to review so the following letters from the Underground do not confuse you terribly. If you need further explanation outside of this preface, we wrote a timeline for you and a list of the nine Officers and eight Isle members for you to reference.

As you know, our world is at war. The treacherous Order of Xenophon (OX) has committed heinous acts of terrorism for years. They are a cult of chaos and must be stopped. The culmination of these attacks is called "the Accident" by survivors. The Order leveled cities, tore apart families, and brought the world to its knees.

A major resistance movement called Resist Rescue Protect Retake (RRPR) has fought back since the beginning. We have strong spirits, but are small in number. Our biggest saving grace has been our omniscient Weapon who gathers intel from his dreams. This Weapon—Blake Bain—keeps us one step ahead.

While the Accident (or the Cleanse as OX calls it) was devastating to the Mainland, it birthed something new. Something full of life. Something that could tear the Order down:

The Isles.

Built upon the islands of Hawaii, The Isles was a nesting ground where seven men raised children as weapons of war.

An Officer of RRPR—Mark Hodgins—lived on the Isles for five years.

THE UNDERGROUND

His purpose was to determine if the leaders of the Isles could become allies. We hoped to form a compact and work together to destroy the Order of Xenophon.

No alliance was forged. Mark and several Isle members—called the Seventeen—joined forces to overthrow their Headmaster Nikita Patya and Keeper Walter "Wally" Jarvis who were part of OX, but had no interest in taking the Order down. Rather, they wanted to overthrow it and dominate the world themselves.

With aid from the other RRPR Officers, the Battle of the Isles was won. Sadly, the Seventeen suffered devastating losses. The fallen included Zita, Harold, Cecil, Marlene, Ava, Usrula, Jeremy, and Becca. Our hearts still mourn the deaths of these young fighters.

Having watched these children fall, the remaining four Keepers opened their eyes to their evil and are now determined to do good. Currently, Keepers Mr. Allaway, Dr. Agro, Mr. Bamber, and Mr. Mallory are converting the Isles into safe havens for the Terrans we rescue on the Mainland: human, Bionic, and Mutant.

After the battle, the living members of the Seventeen have agreed to join us in taking down the Order of Xenophon: Alison, Axel, Sami, Aaron, Yared, Ethan, Lucas, and Donnie. For several weeks they travelled with us to our base: The Underground at Joint Base Lewis McChord in Washington state. This is the third base location for RRPR. The first was destroyed by Nikita Patya and his Keepers. The second was demolished by my rival: PH the Hermes Titan of the English Pandemonium. The man who disabled my youngest sister, Rachel. The man that I can *never* forgive.

During our travels, Royal Veterans (RV) Shane, Aymie, and Mark Hodgins told the Isle members their stories. They shared how they were separated at birth and found one another at Wyght's Home for Young People (WHYP). The triplets' tales intertwined with the other Officers' and mine and are filled with joys and sorrows. The Isle members learned more about us than we knew ourselves.

The most horrific part of the triplets' stories were the acts of the Order of Xenophon which they experienced first hand. Mark encountered the cult the most (Sonny excluded since he is ex-OX). The RV Nerd was the one to destroy the cult's virtual presence around the same time Nikita Patya and Wally Jarvis founded the Isles.

Finally, the triplets shed light on the OX Traitor that RRPR hopes to form an accord with: their father, ex-Titan Marcellus Hodgins. We've been searching for him for years. We feel we're getting close.

With this background, The Isle members now have a burning hatred for OX and are even more determined to stop the evil at the source.

We at RRPR share this same purpose. Not only do we fight head on every day, we have a man on the inside.

Joshua Wolfrum—a Royal Umbrella from WHYP—has immersed himself deep into the cult. He has lived with them for seven years as a subordinate to the sadistic Titan PH. We lost contact with Joshua until I reached out to him a few months ago. Finally, we received the following letter which you're about to read.

Please note that two people are communicating with Joshua Wolfrum. Yared Prinz—Seer Commander of the Isles—agreed to write letters to Joshua with me, Shannon Hollinger, via encoded digital messaging on our electronic tablets. We decided to take turns reading and replying to Joshua's letters in order to keep up with them in a timely manner. Remember Joshua Wolfrum is writing from behind the walls of the Order of Xenophon while Yared and I are writing from the side of the Resistance: RRPR. I will get Joshua to also share a list of terms and acquaintances for you to reference.

Following this preface is Joshua's reply to my letter which simply asked how he was doing.

It's been a while since it was safe to contact our spy. Now we have run out of time and are taking our chances.

Godspeed and goodwill,

Shannon Hollinger
Royal Strategist of RRPR

P.S. Joshua sent his reference sheet after his first letter. I've placed them on 461.

THE UNDERGROUND

LETTER 1

Joshua: I

Dear Shannon,

I am paranoid.

Paranoid, paranoid, always paranoid. I never feel safe. I never feel comfortable. Each breath I take is another closer to my last... which is true for everyone but for me it's worse. They're onto me. I've tried blending in for so long that I'm standing out. They've noticed my existence. Their spider eyes have spotted me. They're getting ready to snatch me up and entangle me in their web.

But I won't let that happen.

Anyway, so that's how I've been so far, Shannon, thanks for asking. I'm glad to hear about these "Isle" people joining our team. If you really have enhanced humans then we might have this war already won. Between Blake's dreams and their invincibility, we'll be unstoppable.

Wow, I can't believe it's been seven years since we've officially caught up. I mean, I've seen you at those gruesome battles. My heart aches thinking about them. I'm haunted by every fight I took part of. In fact, last night my sleeping mind recalled the Battle of North Dakota when my Titan—PH—blew up the RRPR base. While I aided in the survival of many Resistance members, watching the deaths of my old comrades lingers in my subconscious.

My mind replayed the event in my latest nightmare. I think you need to hear this, Shannon. You never knew how your siblings and friends escaped PH's clutches.

Smoke billowed, guns blazed, and blood pooled on the snowy ground.

THE UNDERGROUND

Screams erupted from the lips of the RRPR soldiers as they were slaughtered by the Xenophonians.

And I participated in the carnage.

My heart broke with every bullet fired. I tried to miss intentionally, but the fields were so overcrowded that it couldn't be helped. Even though the soldiers of RRPR were my friends, I couldn't jeopardize my mission. *I am Wolf the faithful Xenophonian,* I repeated to myself. Wolf was my cover. He was who I've had to be for 7 years. I couldn't stop then.

An inhuman scream sliced through the noisy battlefield like a knife. I turned and watched as Nic the Mutant Gorilla dove into the back of Titan PH's beloved Challenger II tank. The Xenophonian was thrown to the ground; helpless as the Mutant smashed the metal beast.

My rank turned and fired at Nic and I had no choice but to do the same. The bullets never reached him. With clenched fists, the Mutant-man roared and leapt into our squad. I scurried backward like a mouse running from a cat. Nic swung his long beefy arms across his body, breaking the ribs and spines of my OX acquaintances. Sweat dripped down my back as I ran away as fast as I could, but Nic kept coming. I thought I was stuck in his line of attack, but then I realized.

He was chasing me.

Oh no, oh no. He doesn't remember who I am, I panicked as I turned a corner and hid behind a crate. I needed to stop fighting. I needed to get away. I pushed my glasses back onto my face and tried to think of a plan.

A chill went up my spine. My body tensed and I slowly looked up. Sharp white teeth stared down at me.

It was Nic.

"Hello, Wolf," he snarled. "I've been looking for you."

My heart flipped. I was certain I'd be killed by my friend, but then I saw the glint in his violet eyes.

He knew who I was.

My shoulders relaxed, but I had to keep an act going. "What do you want?" I croaked.

"Just do what you do best." He gripped my collar, scratching my OX brand with his nails. "Act." He dragged me through the scarlet snow as I kicked, screamed, and begged to be released.

Some of the Xenophonians stopped for a moment to watch the spectacle. Their confusion was apparent and the moment of pause gave RRPR an advantage.

Nic didn't stop there. He tore through a rank of Superior Xenophonians, tossing them left and right while still yanking me along. The soldiers regained their footing and surrounded us.

Which was exactly what Nic wanted.

He held me in the air by my collar and bellowed, "Another shot fired and this Xenophonian blows, taking all of you, me, and him to hell!"

Fear crossed the soldiers' faces and they lowered their guns.

Nic smirked. "Your Titan is practically dead," he lied with conviction. "I suggest you start pulling back your forces before we have a repeat of Fargo."

The Superior Xenophonians were more perplexed than afraid, so I played my part. "Save yourselves; I'm wired to explode!" I screamed. "Protect our Titan; fulfill the Order's mission. In the name of Xenophon!"

That last line caused all the Xenophonians within reach to twitch. Their minds were triggered by the phrase. Nic's command wasn't contrary to their nature; so they heeded. The forces subsided slightly and RRPR received a breather.

Nic dropped me to the ground, bent over, and whispered, "Thanks, man. It may not have stopped the whole battle, but this gives us a chance to get people to safety." He clasped a hand on my shoulder. "Stay strong. We'll see you again soon." With that, he ran off to rescue his soldiers.

I rose to my feet and was ready to run back into the fight when I heard it. The sweet melody of *Scarborough Fair*. My heart leapt and I ran. The last note faded into the air, the tank's turret turned, and—

I screamed and shot up in my bed. Cold sweat dripped off my body.

Like I said, the Battle of North Dakota haunts my dreams. Today marks five months since the event. You know the rest of the story, but my mind couldn't handle it last night. Tomorrow I'll probably dream of the painful ending when PH's tank fired.

So, let me get out of the past and back into the present. Today my spy/acting career is finally on an incline. After seven years, I think I'm actually getting somewhere. Allow me to shed some light on how my life is on the inside.

Oh, and I heard how you love descriptions, Shannon, so I'll do the best I can.

As you know, I'm part of the Hermes Division in the English Pandemonium which is run by Titan PH whom you all know and despise. We Hermes members wear many hats. We scout, deliver supplies, train newbies, and bring messages to Xenophonians across the world. While other members focus on particular tasks, I'm ordered to do anything and everything. Honestly, I feel like an intern. They say they're putting my "advanced skill set" to good use. Do you know what skill set they're talking about? Seriously. I have no idea. Somehow, they see potential in me, and PH gives me more responsibility.

I shouldn't complain. The closer I am to the Titan of the English Pandemonium, the easier it is to betray. Another thing I'll recall about the

Battle of North Dakota was his frustration at how many survived. It would've brought you joy. He was outraged the triplets escaped (and Nic the Mutant Gorilla dented his precious tank). My Titan is determined to bring the Hodginses in. But justice for OX against Marcellus and his children isn't his only MO. He's hiding something. Especially with the missions he's been assigned to.

I bet you want to know more about those. So, I think it's time I shut up with the introductions and let you share in my nightmare.

I sat up in my bed, trying to catch my breath. My dream was so lifelike; I still felt the cold snow beneath me and the scratches on my neck from Nic's nails. When the pain finally subsided, it was immediately replaced with the usual piercing buzzing and humming. I doubled over and routinely slammed my palms into my ears. *Wake up... Hermes... respond,* the Strange Voices whispered in my head amidst the radio static.

"Ready to heed," I growled.

The noise ceased, and I let out a long exhale. They say you get used to the communication methods, but I skipped the Entrance Ritual so I don't think I ever will. And that's okay. A small price to pay for remaining sane.

I crawled out of my rickety bed and grabbed the dirty uniform I had thrown in the corner. Pulling on the black combat pants, I thought over my objectives for the day. I was required by WHYP (and you, Shannon) to discover one new piece of information a week. After the RRPR battle, nothing's been too exciting.

To finish my uniform, I put on the black rimmed glasses I received at the start of my mission—designed by Powell Enterprises. The screens on the lenses glitched and shook before the usual greeting appeared: *Morning, Joshua! Let's get to it.*

Honestly, The glasses are super helpful. I forget a lot of the OX verbiage and this helps me not look stupid. Not to mention it also retains information I find. Its one flaw is only I can review the entries. Either Myles Jr. forgot to add a "send" function or it's too dangerous. He's a boy genius so I'm guessing it's the latter.

I looked through the glasses and at my reflection in the broken mirror hanging on the concrete wall. Staring into my dark eyes, I started my daily encouragement routine: *All right, Joshua,* I thought, *Another day like all the rest. Right now, you are no longer yourself. You are Wolf. The brutal Xenophonian. You are Wolf. You are Wolf.*

As an actor, you have to get yourself to play the part. I repeat this mantra each morning until my instincts take over. The moment I walk out of my cold concrete cell, I am no longer a spy. I am a loyal, heartless member of the Order of Xenophon.

Once my mind was replaced with Wolf's, I twitched my nose to turn the glasses off. I ruffled the curls atop my head and combed the buzzed portion from the top of my ears to the nape of my neck. I hated the bottom-shaved haircut, but Sonny claimed it looks more Xenophonian than my old combed style. Taking a deep breath, I stood up straight and marched out of my room to start the day.

Like always, it was a rush for food. The damp hallways were crowded with Xenophonians nudging each other to get ahead. An ocean of black engulfed me and I struggled to keep my head up to see where I was going. The crowd was frighteningly quiet. Normally there was grunting, yelling, or fighting. This morning I could only hear the shuffling of feet.

What's going on today? I wondered, looking around at the emotionless faces. I twitched my nose to turn my glasses on. *Did I miss something?* Sensing my vibration, the electronic glasses powered up and the usual time and day away from home appeared. No message warned me about something out of the ordinary. *Oh no, what do I not know?*

Pushing the worry out of my mind, I slipped through the soldiers and made my way to the mess hall. The sweet aroma of maple and eggs swirled through the air, making the cold, musty hall more tolerable. I have to tell you, Shannon, out of all the things OX does wrong, food is the only thing they do right. I happily waited in line to receive my share of bacon, eggs, and pancakes.

I was met by the familiar face of my favorite lunch lady. A brute of a woman. I'm not totally sure, but I think she is from the Ares division: our group of trained military/assassins. Her stature and attitude was like that of a bull. Her thick brown blemished face gets her mistaken for a man, but that doesn't bother her. She likes the power.

"Morning, Wolf," she greeted; her voice was hoarse and raspy (like usual).

"How are you, Emel?" I asked, holding out my plate.

She plopped the scrambled eggs onto it. "Eh, fine. My sisters and I fought again."

"About what?" I asked as I slid my tray over for the next item.

"Same old, same old," she replied. "I won though, so that's what matters." She chuckled and fixed the net that protected her thick brown hair which was shaved on the bottom. "So how is little PH doing? I heard he's been kind of grumpy since that fight with the Resistance in ND. His poor girl, Challenger, needs some work done."

"Yeah, he's doing okay, and I think his tank is fine," I replied. I tried not to talk about PH, but Emel would always bring him up. Despite working under him for seven years, seeing what he is capable of is frightening. Especially *after* we destroyed the base... "He's got something planned but none of us know what it is," I explained.

She clicked her tongs before diving into the tray of bacon. "That's how it always is though, Wolf, you know that. You don't know what you're doing until you're doing it. That's how it works." She dropped the crispy slices onto my plate and leaned over the counter. "But if you couldn't tell by your fellow Hermes, the next job is a big one." She winked and went on to serve the next Xenophonian.

I never liked the sound of that. I gripped my tray tighter and went to sit at my usual spot. The table was filthy from the previous Ares members who ate before their assignment. Taking a napkin, I wiped the food onto the floor and sat down.

As I ate, I looked around at my fellow members. They were cold stones that could not be moved. No one spoke. No one raised their eyes. I recognized many worried faces. Normally the newbies fresh out of the Entrance Ritual were the ones to act frightened not these Xenophonians. *Something has to be going on,* I thought, getting anxious.

Then, I heard it. The final verse of a familiar folk tune: *"Come to me my hand for to ask / for then you'll be a true love of mine."* Everyone froze and stared at the entryway. The song had ended and as if on cue, the Titan entered.

PH strode up to the counter with his long green scarf flowing behind him. Even though he wore it over his mouth, he could be heard loud and clear. While his British accent is rustic, his singing is silvery and melodic. The way he performed *Scarborough Fair* frightened and enraptured anyone that heard it. To add to his intimidation, a tall double edged sword was mounted on his back; its hilt hidden in his curly brown hair. Strong yet small hands were shoved deep into the pockets of his long black trench coat. "Emel, how are ya?" I heard him say.

"Fine, PH," she replied. "What're you up to today?"

"Just gettin' some breakfast," he said as she gave him his share (which was more than low Xenophonians received). "I'll see you this evenin'." He spun on his heel and walked to the tables.

And guess what he does next. You think he would walk on through to go to his Titan hall or something. Nope. You know where he sits?

Across from me.

"'ello, Wolf," he greeted, slamming his plate down.

I stared at him, speechless. The man who single handedly overthrew cities, pierced bodies into the sides of buildings, and murdered my friends from WHYP and RRPR sat across from me eating bacon and eggs. I've worked beneath him for seven years and I've barely gotten so much as eye contact.

"Uh, Wolf?" he said, waving his fork in front of my face.

I snapped out of it. "My apologies, Titan PH." I bowed my head.

"Relax, man, it's just PH," my Titan corrected.

I took a quiet breath and discreetly examined him. If you look closely, he doesn't appear to be a heartless brute. He has a soft childish face peppered with freckles. His eyes were bright... and two different colors. Heterochromatic.

I ceased my staring and continued eating quietly. Finally, the Titan cleared his throat and said, "I bet you're wonderin' why I'm sittin' 'ere with ya."

Please don't let him know, please don't let him know, my worried brain repeated over and over. On the outside, I remained as cool as Wolf would. "I am a little curious, yes," I replied confidently.

"Always a curious one, you," PH smirked. "You're the only one to ask me questions." He thought for a moment as his fork hung out of the side of his mouth. "In fact, you're the only one brave enough to even speak to me. Most are tremblin' 'cause I'm in the same room." He glanced over his shoulder at his Hermes subordinates who immediately looked away. PH chuckled and turned back to me. "That's why I like ya," he stated. "You don't fear to be punished for speakin' to a Titan out of turn or not."

That was not the response I expected to hear. Subconsciously, I rubbed the OX brand on the back of my neck. "Well, I'm definitely honored, sir," I replied, "but you didn't come here just for flattery."

"Right ya are," he verified, pointing to me. "You know our previous missions to take in Marcellus' offspring 'ave failed repeatedly. This cannot 'appen anymore. The Order of Xenophon is near the end of its first phase: the Cleanse. The three of them and Marcellus 'ave delayed us long enough. We need to stop 'em before they make it worse." He slid his tray away and rested his elbows on the table. "I need an extra pair of eyes or in your case, two pairs. I cannot give further details. But if you accept, I can guarantee you'll stick around longer than most." He jerked his head to those at the table next to us.

I looked over at their faces. They were Hermes who joined around the same time as me. If an individual didn't fulfill his/her duties as an OX member, they were supposedly reassigned, but we all know that's a lie. Those who are sent away are never seen or heard from again.

"So?" PH said, interrupting my thoughts. "What do ya think?"

I couldn't believe it. Seven years of suffering, lying, and deceiving him and now I'm offered to move up the ranks and possibly work alongside him. *This has to be a trick; this can't be real.* I wriggled my nose to turn my glasses back on. I looked over his vitals, looking for a twitch or clue to expose his lies.

I found none.

If he's telling the truth, I thought, *this could be my ticket to finally finding the weak spot of the Order of Xenophon.*

I let out a deep breath. "I'd be honored to work alongside you in bringing down Marcellus, his children, and the Resistance," I declared.

PH smiled, showing his white teeth. "The pleasure is all mine," he replied. He stood up and grabbed his tray. "Go through the rest of the week as usual. Act like you never saw me. We 'ave no missions scheduled. You and the other Hermes only 'ave training. I will reconvene with ya soon." Without another word, he turned, dropped his dirty dishes onto another table, and left.

Once the tail end of his scarf disappeared, all eyes turned to stare at me. They wanted to ask, but couldn't. Their minds were re-wired not to. That's something PH didn't know.

They're his puppets. I am not.

Still, I couldn't believe what was happening. Seven miserable years here was spent barely getting anywhere. Now, I might have a chance of working in the higher ranks and meeting the other Titans.

The ear piercing buzzing and humming returned in my head. *Breakfast... over*, the distorted voice announced. I couldn't put pressure on my head to stop it while I was in public. Showing weakness would reveal to the Xenophonians that I'm not like them. So, I accepted a migraine, shook off my thoughts, and went about the rest of my day numb to all around me.

That afternoon, I trained some newbies, worked out, did an in-house assignment, had dinner, and then went back to my room. I didn't go to the bar that day to meet up with some of my other acquaintances. I needed time to process the fact that after seven years it was finally time.

Time to begin the Order of Xenophon's downfall.

So, that's how my life's been so far, Shannon. I'm supposed to meet with PH quite soon, but the waiting is killing me. I'll let you know what he says. I can't wait to hear from you and this new kid, Yared, right? Very happy that an Isles member agreed to help you with this.

Also, congratulations on your engagement to Shane! I am so happy for you both. Honestly, it's a relief to hear beautiful, pure stuff like that— especially with the Eros division here... but I won't go into that ever.

To conclude my findings: PH is planning something big for you guys and now I'm in.

How've you been now that the gruesome battle on the Isles is over and you're back after your long journey? I know the Hodginses told those kids their story, but how about you? How are your sisters?

With safety and secrecy,

Joshua Wolfrum

Joshua Wolfrum

LETTER 2

Shannon: I

Greetings Joshua,

Wow, I'm amazed. PH approached you about a promotion? Our prayers are being answered. Hopefully, we can end this war soon.

Thank you for your congratulations! Yes, Shane and I are happy together. I'm just worried about Mark... he says he's fine. Ah, I'm sure he's all right.

Yes, the Isle members are here with us. We returned the other day. To me, they're cute. Their minds are so curious and innocent despite the horrors and battles they've endured. I pray that isn't ripped from them. As for my sisters, mischievous as usual.

Shane, Aymie, and Mark just finished telling their origin story to the Isle members when we returned from the Battle of the Isles. Aaron shut off the voice recorder when we stepped off the stairway and into the Underground. That's where I'll begin.

The Isle members were captivated. Their eyes flew back and forth as they tried to comprehend the concrete city. Our humble huts and buildings bewildered them. When they saw the survivors among them, they lost it. They'd been isolated and captive for so long. The fact that other people were alive and thriving amazed them.

We were walking through the city when Mark asked, "Shannon, where is everyone? You said that RRPR has its own rooms in the Underground?" He clutched his backpack and looked around with wide blue eyes. He was also in awe. Five years had passed and he was a new person. A happier, caring young man with a passion for asking questions and helping others. It made me proud.

"Yes, that's correct," I explained, tying back my short curly hair. "It's set up like our old base in North Dakota so it shouldn't be unfamiliar."

"I can't believe it's been five years," he whispered.

"I can't believe you hid this life from us for so long," Aaron stated. Aaron is one of Mark's best friends from the Isles. He's the Geek with the spiky blond hair and glasses. I sent you his record log. "This life you've had. These people. Man, it's crazy."

"You're bloody right it is," Lucas the Dragonfly said, flying overhead. He went to the tops of the buildings to greet some of the survivors. To his shock, they weren't afraid of him. "These blokes are acting like they've seen a billion dragonfly-men before."

"They've seen worse. I don't think a big bug would scare them," Nic chuckled. Can you believe big Mutant Gorilla Nic is the Co-Director of our operation now? Crazy.

Lucas nodded and landed to walk alongside us.

"Yeah, everyone here's been through so much," Mark thought aloud. "Speaking of everyone, how are your sisters, Shannon?"

I smiled. "Why don't you ask them yourself?"

Mark's eyes widened as he looked towards the center of the city. Clustered around the fountain were six girls in different colored dresses with either brown or dirty blond hair. The youngest one had a brace on her right leg. They were holding balloons, and the cherubs in the fountain were wearing party hats.

One of the girls saw us approaching and did a double take. When she saw Mark, she pointed and yelled, "Clarius the Second is back!" All the heads whipped around to see us. Their sparkling eyes fell upon Mark. Screaming, the six ran towards us.

Mark's eyes watered. He dropped his backpack and held out his arms, ready for the collision. One by one the girls ran into him: Margaret (Peggy), Lucy, Carol-Ann, Rebecca, Agnes, and then Rachel. They sobbed as he held them.

"Girls, I can't believe it. You've grown so much," Mark choked.

"No duh, moron," insulted Lucy. She wore her favorite yellow dress and her hair was tied back into the usual pigtail braids. "That's what happens when you ditch us for five years."

When they pulled away, my youngest sister hobbled forward. Mark choked up when he saw her leg brace. When PH hurt her years ago, she was never the same. "Rachel," he started. "I'm so sorry."

Saying nothing, she buried her face in his stomach and bawled, "Y-y-you promised! You promised you'd take me with you on a mission. Then you left because you didn't love us anymore." She dampened his green shirt with her tears.

Mark rubbed her curly, dirty blond hair. "No, that's not true. I said when you were a big girl. You're eleven now. Almost time." He put his hands on her shoulders and gently pushed her away. He dried her eyes. "I didn't leave because I don't love you guys. I left because I didn't want to hurt you anymore."

"Well, you shouldn't have abandoned us on such a sour note," Carol-Ann retorted, taking one of Sonny's weapons from his belt. The black-haired officer didn't object. He was used to her doing things like that.

"Shane, you lived with all these ladies?" Yared whispered to my fiancé. (He's the Isle member that will write you letters.) He rubbed his dark hair and tried to make his navy combat uniform look presentable. "Any of them, uh, free?"

Shane laughed. "Don't let them hear you. They'll crush you like a soda can."

The Seer chuckled and didn't take his warning seriously. He wiped the dirt off his strong dark brown face and smiled at Peggy who rolled her eyes.

Agnes came to me and rested her head on my shoulder. Her brown hair draped in front of her face. She's taller than me now even though she's ten years younger. "We missed you too, Shannon," she confessed. "You can't scare us like that."

"Yeah, Mr. Wyght was *really* mad," Peggy added, inching away from Yared who tried to stand next to her. "Hopefully, you were punished for that," she continued. "Anyway, let's go see Director Michaelson and Thyme before we get in trouble for tardiness."

The six girls pulled away and ran ahead. Well, Rachel hobbled along while Mark held her hand.

We rejoined my sisters at the far end of the city. Train tracks ran through the different corridors beneath Joint Base Lewis McChord. My sisters piled in the wooden train car. "Hurry up slow pokes!" one of them yelled.

"Don't call me slow, Rebecca," Shane scolded, jokingly. He ran forward and leapt from the ledge and landed in the car on his feet. The Bionics and Mutants flew in while the rest of us hopped on board. It was a tight squeeze with twenty-three of us, but we managed.

I know what you're thinking, Joshua. I'll try to add little reminders of who everyone is. Just note there are nine RRPR Officers, eight Isle members, and my six sisters (but you won't hear of them too much). Do your best to keep them straight.

Aaron threw half his body over the edge, trying to see the undercarriage. "Wait, where's the engine?" He stood back up and readjusted his glasses. "I thought in your story you said you were going to fix this?"

Nic chuckled. "Eventually, but that's why I'm here." He flexed his brawny, hairy arms.

"Oh no, count me out," Alison the Bionic stated. The blue lights in her armor turned on and she reactivated her thrusters, taking off and hovering above the rest of us. Her short gray hair swayed with her movements as she steadied herself. "I'll get there on my own. No offense, Nic."

"None taken," he replied. The Mutant-Gorilla hopped over the railing and grabbed the handle. "Want to race?"

My sisters and Shane cheered while everyone else gripped the railings. The girls tied the balloons to their wrists and braced themselves. Axel—the other Bionic—and Lucas took to the air to join the competition.

On the count of three, we were off, racing down the corridors of the Underground. Thankfully, Nic knew the tracks by heart so we didn't make any wrong turns and smash into a wall or another car.

We skidded to a stop at the end of the line and I teetered forward. Shane grabbed my waist and pulled me backwards. "The only time you can fall is when you fall for me," he joked.

I rolled my eyes and chuckled. "Well, it's a good thing I usually have decent balance," I replied as he helped me out of the cart and onto the ledge. He smiled and tried to kiss me, but I stopped him.

"Ew, ew, ew, stop," Rebecca cringed, covering her brown eyes. She was Shane's Hollinger buddy growing up, and we always teased that she had a crush on him.

And of course, Lucy reminded everyone: "Sorry, Rebecca, he's taken forever now."

She groaned out of disgust. "Let's just go. Michaelson and Thyme are waiting." She dragged Agnes and Rachel forward with her and we followed. She led us to a sealed metal entrance. She entered the code into a chrome pinpad and scanned her retinas. The door slid open, revealing the Hall of Royals.

Stepping onto the polished wooden floors, I looked around at the red hall. A few streamers dangled from the walls. My sisters didn't get to finish decorating for the welcome home party. The paintings of the Royals were restored, but most were moved to the Hall of the Fallen. Honestly, I'm glad they relocated them before the Isle members arrived. If they saw RV Agricola Marian Best's painting, they wouldn't be able to keep it together. They knew she was the sister of their good friend Marlene whom they just lost…

To the left, Interpreter Director Virginia Michaelson stood tall, looking up at the paintings of the current RRPR Officers. She was dressed in the casual uniform: black pants and a white blouse. Around her waist was a blue utility belt that only she and her chosen Interpreters wore. Her golden hair was pulled back into a french braid. She emanated motherly love and authority. A refreshing personality in this trying time.

At her side was a strong man with chocolate skin: RV Combatant Thyme. Despite it being only a few months since I last saw him, his face aged significantly. The creases around his eyes were deep from worry, burden, and loss. He suffered daily from the deaths of his Combatants and Royal Veteran acquaintances: Gregory Flicks, Adeline Zarra, and Marian Best. Guy Vandewater was alive, but he didn't see his best friend as often as he'd like.

I can barely describe his reaction when his dark eyes saw Mark for the first time in five years.

The Combatant ran to see Mark. The one whom he saved from abduction all those years ago. Mark's eyes watered to see one of his friends alive and well. Tough guy Justin Thyme grasped his friend's hand and pulled him in for a manly hug. "What the hell is wrong with you, huh? Leaving all these lovely little ladies alone?" My younger sisters giggled at the compliment.

"Good to see you too, Thyme," Mark chuckled, smacking his friend's back.

He pulled away and yelled to the Interpreter Director. "Virginia! The prodigal son returns."

Michaelson smiled. Her face radiated with beauty. "Too bad I don't have a fattened calf to offer for dinner." Her voice was sweet like a mother speaking to her beloved children. Her light eyes met mine and she jerked her head towards my painting. "Don't we have to change that nameplate soon?"

"Stop talking about it!" Rebecca shouted, pulling Agnes and Rachel.

Michaelson smiled and began walking towards us, but stopped to gawk at the Bionics and Mutant flying above her. In his joy, Thyme hadn't noticed the enhanced Isle members. He followed the Director's gaze and stepped back. Not out of fear but admiration.

"Incredible," Michaelson whispered, lifting her hand to her mouth. She looked back at me. "And they have human consciousness and reasoning?"

"I would hope so," Axel replied as he descended. He, Alison, Lucas, and Sami (the Mutant housecat and sister to Alison and Aaron) went before Michaelson and Thyme.

They weren't startled. They examined their faces and Michaelson asked to touch the Bionics' implants and Mutants' features. The teens consented, and she gently held Alison's arm.

"Amazing," she muttered. She touched Sami's cat ears and gently rubbed Lucas' wings.

"Thank you, ma'am," Sami said as she scratched her ear. "We're here to help. We want to save more lives."

"We want to take down the Invaders—I mean, the Order of

Xenophon," Alison added. "They created the monsters that murdered our brother Jeremy, our friends, and many of your soldiers. They need to be destroyed."

Virginia Michaelson smiled, but there was no happiness in her face. The sorrowful memories flooded behind her eyes. "Thank you all for your service. You'll truly add to our strength and numbers."

"Well, we bloody better," Lucas said. He put his goggles back over his compound eyes. "My name is Lucas, by the way. I was crossed with *Anisoptera* if you couldn't tell."

One by one, they introduced themselves. Here's a quick list as a refresher for you, Joshua: Lucas (Mutant Dragonfly), Sami (Mutant Cat), Alison (Bionic), Axel (Bionic), Donnie (Asset), Ethan (Savior), Aaron (R&D Geek), and Yared (Seer).

"It's a pleasure to meet you all," Michaelson replied, shaking the last person's hand.

Thyme nodded as his greeting. "I wish I could get to know you all better, but sadly I have to leave for my next mission." He looked at Mark. Despite the sorrow this next assignment brought, there was joy in Thyme's face. "I'm happy to have seen you again before I left."

Mark was perplexed. "How long is your assignment?"

"As long as it takes," was Thyme's only reply before he saluted Michaelson and left the hall. The echo of his footsteps hung in the quiet.

Michaelson broke the sad silence. "I wish we could start off on a happy note, but it must be a serious one."

"Like an E flat?" Carol-Ann joked then was immediately elbowed by Lucy. Leave it to my sisters to make a dark mood brighter.

"Yes," she grinned. She was used to my sisters' nonsense. "Come with me and we'll get started on an E flat."

Orderly, we followed her out of the Hall of Royals, down the corridors of RRPR's new base, and into our large conference room. It's similar to the meeting place on our battleships. Maps and newspaper clippings along the side walls, a slim screen hung at the front, and swivel chairs sat around a long mahogany table.

Once we were settled, Virginia Michaelson went to the front. Taking a remote in her pale hand, she turned on the screen. Appearing was a map of Spain peppered with *X*s.

"My Interpreters have been scouting this location for years," she explained, jumping right to it. "Now, it is finally time to infiltrate this Order of Xenophon base." She zoomed into the map, revealing an overhead view of a large circular structure. "It was originally known as *Plaza de Toros de Las Ventas*. A bullring. It is now the center of OX's control in Spain; very similar to what Mark and friends encountered in Guadalajara. RV Guy Vandewater and a small team are already there." She looked at us with serious dark eyes. "He devised a plan to overthrow and destroy the base."

All the Isle members were quiet, shifting uncomfortably in their leather seats. After reading their stories, I don't blame them. The first time they killed another human was when they infiltrated the Guadalajara base. When they realized that most of the Xenophonians were innocent, mindless puppets in the hands of monsters.

Alison placed her metal hands on the table, stood up, and stated, "There has to be another way. We Isle members can't bear taking the lives of the mindless Invaders—Xenophonians." Her mechanical eyes cast downwards. "We don't want to go through that again."

Michaelson looked at the Bionic sympathetically. She understood. The Isle members were no older than twenty. The youngest, Donnie, was ten, but the decision was final. "I know how hard it must be for you all, but this is the only way," Michaelson explained. "Even if we destroy OX's computers and the Xenophonians are thrown into chaos, the sane soldiers will slaughter their own anyway. The only way we can save them is to sever their ties with the Order. We're waiting on our man on the inside, Joshua Wolfrum, for guidance with that."

Alison bit her lip. She remembered the triplets' story and knew it to be true. After Marcellus destroyed OX's computers, the mindless Xenophonian's ears dripped with blood. They screamed and writhed in pain.

Then, PH slaughtered them all.

Alison held her tongue and slumped back in her seat. She knew Michaelson was right.

"If you don't wish to join us, then say so," Michaelson told her kindly. "I understand this is difficult, and I don't want you to do anything against your will. Speak now if you want to opt out of this mission." The crowd was silent. The Isles members promised they would help us even if it brought back painful memories.

"Thank you all very much," Michaelson said sincerely. "You leave in five days. I am sorry you depart so soon, but our time is limited." She turned to our white-haired RRPR Officer. "Bain, from now on I would like you to group with M. Hodgins and our new Isle members. If you dream anything, give them the details first. They need to be aware of these fights more than anyone."

Blake Bain nodded. He was our secret weapon, our saving grace, the one whose precognitive dreams saved lives and helped us get ahead of the fight. Without him, we wouldn't be winning this war.

Which worried me.

"Of course, ma'am," Blake nodded.

"For now," Michaelson addressed the Isle members, "you will rest.

Janelle and Prince have your rooms ready and the Hollinger girls can show you the way."

"Prince?" Yared asked.

"Yeah, the one we saved on our way here before we came to your rescue," Shane reminded as he stood up and stretched.

"You'll meet him soon, but for now, rest," the Interpreter Director said, gesturing to the door.

My sisters led us out and we all went to our rooms, preparing to jump into danger once again.

As I walked, I heard the shuffling of feet then felt a hand on my arm. I turned to see my fiancé smiling at me. "I think you forgot something."

I was confused. "I don't need to prepare for the mission until tomorrow," I told him. "What could I have forgotten?"

Shane chuckled. "Always so serious. You need to lighten up." He reached into his pocket and pulled out our engagement ring. Fear fell upon his face as he slid it on my finger. "You scared me to death," he whispered.

I let out a sigh. "I'm sorry, Shane," I took his hand, "I felt like I needed to be the one to greet Mark after so many years."

He exhaled through his nose. I could tell I upset him. "I understand, but remember Aymie and I need to prove we're there for him, too."

He was right. I kept taking those moments away from them, but I couldn't help it. I knew I was the only one Mark listened to. Or was that my pride talking? "I'll try not to do it anymore," I promised.

He nodded, and his green eyes locked with mine. They were filled with kindness, but something else, too. Fear hid behind his irises.

"What else is on your mind?" I asked. "I know you're stressing about something."

"You're too good." He paused for a moment. "I'm just always worried about you; running into the heat of a fight. What if your mask fails you or something happens?"

I scoffed. "Seriously? I told you not to worry about me. I can hold my own, you know that."

"Yeah, but how many more reminders do you need." He raised my arms and turned them palm up. The wounds that Wally inflicted while I was in custody were finally healing but leaving horrid scars. Red stripes would be painted on my arms forever. "Shannon, things could get worse," Shane said in a low voice.

"They could get better," I ripped my hands from his. "Don't worry about me. I'm fine."

He hated losing, but he didn't want to fight. "Fine. I won't worry about you." Even though he was upset, he grabbed my hand and gently kissed it. Then, he wrapped his pinky around mine. A pinky promise.

SHANNON: I

I couldn't help but smile. Such a childish gesture, but that was my fiancé.

"I'll never break a pinky promise," Shane chuckled. "This seal is permanent." His eyes became serious, but kind. "I'll let you be a big girl, but I'll do whatever I can to keep you safe whether you like it or not." With that, he turned and left.

I took a deep breath. I knew he was right, but I would never tell him. I didn't want him to see me weak. I know he is supposed to take care of me, but I didn't want him to have too much on his plate. He was important to me. I couldn't have him suffer on my behalf.

Anyway, so that's what happened the other day. We're preparing to leave for Spain now. As for me, I'm doing all right. It's tough strategizing these things. All responsibilities fall upon me. If a life is lost, I feel responsible.

Blake hasn't had a dream foreseeing the mission. We're going in blind. If you figure anything out, please let us know.

Godspeed and goodwill,

Shannon Hollinger

Shannon Hollinger
Royal Strategist of RRPR

THE UNDERGROUND

LETTER 3

Joshua: II

Hey Shannon,

Oh, no, you're going to Spain's base? Be careful. I don't know anything, but I have a bad feeling.

On a better note, I met with PH and have more news.

A week later, I awoke to the ear piercing noises as per usual. Getting up, I dressed, relayed my mantra, and went to breakfast. It was the same routine as I previously shared, but PH didn't eat with me this time. I sat at my regular table. I expected to be alone when another member came over and plopped his tray across from me.

I looked up to see a familiar wrinkled golden face with a wiry beard. The short, frail Hermes Xenophonian lowered himself onto the bench with the help of his wooden staff.

"Morning, Solomon," I greeted although I didn't expect a response. Solomon's brain was scrambled, and he only spoke certain phrases. *He sure is a mystery,* I thought. No one knows exactly what happened to him. "How's Diego doing?" I asked. At the sound of its name, the little capuchin monkey hopped onto Solomon's back. "Speak of the devil."

Diego squeaked and shook his head. Solomon held his fork up. The little creature wrapped his thin fingers around the metal and tore off the scrambled eggs with his sharp teeth.

"So, Solomon," I started while the monkey ate, "did you hear that we have a new assignment this weekend?"

The old man nodded.

"Do you know anything about it?"

THE UNDERGROUND

Sometimes, Solomon's words of wisdom gave me insight into OX's plans, but he didn't know anything this time. *"Gold there is, and rubies in abundance, but lips that speak knowledge are a rare jewel,"* he said; his voice was low and slurred.

Frustrated, I exhaled through my nose. Like I said, he rarely spoke. When he did, I had to figure it out. I took that to mean nobody knew what was going on and I was lucky to find anyone who did. "Thanks, Solomon," I replied, slightly annoyed.

Diego made a noise in response, jumped on the table, and proceeded to eat Solomon's breakfast with obnoxious grunts. The old man didn't mind.

After some time of silence, the buzzing and crackling in my head resumed: *Hermes... mission preparation.*

Grunting, Solomon gripped his staff and hoisted himself up. Diego climbed up the stick and perched himself atop, keeping his tail from hitting his master. Solomon nodded farewell and limped off to our meeting spot.

I took a deep breath. *Hope PH is going to meet with me today*, I thought. I disposed of my breakfast remains into an overflowing trash can and went on my way.

As I walked through the cold halls, I longed to see the sun. The concrete walls boxed us in like rats in a cage. There are no windows in our OX base. No one is allowed to see the surface. They don't want to give us a hint of its location. Even when we are sent on missions, we are completely oblivious of our surroundings until we reach our destination.

Yeah, that's right. Still have no idea where I am. That day I left RRPR and met those scouts where Sonny said, I was abducted, blindfolded, and commanded never to make my way home. The Order doesn't trust any of us despite their vigorous Entrance Rituals.

Considering my involvement, I can't say I blame them.

I was about to enter our meeting room when I heard a faint whispering. Placing my hand on the cold wall, I peeked out the doorway to find the source. I wriggled my nose to turn my glasses on and scanned the hall.

The thermal sensors detected two forms: a slender woman conversing with a short man who I presumed to be PH. I tried to listen closely to their conversation, but the walls were thick. I attempted to read their body language, but there wasn't much. The woman was as stiff as a board and PH had the usual hands-shoved-deep-into-pockets pose. Nothing to decipher.

Then, they both turned to take leave. Panicking, I ducked into the room. I was about to scramble for a spot, but luckily, Solomon saved me one. He grabbed me and pulled me down next to him.

PH strode in to give us an overview. With his head held high, he made his way to the front and stood by a blue hologram of a static OX logo. "Mornin', Hermes," he began. "Our next assignment is delivery. An

Ares team is besieging a city that still 'as fightin' Mortals in control." His heterochromatic eyes narrowed. "We can't let 'em win. Startin' tomorrow, we'll be on our way with crates of weapons, food, and warmer clothes: autumn is approachin' fast. Go to your Sub-Division Supervisors for your roles." With the back of his hand, he waved to the side of the dark room where the soldiers were.

The Supervisors are volunteer OX members that chose this life and aren't completely brainwashed. They are tough, rugged, serious troops in the usual dark uniforms. Medals over their hearts distinguished them from the rest. Most of the Xenophonians believe they achieved some great feat to receive such an honor. I know the only feat was betraying their families and countries to join an oppressive movement set on world dominance and "purification".

One by one, my colleagues rose to go to their Supervisors. I was about to follow suit when PH whistled. I turned and saw him jerk his head towards the door. Solomon looked at me confused. "It's probably nothing," I told him. "Let me know what the Supervisor says."

The wrinkled man nodded and limped with the crowd. Diego the Monkey squeaked and hopped off his master. He scurried over and sat at my feet. He wanted to come with me.

"Go back to Solomon," I ordered.

He cocked his head to the side. His brown eyes looked up at me. I wasn't much of an animal person, but Wolf developed an admiration for the little fellow. I scoffed and jerked my head. Squealing with delight, the monkey crawled up my back and perched itself on my shoulder. He was light and didn't smell as bad as I thought. Composing myself, I went out to meet PH.

The Titan leaned against the wall with his sword in hand. He polished it with his green scarf. I was amazed how he could carry the massive weapon around all day let alone wield it with such force and power.

Seeing me approach, he wiped the steel and said, "There ya are, Wolf. Thought you got lost on your way out."

"My apologies, Titan," I replied, bowing. "Someone decided to tag along, if that's all right."

PH chuckled. "Don't worry, mate, the monkey's fine." At the sound of that, Diego cooed and proceeded to chew on his fingers. "Well, as long as he doesn't touch anythin'," PH added. "Come. We have much to discuss." He slid the sword into the sheath on his back and walked down the hall. I followed close behind.

"There is more to this mission than meets the eye," he began as we walked. He was taking me down corridors I've never been. Or have I? Every hall looked the same. We wove around corners like we were trying to escape a maze. "Along with bringing supplies to our Ares troops," he continued as we turned down another hall, "I 'ave my own side assignments in this particular location. You recall the reason why I am recruitin' you, correct?"

I nodded and replied, "Of course. You want to find Marcellus and his children and end the Resistance."

"Right," PH confirmed. "Marcellus' last known whereabouts were Fargo, North Dakota when we were attacked by RRPR the first time five years ago. 'E was off the radar for a while, but finally my scouts 'ave got a new location." We headed down a long dark corridor where I couldn't see a thing. I heard PH's footsteps stop before a door consumed in the blackness. PH tapped a panel and announced his Xenophonian title. Recognizing his voice, it blinked green and the door slid open. I had to shield my eyes from the light. When I could see, my breath was taken away.

It was a bright city full of life. The structures were carved out of white marble and resembled buildings of Ancient Greece. The floor beneath was made of smooth stones. Xenophonians walked to and fro, carrying out their daily duties. To my surprise, there were children playing about as well. I hadn't seen a child since I last saw the Hollinger sisters.

I stood there in awe for a few moments before PH spoke: "Beautiful, ain't it? You're the first of the lower class to feast your eyes on 'er." He raised his arms. "Welcome to New Greece."

As we walked through, I couldn't help but gawk. The rest of our base was a dump. This place was a paradise. I took a deep breath in. The air was clean and fresh and a sweet floral aroma floated through the air. Beautiful flowers and shrubbery of many colors lined our path to the center of the city. We stopped before a circular plaza with five statues around its circumference. I recognized three to be the gods of our Divisions: Hermes, Ares, and Eros.

"There are other Divisions of OX that you may not be aware of," PH explained. He pointed to the statue to my right. It was a wide sculpture of three elderly women sitting in a row. Each had something different in their hands. Carved into the base of the statue were silhouettes of men and women looking up at the three figures.

"This one is for the Moirai and their Children. This other one before us," PH waved his hand to the largest statue of the five, "is in honor of our mighty leader; our god." It was a muscular man with a flowing beard. He sat on a throne and wielded a long staff.

"Zeus," I whispered. I never knew how in depth the Order of Xenophon went with the Greek thing. I knew the Titans spoke the language and we were named after a Greek general, but I didn't realize how far down the roots actually went. I looked past the statues and saw that each had a path leading to a large structure with Corinthian pillars lining the front. "What are those buildings?" I asked.

"Our temples," PH said. "Although, the only one used for worship is the Temple of Zeus. The others are the homes of the Titans." He walked towards the statue of Hermes. The god of mischief was in a running position dressed in nothing but a cloth around his waist and his winged helmet and shoes. In one hand he held a pan flute; the other, a horn. PH patted the base of the statue and followed the stone path up to the steps of the temple.

I followed him up the stairs, glancing over my shoulder at the statutes. Their cold eyes followed me. Past one of the temples I caught a glimpse of two more statues in a garden of pink trees. Other gods? Or just decor? PH called me inside so there was no time to decide.

The interior of the Hermes Temple was vast and branched off to many sections. We walked down a hall that was lined with bowls of fire until we reached the farthest room. Once again, PH spoke into a machine on the side. It accepted his request and the stone door slid open with a low rumble.

On the other side was a round marble table with the OX symbol etched into it. On the back wall hung chrome monitors. To my left hung OX's symbol for Hermes: a circle with two wings.

"Welcome to the Hermes meeting room," PH announced with his arms out. "All the Hermes Supervisors meet me 'ere for meetings and plannings."

I looked at him blankly. I couldn't believe it. *Why is he bringing me here? Why is he trusting me?* I wriggled my nose to turn the glasses on; I felt like I should be paying closer attention. "This is incredible, sir," I told him. "I had no idea our base was so big."

PH chuckled. "This is the main base for the Order of Xenophon. 'Course it's gonna be big." He walked over to the computers and sat down in the large marble chair. I went over and stood behind him. Diego hopped off my shoulder and sat on the console.

PH didn't mind. "This is what I wanted to show ya," he said, ignoring the monkey rummaging through the papers left on the desk. PH powered on the computer and opened documents related to the Hodgins triplets.

For the first time in seven years, I saw pictures of my friends. Aymie was still a beautiful young woman despite her alopecia. The image was of her smiling; her gray eyes shone brightly. Second was Mark. This picture was of him like I've never seen. He was on an island next to a blond boy with black glasses. He had changed. His brown hair was no longer half shaved; it was short and styled up in the front. His blue eyes were happy and full of life. Mark was stronger and confident. Finally, Shane. His picture was the hardest to make out. It was out of focus like he was running out of the frame. From the photo, the only thing identifiable was his brown hair. Thankfully, PH didn't have a clear depiction of him. It would be much harder for the Titan to identify Shane in a line of soldiers. He would be safe.

I helped bring these three together. Now, PH wanted me to tear them apart.

"This is the most recent information we could obtain," PH explained, putting all the images into their own windows. "My sources say that they're closer to Marcellus than we think. Neither party knows exactly where he is, but that's what we want to find out." PH clicked another folder and opened blurred photos of the mysterious man in a trenchcoat and black hat. Nothing was clear; I couldn't see his face.

"Marcellus," I assumed.

"Correct," PH said. "Now that you have an idea, I want you to keep an eye out. The plan is to use one to draw out the other. If we find Marcellus first, we use 'im to get the triplets and vice versa."

"Might I ask why we need them again?" I questioned.

PH's expression hardened. "Marcellus is a traitor and needs to be put to death," he stated coldly. "The triplets on the other 'and can be used; manipulated. Twenty five is still young; the Entrance Ritual can still work on their feeble minds." Gazing upon the blurred face of Marcellus, PH went on, "Marcellus was the greatest Titan we ever 'ad. I wish we could 'ave him back, but he's made up 'is mind now. He's betrayed us and passed 'is skills down to his children through genetics. Together, they're more powerful than Marcellus ever was." He turned back to me. "With them on our side, the final phase can be put into play."

"Which is?" I asked.

PH scoffed, "You're lucky enough to be 'ere. I know you like to ask questions, but you know I can't answer 'em all." He stood up and scolded Diego for nibbling on the papers. Ashamed, the monkey jumped back up onto my shoulder. "Be satisfied with what you do know," PH said.

I wasn't satisfied and never would be until I knew everything. I finally know that I live in the main base of the Order of Xenophon, but still don't know the location. I have a hunch that there are more OX Divisions, but no clues. I caught a glimpse of Marcellus but have no more information. My new life was a constant mystery that I needed to solve.

Not wanting to push my luck, I nodded and replied, "Yes, sir, I am satisfied and eager to start this mission."

PH tugged on his scarf and said, "Good. Now, let's get you back. We leave in the morning." With that, he led me out of the beautiful city and into my cold, damp, lifeless corner of the base. "One more thing," PH added before departing. He took his pipe out of his pocket. "You tell no one about what you saw," he lit his pipe, "Not your buddies from the pub, not your Supervisor, no one, understand?"

I nodded and Diego did the same. "Of course, sir. I would expect no other request."

PH smirked and pointed his pipe at me with his left hand. "Good boy.

Get your rest. You'll need it." He winked, clenched the pipe between his teeth, and spun around to take his leave.

Once he was gone, I took a deep breath. Diego jumped off and looked up at me. "It's been so long," I said to him. "I couldn't stand waiting, but now I feel like it's all happening so fast."

Diego squeaked and ran off to find Solomon while I left to prepare for my first mission under the cold-blooded killer, PH.

I'm telling you, Shannon, this is insane. I had no idea about the city or anything. And if you could please relay the information about Marcellus to Shane, Aymie, and Mark. Whatever I learn, I will share with you,

And once again, please please please be careful in Spain. Best of luck. With safety and secrecy,

Joshua Wolfrum

Joshua Wolfrum

THE UNDERGROUND

LETTER 4

Yared: I

Yo Joshua,

This ain't Shannon. It's Yared Prinz—Seer Commander from the Isles. I know she mentioned that I'd be writing letters to you when she can't. So, uh, she hasn't read this letter yet which worries me. It only came through to my tablet, so I thought I'd take over this one.

Wow, props to you. I hear PH is one sick dude; good luck with him. I'll send over the information about Marcellus to the triplets in time. I'm sure they already know that PH is trying to capture them.

So, back to the problem at hand. I wish we really heeded your warning about Spain… we ran into some complications.

Let me start from the top:

Some Isle members and I were selected to go to Spain. The RRPR Officers joining us were Shane, Mark, Shannon, Nic, and Sonny. We decided last minute that Blake should stay behind so he could sleep. Because last night, he woke up with a start and scared the crap out of me.

I shared a dorm with my Isles' boys and a few RRPR Officers. They ordered us to get our rest, but I couldn't sleep. I was anxious to jump into the action again. I loved every minute of battle. So, I watched the others snore away.

Not creepily, I swear. I was bored.

Blake was across from me, sleeping peacefully. White hair fell around his soft calm face. I wouldn't have watched him for so long if his expression didn't change. I stared as his nose scrunched and breath quickened. His eyes pinched shut and his lips parted, revealing gritted teeth. He tossed and turned, muttering words I couldn't understand.

Mid mumble, he shot up, startling me. Sweat dripped down his temples. His eyes opened; pupils constricted within his light irises. However, his gaze was distant as if he were still asleep. "Something important will be lost. Something important will be lost," he panted. He turned to me, staring with a glass eyed expression. He knows who I am, but he saw a stranger. "Something important... will be... lost," he gasped. His gaze locked with mine. Slowly, his breathing calmed and he fell backward. His eyes shut.

At first I thought he was dead, but his sheets moved as his breathing returned to normal. *That was the freakiest thing I've ever seen.* I'm not the kind to scare easily, but that was something else. I didn't know what to do, so I kept it to myself. I rolled over and forced myself to sleep.

The next morning, Blake didn't say anything about his dream. Since he *supposedly* didn't have a dream, they told him to stay behind.

I didn't fess up that he dreamed. For crying out loud, he stared *right at me* when he said those weird things. I figured if it actually was important, he would've remembered and told everyone... right?

He remained back at the base to rest. If he dreamed of anything, he'd call us.

Unfortunately, he didn't go to bed early enough.

We were scheduled to meet with Mark's old superior: Guy Vandewater, the Royal Veteran Nerd at WHYP. He had a plan to destroy the base located at the *Plaza de Toros de Las Ventas*. The OX members were scarce in that location for now. We had an opening. We planned to scatter them like we did in Guadalajara. My friends despair over that day every once in a while. For most of them, that was their first time taking a life.

That day didn't phase me. I loved every second of it.

Sorry if that sounds heartless, but I love the adrenaline rush. The sights, the sounds, the screams, all of it gives me life and purpose. The problem: I don't know why. I think it's the way I was "programmed" as a Seer under Walter "Wally" Jarvis. He was a sadistic human in nature even though he didn't outwardly appear that way. He taught my colleagues and I well... too well.

Honestly, their deaths were the only ones that brought me sorrow. Ursula and Jeremy were faithful fighters and I miss them dearly.

Just don't tell anyone I told you that, okay? I need my strong reputation. Now, back to the action.

The five RRPR Officers and us Isle members (minus Donnie) were in the remains of Madrid, Spain waiting to meet Vandewater. I hopped off the truck and looked around. I'm sure the city was beautiful once. Now it was reduced to rubble and ash. The air stank of decay and dust. It was no longer inhabited; everything was quiet and still.

Except for Shane. As we waited, he impatiently tapped his foot and glanced at his communicator's clock. "What's taking so long?" he complained. "Scouts should've been here by now."

"Relax, man," Mark snapped, scrolling through his electronic clipboard. "He probably lost track of the time. He can't see the clock after all."

"That still fascinates me," Aaron put in; wonder resounded in his voice. "I can't wait to meet this guy. Being able to use a computer without sight? He sounds brilliant."

"He is quite the genius," Mark replied. "I can't believe how long it has been since I've seen him." A few minutes passed before we heard the murmur of trucks in the distance.

Looking out into the debris ridden streets, I saw three vehicles approaching. "I hope that's the good guys." I looked to my friends for some sort of confirmation, but noticed Ethan had his arms wrapped tightly around him. He was shivering. I scoffed. "They better get here faster; I think Ethan is starting to catch a cold."

"N-no I-I'm n-not," Ethan stammered through chattering teeth. He breathed into his light brown hands for warmth. "I just don't think I'm used to real Autumn weather."

"We were spoiled in Hawaii," Axel added. He rotated his metal legs. "I feel like my prostheses are going to freeze."

"Guys, it's not cold," Nic explained. The Mutant Gorilla had his XXL black combat jacket tied around his waist. "It's not even October yet. It'd be snowing by now if we were still in North Dakota."

The trucks skidded to a halt before us. Coming out of the passenger side was a pudgy man with dark glasses. He tapped the ground before him with a white cane as he made his way towards us. Finding his way to Mark, he held his hand out. "Mark Hodgins?" he asked in a brittle voice.

Our friend shook his hand and greeted, "Hey, Guy."

A tear rolled down the blind man's cheek. He pulled Mark in and hugged him tight. "Welcome back." Mark returned the gesture to his old superior. When Vandewater finally pulled away, he added, "Unfortunately, our time is short. Ready?"

We piled into the three trucks and made our way to the RRPR Madrid encampment. It was located in an old museum less than five miles from the OX base. The vehicles rattled as we drove up the uneven cobblestone and into a small building repurposed as a garage and storehouse.

I flung my rifle over my shoulder and hopped out. "Wouldn't the OX members have noticed this place with it being so close and all?"

"They have no interest in coming this way," Vandewater explained. He carefully exited the truck and led us to the main building. "To them, this place is just as abandoned as the rest. They aren't very meticulous when it comes to city searches."

"But what about all the noise your vehicles make?" Sami asked, scratching her cat ear. "Don't the soldiers hear that?"

"Not everyone has super-human hearing Sami, but she's right. They *are* loud," Lucas put in. "Didn't know OX was filled with drongos."

"If they do hear, they don't care. The higher Xenophonians keep secrets," Sonny put in. "They hide spoils for themselves in many of the buildings. If the lower ranks start sticking their noses where they shouldn't," he made a finger gun and pretended to shoot.

"That explains the family in Guadalajara," I heard Alison mutter. Out of the corner of my eye, I saw her clench her metal fists. Her lip curled and rage shone through her gray eyes. "Vandewater, how soon can we get to work?"

"Immediately." The blind man stopped before the three story building and tapped on the door with his cane. A small panel ejected from the wall and he entered the password, letting us in.

The interior was as run down as the rest of the city. Layers of dust blanketed the museum. The display cases were destroyed. All the artifacts were stolen during the Accident—or the Cleanse. Whatever you call it. The troops at least swept the floor of most of the debris, but there was still more cleaning to be done.

Vandewater led us through the halls and to the main display floor. A dozen computers were set up uniformly, facing the RV Nerd's master console on the back wall. The heavy steps of the Bionics and our commentary were not enough to distract the Nerds diligently working at their desks.

"I'm back," Vandewater announced, sitting in his chair. His computer sprang to life. Beeping and clicking resounded through the speakers. "Let's show our friends what we've been up to, shall we?"

Appearing on screen was security footage of the bullring. Hundreds of OX soldiers marched to and fro, guarding the entrance. The large red flags with the black OX symbol waved in the wind. Pieces of the structure were cracked and broken, but inside was a highly functioning operation of mindless killers.

"They all look the same," Axel said. "The flags, the systems, even the structure shape."

Aaron fixed his glasses and peered closer at the screen. "He's right. Mark, is that how you developed a plan so quickly back in Guadalajara?" the skinny Geek asked.

"Yes," his Commander replied. "I've gone through their layouts and systems dozens of times. I practically know it all by heart." Mark scrutinized the structure again and asked, "And it hasn't changed?"

"It never will," Sonny told him. "The Moirai have had everything just so for over fifty years. They don't see a need in changing it."

"The Moirai?" I asked. "Like, the Children of Moirai?" I recalled the other Divisions you learned about, Joshua.

Sonny shot me a quizzical look. He was surprised an Isle Seer knew more than his colleagues. He forgot I'm communicating with you.

Just between you and me, I'll keep it a secret. Have him think I'm all cool and whatnot.

"Yes, that's correct," Sonny stated. "They are the computer brains behind OX. They are rarely seen or spoken about. These bases house some of them."

"Wait, so those mindless people we killed in Guadalajara were part of the Children of Moirai?" Alison asked.

"Yes. They control the signals and messages sent to the minds of the OX members." Sonny curled his fingers and raised his hand with the palm facing the floor. "Think of the Children of Moirai as the puppeteers. All the others are simply their puppets." He wiggled his fingers as if controlling a marionette.

"Now I don't feel *so* bad," Ethan mumbled. We all had a deep hatred for the Invaders—uh, Order of Xenophon—but the guilt of murder hung heavy in our hearts. This lightened the load a little.

Like I said before, it didn't bother me. Looking at the footage, I recalled the Guadalajara event positively. I couldn't wait to rush into action again.

Vandewater went over the plan in full. I won't tell you the whole thing, Joshua. You'll be bored to death. Shannon strategized most of it, and I have to say, this girl is good at what she does.

"You depart at dusk," Vandewater said, standing from his swivel chair. "We'll hold down the fort here. I ask for some of your members to remain behind; God-forbid OX is led here. This is our first time making our presence known to them. I fear the worst."

"Understood, Guy," Nic said. He tapped his chin with his thick finger as he thought. "You can keep Alison, Ethan, Aaron, Lucas, and Shannon. I'll take the rest."

No one protested. Lucas wanted to argue, but his growling stomach stopped him. "I think that's best. Not sure how long we'll be and a bloke's gotta eat." The Mutant pulled a sandwich out of his backpack and munched away.

Vandewater dismissed us and we left to prepare. We were taken to their storage room where they equipped us with their latest tech and uniforms.

I looked at my reflection in a broken glass window as I zipped my new RRPR jacket. My dark brown skin was rough and scarred from the Battle of the Isles. My crew cut hair had grown in and my dark eyes were worn. In the new uniform and my aged face, I could scarcely recognize myself. I no longer saw myself as Yared the Seer Commander. In my reflection was Yared Prinz; a worn teenage survivor.

Whoa, what's wrong with me? I shook off the feeling of doubt. I was a strong, merciless fighter. I was chosen to lead an army because of my skills. *No. That's gone. They're gone.*

"Uh, Yared?" a voice called, interrupting my thoughts. I turned and saw Ethan waving his hand in front of me. He was out of his combat uniform and dressed back into his long doctor's coat with the Savior's signature red t-shirt beneath. "You have to go now."

I snapped out of it. "Oh, right. Thanks, Ethan."

He half grinned. The Savior still hadn't fully recovered from the battle. He lost his two best friends: Zita and Harold. I saw the sorrow in his brown eyes from time to time. He'd talk with me about it, and I did my best to listen. I couldn't offer advice; I wasn't good like that, but I was honored he trusted me with his sorrows. Our pain made us close.

"Don't mention it," Ethan replied. "I'm happy I'm not going in this time. Just work double for me, okay?"

I flung my rifle over my shoulder. "You can count on that." Saying nothing else, I ran out to meet the others. I hopped in the back of one of the trucks next to Sonny and we were on our way.

The vehicles screeched to a halt about a mile out. OX soldiers swarmed the area. "This isn't normal," Shane whispered as we all hopped out the back. "Why are they all here?"

"It doesn't matter," Sonny snapped, pulling his red scarf over his mouth. "Remember, stay low and keep quiet until it's time. RRPR Officers use code names. Isle members, we'll use your roles such as Seer or Bionic. Understood?"

We nodded. Turning on our comms, we split up into our groups. I went with Sonny and Shane. We crouched along the perimeter; ready to sneak in once the coast was clear. Axel and Sami were to distract the guards while Mark and Nic disarmed the front. Unlike Guadalajara, we didn't need chips to get in. Myles equipped our BoMFs (Bracelet of Many Functions) with a counter program.

Anxiously, I waited for the signal. My stomach tied itself in knots. I was apprehensive but thrilled. I couldn't wait for the bloodshed. I closed my eyes and intently listened to the noises around me.

I heard the whirring and clicking of Axel's Bionic body as he kicked OX members across the streets. The pings of bullets that failed to pierce his armor resounded against the bullring. I listened to Sami's growls and screeches as she slashed enemies left and right. By the sounds of the fight, I knew it was going well.

"*Automatics are down,*" Mark called through my BoMF. "*Let's do this.*"

"Yes," I hissed as I loaded my rifle. Sonny and Shane looked at me with a grin. The two enjoyed fighting more than their comrades.

"I think I'm going to like you, kid," Sonny stated, standing from a crouch. "Let's go."

On his command, the three of us rushed into the line of fire. Axel, Sami, and Nic were keeping the outside troops distracted while we ran to catch up with Mark. Once we were together, we stayed low and snuck inside the bullring. Just like in Mexico, we needed to reach the center of the base, download the information off the mother computer, and destroy the rest.

The soldiers were so concerned with the destruction outside that sneaking in was easy… too easy. Last time they posed more of a challenge. I felt as if we could walk against the crowd and not get caught. Nevertheless, we hid when we heard footsteps approaching.

I dove behind a food counter with Shane as another swarm of Xenophonians marched past. "This doesn't feel right," Shane muttered. He rested his back against the grimy counter and tapped the screen of his bracelet. Its appearance and functionality was exactly the same as our BoMFs.

I looked down at my own bracelet from my Keeper. *I wonder if our design was also stolen from Powell Enterprises.* Aaron found many of Myles' designs in the Nerve Center back at the Isles.

Shane scrolled for a few moments. "There are no notes from the Interpreters or Vandewater that some event or ceremony was happening here."

"Interpreters?" I asked, peeking my head around the counter. I quickly ducked back as more troops passed. When their footfalls receded, a voice resounded in my head, but it wasn't my own. "*Something important will be lost,*" Blake's voice screamed.

"Michaelson's hand-picked group of soldiers," Shane explained, interrupting Blake's warning in my mind. "They go on special missions just for her. They all wear the blue utility belts."

I nodded. Blake's message still swirled. His voice was loud and desperate, but I ignored it and looked down the hall.

The coast was clear. Sonny signaled and the four of us jumped to our feet and raced down the long corridor until we reached the door to the stadium's field.

"Do your thing, bro," Shane said. He and I faced the hallway while Mark worked on the door. Sonny was ready to shoot anyone that came through.

THE UNDERGROUND

As I heard the whirs and clicks of the locks, our BoMFs vibrated simultaneously. It was a message from Shannon who was back with Vandewater. "No time," Sonny ordered. The moment the door opened he ran in with his gun blazing. We followed suit.

The interior layout was the same as the stadium at Guadalajara: the mindless Children of Moirai sat in the stands at their small computers, typing away. The more conscious Xenophonians were in the center of the bullring, encircling the mother computer.

Several of them fell at Sonny's hand before anyone realized what was going on. The alarms blared red and blue, bathing the ring with a purple hue.

"Look familiar?" Mark shouted to me as he knocked a Xenophonian out with an elbow to the face.

It did; that's what I loved about it. The memories of Guadalajara flooded back as I created new ones. I clutched my gun, shouted, and ran into the firefight.

The Xenophonians whipped out their pistols and aimed, but they weren't quick enough. I dove to my right and crawled on my stomach under a few rows of desks. Shane distracted the enemy; I had an opening. Leaping to my feet, I shot them down, but more were coming. I could've waited for the wave, but I had to help the others get to the center.

Gun aimed before me, I busted through their barricade. The rage and adrenaline rushed to my head. I fired left and right, knocking them down with every shot. One snuck up behind me and grabbed the back of my jacket, causing me to drop my weapon. I wasn't out yet. I threw my arms over my shoulder, grabbed the Xenophonian, and bent my entire body forward, throwing him over my head.

His comrade tried to get revenge by lunging at my side with his knife. I quickly stepped back and tripped him, causing him to crash on top of his acquaintance. With a chuckle, I snatched my gun and ran towards my goal.

I looked around to see how my teammates were doing. Frankly, they were doing better than I was. They were already there. Mark had climbed over the glass wall encasing the massive blue hologram. Sonny and Shane had their backs against it, defending their partner. They weren't going to be able to hold them off forever. They were surrounded.

I thought I was going to rush in and save the day when the Xenophonians in the bleachers began screaming in agony. I watched as they shoved their palms into their bleeding ears.

This happened in North Dakota when Mark's dad blew up the main computer and when we wiped the computer in Guadalajara, I recalled as I knocked out another OX soldier. *It's going to blow.*

The mother computer spoke in Spanish which my earpiece translated, "*Self destruct initiated. Five minutes and counting.*" Mark had clambered back over the glass and the three were racing towards me. Even the sane Xenophonians ran out of the bullring. They knew what was going to happen next could not be stopped.

"Let's get out of here!" Mark shouted when they caught up to me. We pumped our legs as hard as we could. Shane had gained some distance and was far ahead, leaving us behind.

Then, it dawned on me. I remembered the only reason we made it out alive. *Alison saved us.* My heart thumped in my chest while my lungs heaved. "Are we going to make it without a Bionic?!"

"Way ahead of you, buddy," Mark smirked.

Then, I heard it. The whooshing of rockets. Axel flew towards us at an incredible speed. He raced over our heads and pushed himself off the wall behind us. He extended his Bionic arms longer than normal and scooped the three of us up. I gripped the metal tightly as we sped out of there, once again barely escaping the blast.

I felt the heat gaining on us as Axel flew us out of the bullring, down the streets, and into a nearby alley. He threw us to the quaking ground and we all tumbled forward. I lay there for a few moments, listening to the exploding OX base. I clutched the ground below me as the blast shook the earth, rattling the buildings around us.

When the earthquake ceased, I wobbled to my feet. My eyes spun and I held a hand to my head. I looked around to count our members. We were all accounted for—even our distraction team. Covered in cuts and bruises, but alive.

Sonny sat up and shook the dust from his slick black hair. "I feel like that was too easy," he mumbled.

"Or are we just that good?" Shane grinned. He tapped his BoMF to see if we got an update from Vandewater.

No *Mission Success* message, but something from Shannon came in during the fight. Shane opened it. The triumph wiped from his face. He covered his mouth with his hand.

"What's wrong?" Mark asked, slowly.

"No…" He shook his head and looked up at his brother. His green eyes filled with worry; something I personally never saw in Shane before. "The Titan of the Spanish Pandemonium is here," he stated slowly. "They destroyed Vandewater's base."

Blake's words rang through my ears: "*Something important will be lost.*"

But I have yet to find out if *that's* what it was.

That's where I'm going to leave you, Joshua. The others are still missing and we have yet to find them. If she's still alive, Shannon will send you the update. We're making our way to the drop off point now, hoping they'll meet us there.

Even though we're still on our way, I wanted to take the time to write this to you; for ours and Shannon's sake since she'll know we're alive. I want you to tell us if you know anything about the Titan of the Spanish Pandemonium: Division, appearance, skillset, favorite color, we don't care. Whatever you can.

Thanks, man, and let us know what your next mission with PH is so maybe someone can stop that, too.

Bravery and fidelity,

Yared Prinz

Yared Prinz
Seer Commander

LETTER 5

Joshua: III

Hi Yared (or Shannon, hopefully),

I'm so sorry that happened. I'm praying everyone is alive.

I knew something was going on in Spain, but I didn't know that the Titan of the Spanish Pandemonium was *actually* there. It was rumored that they would be returning to their base after a long assignment. No one has seen them in four years. The only thing I know is that this Spanish Titan is of the Ares Division. Not good news.

Sorry I don't know more. I wish I did. Hopefully, hearing what I've been up to may lighten your heavy hearts slightly.

The latest Hermes' mission was to bring supplies to the Ares members who were besieging the city of Quebec. That was the last surviving city of Canada. People still had hope; they had faith. Now, it shattered like glass.

The first day of the mission, I woke up strapped to the end seat in an OX plane. As I said before, we don't know where our base is, and they make sure we never find out. Everyone goes to sleep and when we wake up we're on our way. Don't ask me how they dress and move all of us so quickly and stealthily. I have no idea.

I gripped the handles over my head as we entered high speeds. I was terrified as always. Part of me worried I'd slip out of character because I didn't do my normal morning routine.

I'll be okay.

After seven years you get used to it. The real fear is that Wolf will take over and Joshua will be no more, but communicating with you guys definitely keeps me on track.

THE UNDERGROUND

We traveled for an hour before the plane's speed decreased. Buzzing and humming filled my head. I winced as the Strange Voices spoke: *Prepare... to drop.*

PH jumped up from his seat and walked down the aisle. He—like all of us—wore a tight, black skydiving suit over his combat uniform. He pulled a helmet adorned with the Hermes' symbol over his head of curly brown hair. "Ready, Hermes?" he called as he smashed a panel by my head. The bay door opened, and the crisp morning wind rushed against my pale face.

I tapped the sides of my helmet and the handlebars rose. I stood, zipped my glasses into my jacket pocket, and shakily pulled on my helmet. PH looked over his shoulder and smirked. "Ready, Wolf?"

Nope, never. I've done this a million times with WHYP and OX combined, but the idea of plummeting to my death always frightened me. Pulling it together, I nodded.

PH turned back to the front. "Let's go!" He ran forward and leaped off. One by one, we did the same.

I'm going to die, I'm going to die, I repeated to myself (again) as I free fell to the earth. I needed to scout the area before landing, but my brain always focused on not dying first. I counted to ten and pulled the cord. My silk parachute escaped from its prison and caught the air, slowing my descent. I watched as my Hermes comrades pulled their own and the sky was filled with white jellyfish slowly swimming to the bottom of the sea.

Clutching the straps of my chute, I looked around. Below me was the devastated city of Quebec. The sun peeked over the horizon, lighting the citizens' destroyed homes. I could see a ring of black dots circling the densest part of the city. Those were our troops. They drove all of the survivors into one spot and were waiting until they either died out or surrendered. It was too dangerous for the Ares members to rush in and raid. Quebec had a fighting spirit and many Xenophonians fell at their hands.

Which meant the survivors lost twice as many.

I clutched the straps of my backpack as I approached the rubble below. I stuck my legs out and prepared for impact. Closer and closer until my feet touch the cracked pavement. I ran and released my parachute, stopping myself before I fell flat on my face. I gripped the ropes and yanked it back in while my comrades gracefully landed around me.

When my chute and skydiving suit were tucked away in my backpack, I put my glasses on and made my way to our meeting spot where I found PH, Solomon, and the others.

"These folks are tough," PH began, wrapping his green scarf around his pale neck. "They 'aven't cracked and we don't think they will. So we're gonna 'ave to do more than we planned." He pulled a map out of his backpack and cleared a spot on the pavement. He tapped the Ares encampment. "One of the Ares Supervisors' made home 'ere, concentrating his fire forward." He circled the city with his finger and stopped North East of the OX camp. "This is where their defense is the weakest. Most of the women and children are hiding 'ere." PH looked up at each of us. "This is where we strike. We take them for ransom, scare 'em a bit with my favorite tactic, and wait for the surrender."

No, please, not the tactic. I dreaded it. Sometimes he would follow through other times it was a threat. The tone of his voice and the look in his different colored eyes said he was serious.

People were going to die by the hands of the Hermes.

That's not our job. We are scouts, messengers, deliverers. Add murderers to the list and we become a Hermes/Ares hybrid. Only under PH, though. The Hermes in the other Pandemoniums don't do this.

"Understand?" PH said as he finished. I didn't hear the rest of the plan, but I didn't want to. He grabbed the map and stood up. "Right then. Go with your Sub-Division Supervisors. They'll give you your positions."

Everyone understood and turned to take their leave, but I felt a firm hand grip my arm. "Not you, mate," PH whispered. "You're comin' with me." His soft voice struck my soul.

I feared what he had in store for me.

He pulled his scarf over his mouth and led me through the city. Swiftly and stealthily, we made our way to the weak spot of the Quebec barrier. It was closer than PH let on. None of our other members were there yet.

PH pointed to a wall of debris that the survivors made. "Find a way in and see if you can gather any information on Marcellus. My Ares Supervisors report that a man 'as been sneakin' in provisions." He pulled his scarf down. "I bet my tank it's Marcellus; you know 'ow much I love my baby." His exhale became a cloud that touched his lips. "If he's there, don't engage. Find out as much as you can."

I was relieved. I thought he wanted me to take hostages like normal and help him carry out his "tactic". "I won't let you down, sir," I replied, yanking my hood over my head.

PH smirked and pulled his scarf up. "I know you won't, mate. Now get going. Your time is short." With that, he ran back to his subordinates while I snuck my way towards the wall.

I thought I saw a head peek over so I ducked behind the nearest building. I peered around the side and wriggled my nose so my glasses would turn on. With my thermal scanner, I saw bodies clustered around one area. They were armed. *Can't go through there*, I thought. I went out from my hiding spot and farther around the city.

I walked for so long I thought I would end up back where I started. The perimeter was heavily guarded. *There has to be another way in.* I had to think outside the box. I feared what PH would do to me if I didn't return with information. I also needed something to share with you and the triplets... hopefully you're all still alive.

I stopped on the cracked sidewalk to think.

In the silence, I heard faint footsteps. My heart leapt and I hid. Tapping the side of my glasses, I took a look around.

No sign of them.

I listened again and heard a creaking noise. The screen in my glasses confirmed that I wasn't going crazy: *"Noise detected. Someone nearby."*

I couldn't see anyone. Then, I caught something out of the corner of the screen. A faint thermal light in one of the buildings next to me. Cautiously, I made my way forward.

Inside was an abandoned campsite. There was an old cot, empty cans of food, and a fire pit. The flame had just gone out.

Someone was here recently, I thought, scanning the musty room. Nothing. As I walked away, a board beneath my feet creaked. Some were loose. I crouched and tore them away.

There was a ladder beneath.

I pulled a flashlight out of my backpack and cautiously descended.

I hopped off the last peg and into the filthy water. I clicked on the light and made my way down the long, dark corridor. My boots sloshed through the muck; the noise echoing off the walls. The stench of sewage tried to crawl up my nostrils. Covering my nose with my shirt, I held my breath as I made my way down. I followed the graffiti art on the walls, recognizing it to be a directional clue.

My heart jumped when I made it to the end. A rusted ladder led up to a manhole. I stuck the flashlight in my mouth and climbed. Pressing my palm against the cold metal, I slid the cover away and poked my head out.

I was inside a tent within the survivors' encampment. Crates of supplies stacked around me. The space was small and the boxes were light. *I hope this isn't all they have.* Carefully, I crawled out of the hole and slid the cover back. I crouched on the pavement; trapped in a wooden prison. I slipped through two towers of crates and out into the cold camp.

It was deserted and lifeless. I wrapped my arms tight around myself as I strolled through the empty street. In the distance I could hear the faint shouting of the Ares members at the gates.

I can't be out in the open like this. I clutched the patches on my arm, trying to hide my OX uniform.

I stopped before the *Monument Cardinal-Taschereau* when I heard a muffled scream. Whipping myself around, I scanned the damaged buildings until I found a sign within the *Notre-Dame de Québec* Cathedral. Two small figures hid behind a post.

Kids. Slowly, I made my way forward. They tensed as I approached. I called out in an attempt to comfort them: "I'm not here to hurt you, I promise," I held my hands out, "I just need to talk." They didn't respond. "Please, I can help you." I stopped walking before they turned and ran. Slowly, I sat on the ground with my hands behind my head. "See? I don't want to fight."

I watched their bodies loosen up in the thermal scan. They looked at each other until one of them poked their head out. It was a little blond boy covered in soot and dirt. "*Quoi?*" he yelled back.

My glasses translated it for me: What?

"Right, French," I mumbled to myself. I needed to tell him I only wanted to ask a question. I tapped my glasses' frame and whispered my response to which it gave the translation. I read aloud, "*Je ne veux pas te faire de mal. J'ai juste une question.*"

The boy looked over his shoulder at the other one with him. "*Quoi?*" he repeated.

"Marcellus," was my only response.

The boy's eyes widened and he looked around. "*Pourquoi?*"

"*Ses enfants le cherchent.* Shane, Aymie, *et* Mark Hodgins," I replied.

The boy gasped and threw his hand over his mouth. He ordered the other child to run into the cathedral.

I watched as his thermal signal disappeared behind the thick stone. The only fact I paid attention to was that it contained a historic crypt. That meant there *were* survivors and *that's* where they hid.

Time passed before the boy returned. I hoped a tall man in a black hat was with him, but was disappointed. Alone, he poked his head out of the cathedral door and waved me inside. I looked both ways to make sure I wasn't being followed and headed in.

The main area of the church was beautiful despite its brokenness. The cracked brass statues glimmered in the cold light, standing erect and on guard to protect what was left. The paintings were torn and crooked, but the eyes of saints watched carefully as I followed the boy inside.

I was led down the aisle and up to a middle aged woman. Her red crusted hands toyed with the blue utility belt around her waist. She was bruised, dirty, and smelled faintly of blood. She eyed me with speculation and hope.

"You're not Xenophon. You would've taken us away by now," she started; her voice gruff. "But why do you wear the emblems?"

"That doesn't matter," I told her, trying not to sound rude. "Time is short and I need to know. Is Marcellus Hodgins with you?"

"You claim to know his children by name." She crossed her arms. "No one knows that except those he's told. Unless, you know the children themselves."

"I do which is why I seek him."

She arched an eyebrow and raised her pointed chin. "You wear the emblems of the Order. I am forbidden to share. Prove that you are who you say."

I was annoyed at her request but understood. I wouldn't trust anyone in Xenophonian garb. "Fine. How can I prove it?"

Before she could respond, there was a rumbling. The floor shook and the dust fell from the ceiling like snow.

Then, I heard it. The clamor of trucks and the sweet, melodic tune of *Scarborough Fair*. *PH, wait*, I thought in a panic.

The woman's expression turned from speculative to fierce. "You lie!" she bellowed. She pulled out a gun and aimed it at my chest. Her finger on the trigger.

Afraid for my life, I swung my right arm forward, smashing my forearm against hers. The gun fired then crashed to the ground. She winced in pain.

"Please, I'm sorry, I can help you," I cried. "I'll make my Titan call off his troops."

Screams and cries of unfortunate citizens sounded through the high doors and into the cathedral.

PH was taking them.

"It's too late!" she screamed. She gripped her wrist. "They'll all be lost."

I needed to do something, but I wasn't sure what. I thought of one last idea. "I can get him to leave the cathedral alone. Get everyone in here; keep them safe."

Out of options, she agreed. "If you succeed, I'll entrust you with information on Marcellus. Now go!" With that, I spun on my heel and ran out to find PH.

I raced down the streets, following the loud singing of the English Ballad. I found the Titan standing atop one of the trucks while his men threw crying adults into the backs.

He turned to me and stopped his song. "Ah, Wolf! Thanks for distracting them, mate. Was easy to break in with that crazy lady out of the way."

Curse him, I thought bitterly. "PH, I was about to get information on Marcellus."

His eyes widened. "Were ya? Well why didn't ya?"

"You scared the 'crazy lady'," I retorted.

He thought for a moment. "Well, lead us to 'er."

I shook my head. "That'll make it worse. I made a bargain with her for information."

"What does she want?"

I took a deep breath and stared at my Titan. "Leave their other buildings alone and escape now with who you have."

PH looked around at the mess they caused. The perimeter was destroyed, and buildings had crumbled to the ground. Truckloads of citizens were packed and ready to send back to base.

He shrugged his shoulders. "Eh, fine. Ares made the majority of the city surrender. They'll die out."

Hopping back into the truck, he whistled and the vehicle drove away with the rest of his men following.

I let out a deep exhale. I couldn't save all of them, but that was good enough. Racing back to the cathedral, I found the "crazy lady" waiting on the front steps. A hundred survivors huddled shoulder to shoulder in the church behind her. There weren't as many as I'd hoped, but there were some just the same.

"They took so many," she whispered with tears in her eyes, "but you kept your promise." She reached behind her and pulled out a letter. "He left to help another city but gave us this in case we needed to reach him in an emergency."

Carefully, I took it from her calloused hands. "Thank you. I promise to keep this information quiet."

"I hope so," she stated coldly. "Marcellus saved more lives than we could ever know. We can't afford to lose him."

"Well, now you have his children in the fight," I smirked and shook the letter, "things are already changing."

Through her pain and sorrow, she managed a half smile. "I can't wait to see it."

I nodded, shoved the letter in my jacket pocket, and bid her farewell, leaving her to tend to whomever was left in the dying city of Quebec.

I caught up with the rest of the caravan. PH stood on top of his truck and waved his sword to direct the Xenophonians as they yanked blindfolded prisoners into the bay of an Ares plane.

"Hey, mate!" PH called as I approached. He directed an Ares member to take his place and hopped down from the hood. "What's the news?"

I paused. I wasn't going to give him the letter yet, but I had to make up something that sounded legitimate. I needed to get the information to you first. *I can't send letters until I'm out of sight...* "It's too dangerous to share here," I lied. "I feel like this should be something handled by only you and a small team. We don't want to arouse suspicion."

PH took a moment to process it as if trying to see through my lie. "Aight, Wolf. We'll set up a meeting to discuss the info and a course of action." He patted my shoulder. "Nice job." With that, he left to board.

I exhaled and watched my breath fall to the ground in a fog. I thought that would've been my last. I feared he would see through my lie and suspect something. *He hasn't for seven years*, I reminded myself. *Stop worrying so much, Joshua.*

Shaking off my thoughts, I got back into character and made my way towards my designated plane. I put a foot on the bay door and turned to see the city for the last time. I couldn't believe the wreckage the monsters caused.

OX won over Quebec.

PH's Ares members had destroyed the survivors' perimeter and barrelled in with their tanks, guns, and explosives. Despite the billowing smoke and the rubble ridden ground, the city was quiet. No clamor of trucks, no cries, nothing.

Silence.

The quiet after an OX attack filled me with dread and sorrow. Gripping the straps of my backpack, I turned forward and sat down with my murderous comrades. Once settled, they shut the lights, closed the windows, and we were airborne. The vents opened up and there was a faint hissing. Gas poured out and encompassed us in a blanket, causing us to fall asleep.

I awoke in my bed in my night clothes. It wasn't time for breakfast, but something woke me up. I sat up and remembered the letter in my jacket. I ran to my closet to see if the contents within my clothing pockets had been left alone. I fumbled around in the dark until I felt the familiar rough leather of my jacket. I let out a sigh of relief when I heard the crinkling of paper. I pulled the letter out and sat on the edge of my bed.

I put on my glasses and wriggled my nose to turn on the night vision. I turned it over in my hand. I held my breath as I slid my finger under the fold, opening it with a messy tear. I pulled out a damaged piece of yellowed paper. I unfolded it and read it carefully:

> *O Canada do not fret*
> *You are not forlorn yet*
> *Even though I'm not there*
> *You are still under my care*
> *Three gifts given to replace*
> *my being; my mistakes*
> *Understand; all I ask of thee*
> *I am here; you must see.*

I slumped back onto my bed, dumbfounded. *Is this a riddle or was his brain fried to only speak in rhyme?* I read over and over, trying to decipher it. The only thing I got was that the "three gifts" were most likely his children: Shane, Aymie, and Mark. *There has to be something else*, I thought, flipping the page over. *If Marcellus is anything like Mark he would have a code or secret in here somewhere.* I held it above my head and peered closer.

I saw a strange stain in the corner. I rubbed it between my fingers. On instinct, I smelled my thumb. *Soap.*

Then, it clicked.

I tapped the sides of my glasses and chose "UV". The screen turned to a violet hue. Two words and a punctuation mark within the poem were underlined with invisible ink: Three, thee, and a period. The letter was also numbered as if it belonged in a sequence. I had the first poem. I thought for a moment until I realized what they were meant to be. *These are numbers.*

I pulled a notebook out of my mattress and scribbled down what I deciphered: 33.

The start to coordinates, I realized. *He's going to lead us to him.*

So, Yared, that's all I found out about Marcellus. Honestly, it's a big start. He wants us to find him; we just need to put the pieces together. I'll report my findings to you first, but I have to figure out what to tell PH. I'll think of something.

Let me know what develops with the Titan of the Spanish Pandemonium. Forgive me for not having any more information. But, like Canada, the Ares members may besiege your friends until you surrender. I pray you can find the others, Yared.

Shannon, I hope you're the one who responds to this letter. Just so I know you're alive.

With safety and secrecy,

Joshua Wolfrum

Joshua Wolfrum

THE UNDERGROUND

LETTER 6

Shannon: II

Hello Joshua,

It's Shannon. I'm alive... for the most part.

I wish I could say I was excited about the coordinates to Marcellus. Any other day I would be. My heart is too full of sorrow and rage to rejoice.

I'll share what the dangerous Titan of the Spanish Pandemonium did to our Madrid RRPR encampment and what was lost. You must be wary of this Titan.

I was with Vandewater at the computer while our team was out to destroy the bullring. I was watching the screens closely when there was a *ding*. A notification appeared in the corner. Vandewater opened it. It was an urgent message from REM (Blake) back at the Underground.

"Oh no, Blake," I whispered. "What's wrong?"

I read it over and my heart sank to my shoes. It was short but not sweet: *"The Titan is there. It's a trap. Something important is going to be lost."*

I felt a rumbling beneath my feet. Following were a rain of gunshots and screams.

"What was that?" I yelled, turning around.

Aaron and Ethan barrelled into the control room and slammed the doors shut behind them. They pressed their shoulders against it, hoping it would hold.

"Boys, what happened?" I demanded.

"OX troops found us," Aaron told me. He was out of breath and his glasses were missing. His spiky blond hair was red with blood that dripped down his pale face. "I don't know how much longer this museum will hold."

Placing my breathing mask over my mouth, I asked, "Where are Alison and Lucas?"

"In position like you ordered," Ethan replied. Desperation shone in his dark eyes. "I don't know how much the two can take on their own."

"On their own?" Vandewater questioned. "We sent troops to stand guard with them."

Ethan looked downcast, leaning his back against the door. "They're gone," he whispered. "The Titan is ruthless. They don't care about taking hostages. They're out for blood."

My heart raced. Our numbers were dwindling fast; my brain didn't have time to process a foolproof plan. There were too many variables and outcomes. I couldn't think of a logical solution, so I went with my gut. I grabbed a gun and my backpack.

"I'm going out to help them." I put goggles over my eyes and a hood over my head. I covered everything but my breathing apparatus so no one could recognize me.

"No, Shannon," Vandewater cried, grabbing my arm. "Please, we need you."

I tore myself from him and quickly sent a message to Shane and the others. "I'm sorry, Vandewater, but I have to help. Take your Nerds and get out of here. Forward the information; wipe the computers. Blake says we are going to lose something important. Hopefully, it's nothing *too* important." I turned to the boys. "Ethan, Aaron, help get them to safety."

"But what about the others?" Aaron asked.

"Alison and Lucas will be fine. I'll save whoever is left," I told him. "Get them to our drop off point. Aaron, get a message to Director Michaelson back at the Underground. Ethan, be ready for medical assistance."

Not wanting to argue, the two went to work. I ran out the door and up into the chaos.

Surrounding the museum were a dozen trucks armed with automatic artillery. Most of them had been destroyed. The few that were still functioning shot at the museum, waiting for it to come crashing down. Small cracked spheres littered the floor amongst the still bodies of Vandewater's soldiers. As I ran through, I noticed one familiar factor.

A majority of the soldiers weren't shot.

What killed them? I wondered as I ran past another hole-less body.

I followed the sound of explosions and metal clanking to find Alison and Lucas hovering above another vehicle. The enemy shot to take them down but was unsuccessful. Lucas dove, grabbed the operators, and raised them high above the ground before letting go. Alison forcefully crashed into the vehicle, destroying the truck and its weaponry.

She hopped off and faced me. "Detective!" she screamed. "Find the Titan, but be careful!"

I nodded and ran to where her robotic hand was pointing.

I circled the museum until I found a hooded figure looming over a wounded soldier who struggled to get free. On the arm of the Xenophonian were three patches: the OX emblem, the Ares symbol (a silhouette of a vulture's head), and a wasp. The Titan raised a hand above their head and thrust it downward. I heard the *shunk* of a knife piercing flesh and the flailing body went still. The figure threw the corpse to the floor and wiped the dagger on a towel hanging from their belt.

There's no way this person could do such damage with only a dagger.

The Xenophonian turned around and removed their hood. It was a woman. Her braided black hair reached below her waist. Her beige round face was speckled with the blood of her victims. Sharp dark eyes pierced through my mask, trying to fill me with fear.

I shoved it aside.

She flipped her dagger in the air and grabbed its hilt. "*Pareces un reto. ¿Cuál es tu nombre?*" I dropped in a stance and was ready to reach for my gun. "English I'm guessing then," she said with a gravelly voice. "I only asked what your name was?"

"Detective," I spat. My voice was disguised by the electronic voice and crackled with every consonant. "You've done enough damage, now get out of here."

She laughed. "I let you destroy *my* base. It's my turn to return the favor." Placing both hands on her dagger hilt, she twisted until it clicked. She placed its point to the floor, and I watched black liquid drip down the metal.

It's poisoned. "You're going to regret coming here," I threatened, whipping out my gun.

Before I could think, she thrust out her left hand. Silver spheres glistened in the sun. They hit the ground with a snap, and the area was filled with a thick fog.

I swung around, trying to see where she was coming from. She didn't attack just yet. I watched her shadowy figure inch toward me. I speculated that the gas was poisoned and she waited until they were weakened to strike. However, one flaw ruined her favored plan.

I didn't breathe the air.

While she waited for me to drop, I fired. The Titan dove to the side and disappeared in the smoke.

"You're resilient, I'll give you that." Her voice echoed off the buildings. "I am called Sting. The Titan of the Spanish Pandemonium. It's an honor to fall at my hand."

"It's a shame I won't get the privilege." I looked over my shoulder and saw Sting lunge. I sidestepped, grabbed her arm, and thrusted her downward. As she fell, she kicked my gun out of my hand. She rolled and jumped to her feet. A surprised look painted her face; a look I'm sure was unfamiliar to her. She slid her dagger back in the sheath hanging from her waist. She raised her fists to her chin.

"You aren't bad," she scoffed. "Let's see what else you can do." She threw a cross which I deflected and returned with a hook to the body. She wasn't fazed and attacked again until it became a street brawl.

There was a pattern and rhythm to Sting's technique, but I couldn't identify it in the moment. It'd take several fights to analyze her style, but I didn't have time. I needed to get back to the others.

Sting decided the fight should end. She threw a faint punch and reached for her knife with her free hand. *Bad move.* She left an opening. I threw an uppercut, smashing her jaw with a crack. No bones broke, but her brain rattled. She staggered backwards and groaned.

I had a chance.

I snatched my gun off the sidewalk and was about to fire when the ground rumbled beneath me, causing me to lose balance. Seeing an opportunity, Sting took off like lightning. I cursed under my breath and went back to check on my comrades.

In front of the museum, I found Alison and Lucas hovering above the wreckage. The white haired Bionic saw me coming and shouted, "Detective! Where is the Titan?"

"She escaped," I grumbled.

"Not for long," Lucas replied. He flew down and landed on his knees. He panted and looked at me with his purple and blue bug eyes. "She'll be back."

"Then let's get out of here before she does." I gripped my gun and we ran around the building.

We found Vandewater, Aaron, Ethan, and the other troops waiting in trucks on the other side. They were too stubborn to escape without us.

Aaron waved us over. "Guys, we have to get out of here! We think we're in more trouble."

"How can that be?" Alison cried as she lifted a wounded soldier into the back.

"More Xenophonians with heavy artillery are headed this way," he replied. "We're in no condition to win the fight." Aaron banged the side of the truck and it drove off. I jumped on the back of another as it began to roll away. Hastily, we raced down the streets of Madrid, praying Sting wouldn't catch up.

"Where are the others?" I yelled over the clamor of the trucks.

Ethan did his best to attend to a wounded soldier as the vehicles hit every bump and crack in the city. His hands were covered in blood and the Nerd moaned in pain. "They're going to meet us at the drop off," Ethan informed. "Hopefully, they're the only ones. We have to stop for a day or two because of the distance. They're on foot; it will take them a while."

After a few hours, we veered off the road and made camp in the ruined city. I crossed the rubble and into an abandoned store.

Glass was scattered across the floor and the air reeked with decay. Thankfully, my breathing mask helped me with that problem.

As I sat on a rock, I looked around at all my colleagues. They were worn and exhausted. I wanted to get out of there as soon as possible, but they couldn't handle it. I watched as Ethan bandaged all the soldiers on his own. I knew he was exhausted, but the short Savior was determined to heal us all.

The building was quiet as everyone rested. The only thing to be heard was the shuffling of Ethan's feet as he went back and forth from patient to patient. I exhaled through my mask and closed my eyes. I sat down to think in the silence.

Normally, I could come up with a better plan but something was clouding my focus. Something about Blake's message didn't sit right with me: "*Something important is going to be lost.*" I didn't know what it meant and that angered me. I could always interpret Blake's dreams.

This time I couldn't.

Rather than beating myself up about it, I lay down on the hard rubble and fell asleep.

Three days passed and it was time for us to get on the road again. Our friends should've been at the meeting spot by then. I hopped on the back of the truck and held tight as we raced to meet them.

I peered off into the distance to see our six friends waving to us. At first I was relieved seeing they were all right.

But when we got closer, I realized they were waving us away.

There was a loud boom and everything shook. The driver swerved and I fell off the back. I tucked my shoulder in and rolled over the bumpy road. I heard Shane yell and the ring of gunshots. I turned over and tried to get up, but was too dizzy. I opened my eyes to see flames and a building up in smoke. Vandewater's men were aiming towards the blast and firing with no mercy. I heard screams and cries emerging from the fog, but saw no figures.

Bionics Alison and Axel hovered above the fight, scanning the situation first. I watched as they dove into the flames. The RRPR members stopped firing when the Bionics returned.

There was still ringing in my ears, but I heard Alison cry, "Where is the Titan?"

Just then I felt hands on my arms, dragging me to my feet. I was about to put up a fight when I recognized eyes peeking out of the masks of black:

THE UNDERGROUND

Shane and Yared.

My fiancé pulled his scarf down, revealing the rest of his face. "Are you okay?" I gave him a slight nod. I breathed hard through my mask, but felt like I was losing oxygen. I rubbed the scar on my chest where the arrow struck years ago. My lungs burned from the poison that never left. My body wanted to succumb to it.

"What... happened," I tried to say.

"Sting got the jump on us," Yared stated. "We have to go now before we lose anyone else." He pointed behind me.

I turned to see Vandewater's second base in the distance. Our meeting spot. It was a smoking pile of rubble now. I was enraged but had no energy to act. I rested against Shane's chest and removed my mask. "No... she did this," I tried to catch my breath, "Sting..."

"Who's Sting?" Yared asked.

To answer his question, we heard a blood curdling scream. I looked over to see Sami the Cat racing to the flames crying, "LUCAS! LUCAS!"

Two figures stood on the perimeter of the building. Our Dragonfly friend lay on the ground. His body trembled and his wings fluttered anxiously. Hovering above him was a figure with a dagger that dripped a greenish-red blood.

Lucas was stabbed.

The Bionics raced to his aid. Alison snatched the Mutant and brought him back to the others while Axel took on the Titan. The Xenophonian looked almost surprised to see the half-human half-machine. She hesitated for a moment which was her mistake. Axel rammed into her, sending her flying in our direction.

She lay on the rubble two yards from my feet, motionless. Axel believed the job to be done so he flew back to the others. Everyone was gone. They thought the fight was won.

But I knew it wasn't over.

Sting stirred and slowly rolled over. This time I saw she had a gun on her belt. She wasn't going to stall any longer.

As I clutched Shane's chest, I felt his heartbeat increase. I knew he was planning something. He looked at Yared who gave a nod. Then, he turned to me.

His green eyes filled with fear. He placed his hand on the side of my face and pressed his lips firmly against mine. His heart thumped hard and fast in his chest like it always did when he was with me. Quickly, he pulled away and rested his head on mine.

"I told you I wouldn't worry," he whispered. He took my pinky and wrapped his own around it. The pinky promise. "But I told you I'd do whatever I could to keep you safe." Quickly, he shoved my mask back over my face, turned, and bolted in Sting's direction.

Unarmed.

I watched as he slammed into the Titan who just got to her feet. She skidded backwards and kept her balance, but the gun was knocked from her hand. "¡Diablos!" she swore as she pulled out her dagger. She twisted its hilt and gripped it tight.

Shane ran for her again, and she held out her dagger, ready to strike. To her surprise, he dodged it and landed a kick to her gut. She staggered and leaned against a building, gasping for breath. Her brow furrowed, and hatred burned behind her brown eyes.

The Ares Titan was done with being toyed with.

She turned to Yared and me, raising her dagger above her head. Her and my eyes locked, and she smirked. Her arm came down in a fury as she threw the blade as hard as she could.

I closed my eyes and waited for the impact, but all I heard was an exhale. Nothing struck my flesh. I cracked an eye open to see my fiancé.

The dagger stuck out of his side.

I screamed through the electronic voice of my mask as Yared dragged me away. Shane looked at me and managed a smile. He dropped to his knees and rested his hand on the weapon's hilt. Blood dripped, painting the sidewalk red.

No, no, no, this can't be. My heart stopped as his face paled.

Shane's body trembled as he gripped the dagger in his side. He tugged on it slightly, but was too weak. His green eyes met mine and he mouthed, "*Go*".

Screaming, I tried to escape Yared's grasp but it was no use. The Seer Commander had a strong grip, and I couldn't get free. During my fit, I didn't notice the Bionic approaching. Axel swooped down and snatched Yared and me, taking us away from our dying friend.

Below us, I watched Sting approach Shane. Menace across her face. Shane tried to swing at her, but could barely lift his hand over his head. The Titan knelt before him. With one hand, she ran her finger along his strong jawline. She laid the other on Shane's fingers that gripped the dagger. Holding his hand, she yanked the dagger out of him. Blood splattered onto her black uniform. Shane grunted.

I watched my fiancé's eyes roll back, and he collapsed to the ground.

I wailed and tried to wriggle out of Axel's grasp. I couldn't do it. The Bionic flew us high above the smoke and away from the scene. The last thing I saw was the Titan looking up at me and saluting.

I screamed and cursed the Titan, Yared, and Axel. I didn't care if I fell to my death. I needed to get down there. I needed to be with Shane. I needed to stop Sting. The injustice, the inhumanity, it sickened me.

THE UNDERGROUND

We let the Titan escape and left Shane's body to rot.

So, yeah. You can tell why I'm upset. I just... I honestly can't wrap my head around it.

Axel dropped us back off with the others and I had no words to say. No tears to cry. Mark rushed over to me. He was grateful I was okay. He searched for his brother with desperate blue eyes. Then, he looked at me.

All I did was shake my head.

Mark bit his lip and led me quietly through the camp to my tent. He sat me down on my cot and went to tell the others.

Sitting in silence, I pulled the dog tag out from my shirt. I rubbed my fingers over Shane's name. He gave it to me when he proposed. He asked to live the rest of his life with me.

didn't get that chance.

I gripped the dog tag, clenching my fist so tight my knuckles turned white. I wanted to cry, but couldn't. I wanted to scream, but couldn't.

My emotions were dead.

I don't feel sadness or despair. My heart is heavy but there is no outward expression of it. I don't understand. My fiancé was killed in front of me and I feel nothing. *Nothing*. My heart should ache, but it still beats. I loved him. I loved him dearly.

Then, why do I feel so dead?

Outside my tent, I heard the silence of the soldiers. The Officers of RRPR were collected. Mark's voice was steady and calm as he spoke. The Isle members that heard the news were more distraught. They suffered many losses on the Isles, but were never used to it. Shane was a new friend to them. He was Mark's brother; one they dreamed about meeting for months. They wanted nothing more than for Mark to be happy with his family.

I heard Sami the Cat moan and cry in anguish. "Lucas, Shane, Lucas, Shane, Lucas..." she repeated.

From what I overheard, Lucas' heart still beat but he was in critical condition. One life spared out of the many that were lost.

When we returned to the RRPR base in Washington, Mark broke the news to Aymie. I watched quietly as her eyes watered and her lip quivered. Tears flowed down her beautiful face. She pressed her hands into her eyes and wailed. Mark took his sister into his arms.

The three Hodginses were now only two.

"This isn't possible," Aymie bawled. "He's not dead, he's not dead, he's not dead." She repeated.

But I saw him die. He has to be gone. It's the only logical explanation. Blake said something bad would happen. He knew something important would be lost. He didn't clarify what he meant.

I never expected it to be this.

SHANNON: II

I caught Aymie's gaze as she stood in Mark's embrace. Her eyes—though filled with sorrow—narrowed and glared at me. Part of her blamed me. And I know part of her blamed Blake.

I said nothing and let her hatred for me fester.

I know it's not Blake's fault. He *never* knows the whole story. I don't want him to feel like we're holding this against him. Aymie particularly. She refuses to speak with her boyfriend. I hope she comes to her senses...

The only consolation was Lucas. As of right now, he's still alive. His Dragonfly genes saved him from Sting's poison. I guess the Dragonfly beats the Wasp in this round. We aren't sure how yet. He's in the lab for further treatment and study. Hopefully, we can figure out what Sting uses so we won't share the same fate as Lucas and my fiancé.

Of course—after all this—we have no time to mourn. We have to prepare for another mission.

When we were in the Madrid base, we downloaded information on a new location. This one is big and different from the others. In fact, we aren't sure what it is exactly. But we are going to figure it out.

On top of it all, I want to track Sting. Any info you can give me will be much appreciated. I need to find her.

And kill her in cold blood.

Godspeed and goodwill,

Shannon Hollinger

Shannon Hollinger
Royal Strategist of RRPR

THE UNDERGROUND

LETTER 7

Joshua: IV

Hello Shannon and Yared,

First of all, my greatest sympathies to you both. My heart is sorrowful. I will never forget the first day I met Shane; when I led him back to Mark at WHYP. That was a proud moment. The day I reunited a family that would remain together for as long as they lived.

I never anticipated one of the lives would be cut short.

I wish I would've known more to give you an advantage. I am so sorry, forgive me, please.

Shannon, don't let revenge consume you. Justice comes in time. I promise Shane's death will not be in vain. Today, I met an important member of the Children of Moirai and someone else who will be of interest to the remaining Hodgins triplets.

After our mission in Quebec, PH ordered that I report my findings on Marcellus. Honestly, I wasn't sure what to do. I didn't want to give him the letter, but I knew if I tried to relay the information orally he would never believe me. PH needs hard solid evidence if he was going to believe anything.

A week after the mission, I went to our pub which is called "Lucky's". Dead giveaway that it was founded and run by the Hermes Division. The furniture is made of the same marble from New Greece. The bar was kept neat and tidy but the rest of the place was filthy. Xenophonians got smashed and the stench of body odor and alcohol hung in the air. Germs and diseases lurked about like monsters. OX is disgusting. I refuse to sit anywhere else but the bar.

THE UNDERGROUND

I sat atop the high marble stool with my elbows on the counter. Resting my chin on my fist, I shook an empty glass in my other hand. I drank to rid myself of my sorrows, worries, and pains. Shane was gone and I had no time to mourn. I had to think about PH. I played over every scenario in my head, but couldn't come up with anything that would keep me alive.

"Hey, what's bugging you, Wolf?" a voice interrupted. I raised my eyes. The red headed bartender looked at me as he shook another drink. "You seem down."

"It's nothing, Leprechaun," I sighed as he re-filled my glass, "My mind is always lost after these missions."

He grabbed a cup and poured himself a beer. It bubbled and foamed like the sea. "I getcha," Leprechaun replied. "Your missions are tough and you usually never come back the same."

I scoffed. "You don't know the half of it."

"Well, you know you can spill your secrets here," he winked and raised his glass. I tapped mine against his. "*Sláinte*," he said and took a drink.

Leprechaun was one I could turn to besides Solomon. He had a good nature. His eyes were kind and he was always cheerful, despite the bar fights, screaming, cursing, and putrid stench. His voice was accented, but I've been away for so long that his homeland slips my mind.

One thing that always surprised me was how much he knew. He was one of my main sources of information. If he heard anything, he'd tell me. I don't know why, but I never dwelt on that part. I just accepted the intel.

I took a sip and looked around, making sure no one was listening. The pub was quiet this time of day. A few Hermes members gambled in the corner while another was passed out on the table behind me.

I rested my glass on the torn coaster and shifted in my seat. "Well, maybe there is something you can help me with."

He wiped his mustached lip with his left forearm. "Story horse?"

Thankfully, I've been around Leprechaun enough to understand his -isms. He basically asked "*What's up?*"

"So, I'm supposed to present something to our Titan," I started, "and I'm worried it might not be enough for him."

"What do you have to present? Or am I not allowed to know."

I paused, thinking of how to word it. "I found information on a certain person in exchange of PH sparing a dozen lives. If the information doesn't meet his demands, I fear he may have my head for it."

The bartender chuckled and scratched his head. "That's a fret, but why worry? If you're honest and you die, you die an honest man. No one wants to die a liar."

That's not very helpful.

By my expression, he could tell I wasn't pleased. Rather than offering consolation, he just laughed. "Not sure what to tell you. Just show him what you've got."

I didn't know what to say. I sat quietly while Leprechaun attended to some other customers. Several minutes passed and I still had no words. I was about to get up and leave when I heard the familiar shuffling and thumping of feet. Two figures I knew too well sat on either side of me at the bar.

"Afternoon, Wolf," a deep, gravelly voice said. It was Goliath. The giant of a man had returned with us from the Quebec mission. He was besieging with the Ares Division and I'm sure he caused a lot of the damage. He rested his brawny inked arms on the bar and tapped his sausage fingers. He'd received three new tattoos within the past year. One was the Mark of Ares, a double edged sword that started behind his left ear and crawled down to his heart. Only the most sadistic, loyal, heartless assassins received those marks.

The man, Gerrior, who was after the triplets had one, too. My heart sank as I thought about the triplets again. WHYP worked so hard to protect them from the evils of the Order of Xenophon. We thought they were safe, but the Order still won in the end…

Will they always win?

I shook off the feeling. I couldn't mope around my OX peers. Wolf was faithful, loyal, and fearless. Joshua had to be tucked away for a while. I took a deep breath and greeted my companions with confidence. "Hey, Goliath." I turned to my other acquaintance. "Solomon. You both look well."

The wrinkled man nodded. His pet monkey jumped onto the counter, reached over, and grabbed a clean glass.

"Hey!" Leprechaun ran and snatched the cup from him. "Diego, quit acting the maggot."

The monkey squeaked and hopped onto my back for protection.

Goliath let out a deep chuckle. "You know he'll forever bother you, Lep."

Leprechaun sighed. "I should be used to it by now. Anyway, men, the usual? Minerals?"

"My usual," Goliath informed, picking his teeth with his fingers.

"*Wine is a mocker, strong drink a brawler, and whoever is led astray by it is not wise*," Solomon replied.

"Minerals it is then," Leprechaun interpreted, sliding the old man his club soda. "And the Long Island Iced Tea."

Goliath took his glass and raised it. "To another victory over the world."

As much as I didn't want to, I lifted my drink.

The Ares member gulped down his tall cocktail like water. He slammed it down and waited for his refill. "What are you boys doing to celebrate our success?"

Diego cooed and jumped on Solomon's head who nodded in agreement. Not that we understood what that meant.

"Sounds good, Solomon. As for me, I have an appointment tonight," Goliath winked.

It took every ounce of my body not to gag. The "appointments" Xenophonians spoke about were "meetings" with the Eros members. I didn't mention this in my first letter, but the purpose of the Eros Division is for member satisfaction and selective reproduction.

That's all I'll say.

"I have some things to report to PH," I butted in, changing the subject. "Remember that group we encountered in North Dakota the first time?"

"When you hit me in the head with a rock?" Goliath's voice sounded menacing but I could tell by his dark eyes that he was kidding... I think. If you recall, I only hit him so he wouldn't hurt the little Hollinger girl, Rachel.

"Yes, that day," I quickly replied. "I found out more information about the one who blew up our tent."

Goliath, Solomon, and Leprechaun all stopped what they were doing to look at me. It made me uneasy. *Stupid, Joshua. You can't go around telling people this stuff.*

The Ares member leaned closer; the alcohol on his breath wafted towards my face. "You know more about Marcellus?"

I didn't back down. "I do," I stated, flatly. "Is there a problem?"

The giant man smirked. "Not at all." He leaned away. "Just make sure you catch that son of a —"

"Wolf!" a voice called, causing everyone to freeze. I turned to see PH standing in the doorway. "Come with me," he ordered.

I looked at my comrades and then hopped down from the stool. The monkey jumped onto my shoulder, insisting on tagging along again. I couldn't shake him, so I let him come. Fixing my jacket, I strode to meet my Titan who was already down the hall.

I followed him silently down the dark corridor. He led me through rooms, halls, and other areas of the base I'd never seen before. Not as many twists and turns as if we were heading to New Greece. We came upon chrome doors that slid open as we approached.

Behind them, a woman stood in the center of the hallway, looking out the glass windows before her. I turned to see what she was watching.

We overlooked some sort of experimentation room. People in all black sat in rows facing a wall that was hidden from the observation deck. They were strapped down and staring. Their eyes were wide and mouths open. I thought I recognized some of the faces, but couldn't be sure.

PH stopped before the woman and announced, "Arata. Always a

pleasure to see ya.”

She didn't turn to greet him. Her almond eyes were fixated on the scene. Her slick hair was cut to her ears. A black dress suit fell straight around her figure. Sewn onto the left sleeve of her jacket was a patch I didn't recognize. It was criss crossing lines like tangled strings.

“This is my favorite part of the Entrance Ritual,” she whispered, pointing to the scene. “The part where they are given new life. They are children now; unsure of the new world around them.” She raised her arm and tapped the metal watch on her wrist. Below us, Xenophonians entered. They wore dark face shields to match their all black uniforms and stood behind the seated individuals. With needles in hand, each one violently shoved an unconscious Survivor's head down and stabbed their necks.

Despite the pain it inflicted, those being branded didn't flinch. It frightened me. They were getting the chip that put the final touches on their new nervous system. They made no movements. They were still.

Peaceful, almost.

“They should be done shortly,” Arata said sweetly. She finally turned her attention to us. She was surprised to see me and took a slight step back. “Oh, who is this, PH?”

“This is Wolf and the monkey is Diego.” PH held his arm out in front of me. I bowed and the monkey cooed at its name. “Wolf 'as information on Marcellus for us.”

Her thin eyebrows raised. “Fascinating. No one has been able to get anything concrete on him for years.”

PH smirked, clearly proud to be my Titan. “He's a clever one and also the reason for this meeting.” He cleared his throat. “I wanted to ask for your permission for Wolf to attend the next Titan meeting to present his findings.”

My heart raced. *Is he serious?*

Arata looked at me, her dark eyes tried to be kind, but something else hid behind them. “I think that should be fine,” she replied. “I will ask the others, but I don't think they'll mind. I know one is good friends with Wolf.”

Who's friends with me? What others?

PH cracked a smile. “Thank you, Arata,” he shook her hand, “Ya won't be disappointed.”

“I know I won't.”

We were about to turn to take our leave when the door opened behind us. “Arata! Arata!” a female voice called. I stepped back as the woman ran up to her. She had a long brown braid and wore a combat uniform. On her arm were three patches: the OX emblem, the Ares vulture, and a wasp. Attached to her belt was a sheathed dagger.

Sting.

I held my breath as the Ares Titan rambled to Arata in Greek. Beads of sweat dripped down my neck. My mind envisioned her mercilessly tearing a poisoned dagger out of Shane's flesh. She killed the son of Marcellus in front of his fiancée and friends. Now, she stood before me, babbling gleefully like a child to its mother. She was so close that I could snatch her dagger and avenge Shane right there and then.

But I couldn't. My primary mission is first, always.

"I have made a great discovery," I finally heard her say. "It'll help move phase three along faster than we could imagine."

Arata was intrigued. "I would hope you found something after your long absence. Now what is it?"

She was about to say when she caught me staring. Her brown eyes met mine. Her brain processed my features for a moment until she finally gave me a look that knotted my stomach.

"Sorry, PH, I didn't mean to interrupt your meeting," she said, trying to make her voice sound lower yet sweeter somehow. "Who is your friend?"

"This is Wolf and the little bugger is Diego," PH introduced. "He's gonna be presenting new information durin' the Titan meetin'."

She nodded at PH but her eyes were locked on me. I didn't like it. Clearing her throat, she returned her attention to Arata. "On second thought, maybe I'll present my discoveries at the meeting."

Arata smiled. "That sounds like a better idea. I'm sure whatever it is will be worth listening to." Her watch beeped and the prisoners below us were alone again. They were branded, chipped, and real Xenophonains.

"Oh, good," Sting exclaimed, tapping the glass with her gloved finger. "You put mine in the lineup. Thank you."

"Of course," the other woman said. "I don't believe they'll go into your suggested Divisions, but it's the best I could do. It's the least you deserve for your success."

Hearing the two talk about the mission as if she was a hero made my blood boil. This woman—no, monster—murdered my friend Shane, and I couldn't do anything but rejoice in her victories.

The lights dimmed on the Xenophonians below us. "I look forward to seeing what you both have to offer," Arata said, bringing the meeting to an end. "The other Moirai will be as well."

Even after she left, her words hung in the air. Then, it hit me like a freight train. I stood motionless. *Wait, wait, wait. She's one of the Moirai?* My head spun. *She's one of the heads of the Order of Xenophon.*

"Yo, Wolf?" PH asked, waving his hand in front of my face. I snapped out of it and he chuckled. "Relax, mate. Everyone gets nervous when they meet our Moirai. Sometimes we Titans get intimidated. I know the Titan of the French Pandemonium shakes whenever they're around. Our Moirai could get rid of us like that," he snapped his fingers. "Ain't that right, Sting?"

Sting eyed me. "Absolutely, PH," she purred, the words rolling off her tongue. She stood up straight. "Well, I'll see you boys later." As she walked past, I felt her brush up against my arm.

My cheeks burned and my stomach hurt. Noticing my discomfort, PH laughed. "Oh, mate, you should consider yourself lucky." He patted me on the back. "When Sting looks at men like that there are only two outcomes. You're still alive so I'm pretty sure it's the second one." He winked and left the hall.

I let out a deep breath and looked at the prisoners below. Their dead eyes glowed in the dim light. They saw nothing, felt nothing, and slowly were becoming nothing. Looking at their faces snapped me out of it. They were the reminder as to why I endured what I did.

I needed to shut OX down.

I followed PH who led me out and back to our Hermes meeting room. I wasn't sure why, but I obeyed and went inside. Shutting the door behind him, he asked, "So, are ya able to show me this evidence, Wolf?"

Here we go. Just do what Leprechaun said. "Of course, sir." I reached into my pocket and pulled out the yellowed letter. "I don't think it's much."

"It's better than nothin'," he replied, taking it. Gingerly, he lifted the envelope flap and pulled out the letter. He read it over. Then again. And again. His brow furrowed and he had a puzzled expression. He couldn't quite grasp the poem.

"The *'three gifts given to replace'* are obviously the triplets," he stated slowly. He peered at the rhymes again. "Wait a mo." He held the letter above his head then pulled it closer to his face and sniffed.

My heart dropped to my shoes.

PH laughed as he smelled the familiar scent. "Clever, Marcellus. Always playin' his tricks on me." He strolled to an old cabinet in the corner. Diego hopped off my shoulder to follow him. The creature scurried its way to the top and watched PH search. Rummaging through the drawers, PH hummed a tune that I recognized somehow. I didn't know where.

"Aha!" he exclaimed as he pulled out a small UV light. He clicked it on.

Frightened, Diego clambered back down the cabinet and hid behind me.

"Let's see what secrets you're hidin', mate." PH hovered it above the letter and found exactly what I did: the beginning to coordinates. "Marcellus," PH chuckled. "Your love for these blokes will be your downfall." He turned to me and smiled. "Wolf, you are brilliant. Absolutely brilliant!" Patting my shoulder, he shoved the letter and light towards my chest. "You present this at the meetin'." His different colored eyes sparkled. "I 'ave a feelin' you and I will be workin' alongside one another for a long time." With that, he winked and left me alone.

Dazed, I stood in the silence.

I would've been there for a while if Diego hadn't jumped on my back and startled me. I clutched the letter and light closer to my chest. Holding my breath, I made my way back to my room to prepare what I was going to say.

Many questions swirled in my head. I couldn't believe PH figured out Marcellus' code. I also wished I could have avenged Shane when Sting was within reach.

And yet, on top of all of it there was a bright light shining in the darkness. After seven years, I finally met one of the Moirai: a leader of OX. I would also be introduced to the other Titans *and* Moirai. This was the opportunity I've been waiting for. I get to meet the others in charge of the Order of Xenophon.

I will find the head and crush it.

I hope that your mourning will be turned into dancing soon, Yared and Shannon. Again my heart goes out to you all. I will give you anything else I find on Sting and the Titans.

They will be avenged.

With safety and secrecy,

Joshua Wolfrum

Joshua Wolfrum

LETTER 8

Yared: II

Hey Joshua,

It's a good thing Shannon and I are taking turns replying to you. She is in no condition to do anything right now… She's more depressed than she lets on. Her nature is cold and her words are sharp as icicles. They'll pierce through anything no matter how warm.

Man. After re-reading your letter, I have to say, those Entrance Rituals are messed up. I knew they were bad from when we encountered them in Guadalajara, but I think they might be getting worse. It's great to hear about you meeting with the Titans and the Moirai. Let us know what Sting has to say to everyone. One of my biggest fears is that Sting knows she killed a Hodgins. I'd rather keep OX and PH on their toes, thinking all three of them are still actively fighting.

Let me continue from where Shannon left off. Shane was killed-in-action and Lucas had been stabbed. I wish I felt more pain, but to me they're nothing but casualties of war. Sucks that I feel this way, but that's how I was raised.

A week after we returned from the mission, I waited in the observation room of the RRPR lab. Lucas was behind glass and strapped to a table. His long membranous wings draped off the sides and gently brushed the cold floor. His bug eyes gazed at the ceiling, but I couldn't tell if he was sleeping or not. Bandages secured the shoulder that was stabbed by Sting's dagger. She missed his heart, expecting the poison to take his life. His pale chest rapidly moved up and down. His breathing was unable to be steadied.

But he was alive.

THE UNDERGROUND

Ethan sat at the desk in front of me. Dark eyes peered through a white microscope at one of the Dragonfly's blood samples. The Savior worked for hours with no rest. He was doing his best to find out what poisonous compound was running through our friend's veins, but it was hard to tell. Lucas' blood was impure. Ethan was the only one at the base familiar with Mutant makeup so he had to do it alone.

"GAH!" Ethan exclaimed, startling me. He dug his nails into his skull, tousling his short dark hair. He leaned back in his chair and groaned, "It's too contaminated. I can't figure out how to help him."

I rested my back against the table. I didn't know what to say, but I had to say *something*. "C'mon, man, you can't give up."

"I'm just about to," he shot. "There has to be something I'm missing. It's hard to find with only one pair of eyes." He let out a deep breath and looked longingly at the microscope. His face fell as the memories of his comrades flooded his mind.

I couldn't help but remember with him. Zita's kind face and frizzy red hair; Harold's self-deprecating jokes and dry wit. They're in the past now. *Casualties of war…*

I shook my head. Ethan needed a friend, not a general. I patted him on the shoulder. "But one pair of eyes is all we've got. And I have to say, they're good ones," I told him as comfortingly as I could.

Ethan managed a half smile. "Thank you, Yared. I'll keep trying."

"And you'll succeed. Don't doubt yourself."

He dismissed my remark with his hand and went back to the microscope. "I feel like I know this makeup, though." He tapped a few buttons on the medical analyzer next to him, hoping it would give him a clearer reading. It failed him, again. The machine wasn't programmed for Mutated genetics. He needed his old equipment, but that was destroyed during the Battle of the Isles.

He grew frustrated again. Fist clenched, he was about to slam it on the table, but stopped himself. Peering more intently into the microscope, he asked, "Yared, does Sting associate herself with anything?"

"Uh, well she's the Ares Titan of the Order of Xenophon."

"No, that's not what I mean." He twisted some knobs. "I'm starting to recall something. I thought this was poison, but it's a venom. A natural one at that. I don't know if it's mammalian or what." He looked up at Lucas. "If he was awake, he could give me a clue." Tapping his head, he picked up a pen and scribbled some notes.

"Well, we're lucky he's still breathing." I crossed my arms and thought. I didn't get a close look at Sting, but I needed to think. I recalled the battle in my head, envisioning the enemy before me. I watched as she raised her arm, throwing the dagger into Shane's side.

I shook off that last part and focused on her arm.

Her black uniform was covered in blood. Splattered red were her embroidered emblems.

Then, I remembered.

Each Titan that rules over a Pandemonium has three patches on their uniforms. The last one is specific to that Titan. PH's is a snake wrapped around a sword…

Sting's is a wasp.

The words almost caught in my throat. "It's wasp venom," I whispered.

Ethan's pen stroke jerked which streaked a long line across the paper. Abruptly, he looked back into the microscope, rattling the tools on the metal counter. He entered a new code into his analyzer. "I think you're right," he mumbled. He looked at Lucas and laughed. "You've got to be right. That's why he's alive." Ethan jumped from his chair and raced to the medical cabinet. He flung the door open and grabbed supplies.

"Ethan," I started in a low voice, "dragonflies lose to wasps."

"Yes, you are correct," he replied, unfazed. I didn't know what he was doing, but his hands moved lightning fast as he tore things out of the cabinet. "Wasp venom melts the insides of any insect. When it's injected into a human, it basically tricks the nervous system into thinking it's in severe pain until the bloodstream can carry the diluted venom away."

"Okay, but that doesn't explain why Lucas is alive and everyone else isn't. If it's a trick, why did they all die?"

"Sting's venom is given at a higher quantity," Ethan explained, shaking a syringe. "This particular makeup is mostly MCD peptide and hyaluronidase. Together they eat through cells and tissue while sending tricking signals to the brain. It's basically extensive nerve damage. With this enhanced venom, people *think* they're dead before the venom and stab wound fully do their job." He pulled on gloves and made his way to the door.

"So, it's paralysis," I concluded.

Ethan nodded. "Lucas is still alive because the venom is having a harder time destroying his cells. It's as if it's confused, you may say. Dragonflies aren't supposed to have the makeup of a human. He can withstand more than the average bug and human combined. His Mutated genes aren't going down without a fight." He entered Lucas' chamber and I followed.

I looked at our bug friend and froze mid-step.

Lucas stopped breathing.

Ethan grabbed our friend's arm and prepared the syringe. We weren't sure if it'd work.

"Hold him in case he starts convulsing," Ethan ordered. I stood beside him while he stuck the needle into our friend. The medicine decanted into Lucas' bloodstream. Gripping the Mutant's prickly arms, I waited for something to happen.

Nothing.

We waited patiently, hoping it would take a little while.

Lucas' body felt cold.

I hung my head down and Ethan bit his lip. "No, no, no," he said, shaking our friend. "Wake up, Lucas. It's a trick. Just a trick."

Letting go, I took a step back. "Ethan, he was fighting the venom for a week. I think we're too late."

His brown eyes welled up with tears. "No. He was strong. He couldn't have given up yet." He stepped back and clutched the syringe. "It should've worked." Growling, he threw the needle at the wall in a fit of fury. It shattered and the glass fell like hail. "It should have worked!" he exploded. He threw his hands back on our friend's cold arms and vigorously shook them. "WAKE UP, LUCAS!"

I heard the faint clanking of metal and then watched Axel burst through the door. He looked at us speculatively through the glass. Realizing the situation, he entered the chamber. "Oh no," he whispered.

"He's not dead!" Ethan bellowed. "He's sleeping. His brain thinks he's dead. His Dragonfly genes saved him." Sweat dripped down his tan forehead. His voice softened and he shut his eyes tight. "His Dragonfly genes saved him," he sobbed.

I ran around the table and tore the Savior off of Lucas. I dragged Ethan thrashing and screaming out of the chamber and down the hall, leaving Axel alone with the body.

"Let me go, Yared," Ethan threatened, clawing at my arms.

Mark heard the shouting and ran down the hall to see what was the matter. "Whoa, guys, what's wrong?"

"He's not dead!" Ethan yelled, kicking me in the shin. "He can't be."

"Who's not?" Mark asked.

I squeezed Ethan's torso. I looked at Mark and whispered, "We lost Lucas."

Mark's face fell. He couldn't believe it. He just lost his brother and now one of his close friends.

Or so we thought.

"What's all this screaming about, mate?" a voice said from behind us.

I looked over my shoulder to see Lucas standing in the doorway with his arm draped over Axel's shoulder.

Ethan laughed and wriggled out of my grasp. "I told you! I told you! It worked," he exclaimed. He ran to our bug friend and shook his hand. "Nice to have you back, man."

Rubbing his shoulder, Lucas replied, "Happy to be back. That was the worst sleep ever. I'm still knackered."

"How are you not dead?" I asked in utter disbelief. "And how are you up and walking?"

He weakly waved his hand. "I've been laying down for too long. I was pretty much dead if this guy hadn't given me a kickstart." He jerked his head to Axel. "Thanks to you all, I'm still ticking."

"You zapped him back to life?" Mark chuckled, wiping the tears from his eyes. "I thought zappers killed bugs."

"Not this one, mate." He rubbed the marks on his bare chest where Axel shocked him. "Now, let's tell everyone Ethan found a cure for Sting's venom."

Mark looked at Ethan with wide blue eyes. "It was venom? What kind?"

The Savior let out a deep breath and briefly explained.

It took a moment to process. The Hodgins brother rubbed his hands through his brown hair and leaned against the wall. "So, Shane would have survived," he croaked. Sadness changed to fury like a spark igniting a fire. He whipped around and smashed the concrete wall with his fist. "He was STILL ALIVE!" he bellowed.

I hadn't thought of that. Shane's stab wound didn't appear fatal but we assumed the poison killed him instantly. We didn't take into consideration he was only paralyzed.

"Can we go back and check for him?" I suggested. I wanted to be hopeful even though it wasn't in my nature. "Ethan can whip up some more antidote."

Mark's back was turned. I couldn't see his face. "It's too late," he croaked. His voice was cracked and broken. "The Interpreters swept the area and there was no sign of his remains. Sting blew up the block after we left."

I had no words. I was never one to console. I made things worse.

Mark cleared his throat. "Let's get Lucas something to eat. I'll inform everyone about Ethan's discovery." Standing up straight, he strode away in silence.

The boys and I stood there quietly.

"I feel so bad for him," Axel whispered. "He returns home after five years and then loses his brother."

I wanted to repeat to myself that it was a casualty of war, but for some reason, I couldn't. My mind flashed back to my Seer comrades: Ursula and Jeremy. They were good fighters like Shane. They did their duty until the end, no matter what the cost.

But was the cost worth it? Leaving me to mourn and doubt?

The rumble of Lucas' stomach snapped me out of it. "Sorry, mates." The Dragonfly clutched his belly. "Let's not dwell on this now. There's always plenty of time to suffer." He tried to walk, but his knees buckled beneath him and he almost collapsed. He was too weak, but he didn't want to rest. Axel aided him forward and the four of us made our way back to our corner of the RRPR base.

Entering the lounge, we found the Isle members and Aymie seated around the kitchenette's table to our right. Ahead, Blake was out cold on our couch. After what happened to Shane, he'd been afraid to sleep. He kept himself up every night. To my surprise, he lasted several days, but exhaustion took its toll and he passed out.

Sami was the first to see us. Her cat eyes welled up with tears when she noticed Lucas wobbling in with Axel. Leaping from her seat, she ran and embraced her Australian friend. "Lucas, I thought we lost you," she whispered as she wet his bare back with her tears.

He didn't care. "I thought I lost me, too," Lucas replied.

The rest of our friends jumped to their feet to greet the resurrected Dragonfly. I looked over and saw Aymie smiling. She was joyful at his recovery, but sadness and jealousy shone in her gray eyes. I knew she missed her brother terribly, but she'd never outwardly show it to us. She was the strong, motherly face of RRPR. Big girls don't cry as they say.

"You must be starving." Aymie rose from her seat, went to the counter, and fixed Lucas a hearty sandwich. "You're all just in time for us to go over the plan of the next mission."

"We have another one already?" Ethan asked, sitting in a vacant seat.

"With RRPR there is no time to rest or mourn," she said solemnly. "One of the things I hate about it."

Silence filled the room. The only sound was the *swish* of the knife slicing through bread. Aymie finished and brought Lucas his sandwich. He inhaled it. His obnoxious manners lightened the mood slightly.

"We have information on a new OX base," Aymie continued, sitting back down. "We downloaded information from the Xenophonian base in Madrid which hinted at new structures somewhere in Europe. We aren't certain the exact location yet."

"What do you mean 'new structures'?" Axel asked.

"That's just it, we don't know." She pulled out a tablet and slid it to the center of the wooden table. I peered over little Donnie's shoulder. Blueprints for strange buildings flashed across the screen. It appeared to be homes, schools, stadiums, all different yet all advanced and appealing.

"This is all the Madrid base had to offer." Aymie tapped the screen to make the slideshow pause. "They aren't your standard OX buildings like Sonny is used to or that Joshua Wolfrum has informed us of. We don't know what their next phase is."

Alison looked up at our bald friend with wide mechanical eyes. "Wait, so the Accident," she paused, "is officially over?"

We all turned to her. Aymie's gaze reached us individually. "Yes. The Cleanse—or as you call it, the Accident—has been successfully completed." She let out a deep breath. "We couldn't stop it."

We were silent again.

OX had won the battle, but we weren't going to let them win the war.

"So what's next?" I demanded, breaking the quiet. "What are they calling this next phase? What are they doing?"

The RV Polymath shook her head. "We aren't sure. We have no insight from Sonny or Joshua."

"What about the Weapon?" I jerked my head towards the couch.

"Blake's in a bit of a slump." She turned to her sleeping boyfriend. You could tell she didn't want to blame him for Shane's death, but part of her couldn't put it aside. She trusted his precognitive dreams. Now, Aymie felt something she couldn't describe.

Betrayal.

That's the word she was looking for. I glanced over at resting Blake. I felt sorry for him. He had no control over his dreams. He slept peacefully. Too peacefully. Exactly like he had the other night.

And once again, he became restless.

Aymie's discussion became an inaudible mumbling as my focus was on the tossing-turning Blake. His peace turned to frustration and he began to sweat. His lip curled and his eyes tightened. His breathing turned to a growl. Suddenly, he shot up and faced me. His glass eyes found mine again. "MOSCOW!" he screamed. His breathing was heavy and his blue eyes became distant. His white hair clung to his damp forehead.

Everyone stopped. "Blake, what is it?" Aymie asked softly.

His constricted pupils dilated at the sound of her voice. He shook his head and groaned.

He was awake.

He turned to his girlfriend; his breathing slowed down. "They're in Moscow," he panted.

She snatched her tablet from Donnie and entered the location. "It's in the region OX gave us," she whispered. Saying nothing, she rose to her feet and strode out of the room.

Blake slumped back on the couch and caught his breath. With a hand on his forehead, he mumbled, "I hate this."

Something tugged inside me, telling me to talk to him. I crossed the room and stood at the foot of the couch. "Chill, man. Your dreams are what keep us one step ahead."

"Not all the time." He wiped his face with his gray shirt. "I hope this one's worth it."

THE UNDERGROUND

Slowly, I seated myself on the coffee table that creaked under my weight. I looked over to see if anyone was listening. The rest of the Isle members whispered amongst themselves. I turned back to the white-haired young man. "Why would it not be worth it?"

"Some people might end up *liking* what we find." Blake's gaze caught mine. A scene reflected in his light blue eyes. A scene of sorrow and confusion. "This next mission," his voice was a low whisper, "will cause division amongst us."

My heart raced in my chest. It wasn't out of anxiety or fear of our team being torn apart. No.

It was excitement.

The danger, the suspense, the fights. I never wished for them to happen, but when they did come... I loved every moment of it.

With that being said, my words would've been of no comfort to Blake. He needed someone to tell him something positive like "We'll all stick together" or "We know what OX is capable of. Nothing will sway us", but I wasn't that person. That kind of person would've been Mark or Shannon... or even Shane.

But he was gone. Perhaps the division had already begun.

Unsure of what to say, I gave an awkward smile and patted his shoulder. Blake nodded. He knew my intentions. Deep in my gut, I felt the two of us were connected somehow. Standing up, I returned to my friends who were discussing the matter.

"What is a Moss-cow anyhow?" Donnie asked, confused. The little boy had been so brave after losing his friends: Marlene and Ava. He was the only Asset left in the group. He represented his Isle as did Ethan and I, but he was only ten.

"It's a place in Russia," Alison explained with her clipboard in hand. She used it more than ever now. "Part of the Soviet Union a long time ago; whatever that means."

"But what is it now?" Sami asked, peeking over her sister's shoulder.

Out of the corner of my eye, I saw Blake's head hang low.

Before I could ask, Mark walked through the doorway with Sonny.

Aaron jumped to his feet; his new glasses almost fell off his face. "Mark. What's going on?"

"Pack your bags everyone," he ordered. "We leave now."

That happened yesterday. Right now, we are traveling to Moscow and unsure of what to expect. I feel like Blake knows though. I've kept an eye on him this whole plane ride and he's acting stranger than normal. Distant. Quiet.

Blake is hiding something, but I don't know what it is.

You have quite the list from us: Sting, Moscow, Marcellus, the Titans, the Moirai, PH, the whole shebang. Let me know how your Titan meeting goes. Best of luck, man.

Bravery and fidelity,

Yared Prinz
Seer Commander

THE UNDERGROUND

LETTER 9

Joshua: V

Hello Yared and Shannon,

I can't believe Sting's poison—I mean, venom causes paralysis. My heart mourns for you, but I'm thankful for your discovery.

In addition, I hope you arrived in Moscow safely. I found out more about what you'll encounter, but I fear this information will be useless by the time you receive it.

The day of the Titan meeting, I awoke to the Strange Voices, got dressed, repeated my mantra, and went to the dining hall. I wasn't sure what to expect. *I'm going to present in front of OX's authoritative figures… What if I screw up?* I worried as I approached the food counter.

"Morning, Wolf," Emel greeted as she slopped oatmeal into a bowl for me. "You look on edge today."

I hated how she knew me so well. "I have some stuff going on, I guess," I replied, trying to push my worry aside.

She scratched her round face with the back of her gloved hand. "Going to that meeting with PH, aren't ya?" I stopped abruptly; the bowl of oatmeal almost slid off my tray. She snorted. "Of course I know. PH wants you to meet him in the hangar. You'll know the section."

I nodded and followed her down the line. "Have you had any recent fights with your sisters?"

"Nope, thank goodness." She handed me surprisingly clean utensils. "I think they've given up. We all have so much to do they just leave me alone now."

Honestly, I wasn't sure how much power a little—well, big—lunch lady had in an operation such as OX, but I wouldn't underestimate her. I feel like there's more to Emel than meets the eye.

I wanted to remain on her good side, so I flattered her: "I don't know why they'd want to mess with you. I'd like to meet your sisters just to find out."

She smirked. "One day." With that, she returned to the front of the line to assist another Xenophonian.

Gripping my tray, I went to my table. I sat across from Solomon and Diego again. This time, Goliath squeezed next to them on the bench. "Hey, guys," I greeted.

"So what's the story? You can't keep hiding from us," Goliath replied, snapping his banana in half. The fruit's scent floated through the air and met Diego's nose. The monkey squeaked and leapt onto Goliath's bald head. The big guy didn't mind giving some to the little critter. That was a shock. He never shared anything with anyone.

I looked around. No one was paying attention. *If I don't tell them, Goliath might pummel me.* I was about to share when Solomon's and Goliath's eyes glanced above me.

"Hey boys, what's the craic?" a familiar voice chirped. I turned to see the bartender seating himself beside me.

"Wolf here is about to tell us what happened with PH, Leprechaun," Goliath explained.

"Ooh," his light eyes widened, "do tell."

I let out a deep breath. "PH and I interpreted the information I found on Marcellus," I said in a low voice. "Now, I have to present it at the Titan meeting today."

Jaws dropped and eyes widened. Even Diego listened intently.

"No one within our low ranks has ever stood in the presence of more than two Titans," Goliath whispered. "Now, you'll be before all of them."

"What an honor," Leprechaun declared. Grabbing his fork with his left hand, he stabbed his breakfast potatoes and waved them at me. "You sure do have a promising future ahead of you."

"Thanks," I mumbled. "I'm just not sure what to expect."

"Well, at least you'll have some familiar faces there." Leprechaun ate his potatoes and scraped his white teeth on the utensil. "You'll have PH, Emel—"

"Wait," I interrupted. "What do you mean 'Emel'?"

He scratched his head of reddish blond hair. "I thought you knew?"

"Knew what, Leprechaun?" I asked.

He clicked his tongue. "Not sure if I should say." He paused. "She's got more power than you think she does, let's just say that."

I turned and looked at the brute lunch lady. She laughed heartily as she served a low ranking Xenophonian. Her gaze caught mine and she winked. *I knew she had more significance.* I just have to find out what it is.

"I'll keep that in mind," I told him, taking a sip of rich coffee. Emel made it perfect once again. "I just hope I don't screw this up."

"You better not," Goliath threatened. "You need to get promoted so you can put in a good word for the rest of us."

Once again, he surprised me. Most Ares members were cruel, jealous, and competitive. Goliath *wanted* me to succeed. Of course he hoped to get something out of it, but he didn't want to race me to the top. He was different from the others. Despite his villainous, disgusting nature, not having to worry that he'll snap my neck was comforting.

I nodded and finished my breakfast. Standing from my seat, I bid my acquaintances goodbye. I started to walk away when a wrinkled hand grabbed my arm.

Solomon looked up; his distant eyes were serious. "*To answer before listening — that is folly and shame.*"

"I'll be careful," I told him. Diego chirped and hopped up on my shoulder. I was about to complain, but something in Solomon's gaze made me hold back. He wanted Diego to accompany me again. Not sure if it was for good luck or what. Saying nothing else, I took my leave.

I walked down the dark corridors until I came upon the hangar door. Taking a deep breath, I patted the letter in my breast pocket. *You got this, Joshua. Remember, you are Wolf. PH is fond of Wolf.* I entered the code into the panel and the metallic door slid aside.

OX aircraft and artillery filled the hangar. Planes, helicopters, tanks, trucks, weapons, you name it. The sound of mechanical whirs bounced off the walls. Automated robotic arms hung down from the ceiling, repairing the vehicles. Diego squeaked and covered his ears with his hands. I scratched the creature's head and made my way to the back where the English Pandemonium weaponry was kept.

PH sat on top of his beloved Challenger II with his pipe clenched between his teeth and his sword across his lap. Robotic arms hung around him, finishing the repairs of his tank. Sparks flew as they welded, but PH didn't care. He wouldn't dare leave its side despite the fact that his arms were exposed and could get burned.

I had to do a double take. In seven years, I never saw him without his combat jacket. He wore a white t-shirt, and my eyes widened when I saw his arms.

Tattoos of red, black, and brown hues crawled up from his wrists to his shoulders, hiding beneath his shirt. Greek styled designs covered his body. *I didn't know Titans were marked for their kills like the Ares*, I thought looking at his ink. PH's body was a canvas painted with the blood of those he slaughtered.

The robotic arms made an ascending tone and lifted away from the tank. With the noise subsided, the Titan heard me approaching and lifted his eyes. Blowing out a puff of smoke, PH called, "Wolf! Emel got my message to ya."

"Of course, sir." I stood next to the tank and patted its tracks. It was sure an impressive hunk of metal. Modeled off of the third generation British main battle tank, but with OX modifications of course. "She's looking better."

"Ain't she?" He stood and grabbed his sword with his left hand. He pointed its blade towards the back of the armored vehicle. "She's all better after that Gorilla-Man 'andled her. No more dents." Swiftly, he slid the sword in the sheath on his back and hopped down from the hatch to the hull then to the floor with the pipe still in his mouth. "Brings me joy that you ask about my girl, mate." His heterochromatic eyes sparkled. "She means everythin' to me."

I managed a smile and nodded. I was surprised that the cold blooded killer had a soft spot for anything even if it was mechanical. His passion for his possession made me wonder if he had feelings for anything else. *Maybe he isn't so cold hearted after all*, I thought, but had to shake it off. I couldn't let my vision be blurred. My focus needed to be sharp and my will like stone.

PH grabbed his scarf and combat jacket off the bench. Before he put them on, I forced myself to say, "I didn't know you were marked, sir."

The Titan chuckled and slid his arms through the jacket sleeves. "If subordinates are inked for their victories, their leaders should 'ave nothing less." He flung his scarf around his neck. "All Titans 'ave tattoos. It's an 'onor. Our backs are the most decorated with our emblems at the center. Once you're a Titan, there's no goin' back. You're all in," he zipped his jacket, "or dead."

I tried not to show discomfort towards his last comment. "Understood, sir."

He slid his sheath back over his head. "So enough about me. Are ya ready?"

"As ready as I'll ever be," I told him and Diego squeaked in agreement.

He chuckled. "You're lucky I like this monkey," he pointed his pipe at it. "Otherwise he'd be dead for accompanying ya all the time."

Diego snatched the pipe and curiously played with it. PH whistled and the creature returned it.

"Also a good thing he's obedient." PH smiled, sticking the pipe back in his mouth. He puffed out a cloud of smoke, filling the hangar with the aroma of sweet tobacco. "Let's crack on," he declared as he spun on his heel and led me out and down deep into the base.

JOSHUA: V

We twisted and turned down corridors that grew darker and darker until I couldn't see. I knew where he was taking me.

New Greece.

PH granted us access and the door slid open. I shielded my eyes so I wouldn't be blinded by the light reflecting off the white city. We passed through and up to the main plaza where the five statues of the gods of our Divisions stood. Rather than going to the Hermes temple, we continued straight towards the Temple of Zeus.

My heart thumped and my hands quaked as we walked up the marble steps. PH claimed it was used for real worship. I was blessed at OX never having to betray my religion. I was afraid today would be the day I'd fail Him.

Entering the Temple, I found it to be one long hall. The perimeter was lined with marble throne chairs between its pillars. Two emblems were etched above each seat: the Division symbol and the Titan's personal emblem. All the Titans sat in their respective places. Most of their faces I didn't recognize. The only one I knew sat beneath the Ares vulture and her personal wasp emblem:

Sting.

She eyeballed me as PH and I crossed to the center of the room. We approached a massive bowl of fire. The flames climbed high like hands reaching for help. PH stopped before it, and I remained behind him.

Closing his eyes, he whispered some things in Greek. He reached into his pocket and pulled out a closed fist. He took a step back and I copied. He raised both arms. His eyes popped open and he tossed what he was holding into the bowl. The flames roared and crackled, shooting up into the air as if his offering frightened them. The color changed from its fiery red to a bright green, resembling the color of the Hermes Division.

The flames died and PH led me over to his throne. I thanked God I didn't have to make an offering. I was safe.

Removing his sword from his sheath, he placed it in a holder beside his marble chair. With a grunt, the short Xenophonian hopped up and took his rightful place. I stood at his feet, facing outward.

I wriggled my nose and looked around, wanting to further identify what I was seeing. The Titans sat still and silent in their cold thrones. In the front of the room were three women's statues: two slender ones and a larger one in between them. They all had a haggard look and were each posed differently. The first had what appeared to be a spool of thread; the second had her arms out as if she were measuring; the third clutched cutting shears.

The Moirai, I thought, looking at the empty thrones beneath. *Now I'll find out the truth about Arata and the others.*

I looked past the three to the giant statue of Zeus sitting on his throne.

It was a replica of the one outside the plaza but scaled up. His lifeless eyes met mine, challenging me. I was terrified, but Wolf returned the glare.

"Beautiful, ain't it?" PH whispered.

I gave a quick nod. I averted my gaze from Zeus and back to the Moirai, hoping for the three figures to appear at any moment.

"The Moirai won't join us in person today," PH explained. "Since you're 'ere and all."

I held back a curse. "I apologize if I'm changing your meeting routine."

Sting leaned towards me; her long braid dangled over the edge of her throne. "You're a good change," she purred. "I get tired of looking at three old bags." She winked and sat upright.

Diego chirped in my ear. *Shut up,* I mentally told the monkey.

Then, I felt my legs quake. Not from nerves. A rumbling gently shook the floors of the temple. Smoke billowed from beneath the statues of the Moirai, encompassing them in their cloud.

A light shone on the first Moirai statue. "I, Clotho, wish to welcome you to this gathering." Her voice was sweet but also familiar. "It is a glorious day for the Order of Xenophon. Zeus has been kind to us. Our missions have been successful and the Cleanse is nearly complete."

The Temple filled with roaring acclaims.

My heart sank. I had no choice but to add to the cheers.

The first light went dark but another shone on the third statue. "Our final stage, the Annex will now be put into effect." This woman had a kind voice, but I didn't recognize it. "We gave millions a new purpose. They now have a chance for a new life. The world was once disgusting, inhumane, imperfect. We cleansed it of those impurities." She paused.

Lights shone on all three statues. Voices spoke simultaneously: "Time to make the world perfect again."

The Titans shouted in agreement. I tried to smile but was terrified. *"The Annex"... does that mean what I think it means?*

The light shone solely on the statue of Clotho again. "While this stage begins immediately, there are still some final insects to squish. Two of the obstacles were removed: former Titans whose Mortal names were Nikita Patya and Walter Jarvis. However, we must silence the first traitor: former Titan Marcellus. Let's also not forget his treacherous children and their Resistance."

Sting's announcement interrupted the Moirai: "Madams. Some good came out of the betrayal of Patya and Jarvis." Hopping down from her throne, she marched with confidence to the fire. She threw something into it and it spread. The flames were red and a picture was displayed within it.

It showed clips of two figures made of metal. They were flying and fighting, taking down more OX soldiers than a normal man could. Blue lights shone amidst the dust and debris. Power and strength emanating from them both.

A power I dreaded OX obtaining.

"These two are called Bionics and they come from the Isle of Biomechatronics Testing," Sting informed. "They are currently siding with the triplets, but I believe they can be swayed." Her eyes raised to the statues. A smug look crossed her face. "Clotho, I know you can give them a new purpose. Lachesis, you say the word if they get out of line. Atropos, you can end them."

The statues were silent, pondering her words.

A bead of sweat dripped down the back of my neck. While Axel and Alison were strong, I feared that their technology made them vulnerable.

"Brilliant, Sting," the third Moirai—Atropos—said. "They would be a great addition, but aren't required to fulfill the plan. You may retrieve them if you desire. The rest of the Titans will only take part if they volunteer."

Sting bowed and walked back to her throne. *She didn't say anything about Shane*, I thought, relieved. If she knew she killed a Hodgins, she would've said… right?

Clotho's statue lit up again. "Now, PH. I believe you and your soldier have some developments on your predecessor?"

The British Titan nodded. "Wolf 'ere discovered that Marcellus 'ad connections to the crazy lady who gave us trouble in Quebec." His eyes darted to me and then back at the statue. "Present what you got, Wolf."

My body trembled with every step forward. Diego abandoned me and perched at the top of PH's throne. The company would've been nice. *Coward*, I thought, looking at the creature.

Nevertheless, I approached the statues with what appeared to be confidence. Wolf was braver than me. I pulled the letter out of my jacket pocket and held it up. "This was given to me by the woman in Quebec in exchange for one building to remain standing," I began in a loud voice. I took out the black light. "This is written in Marcellus' handwriting. The poem as a whole means nothing. But," I illuminated the letters, revealing its secrets, "it means more when it's taken apart. The beginning of coordinates." I clicked the light off. "Marcellus shall lead us to him."

The statues were silent. I feared I messed up.

As I was about to scurry back to PH, the center statue of the larger woman lit up. She laughed heartily. She was about to say something when she was interrupted.

"That is magnificent, Wolf," Clotho put in. "We are pleased. Lachesis most of all. She decided the date for Marcellus' end a long time ago. Thanks to you, her request is closer to being fulfilled."

I bowed. "Thank you for the compliments, ma'am, but PH instructed me. He gave me the hints to the perimeter's weak spot and followed through with the bargain for the letter."

"Your modesty is held in high esteem," Clotho replied. "Great work."

I returned to my place and looked up to see PH eyeing me. Satisfaction spread across his freckled face. Diego was also pleased. He squeaked and cooed as he climbed down the marble and onto my shoulder.

To conclude the meeting, the Moirai and Titans spoke in Greek; probably so I wouldn't understand. My glasses tried to translate, but the different accents and overlapping speech were difficult to decipher.

An hour later, the meeting reached an end. The Titans rose from their seats and made their way to the fire pit in the center. Murmurs fell from their lips. Their eyes closed, and they held out clenched fists. One by one the Titans threw their offerings into the pit causing the flames to rise high to the heavens.

I forced a smile as they celebrated their victories.

When their ritual concluded, I followed PH back out to the plaza of New Greece. Thinking we were returning to the lower Xenophonian section, I headed straight while PH turned to the Temple of Hermes. Diego squeaked and tugged on the long part of my hair. I did a double take and chased PH up the steps.

"Thought we were done, mate?" he chuckled when I caught up. "We have to find the other letters from Marcellus."

"Do you have an idea?"

"I've got a few," he said smugly. We entered the Hermes Temple and went to the computers. PH sat and typed at the console, pulling up his other findings on Marcellus.

"We only have to focus on 'im now," PH explained. "Sting is now in charge of the triplets."

My heart pounded in my chest. That was the last thing they needed. "Does she know something about them that we don't?" I asked, calmly.

He scoffed. "That lady don't even know 'er Mortal name. She's just not stealthy enough to catch Marcellus."

"We're not instructed to catch all of them?"

He shook his head. "No, we're runnin' out of time. Phase Annex is the most important. We can't have 'em screwing this up." He pulled his pipe out of his pocket and lit it. "Let's get started." With the pipe clenched between his teeth he started his search and together we found the most recent known whereabouts of Marcellus Hodgins.

Shannon, Yared, be careful when going to Moscow. I think that's the original starting point of the Annex. If it means what I think it means, you're in for a surprise.

Also, tell Ethan to whip up some more of Sting's venom's antidote. You're going to need it.

With safety and secrecy,

Joshua Wolfrum

Joshua Wolfrum

THE UNDERGROUND

LETTER 10

Shannon: III

Hello Joshua,

We were blessed. Your letter came through before the mission to Moscow. At least we had some idea what to expect. Unfortunately, what we saw was worse than we could've imagined. I fear what Blake said will come true.

RRPR will divide.

As soon as I stepped off the plane, I couldn't believe my eyes. Frankly, no one could. The ruined city of Moscow was rebuilt. Marble structures erected where rubble should've been. The roads were paved with smooth stones. The sky was bright, the air was clean, and there was peace.

A peace meant to cloud lies.

Cautiously, we made our way towards the new city. "What is this?" Sami asked nervously as she crept along the ground on all fours.

"Not sure, but gosh, it's beautiful," the farmer boy—Donnie—marveled. I disapproved of his accompaniment, but he was stubborn and persistent, so we compromised. He was only going as far as Virginia Michaelson's Interpreter camp where he'd stay until the mission's end.

Sonny gripped his weapon tighter. "Don't let this fool you. This is the beginning of the Annex. It's not as promising as it seems."

We moved around the outside of the city in silence. There was no sign of OX anywhere.

Finally, we met an Interpreter on the perimeter. She waved us into an abandoned house that was untouched since the Accident. One by one we followed her inside.

Within the dusty stone building were only a few Interpreters, and they didn't look well. They were beat up, bruised, and in poor spirits. "What happened?" I asked.

She responded in Russian to which Sonny interpreted: "OX found their encampment years ago when they started rebuilding the city. This is all that's left of Michaelson's forces here."

Their condition made my heart heavy. *We were never winning this fight, were we?*

Mark took over the conversation for me. "Do you know about the Annex?"

She nodded and explained which Sonny translated, "She says it's the final stage of the Order of Xenophon's plan. The world is cleansed and now it's time to return those who are worthy."

Mark had a speculative look. "Wait, Sonny, what does that mean? Who do they deem worthy?"

The ex-Ares member turned. His red eyes glowed. "All those that OX captured, if they survived, will be released and given a new purpose. A new start."

If my parents are alive... they'll come home? I thought.

"Is this a good thing or a bad thing?" Ethan asked as he unpacked his medical kit.

Letting out a deep breath, Sonny replied, "It will only be good if we can deactivate OX's chips in the survivors' necks. Then they'll be freed from the Order mentally and physically."

"And what if we can't free them?" Mark questioned.

"Those who were captured are no longer your friends or family." Sonny didn't meet Mark's gaze. "They are Xenophonians. They may not be soldiers but can fight if they have to."

Yared held up his hands. "So, let's say the Annex is successful and all the survivors are out and about. There are two outcomes. First," he lifted one finger, "we release all survivors, saving them from mental captivity. Second outcome," he paused; his eyes darted back and forth from Mark to Sonny, "our little RRPR is up against millions of OX zombies?"

Sonny's lips tightened. "Pretty much." He thanked the Interpreter and slung his rifle over his shoulder. "Well, they're not going to be much help. Let's keep moving."

"I'll come with y'all," Donnie stated. He pulled Marlene's sheep shears out of his pocket with a *shing* like a knight drawing his sword. He was ready for battle.

"No, Donnie. You stay here," Alison ordered. She put her metal hand on the boy's shoulder and nudged him towards the Interpreters.

He wriggled from her grasp. "Alison, I beg ya." He stared up at her with his big eyes. His freckled face was almost too cute to deny.

Lucas put his arm around the boy. "Hey, cobber, you can stay behind with Aaron, Ethan, and me." He pointed to the wounded Interpreters that lay still on their cots. "We need to protect these folks here."

"Please!" Donnie cried, running away from Lucas. He dropped to the floor at Alison's feet and wrapped his arms around her armored legs. "I need to help. I need to fight." Tears tore through the dust on his cheeks. "For Marlene. For Ava," he choked.

My heart broke hearing their names. Marlene was the one my fiancé Shane searched for for years. He promised her big sister—RV Agricola Marian Best—that he'd return her pocket watch. A day later, she was killed protecting her friends. And little Ava... she was nine when she was murdered. My stomach tied itself in knots as I remembered her little face as she was shot by that Seer. Despite her pain, Ava was peaceful knowing she was going home. Knowing she would see Marlene.

Donnie can't go home yet, I thought, biting my lip. *We can give him the future his friend's would want him to have.*

I stifled a gasp when a firm hand clasped my shoulder. I turned to see Mark. His blue eyes filled with kindness. "*It's okay,*" he mouthed.

"Guys, don't worry. I'll stay with them; take Alison this time," Nic decided. The Mutant Gorilla scooped the sad Donnie up. The boy flung his slender arms around Nic's neck and wept. Even though Donnie was ten, he looked like a toddler against Nic. "If you need our help, give us a call."

"Thank you, Nic," I said, placing my breathing mask over my mouth. I covered the rest of my head and face to disguise my appearance. "We'll keep you posted." With that, the rest of us went out to find the Xenophonians.

Our footsteps sounded like screams as we marched down the quiet streets of the remains of the Red Square. Classical marble replaced the colorful domed structures. In the center was a massive temple-like building. Above the entrance were two emblems: the OX symbol and the Ares vulture. There was a spot for a third but it was blank. At the base of its steps was a tall statue of the God of War himself.

"This would've been my temple," Sonny muttered.

He spoke a little too loudly, and Yared did a double take. "Whoa, hold up," he sputtered. "You would've gotten your own temple?"

Sonny nodded and pointed a pale finger to the vacant emblem. "That last mark is for the Titan that rules all the lands within his Pandemonium. He has one location to call home and this," he looked longingly at the marble structures, "would've been it."

I marveled at the thought. If Sonny didn't have a change of heart due to his mother, we would've fought against him (if we even got that far).

"What did your emblem look like?" Mark asked, curious. "I know PH has the sword and snakes; Sting's is a wasp. Were they all creatures?"

To my surprise, Sonny wasn't annoyed by the question. In fact, pride and pleasure crossed his face. After making sure the coast was clear, he unzipped his jacket. I blushed as he lifted his shirt, but my red face turned white as I saw his marks for the first time.

Tattoos of black, red, and brown hues crawled up the right side of his body like moss on a tree. His entire torso was covered in ink and white scars. From your description about PH's tattoos, I figured Sonny was also marked for his killings and achievements in OX, but I never suspected it'd be so intricate and vast. Each tattoo, every detail meant someone fell at *his* hands outside of mass battles. Sonny was only twenty-five and hundreds of deaths were marked on his body. *And he left when he was young*, I thought with a shudder.

Raising his shirt a little more, Sonny showed the most important tattoo. In the center of his back was the profile of a large black and red galea—a Roman helmet.

"That's my emblem. My mark," Sonny explained. "Any Xenophonian that saw it trembled with fear." Covering himself up, he turned back to us. "They knew *I* sought their blood." Memories of OX shone through his red eyes. I sensed the Erik Patya part of him missed his old way of life. Even though he was a Wilcox, the menace of being a Patya still burned within him.

Will Erik Patya ever take Sonny over? I wondered. No, he's done so much for us…

Mark whistled, interrupting my thoughts. "Man, that's freaky," he confessed. "Please don't slip me a card with your mark on it anytime soon."

Sonny smirked. "You're lucky you won't get the pleasure." He turned around, bringing our attention back to the moment at hand. Gripping our weapons, we made our way forward.

The city was still. No birds chirping, no water rushing, not even the breath of wind.

"I don't like this," Alison muttered. Her armor gleamed in the white marble's reflection. "Where is everyone?"

"Not here yet," Sonny replied. "We have time."

"Time to do what?" Aaron asked, clutching his backpack tighter.

Sonny peered around a pillar. "To destroy the temple. Their technology and supplies must be there. The temples are more like bases than places of worship."

"Wait, we can't destroy it yet," Mark protested. "We should infiltrate it and gather information. Maybe it communicates with the other temples. We need those locations."

"He's right," I chimed in. "We can't wait for Joshua. Who knows how long it will take before that information is revealed to him?"

Sonny grunted. "All right, but we don't have long." He desired to destroy the base for personal reasons. He craved the power OX gave him.

If he couldn't rule, no one could.

Quickly, we devised a plan. Aaron, Mark, Axel, and Sami would go into the temple, find the computers, and get whatever information they could while the rest of us kept watch. It wasn't well thought out, but we had no choice.

They took their leave, and the four remaining spread out. The eerie vacancy of the new country frightened me. Something worse was in store.

I crouched on the steps of a new marble shop. My hands were clammy and my breathing was shallow. I felt disturbed like a paranormal presence surrounded me, unnerving my soul. The ghosts of our past world awoke today. To either seek revenge or welcome the changes of the Order of Xenophon.

I prayed it was the former.

I keenly watched as the rest of the team raced towards the building. We had no idea of its defenses or what was inside, but so far so good.

I waited patiently as Axel stopped before entering. He stared intently at the Temple and scanned it. He paused and a confused look fell across his face. I sent him a quick message to ask what was the matter. He stared off into the distance, reading the text that flashed before his eyes. He mentally sent back, *"There's no one inside."*

The discomforting feeling weighed heavier in the pit of my stomach. I watched my four friends cautiously enter the temple.

The minutes felt like hours. I anticipated something terrible to happen, but all was quiet.

"Did I miss anything?" a little voice behind me whispered.

Startled, I aimed my gun. It was Donnie. His hood was pulled over his dirty blond hair, and Marlene's sheep shears were tight in his grasp. He wanted to fight.

"What are you doing here?" I whispered, trying not to let anger slip through my electronic voice.

"I told ya," he shot, "I have to do this. For Marlene. For Ava."

"No, you can't. Not here." I sent a message to Nic.

"It's too late. I'm here now. You can't send me back."

I was about to argue when a chill went up my spine. Donnie saw me pause and looked over my shoulder. His light eyes widened and he staggered back.

I turned and saw the person I hated most.

A fake smile spread across her face. "What's the matter, kid?" Sting asked, "I won't hurt you."

I glared at her through my goggles. I wanted to end her, but Donnie was too close. One false move and he could get hurt.

Careful to only seek justice and not revenge.

I ignored that voice.

Sting faced me and stood up straight. "I know you. You're Detective."

"What do you want?" I demanded.

She shook her head. "Always wanting to solve the problems quickly. I'm not here to fight. I'm here to offer you something." Sting reached into her pocket, and I dropped into a stance. She scoffed. "Relax." She pulled out a small scroll and threw it at my feet.

Holding her gaze, I picked it up. She gestured for me to read it. I ordered Donnie to keep an eye on her while I went over it.

It was an offer. A possibility of peace. The Order of Xenophon and RRPR living side-by-side in this new world. They offered us a home, resources, a new way of life. We would receive a temple built specifically for us. The masters of war and destruction were presenting an option that went against the very nature of their order.

But there was a catch.

RRPR must hand over their Bionics.

Not only is this unacceptable, it's a trick, I thought. *OX would never live in peace with us.*

I raised my head. I locked eyes with Sting as I crumpled the parchment and threw it at her feet. "Not a chance," I snarled.

Her mouth became a straight line. Disappointment crossed her face. "Are you sure? This seems like a pretty good deal." She picked it up. Her gaze lifted and met Donnie's. "Catch, *niño*." The crinkled ball soared and landed in the boy's hands. "I think you have more sense."

Without flinching, Donnie caught it. Hesitantly, he unfolded it and read. His expression remained neutral as he shoved the paper in his jacket pocket. Gripping his shears, he pointed at the Titan and sneered, "Thanks for the offer, miss, but our friends ain't going nowhere with ya."

Sting sighed. She took a few steps closer, but Donnie didn't budge. He kept the shears pointed at her chest. "I thought you'd make the right choice," she hissed, eyeing him up and down. "Who knows? You still may." Standing upright, she glared once more at the boy and me. She spun on her heel and disappeared behind the marble building.

Donnie gasped as if coming up for air. "What was that about?"

I shook my head. "I'll figure it out soon. There's much more to it." My gut wrenched at the sight of her walking away. That sadistic monster murdered my fiancé in front of me. I wanted her to know the pain she had caused me.

But I couldn't do it. For the sake of the operation.

We waited anxiously to hear from Mark and the others. They were still inside the Temple, and no ruckus was caused. I tried to contact them, but no response. I started to worry.

I messaged Sonny who replied, "*Let's move in. Be careful.*" I ordered Donnie to stay behind, gripped my pistol, and went to meet the others.

I saw Sonny, Yared, and Alison slowly making their way forward. I was almost to the base of the steps when I heard the clamor of trucks. I couldn't pinpoint the exact direction. The sound came from everywhere.

I met up with Alison first. "What is that?" she asked; a frightened tone in her voice. Normally, she was strong and brave. Something unnerved her, too.

"I don't know," I confessed, "Did you see anything?"

She shook her head. "I have this weird feeling, though."

"Glad I'm not alone."

The hum of engines grew louder until the vehicles drove into view. Coming from all directions were dozens of trucks spotless from dirt and grime. Alison grabbed me and flew us atop a building. We dropped to our stomachs and watched them circle the statue of Ares in the center of the plaza.

They stopped simultaneously. Emerging from the backs were hundreds of people. Their ages ranged from twenty-five to sixty-five. Bright white togas draped off their slender bodies. Their eyes widened as they looked around in awe at the new city. Happy exclamations escaped their lips. They cried, rubbed their hands across the buildings, leapt for joy, and explored the new land around them.

Sting emerged from a side street. The sea of white parted as she went to stand before the statue of the war-god. She raised her hand and everyone silenced. She spoke aloud in Greek: "*Citizens, welcome to your new home. The war is over. You have won. It is time to take your rightful place here in the New World.*" She gestured towards the temple. "*Your place of answers. Your place of protection. Your place of worship.*"

Their curious eyes scanned the building. Slowly and mechanically, they lumbered into the temple like it was calling them.

"What's going on?" Alison whispered.

Before I could answer, my watch beeped. It was Mark. I held my breath as I read the message. For some reason, it was received in fragments: *There wasn't... found... rigged ... blow. Permission?*

My fingers hovered over the keypad. I was ready to say "Yes", but my conscience stopped me. I watched the childlike survivors climb up the steps and into the building. I growled and slammed my fist on the roof.

"What's wrong?" Alison asked.

"They want to blow up the building."

"And?"

"We can't." I pointed to the people. "We'd slaughter them all."

I ordered Mark to get out of there and leave the charges. Hopefully, they won't be found and we could finish the job at a later date. He understood and his team would meet us back at the camp. I sent a message to Sonny and Yared, briefly explaining the situation. We were to retreat, leaving the new city untouched.

Alison flew me back to the shop where I left Donnie. Sonny and Yared were there, but Donnie wasn't. I tried to remain calm. "Guys, you haven't seen Donnie have you?"

Their eyes widened. "What do you mean?" Yared asked.

I bit my cheek. "He escaped the camp and found me. I left him here when the survivors arrived."

"What?!" Yared fumed. "I thought Nic was supposed to watch him."

"That doesn't matter now!" Sonny snapped. "Let's find him."

It occurred to me that I hadn't heard from Nic after Donnie arrived. I sent another message to see if they were okay. Still nothing. I kept that detail quiet.

Sonny gave the order and we split up to search for the boy. I raced down a few sidestreets until I found him at a new home near the Red Square.

Donnie stood on the steps, staring into the doorway. His mouth agape and his arms were limp at his sides. Marlene's shears slowly slipped from his grasp. I watched as a slender arm reached out and gently took the weapon from him. The boy's breathing quickened and he teetered back and forth.

I raced towards him, shouting his name. I didn't care who heard me; only, he didn't. He remained in his trance-like state. I couldn't understand what was going on, but I didn't stay to watch. I snatched him and ran around the back of the building. His thin body was limp and his arms were going cold.

I lifted my head and screamed for Alison. In an instant, she tore through the air until she hovered beside me. Her mechanical eyes widened, but she didn't ask. Gingerly, she took Donnie from my arms and flew to meet the others.

I raced behind her, not looking back.

Returning to the Interpreter's hideout, I watched Alison lay Donnie on the ground. Ethan stood over the boy, pressing a stethoscope to his chest. The other Isle members watched over him. Everyone was accounted for except Nic.

"Shannon, what happened out there?" Sami the Cat quavered. She stood from Donnie's bedside. The boy's eyes were shut tight and his nose was crinkled. He was having a bad dream, but couldn't wake from it.

"I'm unsure," I confessed. "He stood in a doorway, staring at some woman who took his shears from him. That's all I know."

"Did you see what she looked like?" Sonny inquired.

My observation skills failed me, and Donnie would pay the price. "No. I feared for Donnie's life. I grabbed him and ran." I lowered my voice. "I'm sorry."

Axel the Bionic clasped a metal hand on my shoulder. "It's all right. You did what you had to."

"What else happened while we were in the Temple?" Aaron asked. His blue eyes darted back and forth.

We shook our heads. Other than Donnie's trance, there was nothing but the survivors' arrival.

"There must be something we're missing," Mark said, rubbing his chin. "We found a clue for two of the other temples, but that was it. No speakers, no screens, nothing. Just supplies and a few maps."

I sighed. "A clue is a start. We'll revisit this place later."

Sonny, Yared, and Alison stated the only thing to report were the trucks with the citizens and Sting's appearance.

"I can't believe we didn't take her out," Mark muttered. "She didn't know we were there."

My eyes couldn't meet theirs. I didn't want to tell them about my encounter with her or her offer of peace.

If they find out, chaos will break out amongst us. A division will arise.

Sami's ears perked up and she turned towards the door. "Someone's coming."

We dropped to our stances and aimed our weapons.

The doors burst open and Nic barged in with a few Interpreters. He panted and fear shone in his violet eyes. He opened his mouth to speak but shut it when he saw Donnie. He let out a long exhale. "Thank God. Where was he?"

"He followed us. I thought *you* were supposed to watch him," Yared spat, lowering his rifle.

Nic sat down on a chair too small for him and caught his breath. "He ran out when my back was turned. I've been looking for him all over."

"It's okay, Nic, it's not your fault," Mark consoled.

"You didn't get the message I sent?" I asked.

Nic looked perplexed. "I tried sending *you* messages." He tapped the screen on his communicator and shook his head. "Nothing came in."

I looked at my own. "I didn't receive anything from you either."

Aaron tapped the side of his cheek and said, "I wonder if the Temple has anything to do with that."

"What do you mean?" Nic asked.

"We didn't find technology of any kind, but we know the Xenophonians use chips to keep track and communicate, right?" Aaron said.

"So there must be a signal from somewhere to keep the survivors in check."

Mark patted his friend's back. "Great theory, Aaron. I think someone might be scrambling other signals that could interfere with OX's hold of the survivors."

"Well, get on it, mates," Lucas ordered, rubbing his wounded shoulder. "So we can figure out what happened to Donnie."

After that day, we stuck around Moscow for the rest of the week, watching from the shadows. The citizens were content with their new lives. They received their goods from the temple and all lived equally. On the outside, they appeared happy.

Their happiness isn't meant to last.

Now, we're traveling back home. We learned nothing more about what happened to Donnie. He is still in a coma, and we are distraught. He can't wake up from his nightmares.

Please, seek the slender white woman in possession of Marlene's sheep shears. Find out what she did to Donnie.

Also, watch Sting. I fear that our encounters with her will be more frequent. It'd be best if she wasn't in her right mind when she faced us.

Godspeed and goodwill,

Shannon Hollinger

Shannon Hollinger
Royal Strategist of RRPR

LETTER 11

Joshua: VI

Hello Shannon and Yared,

That poor boy. If I find any further information, I'll let you know. I do have some news. I found more letters from Marcellus.

You can decide whether it's good or bad since I handed the information over to the Titans. They'd know if I was hiding something, but I documented my findings to share with you: 33._ _ _ 35 _ x - 1 _ _ . _ _90_ _. More numbers are needed which gives me a chance to come up with a plan.

I hope my time isn't shorter than I thought, because I encountered someone who added more pressure.

I was on another hunt for Marcellus' letters with the usual group of Hermes: Titan PH, Solomon, me, and some of the standard Supervising Officers. However, this time I was a little surprised. Leprechaun the bartender was ordered to assist.

He was buckled across from me in the back of the truck. I watched him sit still, unaffected by the bumps and harsh movements as the vehicle drove across the ruined terrain. I held the seat beneath me so I wouldn't topple on Solomon and his monkey companion.

We sat in silence, but it wasn't peaceful. Something about Leprechaun unnerved me that day. I felt the need to be alert. Every so often his gaze would catch mine. He flashed a simple smile, maybe gave a wink, and then turned away. Even those kind gestures made me uneasy.

Don't show it, Joshua, don't show it, I repeated to myself. Subtly, I took a deep breath and got back into the character of Wolf.

Ringing and humming pierced my ears immediately followed by a monotonous message: *Grab your weapons and head to your designated areas.* The truck came to a stop and our buckles unlatched. I stood up, flung my rifle over my shoulder, and hopped off the back, running to my mission's destination.

I didn't have time to take in the sight. Frankly, I didn't want to. The city had crumbled into rubble and fire had scorched it to ash. The remains of citizens lay scattered like leaves during autumn. It made me sick.

Ducking behind a building, I caught my breath and hid my face; careful not to look at the skulls and bones at my feet.

I pulled a folded yellowed paper out of my jacket pocket. A crude drawn map offered direction. Not very clear, but it was a start.

"Hey, boyo," a voice called.

Startled, I turned and aimed my pistol. It was Leprechaun. He calmly raised his hands. "Geez, man, you almost gave me a heart attack," I said on an exhale, putting my gun away.

He chuckled. "Sorry, Wolf. My drinks have that effect on people; not me." He peered over my shoulder. "Where are you off to?"

"Classified." I turned and faced the other way.

"All right. Good luck finding Marcellus then." I heard the rubble crunch beneath his boots as he started to walk away.

I cursed myself. *This is why you must keep secrets, Joshua.* I forgot I told him, Goliath, and Solomon everything before I attended the Titan meeting. I should've let him march back to camp, but something made me call out to him. "Wait, Leprechaun." I didn't know why, but I got the impression he knew something I didn't.

The bartender halted mid step and turned around. "Want some help?"

"I don't need it," I replied, confidently, "but since you're here, the companionship would be nice."

He managed a half smile. "All right. I'll keep you company."

The two of us ducked through the streets until we reached the spot PH marked. "Let's split up," I ordered, shoving the map into my pocket. "Meet back here in an hour."

Leprechaun nodded and we parted ways.

Wriggling my nose, I turned my glasses on to search the buildings for any clues. I found nothing but death among the rubble. My stomach churned and I gagged at the scents and sights. I hastened my search, but came up dry. No clues, no letters, nothing.

With a sigh, I made my way back to meet Leprechaun, but he was nowhere to be found. I was about to call his name but bit my tongue. I didn't need to bring attention to myself, so I quietly went to search.

As I strode down the ruined streets, a chill went up my spine. A weird presence floated through the air. I spun around with my guard up several times, but no one was there.

I reached the edge of the town when I heard a low murmuring. Crouching, I made my way to a nearby building and hid behind it to listen.

A male voice spoke a language my glasses didn't translate. *"Quam multum tempus est reliquit?"*

No answer; at least I thought. The voice continued as if it were having a conversation. *"Sciunt aliquid?"*

Again, silence.

Nothing more was said and I heard the light treading of feet. They were leaving.

Gun in grip, I peeked out from behind the building. No one was there. I tiptoed over and looked around. Out of the corner of my eye I saw a figure. I aimed, but all I saw was a streak of black as the figure ducked into an alley. I could've sworn he was wearing a cap.

My heartbeat quickened. *No… it can't be.* I chased the shadow.

I couldn't see him, but I heard his feet digging into the rubble as he ran. I wriggled my nose and turned the thermal scanners on in my glasses.

I spotted him.

He was scaling the side of a building. As fast as I could, I did the same. I thought I lost sight of him.

But he waited for me.

I screeched to a halt on the rooftop. The figure stood with his back to me. He propped his foot up on the ledge and looked out. Underneath his ratty black trench coat coat was an old Order of Xenophon uniform. His black cap covered a head of thick brown hair streaked with silver from age.

I was frozen with fear, awe, and confusion. I stared blankly at the back of the figure. *C'mon, stupid, say something!* I commanded myself, but I was so scared that Wolf couldn't act.

The man spoke first: "So, you're the one collecting my clues, correct?" When the last word reached my ears, my body trembled. He was responsible for the weird presence that hung in the streets. Now, I was engulfed in it and frightened out of my wits.

"Y-yes, sir," I stuttered with my voice cracking. I mentally scolded myself. I showed a sign of weakness.

What I thought was a mistake turned out to be my only saving grace.

He hesitated before reaching for his gun. Without turning, he asked, "Who are you?" His voice was husky and it rang with authority and confidence.

I wondered how to answer. *Do I tell him the truth or hold on to the OX act?*

I took too long to reply. Still facing away, he ripped his gun out of its holster and aimed it at my chest. Trembling, I threw my hands up and stepped back. I kept my eyes locked on the barrel until something else caught my gaze. On his arm I saw three patches: OX, Hermes, and an emblem that was somehow *familiar*. It was an illuminated green letter "*H*". My heart remembered before my mind did.

A whisper fell from my lips: "Hodgins."

The quiet murmur was a scream in the man's ear. His head shot up and he whipped around to stare at me, showing himself for the first time.

High cheekbones stuck out of his pale face and stubble covered his strong jawline. His large eyes were striking and their color a familiar shade of gray.

I knew his face, but not because it was his. I knew it because it belonged to his three children.

"You're Mr. Hodgins," I gasped, pointing to him.

"How do you know that name?" he demanded, stepping forward. "No low Xenophonian has ever known of me by that name."

I wanted to turn and run. His demeanor was intimidating. His gaze cut like knives, but I held my ground. I decided it was his right to know who I was.

"That's because I am *not* a Xenophonian." I stood up straight and put a hand on my chest. "Known to OX I am Wolf. My Mortal name is Joshua Wolfrum, and I am part of the Resistance known as RRPR."

Marcellus halted. His head cocked. "I don't believe you."

"Your children and I have searched for you for over seven years," I explained.

"What makes you assume I have offspring?" he spat.

My mouth went dry. *Say it, stupid. Say it!* "Their names are Shane, Aymie, and Mark Hodgins," I managed. "You saved one of your sons five years ago after you blew up PH's base in Fargo."

His eyes widened. "My son," he whispered, clutching something around his neck. He became lost in thought. A bittersweet joy fell over his face.

The moment quickly faded and he sharpened his gaze. "That doesn't matter," Marcellus snapped. "I don't trust you, but I won't kill you. If you are who you say, make sure my children find me first." He spun on his heel and headed back towards the edge.

"How will they find you?"

"I'll give you nothing more," he replied. "If they are my children, they'll find me. You keep the Xenophonians at bay." He looked at me one last time. His familiar gray eyes gleamed in the sunlight. His gaze said he *trusted* me.

Saying nothing more, he leapt off.

Just like that, the man I was searching for disappeared in an instant.

He slipped through my grasp like water. Now, I had to dry my hands and try again. Only now, my time was short.

After standing in awe for a few moments, I shook it off and headed back. Wolf needed to act like nothing happened, but Joshua couldn't believe it.

Throughout that encounter, I forgot about Leprechaun. When I returned to our meeting spot, he still wasn't there. I groaned, impatient. "Leprechaun!" I called. My voice bounced off the broken buildings. There was a whistle in response.

I walked around the block to find the bartender sitting on a broken statue. In his left hand was a beaten old pipe and in his right was a small piece of paper. He raised his eyebrows at me. "How's she cuttin'?"

"Where have you been?" I demanded, ignoring his question.

He blew out a smoke ring, filling my nostrils with the spice of tobacco. "Letter hunting." He handed the paper to me. "Isn't that what you're here for?"

I read it over. It was certainly one from Marcellus. I wasn't going to take out the blacklight in front of Leprechaun, so I changed the subject. "I didn't know you smoked?"

He chuckled. "There's a lot about me you don't know."

"Well, I guess I never had a reason to find out," I replied.

"Touché." Clenching the pipe between his teeth, he rose and stretched. "Well, we should probably leg it in case someone shows up."

I nodded and the two of us headed back to the caravan. PH waited by one of the trucks. He waved for me to come over. I obeyed and Leprechaun followed.

When we approached, PH glanced at Leprechaun first. His expression was confused rather than upset. He didn't acknowledge the bartender's presence and turned his attention to me. "What did ya find, Wolf?"

"Actually, Leprechaun found it," I confessed, pulling out the paper. "We returned immediately, so I didn't go over it."

He didn't take the letter. He glared at Leprechaun who still had his pipe clenched between his teeth. PH patted his jacket pocket as if to check for his own. His expression showed it remained in his possession. "Well, thank ya, Lep," PH said as politely as possible. There was distaste in his voice, but Leprechaun didn't react.

"My pleasure, sir." He bowed. "If I'm ever needed again, please let me know." He took his leave.

Once he was out of earshot, PH gripped my arm and walked me away. "Never trust that Mick," he growled. "He's hiding somethin'." He looked at me and ordered, "Keep him close. If anything's suspicious, report it immediately."

I nodded and the Titan left.

I shoved my hand in my pocket and fiddled with the letter. I wanted to read it, but my brain was rattled enough for one day. Between Leprechaun, meeting Marcellus, and PH's strange suspicion, I couldn't process anything.

Hopping back in the truck, I sat down and buckled in, ready to return to base. Leprechaun was already there as was Solomon. The monkey Diego jumped off his master and onto my shoulder. I felt his tiny fingers jabbing at my scalp as he removed the dirt.

Leprechaun looked up at the creature, smiled, and turned his gaze away.

I can't look at our bartender the same ever again. I learned more and less about him in one day. I noticed more features and habits but understood nothing about what they meant. I learned he's Irish, left-handed, and smokes a pipe. I didn't understand his true intentions, his demeanor, or how much he knows.

For some reason, it worries me and I don't know why.

Well, now I'm back at base after that journey and waiting for the next assignment. The letter Leprechaun found revealed the last few digits I informed you of earlier. I also didn't encounter Sting or the slender woman who might have harmed Donnie. Hopefully, he is all right.

I still can't believe it. After so long, I finally met Marcellus. Why was he so reserved? Why did he make me feel so afraid? Isn't he supposed to be the survivors' savior? The one they can count on in times of trouble? I can't wrap my head around it. If you figure it out, let me know.

With safety and secrecy,

Joshua Wolfrum

Joshua Wolfrum

Letter 12

Yared: III

Yo Joshua,

I'm blown away. Marcellus' features resemble the triplets. It must be their dad. I can't believe you actually met the guy. I wanted to tell Mark and Aymie (and Shannon) about this, but it wasn't the right time. Everyone continued to mourn after Shane's death and are worried about Donnie. I hope we find Marcellus soon. We're in more trouble than I first anticipated.

When we returned to the Underground, Donnie was still recovering. His encounter with the slender woman left him in a coma filled with nightmares. His body remained still, but his tight eyed expressions showed terror and sorrow.

"How much longer will he be like this?" I asked Ethan as I sat on the edge of the couch. We brought him into our corner of the Underground: a small lounge with a kitchenette. The infirmary, sadly, was full and Donnie needed immediate attention.

The Savior rested a cool cloth on the boy's forehead. "I'm not sure," Ethan whispered. "I've never seen anything like this. I don't know what happened."

Mark poured glasses of water and rested them on the counter behind us. "My theory is he encountered a brief yet powerful mind wipe transmission."

"No, no," Axel denied, stepping out of the corner. "Donnie will wake up the same. He's fine."

Mark looked downcast. Axel rubbed his fingers through his curly hair and muttered something in Spanish.

Ethan rose and took a glass of water. I watched as a bead of sweat dripped down his face. "What could they hope to gain from this?"

"Division," a soft voice said. I turned and saw the white haired RRPR Officer standing in the doorway. "They want us to fight and turn against one another."

"Blake, of course," I retorted. "But, no offense, wouldn't they have killed him if they wanted us to fight?"

"No, no," he shoved his hands in his jean pockets, "they're smart. This has been done before. It's successful." He adjusted his gray beanie as he thought. "Think of Donnie as OX's Trojan horse."

We Isle members looked at him confused. He made a reference we didn't understand. We have no memory of the past let alone history.

Mark understood and his face fell. "You think they're using Donnie as a puppet? A pawn to get us to disperse?"

Blake nodded slowly. "I sense they left something in Donnie's mind. I don't believe they wiped him, but rather planted a seed."

"A seed that'll become overgrown and untamable," Mark growled. His grip tightened around the pitcher of water. His knuckles turned white and I thought the glass would shatter.

"What can we do about it?" Axel asked, crossing his arms.

Mark and Blake looked at each other, waiting for the other to come up with an answer.

"I don't know," Blake confessed. His blue eyes filled with sadness. "I want to warn everyone, but will they still believe me after what happened?"

"You redeemed yourself with Moscow. I think that's enough," I replied as nicely as I could. I told you, I'm not one for sympathy.

He bought it: "Thank you, Yared. Although my warning may not do anything anyway."

Mark let out a deep breath. His grip loosened and he gently placed the pitcher down. "Well, man," he started, walking over to Blake, "we believe you. You can say you tried." Mark put his hand on his friend's frail shoulder. "It's better than nothing."

Blake managed a smile. I could tell an invisible wall erected between him and Mark after what happened to Shane. So, the white-haired young man said nothing and turned to take his leave.

The moment the door slid closed behind him, a weak voice spoke up. "H-hello? Golly, what happened?"

I turned to see Donnie's eyes fluttering open. His pupils dilated back to their appropriate size and the color returned to his cheeks. Slowly, he sat up, and the room's tension receded.

"Take it easy," Ethan warned. "You were sleeping for over a week."

The boy shot a speculative look. "I was?"

"Yeah. It wasn't a nice sleep," Ethan added.

Donnie cocked his head to the side. "What're you talkin' about? Whatever nap I just had was the best in my life. I had the most amazin' dream." His eyes sparkled in a way that unnerved me. "It was a dream of peace. A dream of happiness. Things ain't as bad as we think." He sat on the edge of the seat and thought. He looked around the room for something. When he espied it, he leapt up, grabbed it, and ran out the door.

The four of us looked at one another.

"This can't be good," I grumbled. Immediately, we chased after him.

We raced down the furnished corridors of the RRPR section of the Underground. We searched every room, but there was no sign of him.

"Where could he be?" Axel called as he hovered above us.

Ethan grabbed his Bionic leg and dragged him down, causing him to shut off his thrusters and land. "No jets down here, you know that," he scolded.

"Do you think we have time for that?" Axel replied, harshly. "We have to talk some sense into him before he starts spreading lies."

"Guys, relax," Mark spat. He put his fingers to his temples and thought. "Okay, if I wanted to infiltrate a base as a little boy who would I tell first?"

"OX usually attacks members in power first, right?" Ethan asked. "He might've gone straight to Virginia Michaelson."

Axel agreed. "She's too sweet not to hear him out."

"But she's too smart," Mark added. "She'd try and talk some sense into him."

"So he'd go to someone dumb?" I asked. I could think of a couple people, but it obviously wasn't correct (nor will I tell you who came to mind).

"Not dumb," Mark said slowly. A worried look crossed his face. "Innocent." Without another word, he raced down the corridor and we blindly followed.

He brought us out to the tracks connecting the Underground. Leaping over the rail of a cart, he commanded, "Axel, push us as fast as you can back to the main plaza."

"Will you tell us why?" I asked, hopping onto the cart.

"I thought corrupting the innocent was Mr. Nik's thing," Ethan said, bracing himself.

"They must've learned from his ways or something," Mark panicked. "We have to hurry. Donnie could've gotten to them already."

Axel gripped the railing with his bare hands as he hovered in the air. His thrusters shot flames, bathing the dark corridor in blue and yellow. "I'll do my best," he promised. "I don't have my armor. My upper body strength is average now."

"Don't strain yourself too much," Ethan warned. He went over to the cart pump and grabbed a side, commanding me to do the same. I obeyed and Mark counted down. With force and fire, the three of us sped the cart down the tracks.

The lights of the concrete city illuminated the end of the tunnel. Mark grabbed the brake handle and yanked it with all his might before we crashed into the station. I held tightly onto the pump as the cart jerked back and forth, causing us to lose our balance. Mark leapt over the rail and ran with the same momentum as the racing cart. Before I could steady myself, I chased after him with Ethan and Axel following.

We raced through the rustic plaza, calling for the boy. Axel flew above the huts like a hawk seeking out its prey. Our search was frantic but not in vain. We found Donnie sitting on the edge of the fountain.

Those around him made Mark nervous.

At Donnie's feet were the children of the Underground. Most no older than the age of 6 with the exception of Shannon's sister, Rachel (the one with the leg brace) who is 11.

Donnie sat with wide eyes and talked with his hands. A smile spread across his face as he pantomimed what appeared to be buildings like we saw in Moscow.

Mark halted and caught his breath. Ethan skidded to a stop and almost crashed into him.

"What are we waiting for?" Ethan asked, regaining his balance.

"I hope we're not too late," Mark whispered. His blue eyes filled with frustration as he marched up to Rachel. Harshly, he grabbed her arm and pulled her away from the crowd, trying to talk some sense into her.

I looked at the group of kids. They were enamored by Donnie's story. Despite his mannerisms and Asset vernacular, the children were attentive and engrossed. It was like he was bringing them into his dream world.

It made me sick.

I rolled up the sleeves of my Seer's jacket and stomped towards them. Donnie paid no attention as I hovered over the line of kids at my feet. I crossed my arms and stared at the Asset who continued rambling. I cleared my throat and he stopped, looking up. He wasn't surprised to see me. He was disgusted.

"What're you telling these kids lies for?" I scolded. I clasped his arms and yanked him to his feet.

"Hey! What's the problem, Yared?" Donnie tore himself away. "I ain't tellin' lies. Gosh, I'd never kid about something like this."

"He said he saw it!" a little girl cried. "It's a beautiful place."

"No, it's not," I snarled. I looked at each one of them. I wasn't fond of kids, so disciplining them was easy. "Don't be fools. Donnie was out in a coma—a deep sleep—and he had a nice dream. That's all it was. Nothing more."

The kids whined with disappointment. They stood up and yelled at Donnie for being a "fat liar" and "meanie pants" and dispersed. Ethan and Yared chased a few of them down to talk to them. Mark thought he got through to Rachel so he went to help the others.

As they left, Donnie cried, "Wait! I'm tellin' the truth! You gotta believe me." The last one went out of sight and the little Asset became bitter. He clenched his fist and drove it into my stomach. It didn't hurt, but it caught me by surprise.

"Yo, what's your problem?!" I grabbed his fist and held it to prevent him from attacking again.

"You don't believe me!" he shouted, trying to get free. "You don't wanna believe we have a chance at peace. I have proof." Yanking his hands away, he pulled out a wrinkled piece of paper. "This was offered to us by Sting of the Ares Division. There's a home for us. We can be happy again."

The way he spoke almost made me pity him. We'd known false happiness for a time, but it was nothing but lies. I can never go back. None of us should have to.

"The only way we will be genuinely happy is by killing every Xenophonian we cross," I growled.

I reached for the paper, but Donnie pulled away. "You ain't worthy," he grimaced. He turned to Rachel who rested silently against the fountain. "You believe me, don't ya?"

The girl was quiet; her light eyes looked downcast. She wasn't sure what to believe after Mark's talk. Donnie walked over to her and patted her arm. "It's possible," he whispered, placing the crumpled paper in her hands. "Trust me."

Gingerly, she opened it and read the offer.

I didn't want her to get any ideas. "That's enough." I tried to snatch the paper from her, but Donnie pushed my arm out of the way. Within those few seconds, Rachel read it all.

"He's right." She looked at me; hope sparkled in her eyes.

"You don't understand; that's a fake," I lied.

"You don't even know what it is!" Donnie yelled.

"I don't have to," I retorted, reaching for it again.

Rachel swatted my hand away. "You want to keep this from everyone?" she asked. "They're not asking for a lot."

"I'm sure your definition of 'a lot' is different than mine." I didn't know how I could convince her. I spun around and yelled for Mark, hoping he'd scold her again, but he was out interrogating another child. When I turned back, they were gone. I cursed aloud and screamed, "Donnie!

Rachel!"

Mark raced back. "Yared! What happened?"

I let out an exasperated breath. "Donnie made up some sort of 'peace treaty' thing and gave it to Rachel. She's all for it."

"What did it say?"

"I don't know." I rubbed my black crew cut hair. "She said there's a price for peace, but I have no idea what it is. Donnie wouldn't let me read it."

Mark held his forehead. "Oh no, this is bad. This is *bad*."

Axel and Ethan returned. "Some of the kids believed Donnie was joking," Ethan explained, "but I don't know about the others."

Mark shook his head with disbelief, trying to comprehend it all. "I hope Rachel finds some sense."

Before they could ask, Axel announced, "Wait, I'm getting a message." He stared off into space as it flashed before his eyes. "Joshua sent information on more temples. We're going to split up and scope them out."

"How soon are we leaving?" Mark asked.

"We go for a briefing now and then first thing tomorrow."

Without another word, we returned to the RRPR section. On the way, I kept an eye out for Donnie and Rachel.

I was about to follow the others into the conference room when I heard racing feet. I turned around and saw Shannon's other sisters—Agnes and Rebecca—running down the hall calling for their older siblings. "Girls! Rachel has great news!"

Oh no, I thought. I was about to chase after them but Co-Director Nic ordered me to come. As a trained Seer, following orders was second nature. Not able to disobey, I stifled a sigh and closed the door, letting the girls spread lies deep within the Underground.

I feel so guilty. I haven't told anyone. The more they don't know, the better. I've always been a cold-hearted, serious Seer. So far, that's how I think I will remain.

Thank you for the tip on the temples. I hope us going to them doesn't make this situation worse.

Bravery and fidelity,

Yared Prinz

Yared Prinz
Seer Commander

LETTER 13

Joshua: VII

Hey Yared (and Shannon),

I don't know what to say. Hopefully, RRPR can see through those lies.

I'm glad you received the information on the temples. Good luck and be careful. What you find may divide you further.

After the Marcellus encounter, I grew uneasy around Leprechaun. PH told me to keep an eye on the bartender. He planted a seed of uncertainty that started to grow.

I sat at the bar with my bare arms pressed against the cold marble, waiting for Solomon and Goliath for our end-of-week meetup. They think it's a friendly chat, but it's more for my benefit. They're my eyes and ears throughout the rest of the base.

Normally, I'd make conversation with Leprechaun, but I sat in silence, watching him work. Recently, I noticed different things. His stature was below average (not as short as PH, however), he fought mostly with his hands, he was careful with his words and actions, and a tune that he'd always hum was painstakingly familiar.

I drummed my fingers on the counter as I tried to recall where it was from. Leprechaun hummed the melody as he cleaned the glasses. I closed my eyes. After a few moments, I saw a face in the blackness.

PH.

I opened my eyes and stared at the bartender as he replaced the cups he washed. *Scarborough Fair* wasn't the only song in the Titan's repertoire. PH and Leprechaun both knew the same song. Neither of them knew the lyrics. At least I don't think. PH would hum it as a vocal exercise. Regardless, they knew the song.

That's gotta hint at something, I thought as I eyed him. Leprechaun joyfully wiped the counter, humming the light hearted tune. He seemed happy... too happy for a Xenophonian. Everyone at OX has a depressed side.

For me, it was easy to fake. Wolf's depressed side was Joshua. Those moments I'd slip out of character didn't alter anyone's view of Wolf.

When I was depressed is when I showed my true self.

Don't worry, this state of mind doesn't last long. I snap out of it quickly. But working undercover as a cold-blooded killer named Wolf takes its toll on you. I get down in the dumps every once in a while.

"Hey, mate, you all right?" I heard Leprechaun say.

I snapped out of it. "Yeah, sorry." I put my head in my hands. I decided to be myself for a minute despite my suspicions. "A lot on my mind I suppose."

To my surprise, he noticed I wasn't right. "That doesn't sound like Wolf at all. Something eating at you?"

My face flushed. *Stupid, Joshua,* I repeatedly scolded myself while he stared at me with his bright eyes. Quick as a whip, I thought of something. "Yeah, I suppose. That song you were humming. Where is it from? I hear it all the time."

He was taken aback. He couldn't believe I'd heard it before. He shot me a look that I'll never forget: wide eyes, eyebrows raised, and lips parted.

I hit a nerve, I thought.

I didn't hit hard enough. He shook off the feeling and stroked his short beard. "It's a song from my younger days." He started wiping the counters again. "Where did you say you heard it?"

He's hiding something. "I know I've heard it more than once. The only one I can recall singing it," I paused and eyed him, "is PH."

He froze mid-wipe.

Gotcha.

In his pause, he thought of an answer. "He probably heard me humming last time he was here. It's a very catchy tune."

"Sure is." I knew there was more, but wasn't going to push it. Something's going on between him and PH, but I must find out what.

Breaking the awkward silence was the squeal of Diego the Monkey. I turned to see Solomon limping his way to the marble stool. In the field he was a machine, but at the base, he's frailer than a china doll. He gripped his wooden staff and hoisted himself up. Without asking, Leprechaun slid him a cold glass of club soda.

He removed his fingerless gloves and wrapped his wrinkled hand around the condensation covered glass. He nodded to say thank you and quietly drank.

Diego hopped off his shoulder and looked at his reflection in the clean marble. He patted the sides of his white bearded face and cooed, approving his appearance.

"Lookin' sharp, mate," Leprechaun chuckled. He took a banana out of a fruit bowl and gave it to the creature who snatched. Diego climbed up on my shoulder and chewed it in my ear.

Why do you like me so much? I wondered as Diego nibbled at his berry.

A few moments of silence passed before I asked Solomon where Goliath was. The old man sighed. "*He who commits adultery lacks sense; he who does it destroys himself.*"

I held my hand up. "Say no more." He had an appointment with an Eros member again. Disgusting.

The subject quickly changed which always surprised me. All the other Xenophonians had such vulgar speech, but not this crowd. Even though Leprechaun raised suspicions, I appreciated his censorship and respect. *I guess that in itself is suspicious*, I thought. As for Solomon, he couldn't converse unless there was a line about it from the Holy Book that was jumbled in his brain.

"So, Wolf, you ready for your next assignment?" Leprechaun asked as he slid me a drink.

"What assignment?"

He jokingly covered his mouth as if he spilled a dirty secret. "Didn't you hear? You have to train a fresh Hermes member on the next mission."

I shot him a speculative look. "How do you know? Shouldn't the Supervising Officers do that?"

He shook his head. "Heard your name come around. I wasn't earwigging, I swear. I just hear everything."

I didn't believe him. They never put an "involuntary" Xenophonian in charge of a newbie let alone on a *mission*. Normally, they'd train on base. To change the system would mean they were making an exception for me.

They've started to, though. Regardless, I wouldn't believe it. If it was true, how did Leprechaun come upon such classified information? Sure a bartender hears things, but not those kinds of things.

Leprechaun was about to explain further when he stopped mid sentence. His gaze fixed on someone behind me.

Before I could turn around, I felt a hand rub across my back. Rough fingers traced my spine. Frightened, Diego went back to his master. My stomach turned.

"*Hola*, everyone," Sting purred as she sat beside me. She jerked her chin towards Leprechaun. "You know what I want." In silence the bartender fixed her Sangria. She eyed me up and down and bit her lip. "Aren't you going to salute your Titan?"

Don't look at her. She made my skin crawl. Knowing what she did to my friends made me sick and terrified. The further I stayed away from her the better.

Then, an old saying crossed my mind that made me think twice: *"Keep your friends close and your enemies closer."*

If I wanted to avenge Shane and all the RRPR members she killed, I had to get close to her. If that meant her viewing me as an object, so be it. I promised you, Shannon, I'd find out as much about her as possible. *But I'll never become her "play thing" or let her into my head*, I vowed to myself.

I breathed in through my nose. Joshua wasn't brave or charming, but Wolf was. *Wolf can do this. Wolf can do this.* I turned to her, locking eyes. "I apologize, but PH is my Titan. I've been taught to solely salute him and the Moirai. But if you desire, I can make another exception."

Her mouth turned upward. "Yes, I do desire."

I bowed and gave a casual salute.

She smirked and drank her Sangria as we sat in silence. No one spoke as she gulped down the alcohol. Four empty cups were stacked before she stopped. Slamming her last glass on the counter, she laughed. "*Gracias*, Leprechaun; you are the best." She hopped off the stool and wobbled a little. She was functioning just a tad crooked. "Wolf, I hope you're at the top of your game. PH and I were talking and we agree you have potential." She stepped forward and rubbed my arm. "We're going to push you a little more," she whispered. "See what you can handle. Just don't," she leaned in; her breath reeked of sweet wine, "break." With that, she walked away as straight as she could.

When she was out of sight, all the eyes in Lucky's watched me. I felt like an animal in a cage. Wolf, however, was not shaken. We were both confused, though.

Leprechaun chuckled. "Told ya. Someone is planning something."

Now, I needed to know. I said goodbye to Leprechaun and Solomon and went to find PH.

I ventured down the corridors until I heard two distinct voices. One was PH; I'd recognize his rustic British accent anywhere.

I turned the corner and stopped dead in my tracks. PH was conversing with Arata, the Moirai Clotho. Her dark eyes noticed me, but they didn't narrow. She smiled and waved me forward.

I took the first step when I was startled by a little body latching onto my back. Diego chased me down and climbed on top of me. "Geez, don't do that," I whispered through gritted teeth. He squeaked his response which sounded sarcastic (if that's even possible).

"I don't think this little one wants to leave you alone," Arata grinned.

"No, ma'am," I replied. "I don't know why he likes me so much."

"These creatures have odd yet sometimes unique instincts. This one in particular." She pet his furry head. "Always amazes me. That's why we allow him to live here."

PH crossed his arms. "I don't mean to be rude, but I've got a mission to prepare for."

"Yes, right." Arata cleared her throat and clasped her hands together. "Wolf, we have a task for you. It's not one we usually assign to lower Xenophonians such as yourself, but I feel like you've shown great dedication and loyalty to the Order."

I bowed. "Thank you, ma'am. It's my sole purpose."

That pleased her. "As it should be. If you succeed with this task, greater things shall be expected of you."

PH nodded. "Along with your search for Marcellus, you'll need to train a Reborn."

My body froze. *Leprechaun was right.* "That is unheard of. What is the reason?"

"This one has too strong of a will," Arata explained. "Sting picked him up during a previous mission. His subconscious mind is attached to the old life. You must show him our ways. Show him his new purpose."

"If 'e remembers *anything*, report it to us," PH interjected. "Who knows what may come out of 'is mouth. We don't know who 'e was in the old life. He'll be a strong, powerful member once 'e understands."

Me? Break someone's will? That's something I've never done or wanted to do. I've aided Hermes who were practically walking vegetables. As depressing as it was, it was easy. They knew nothing and desired to be guided. They needed a purpose, a will, a master. To change someone's state of mind—especially while they are struggling to hold on—is an entirely different situation. Not to mention he's probably fighting for good and not evil.

"Is there anything else I should know?" I asked, steering away from those thoughts.

They both looked at each other. "Yes, actually," Arata said hesitantly. "Keep him away from Leprechaun. No further comment."

What, why? I wondered, but couldn't say. Not wanting to push it, I told her I understood the responsibilities and accepted the task.

A smile spread across PH's freckled face. "Excellent. You'll start first thing tomorrow. I'll point 'im out to ya today but don't engage until after the briefing."

"Understood."

"Thank you, Wolf," Arata responded sincerely. "I was afraid that Lachesis would have him executed. I normally don't interfere, but he's one of Sting's prisoners. Keeping him alive was the only reward I could offer. I couldn't even put him into her desired Division, but she has plenty of other toys."

I held back a shudder. Despite the tortures, responsibilities, and lies, I held onto whatever goodness I had left, but Wolf was unfazed.

PH and I (and Diego) bid our farewell and we left to find this new Xenophonian. To my surprise, PH conversed with me as we walked. Usually we strode in silence but today I couldn't get him to shut up. He chatted like I was an old friend. He spoke mostly of his tank but we went on a few tangents. Somehow we stumbled upon the topic of Leprechaun.

"I don't trust that Mick, I told ya," PH spat as he pulled his pipe out of his trench coat pocket. He pulled down his green scarf and clenched the wooden bit between his teeth. "He's up to somethin'. Not to mention he's always copying me. It creeps me out."

"What do you mean, sir?"

He blew a smoke ring up to the high ceiling of the cold corridor. The dank air filled with a sweet smelling cloud. "Ya 'aven't noticed? He smokes a pipe, does stuff with his bloody left 'and, *and* he stole a song from my repertoire."

"*Scarborough Fair?*" I asked, playing dumb.

"Nah, another song I've known for ages."

I was utterly confused. *Is PH telling the truth? Is Leprechaun lying to me?* It didn't make any sense, but I had no choice but to go with it. "I'm sure we'll learn the truth soon enough."

"Sure 'ope so."

Finally, we reached the largest common room. It was damp, uncomfortable, and crowded. Several tattered sitting areas were scattered across the floor. This was the one place that the lower Xenophonians of all Divisions gathered.

We walked through unnoticed. Not a single one acknowledged PH's presence. The other Titans would've been infuriated at the lack of respect, but PH didn't mind. From what I gathered, he's the most down-to-earth Titan. He's practical and knows how to not make a scene if he didn't need one.

PH stopped at the edge of a Hermes sitting area. In the center of the broken chairs and torn couches was a crowd of people surrounding one man on a high stool. His back was towards us as he patted his leg and sang. His voice was strong and silky; it mesmerized everyone. Something about him was oddly familiar.

"You see what I mean?" PH whispered, gesturing to the scene. "Too much enjoyable fellowship. This bloke is too well liked. He's already got a followin' and it's only been a few days. He's wounded so 'e shouldn't even be out and about. If he remembers too much, he already 'as an army to back him up."

I understood the threat. For me, it was an advantage. *If I can convince him to side against OX, he could be a valuable ally.* That was a plan to develop at a later time. "What is he called?"

"They call 'im *Sinatra*," he said, mocking the man's Godly name.

The name sounded familiar. I think it was a musician from a time before, but I wasn't sure.

I watched Sinatra intently as he sang and enchanted the crowds. He turned his head. He had thick brown hair and a beard that covered high cheekbones. I caught a glimpse of his eyes. Emeralds gleamed in the dim light.

My heart stopped. *No, that's not possible. It can't be.* I refused to entertain the thought. I won't tell you what crossed my mind. I can't. I don't believe it. You shouldn't either.

PH chuckled, interrupting my internal crisis. "Make sure he doesn't steal my songs, eh mate? I don't need more than one competitor."

Diego squeaked as if to mock PH. The Titan glared at the monkey, gesturing that he'd keep his eye on him.

Saying nothing more, we turned and left.

Today was too eventful. First Leprechaun, then Sting, now Sinatra. Too many mysteries, not enough clues. The puzzles seem unsolvable.

But I won't give up.

With safety and secrecy,

Joshua Wolfrum

Joshua Wolfrum

THE UNDERGROUND

LETTER 14

Shannon: IV

Hello Joshua,

I wish I could help solve your puzzles. You know I love them. Leprechaun and Sinatra are intriguing. I could crack the case in a moment if I saw their faces and heard their mannerisms, but I'm too busy holding RRPR together by a thread.

We took on two temples at once. I traveled to Algeria with Mark, Myles, Alison, Lucas, and my sister Lucy. Lucas and Lucy both came against my will. The Dragonfly insisted he was fine despite his stab wound from Sting. As for Lucy… honestly, she's so stubborn sometimes I don't have a choice.

We arrived in Algiers, Algeria under the cover of darkness. The pristine marble buildings glistened in the starlight. The city had been rebuilt and the Annex was in effect. In the distance, lanterns glowed like fireflies in the windows of the neoclassical style homes. The Titan had brought in the refugees the day before, ruining our chance of destroying the temple. They wouldn't survive without it.

We camped at the top of a vacant building on the outskirts of the city, overlooking the sea. The waves gently brushed up against the sandy beach. The quiet sounds were like screams in the silence of the night.

I looked longingly out at the scene. Water always reminded me of Shane. He watched his Uncle Chuck and Aunt Monika drown in a river when he was six. Ever since then, water petrified him. But when he was with me, he didn't mind the ocean. He appreciated the beauty of nature even though the memories were ugly and terrible. *And I took him for granted.*

Noticing my distant eyes, Mark sat next to me. He rubbed his thick brown hair and sighed. "I know it's hard. I miss him too."

We sat quietly while Alison, Lucas, Myles, Lucy, and the other soldiers slept. We were to wake at dawn and rush into unknown dangers. They needed all the rest they could get.

I wanted to say something to Mark, but I didn't know what it was. I missed the times we worked on missions together; back when he had a half-shaved head and bitter attitude. We worked well as a team—sometimes better than Shane and I.

I looked at him. His crystal eyes sparkled like the night sky.

"I wish we could return to the past," I whispered.

"Oh yeah? What part of the past."

"Those brief moments where we were all together; happy and unified."

Mark chuckled. "Sweetheart, you know our lives weren't always filled with joy. While we had our moments of happiness, sorrow and anger always crept in."

The way he spoke made me realize he changed so much yet not at all. His speech and mindset had grown but his attitude and doubtfulness remained the same in its own way. While I was practical and viewed things as they were, he saw everything in a negative light. Never around the Isle members mind you. He puts on a good act for them. But deep down, he didn't believe himself at times.

I knew he was right, but I didn't want to be wrong. "I want to go back to those good days. Before Zander's betrayal and Nikita and Walter. The times where we'd perform as *Left Lane Only* or work on missions with Sonny and Myles."

Mark placed his hand on mine. I didn't flinch. His touch was soft and warm. It radiated a comfort I desired but never asked for.

"I'm sorry, beautiful. It'll never be like that again." Mark pushed my curls out of my face and looked into my blue eyes. "We're not going to make it how it was." He shook my hands. "We're going to make it better."

I managed a smile. I was grateful for Mark being there. He's no Shane, but he did his best.

I miss my fiancé so much. I loved him, and I pray he knew that to the end.

Not wanting to dwell on the pain, I pulled myself away from Mark and told him to rest. Being stubborn, he insisted I slept while he kept watch. Exhaustion consumed my pride and I lay down and went to sleep.

Mark shook me awake the next morning. "Hey, babes, it's time to move." I sat up and looked around. The sun peeked over the horizon. I gathered my things while the other officers arose.

Alison stepped into her armor. Her teeth grit and she hissed at the pain as it clamped around her body, connecting to her bionic limbs. Its lights turned on and off excluding the white circle around her heart that led down to her ring finger. I remembered how that white light held a dark significance. It was designed to kill her, but after Mark cut off the connection, it became a symbol of life.

When she was ready, she came to me and asked, "What's the strategy, Shannon?"

I pulled out my tablet and went over the plan.

When I finished, Lucy said, "Seems pretty straight-forward, sis." She finished braiding her long brown hair. "But why am I only on patrol? You know I can handle going into the Temple."

Myles chuckled. "That's not the smartest idea. You'll probably break something important."

Her hand flew up as if she was about to slap him, but he flinched (as always). She scoffed. "That's what I thought."

"You both haven't changed a bit," Mark smiled. He flung his backpack over his shoulder. "Lucy, listen to your sister for once. She knows what she's doing."

She wasn't going to answer that.

Once everyone was ready, we spread out. I led the patrol team (that included Lucas and Lucy) while Myles, Mark, Alison, and their soldiers went into the Temple located at what used to be Alger Center.

My team and I climbed up the side of a building overlooking the Temple. Crouching by the edge, we watched our ground team sneak towards their target.

Lucas dangled his feet off the side and pointed to the massive structure. "Cobbers, look. They've chosen a bloke to run the place."

I pulled binoculars out of my backpack. I saw *three* emblems on the temple: the OX, the wings of Hermes, and the Titan's personal emblem which was an open book.

"Would've been my kind of Titan," I said, "if the citizens were allowed to read."

"Looks like they have a library of some sort," Lucas stated, pointing to the other side of the city. "Either that or he's bloody obsessed with his symbol."

I looked and saw another building with three book emblems across it. *If they do read, the books' messages are all in OX's favor.*

"Books shmooks," Lucy interrupted, "they probably don't remember how to read anyway. Let's focus on finding this dude, please?"

Lucas would've rolled his eyes with me if he could. Cautiously, we moved from roof to roof in search of the Titan. The citizens wore white togas so it'd be easy to identify them. As far as I know, the Titans always wear their field uniform. In fact, I don't even know if they own any other outfit. Correct me if I'm wrong, Joshua.

Hours passed and we simply observed. The citizens went about their day quietly. What surprised me was how uniformly they moved from place to place. They traveled in organized groups and only stayed at each location for a certain period of time. At one point, the streets were barren because everyone was in a different building.

"Are they on a schedule or something?" Lucy whispered as we watched another group march by.

"The other place wasn't like this," I explained. "They were free. This seems too regulated."

"Maybe this bloke has OCD?" Lucas thought aloud.

Lucy scoffed but I didn't dismiss his idea. "You never know," I replied. "The Titans all have a certain trait. Being a Hermes, I wouldn't put it past this one."

My watch ticked noon and the citizens were out and about again. Rather than moving to another spot, they intermingled in the streets. Smiles spread across their tan faces.

"Where are the ankle biters?" Lucas asked, looking out at the sea of adults.

"OX hates children, remember?" I reminded him.

"They also hate old people," Lucy butt in. "Don't you see they don't look a day over sixty?"

She was right and it made me bitter. God only knows what they did to the rest of the world...

"Crikey!" Lucas gasped. "There he is! There's the bloody demon."

I spotted a figure in all black swimming through the sea of white. He had a tan face with a thick beard and dark hair pulled into a bun. On his arm were three patches—one was the open book symbol. Under his arm was a folder. With a smile, he strolled along and greeted the citizens. They saluted him with a grin and some made friendly conversation.

"Why is he so nice?" Lucy complained. "He's supposed to be an evil monster."

"It's an act," I told her. "Nothing more."

"He's a bloody good actor then," Lucas growled. "Let's put an end to his fame, shall we?" He was about to abandon his post and attack when I grabbed his prickly arm and yanked him back.

"Wait, we should observe first," I explained.

The Dragonfly whined. "Ugh, fine. You're probably right. Maybe he—" he trailed off and sniffed the air. Delicious aromas of meat and bread filled our nostrils. Lucas' insatiable appetite couldn't resist. In an instant, he pulled on his goggles, hid his wings under his cape, and ran out into the streets.

"Lucas, stop!" I called without thinking.

"What a moron," Lucy grumbled, palming her face.

The citizens' noticed, but they didn't stare as the Dragonfly ran into a restaurant. He did, however, catch the gaze of the Titan. The Xenophonian politely excused himself from his current conversation and ran up the steps and into the building.

My heart fell into my shoes. I didn't know what would happen next. I threw on my breathing mask and Lucy and I quickly disguised our appearances. I ordered the soldiers to remain put for backup. Once my sister and I were unrecognizable, we followed him in.

As much as I hate to admit it, the inside was beautiful. The floor was covered in shiny maroon and white patterned tiles. Gorgeous paintings of the greek god Hermes looked down from each wall. Bowl lanterns filled with fire hung from the ceiling. The charcoal scent of freshly grilled meat hung in the air. My stomach growled.

I shook off the feeling and pulled Lucy forward. Thankfully, Lucas was easy to find. Along with being a bug, he was the only blond. I spotted him seated at a high marble table at the far end of the establishment.

The Titan sat across from Lucas, eating lunch. He conversed in English and acted proper while Lucas scarfed down his food. The Dragonfly was half paying attention. The parts he did get, he nodded in agreement.

No, no, no, he's lying, Lucas. I didn't want to panic. Taking a deep breath, I stood up tall and marched over to the table with Lucy quietly following.

Pleasant surprise crossed the Titan's face when he saw us. "Ah! Welcome, friends." He motioned for a waitress to bring over two stools. Hesitantly, I sat atop the marble seat she brought over.

The Titan wiped his mustache with a napkin. "So, you're our new visitors. Might I ask whom I have the pleasure of speaking to?"

"They call me Detective," I stated coldly with my electronic voice.

He eyed my breathing mask and goggles. "Why all the secrecy? You and this gentleman here. Only this one shows herself freely… her eyes, anyway," he pointed to Lucy.

"My stare is more intimidating than any weapon," she replied with confidence.

The Titan chuckled. "Understood, Miss. Well, allow *me* to introduce myself." He folded his hands and rested them on the table. "My Godly name is Munazam. I oversee the Arabic Pandemonium, Algeria, and the Reborn in my care." He looked at those in the restaurant. "They were so lost before. No order. No purpose. Between the Order of Xenophon and myself, their lives are now meaningful and organized," he patted the folder that lay on the table.

"Everything is perfectly arranged and peaceful."

Lucas was right. Hurrying the conversation along, I snapped, "What is it you want from us?"

Munazam arched an eyebrow. "You infiltrated *my* Pandemonium," he replied as kindly as possible. "I should be asking you that question."

"Answers," I stated. "What is your intent?"

He took another bite of his Mechoui. "All this running around and fighting nonsense annoys me," he explained with his mouth full. He swallowed. "I've conversed with others and realized there is no longer a need to be rivals. As you can see, no one notices your presence. I know you're searching my Temple right now. Am I trying to stop you?" He shrugged. "No. It's to show you I'm not afraid and I don't want war. I want organization. No more chaos and changes to the schedule." He gently placed his utensil down and looked at me. His gaze found their way through my goggles. In his chocolate eyes was an unfamiliar power that struck my soul.

It was like I wanted to believe what he'd say next.

He stated in a low voice, "Stop this nonsense. Make peace with us. There's enough room for all. Why, you can stay here if you'd like. As a Detective you enjoy your research, right? Well, our library is beautiful and the assortment of knowledge is vast."

Lucas and Lucy were silent as they watched me, waiting for me to do something. Munazam's offer was enticing, but it wasn't practical. It wasn't true. We needed to put an end to their lies. I could've pulled a gun and killed him there and then.

But I didn't.

I couldn't. OX had the upper hand. The citizens were programmed to believe that Munazam was the good guy. Killing him before releasing them would prove their point.

I took a deep breath. "We appreciate the offer, but we decline. While the surface is calm and beautiful, deadly dangerous creatures are swimming below."

Munazam nodded. "I understand your caution. I won't persuade you nor will I hurt you. Rather, I'll give you time. Consider it." He turned to Lucas and Lucy. "If you like this food, imagine all cuisines in the world at your fingertips. Everything handed to you on a silver platter. You could enjoy luxury rather than eat scraps to survive." Without another word, he stood, bowed, and took his leave.

We sat at the table for a moment, taking it in. Lucas swallowed his last bite and said, "This guy's good. Almost had me convinced."

I was relieved. Lucas' reply seemed genuine.

My sister, however, not so much. The loud, boisterous Lucy was quiet as a mouse. I feared she was internalizing it.

SHANNON: IV

My communicator beeped. It was Mark ordering us to rendezvous back. Casually, we stood up and left. The hostess bid us farewell in Arabic and we took our leave.

When we arrived at the meeting point, Mark claimed to have good news. They found something that'd be useful. However, it's complicated so he said he'd explain everything when we reached the base.

When it was my turn to recap our findings, I withheld the information about Munazam. Privately, I ordered Lucas and Lucy to do the same. I didn't want to cause a scene. I needed to talk with Johanna before saying anything. Hopefully, she can provide good counsel.

We're on the plane, heading back to the states now. I have a feeling that something will be different when we return.

Godspeed and goodwill,

Shannon Hollinger
Royal Strategist of RRPR

THE UNDERGROUND

Letter 15

Joshua: VIII

Hi Shannon (and Yared),

I think I remember seeing Munazam at the Titan meeting. He didn't say much, just quietly observed. I'll add him to my never ending list of people to keep an eye on.

So, I had my first training session with Sinatra. I'm not sure how it went, so you tell me.

I thought PH would have me work with Sinatra at the base for a little bit first. Nope. They drugged him like the rest of us and threw him on a plane next to me for an assignment.

To my surprise, Sinatra was quiet. He looked around curiously with his familiar green eyes. He sniffed the air and immediately regretted it. He didn't know me but acted like he did. Leaning in, he whispered, "This plane is filthy. You think they'd have the decency to put an air freshener in the cockpit."

I stifled a chuckle. He was right but wasn't allowed to be. Lower Xenophonians never questioned *anything* about OX. Not even health hazards.

He was about to make more comments when the droning, humming, and buzzing rang in our heads. A message was coming in, and Sinatra wasn't used to it somehow. I still felt the pain, but learned to hold it in. He didn't. He yelped aloud and jammed his shoulder into his ear.

Prepare… for… jump. All Hermes… to rightful positions, the Strange Voices whispered amidst the radio static.

The noises ceased and Sinatra breathed heavily. "Geez, that was the weirdest thing," he muttered. "Why does it do that?"

I faced forward, not answering.

He didn't like that. "Helllooo? You gonna talk to me?"

Keeping my head straight, I growled, "You have to be quiet. We'll be punished if we don't follow orders."

"I didn't get any orders telling me to keep my trap shut," he retorted.

I was about to scold him when PH stood up and walked to the back of the plane. The hatch opened and starlight pooled in.

"All right, mates," PH began, "grab a torch and follow me. I'll brief you outside."

Unlatching my seat belt, I picked up my flashlight and followed suit. I turned to see if Sinatra was tailing, but he stood on the hatch door, staring at the sights. He peered into the distance and pointed, "Whoa, I've never been to Australia before."

Some of the members looked at him; amazed he knew the location before the Titan revealed it. I panicked internally, but kept my cool. I wanted Sinatra to remember everything, but no one could know. I ran up, grabbed his muscular arm, and dragged him towards the group.

Before he could protest, I hissed, "You need to keep your voice down. You know more than anyone else here. Don't let them find out."

"Why?" he replied, confused. "I know I'm pretty smart, but why should I hide it?"

"The kind of 'smart' you have is unacceptable here." I looked around, waiting for other Hermes members to stop staring. "I can't tell you now, but know you have to pretend like you know nothing. Stay quiet, stay hidden."

"You're asking a guy who loves attention to do the opposite of everything he believes in," he chuckled.

I shot him a glare. "Sinatra, in the name of Xenophon, do as I say."

Something inside him clicked. His face went expressionless and he shut up.

Ah, crap. I didn't want to use it, but I had no choice. It was a trigger word for Xenophonians who still had Mortal tendencies. It was never proven to be permanent but was still effective. I hoped I wouldn't need to use it any more.

"All right, listen up," PH announced, standing on top of a truck. The encampment was lit by actual flaming torches around the perimeter. In the dim light I saw the Irish bartender and Solomon standing on the other side of the crowd.

I have to hide him from Leprechaun, I remembered. *Geez, PH, way to make it challenging.*

Thankfully, all eyes were on the Titan. "There is a Resistance encampment 'idden in Sydney. We're scouts this time around; no engagin'. My Ares will return and finish the job. Break into your chosen groups and 'ead out. Hide under darkness."

With that, everyone left, save Sinatra and me. Well, I forced him to stay put. He wanted to run off, but I grabbed his jacket and jerked him backward. He was about to comment when PH hopped down and came over to us.

Sinatra stared at PH's face. He pointed a finger; his mouth agape. "Hey, I know you."

"You should. I'm your Titan." PH pulled a map out of his trench coat pocket and handed it to me. "Wolf, 'ere are the last known whereabouts of the subject. Find the next letter." He turned to Sinatra. "You are goin' with 'im. Ask no questions and there'll be no consequences. Understand?"

PH didn't let him answer. He left to fulfill his Titan duties.

"All right, let's see what we've got," I said aloud. It was going to be hard to find Marcellus without talking about Marcellus. PH didn't want Sinatra to know his name either in case he spilled.

Why'd he accompany me then? No idea.

Sinatra stroked his dark beard. "So, what're we doing?"

"We're looking for something without getting caught," I replied, folding up the map. "We need to find a series of letters that reveal the location of an enemy."

"Ooh, sounds fun," he replied, genuinely excited. "I love the thrill of adventure. Where to first?"

I chuckled. "Hope you like books." With that, we hopped in a truck and drove to the State Library of New South Wales.

The entire journey, Sinatra sang his heart out. I didn't mind. It had been seven years since I heard music. I loved every minute of it. His silky voice reminded me of an older era. With every verse he sang, hidden memories resurfaced inside me. Memories of joy, happiness, and peace. Memories of people I used to know…

I didn't want to believe it. I shook off the feeling.

We arrived at the side of the library and parked the vehicle. I hopped out and made my way towards a tall statue of Matthew Flinders. I was surprised it was still standing after OX raided Australia years ago. I crouched beside it and kept a lookout.

Sinatra stopped before the structure, scanned it, and whistled. "Pretty nice. This guy seems like he was a cool dude. A shame he's dead."

"We'll both be dead if you don't keep it quiet," I growled. I grabbed his arm and pulled him around the building until we found the entrance. Another statute lacked a head, but I didn't let Sinatra stand and stare. We raced up the steps and went inside.

The once beautiful interior was overgrown. Vines wrapped around the neoclassical columns. Weeds cracked the tile floors, wriggling their way to the surface for air. The building once held knowledge and wisdom, but now reflected lies and manipulation.

Sinatra ruined my dramatic moment. "Eesh, they should've kept the maintenance guy around." He crushed the weeds with his long feet. "I mean I'm no bookworm, but they shouldn't have let real worms run the joint." He knelt down and pulled out some of the vegetation. He paused and glanced at the floor as a whole. "What a cool map," Sinatra muttered.

There was no time for cartography. I dragged him to his feet and pulled him forward into the main library. I lit my torch—err, flashlight—and looked around.

Books were thrown off the shelves and scattered carelessly across the floor. The mezzanines were cracked and unstable. The tables overturned and the chairs were broken.

It was heartbreaking, but I couldn't show it. The Xenophonians did it and I was supposed to be proud. Taking a deep breath, I searched among the wreckage.

Sinatra pulled up a swivel chair with the wheels still intact. He sat down and I thought he'd stay put. Nope. With strong legs, he scooted himself up the ramp and into the hallway. With a grunt, he rolled from one end to the other. I glanced up from my work to watch his figure appear and disappear in the doorframe. He overshot and I heard a *thud*. "I'm okay!" he called.

I rolled my eyes and continued my rigorous search. I thumbed through pages of books, rummaged through drawers, and looked in every nook and cranny. Nothing.

Sinatra rolled back into the room. He was bored. Spinning in his seat, he asked, "Uh, so what're you doing exactly?"

"Searching for a special poem," I stated.

He chuckled. "If you want to get with a girl, Wolf, I don't think a poem is gonna cut it."

I shot him a look and he shrugged. "No, it will lead us to a dangerous individual," I retorted.

"Ooh, cool. Who is it?"

I almost slipped. I growled and snapped, "You're not allowed to know."

"Why not?" he groaned.

Before I could answer, there was a rustling coming from one of the mezzanines. I whipped out my pistol and aimed. Sinatra jumped to his feet and clenched his fists.

"Hold," I ordered, shining my flashlight across the top shelves. I held my breath when I caught a glimpse of two glowing beady eyes hiding behind a post. They stared right back, not blinking.

Then, I saw fangs and heard a squeak.

"Diego?!" I exclaimed.

At the sound of its name, the capuchin monkey jumped off the platform and grabbed onto a leaning bar with its tail, swinging itself around. It grunted and tried to motion something to me. He was pointing to the room next door.

"Is someone else here?" I asked. It nodded. "Solomon?" It screeched happily hearing its master's name.

PH didn't say anything about Solomon not seeing Sinatra, I thought. Unfortunately, nothing is ever easy. I heard a familiar Irish brogue.

"Where is that little monkey of yours? He's gotta stop acting the maggot," Leprechaun said.

Oh no, what am I going to do? I panicked. I turned to Sinatra who watched Diego with fascination.

Quickly, I thought of something. "Sinatra, check over in that pile of books," I pointed to the far corner, "you'll know the poem when you see it."

"Sure thing, chief," he replied with a joking salute.

While he was busy, I pulled fruit out of my provisions bag. I clicked my tongue a few times to get Diego's attention. The white faced monkey cocked its head and stared. I waved a berry and he chirped with excitement. Slowly, I backed towards the entrance and peeked my head out the doorway. The foyer was empty. I teased the monkey again and chucked the berries down the hall.

The monkey screamed as if I committed a heinous blaspheme. It leapt off the pole and ran like a bat out of hell.

"Sinatra!" I exclaimed. "Diego ran off, and I can't catch him. Are you fast enough?"

The question offended him. "*Fast enough?*" he repeated. "You don't know the meaning of fast." With that he took off like lightning.

That mentality is awfully familiar, I thought.

Then, it dawned on me.

Shane.

My heart raced. It couldn't be true. Shane was dead. Sting stabbed him; Shannon and Yared watched him die. *But that's how he'd talk about his incredible agility,* I thought, but shook it off. *Anyone can be that cocky...* I didn't shake hard enough. *But, not everyone can be afraid of water.*

A light bulb went off. A way to put my mind at ease. I knew Sinatra wasn't Shane, but my stupid brain wasn't going to be satisfied until I knew for sure.

"Ay, Wolf!" Leprechaun yelled, interrupting my thoughts. He and Solomon approached; papers and books under their arms. "What're you doing here?"

"I should be asking you that question," I retorted.

"I asked you first." Leprechaun smirked.

I didn't know what to say. I've told them about my Marcellus missions for PH before, but I couldn't tell them anything about Sinatra.

The bartender chuckled. "I know you're here on secret Titan business."

"The Lord detests lying lips, but He delights in people who are trustworthy," Solomon added with a smile.

"Of course you can trust me," I replied. "Yes, you're right, Lep. Do I make it that obvious?"

"It's not obvious whom you're searching for," he answered. "But you've confessed to Solomon and I before. Why bother hiding it?"

He was right, and it was my own stupidity. I shouldn't have shared anything with them. *Although Leprechaun would have found out on his own somehow.*

Before I could make any other assumptions, there was a squealing down the foyer. I ran over to see Diego waddling on his hind legs towards us. He waved and jumped up and down, screeching like I knew what he was saying.

At the end of the hall, I saw shadows racing back and forth behind frosted doors. There was grunting, yelling, and crashing.

Oh no, Sinatra. "Lep, Solomon, stay put as backup!" I yelled, racing towards the scene with Diego hopping onto my back. I needed to save Sinatra then hide him.

I flung open the door to the *"Friends Room"* to find it in shambles. Resistance members stood about the room with weapons in hand. By their blue utility belts, I identified them as Interpreters: Virginia Michaelson's soldiers.

They were too preoccupied with Sinatra to see me. In turn, they went after him. To my surprise, the new Xenophonian could hold his own. He fought back with such dexterity and skill that I couldn't help but stare.

One lunged for his chest but Sinatra quickly stepped out of the way and dragged him to the floor. Another tried to save his friend, but my ally stopped him with a right hook to the ribs. Another fired a shot, but Sinatra rolled and flung a piece of marble at the soldier's face, knocking him out. One after another, five members were on the young man at once, but he wasn't fazed. He kicked, punched, grabbed, dodged until they were spread out at different corners of the room.

They had him surrounded. Heaving and panting, the five Interpreters jumped to their feet and charged towards Sinatra, knives in hand.

Sinatra smirked as he faced his attackers. He dropped into a stance and clenched his fists. He waited until the last second to make a move. All weapons were on him and he did something that made me give into doubt.

He jumped.

The scene moved in slow motion. With little effort, Sinatra bounded off the ground like a frog. His spine arched as he did a back handspring over the five tall Interpreters. These strong fighters collided with bloody casualties. Sinatra landed on his hands behind the dog pile and flipped himself once more to stand upright. Not a scratch.

Time returned back to its normal state. I stared at the sight. I couldn't believe it.

I've only seen one human pull off a move like that, I thought. *It must be him.*

Sinatra brushed the dust off his combat jacket. "Hey, Wolf. Your monkey needs to stay out of trouble."

Diego who was still perched on my shoulder screeched at him.

"Yes you do," Sinatra chuckled. "But, he was of some use." He pulled two halves of a piece of paper from his jacket pocket. "Is this what you were looking for?"

I lumbered forward and took the letter from him. I kept my eyes locked onto his. The emerald irises glimmered in the faint light. They were familiar, but I didn't want them to be.

I turned away and held the papers close together. I wriggled my nose to turn my glasses on and scanned the poem.

"This dude is good at poetry," Sinatra added. "*He'd* pick up a chick with his writing skills."

"Wolf!" Leprechaun called.

Sinatra's ears perked up. The sound of Leprechaun's voice intrigued him too much. "Ooh who's the Irish dude?"

Why do you know so much?! I wanted to yell at him, but I feared to use the phrase again. "Things are fine, Leprechaun," I called, "take Diego and head back to base with Solomon. We'll be right behind you."

"Who's we?" he asked. His footsteps came closer and closer.

Casually, I stepped outside and closed the door behind me, locking Sinatra inside. "Hey!" he protested.

"What happened? You never called for us," Leprechaun said, crossing his arms. Solomon arched an eyebrow and gripped his staff tighter.

"I took care of the issue," I lied. "There were only 2 enemies and I neutralized them." Diego chirped in agreement. He knew how to keep a secret better than Sinatra.

Leprechaun looked impressed. "Fair play, mate." He patted my shoulder. "No more questions. You finish PH's mission and we'll crack on, eh?" He winked.

Solomon clicked his tongue and Diego hopped onto his master's staff. The wrinkled man bowed and the two took their leave.

Once they were out of sight, I let out a deep breath.

"Uh, Wolf, can I get out of here now?" Sinatra called. "I'm bored."

He's like a five year old. I turned and opened the door. Within that brief time, Sinatra straightened up the small library and gagged, bandaged, and tied up the Interpreters. He stood in the center of the room with his muscular arms crossed and his foot tapping like nothing happened. "Well?"

"Well, what?"

"What are we supposed to do now?"

We needed to go back and report to PH but I wanted to do another test. "We're supposed to get you cleaned up." I pointed to the blood that was on his neck.

He touched it and examined the red on his hands. "Not mine," he smirked.

"Doesn't matter. You must be presentable." I rummaged through my bag. "Come here, Sinatra."

Obeying, he walked over and was not expecting what was to follow. I opened my canteen and flung water on his face.

I didn't want him to, but he did *exactly* as I expected.

He staggered back and swatted at the water as if bugs crawled on his face. He cursed and swore. His chest heaved; his breathing grew shallow. He had a panic attack. He sank to the floor and wiped his face with his shirt.

My eyes widened as I watched him calm down. *I can't believe it...* The appearance, mannerisms, abilities, and now fears. Everything matches an Agricola I used to know...

But my mind *still* refused to believe it.

Sinatra took a deep breath and stared. He was confused, not upset. "Why'd you do that?" he asked calmly. "And what was that? It was like I had a weird nightmare."

"It was a test," I lied. "You passed."

He jumped to his feet. "A test for what?"

"That doesn't matter," I snapped. "Just know you passed. Now let's get out of here."

He didn't argue, and we left the library and returned to the encampment where I gave PH the torn letter. At a quick glance, he couldn't figure it out. He said that I would go over it with him in the near future. For now, I had to focus on Sinatra.

Thank goodness, because I couldn't keep my eyes off of him. (Not in a creepy way, I swear.) The more I watched, the more I recognized other Shane-like tendencies. His smile, his speech, his humor, his fighting style, everything.

My heart said he was Shane, but my mind refused to believe it.

There was one more piece of evidence that I needed. One that'd solve the mystery once and for all.

I needed Sinatra to sing for me. A melody only a WHYP or RRPR member would know. Verses only *that* Hodgins would know because of his beloved Hollinger.

I don't remember what it was called or exactly how it goes, but once I hear it I'll know for sure.

But for now, he's Sinatra. Hopefully, that's how he'll stay.

So, yeah it was crazy. This guy has everything Shane had but I don't believe it. Okay… I do believe it. Maybe. I don't know. You know us humans, doubtful.

Hopefully, Yared, it's your turn to read these letters. I'm not sure if Shannon should be distracted yet with all that's going on.

Please let me know how your mission report went. After what Shannon told me about her Titan encounter, I fear things won't go well.

With safety and secrecy,

Joshua Wolfrum

Joshua Wolfrum

THE UNDERGROUND

LETTER 16

Yared: IV

Yo Joshua,

It's me. Don't worry, your Shane secret is safe. Honestly, I don't know why you need more proof, but you do you. If Sinatra is Shane that'd make our situation easier. But for now, RRPR will keep doing things the hard way.

So as for *me*... today was great. Absolutely fantastic. Couldn't be better.

If you couldn't tell, I'm being totally sarcastic.

Both teams returned to the base from the RRPR temples. Mine was located in Paris, France where a nasty Eros Titan ruled. By nasty I mean a number of things. I won't get into details.

The (now) eight RRPR officers, eight Isle members, and three of Shannon's sisters were seated around the table in the large conference room (uh, that's nineteen I believe. Math is fun.). Virginia Michaelson stood at the head, facing a blank projection screen. Her golden hair was perfectly wavy and her blue utility belt wrapped tightly around her waist.

Out of all my superiors, I admired her the most. Whether it was her beautiful face or motherly nature, I was drawn to her. I felt like I could tell her everything I experienced and she'd help me no matter what.

I'd *never* tell anyone else that, so you better keep your trap shut, Joshua. I'm the Seer Commander, not some baby crying for a mom.

Once everyone was settled, she started the meeting. "Welcome home, everyone. We'll jump right in. M. Hodgins has important information."

Mark nodded and stood up. "After gathering intel across three missions, I've come up with a theory as to how these new temples work.

Since there are no computers to control the citizens, I believe the chips within the survivors' necks are controlled by the main OX base—location still unknown. However, the frequency can't reach all the survivors without communication towers." He gestured towards the front of the room where a blueprint of the Algeria-Hermes temple projected. "Somewhere in these temples is a complex receiver that routes the transmissions and ideas to the chips. It's well hidden, but we detected a faint signature. It definitely exists."

"Why don't we just blow up the entire thing?" I interrupted. "Cut off the transmissions?" This constant back and forth between OX and RRPR irked me. We needed an upper hand.

Mark clicked his tongue. "That's the thing. Do you remember when I told you what happened when Marcellus—we believe—blew up the computer at PH's encampment?"

I remembered. All the chipped soldiers were in excruciating pain. Blood trickled from their ears; unable to withstand the ceaseless screams and noises in their heads. Then, PH and his men slaughtered them all.

"What do you think we should do?" Aaron asked, cleaning his new glasses.

Mark pressed his hands against the table. "Use this to our advantage. Get a step ahead. I know Joshua is working on finding the source, but let's see if we can help. If we can code or develop something even more powerful than OX's frequency, we can cancel it out."

Everyone was silent.

Seems like a reasonable plan, I thought. Of course I didn't understand the science behind it.

Thankfully, we had a blond boy-genius. Myles Powell Jr. graduated with a Masters at age 13 and invented most of the RRPR's tech. "If we gather enough information and more sample chips, it *could* work," he explained. "It's risky though."

"Risky how?" Johanna asked. "I don't want to give therapy to more patients than I have to."

"Well," Mark started, standing up straight, "if we make a wrong move, it could potentially cause both frequencies to go silent."

Johanna cocked her head. "Which means what?"

"In theory, if that happens," Mark took a deep breath, "the citizens would go brain-dead."

Quiet gasps filled the room.

"I know, I know," Mark replied with his hands out. "But if it does work, think of the possibilities. We could end this war sooner than anticipated."

"Or kill half of the population!" Aymie cried. "Mark, I don't care what the numbers are. It's too dangerous."

YARED: IV

The Officers started to bicker and argue, but Michaelson held her hand up, silencing them. "Everyone, please. I understand how hard this is to take in," she began kindly. "I don't want any tragedies, but I think it's a considerable option. If anyone has another idea—other than waiting on Wolfrum—please speak up now."

Unfortunately, someone did.

Donnie's hand shot up like a rocket. "I have an option, Director Michaelson." Granted permission, he rose, quickly fixing his dirty blond hair and oversized combat jacket. "There's another way we can do this. A way y'all haven't said."

"Which is?" Johanna asked impatiently.

The Asset met each members' eyes. When he looked at me, he shot a menacing look. "I think we should take up Sting's offer for peace," he declared.

Sonny didn't give anyone time to think. "Absolutely not," he spat. "Peace is not an option. 'Liberty or death'."

Michaelson held her hand up again, preventing further rebuttal. "What do you mean by 'Sting's offer of peace'?"

"Oh, didn't Shannon tell ya?" he mocked, glaring at the RRPR Strategist. He looked to Carol-Ann—one of Shannon's sisters—who tossed Director Michaelson a crumpled paper.

Gingerly, she opened it and read it over several times. An eerie silence hung in the air. Out of the corner of my eye, I saw Blake's face darken. It unnerved my soul. In his light eyes I saw *everything*. Something bad was coming and there was nothing we could do. He averted his gaze, not wanting to look at any of us. *He dreamt all of this*, I thought.

Michaelson finished reading the letter for the third time. "I'm sorry, Donald," she replied finally, "their conditions are unacceptable."

"Why not?" he growled. "What happened to 'sacrifice one for many'?"

"It's not sacrifice, it's murder," Shannon snapped. "OX will do whatever they can to break them and use them against us. You're asking our friends to lose everything and ultimately for us to destroy them."

"No one said anything about fightin' 'em!" Donnie shouted. "It's a peace offerin'. We won't have to fight anyone anymore."

"What's the cost?" Sami asked timidly. She nervously played with her black tail while we waited in agony for the answer. Even I was on the edge of my seat. I didn't know the conditions of the treaty until then.

Frankly, I wish I still didn't know.

"It says that to ensure peace," Michaelson explained, slowly, "we must hand over the Bionics."

"What?!" Axel spat. He turned to Donnie. "You can't be serious."

"Yes, I am," he replied, sternly.

Axel was the more offended Bionic. "You'd rather hand us over to our enemies than fight a little while longer?" he snapped.

Donnie's stare cut like knives. "Absolutely."

Axel and Alison were taken aback. Their gray mechanical eyes grew distant. The little boy that we cared for and fought beside wanted to trade his own friends. We would've died for him and now he wanted to stab us in the back.

Alison remained calm and asked, "Donnie, why do you want to get rid of us? We've done so much together." Her eyes met his and she held his gaze. "Isn't our family broken up enough?"

I thought for sure the family part would get him; it touched some of the other members. Despairingly, it didn't work on the little brat. That Xenophonian changed him.

She turned his heart to stone.

"I'm sorry, Alison," he replied unapologetically, "but it's because we've lost so much that this has to happen. I've seen the peace. I've seen the joy. We deserve that more than anyone." Turning to Lucy, he pointed and shouted, "You told me you saw it! You saw what I'm talkin' about!"

Lucy hung her head low; her braids fell gently onto her lap.

Myles was the most hurt. "Lucy," he began, "the Bionics are our friends not to mention our strongest members. You want to hand them over and live alongside murderers and liars?"

She didn't look up. "I'm sorry, blondie. I saw how beautiful everything was. How happy the people were." Tears rolled down her cheeks. "We can find my parents. We can be happy again alongside OX. I miss Mom and Dad so much. I think about them every day." Her voice cracked and she cried, "I want our old lives back! I want to be innocent. To be free." She broke down and sobbed.

Her performance didn't help the situation. Aymie turned to Shannon. "Donnie said that you knew about the treaty. Why didn't you tell us?" she demanded.

"I thought it'd be best not to share it," the Strategist replied mechanically.

"This was kind of a big deal, Shannon," Aymie chided. "We could've worked something out before everyone got their hopes up."

"Wait, you encountered Sting?" Peggy Hollinger put in, grasping what Donnie said previously. "Why didn't you kill her?" She didn't mean it as an accusation, but it came out that way.

Her sister was silent.

"That's right, you could've avenged Shane!" Aymie exploded. Shannon hid more than she realized, and it boiled Aymie's blood. "Why didn't you?! Our brother died at her hands. Shane was your fiancé! Didn't you love him?"

YARED: IV

That hit a nerve. Shannon slammed her hands on the table and shot up. "Of course I love him!" she screamed. Shannon never lost her cool. Her face was red, her chest heaved, and her eyes watered. "That's why I didn't bring you the treaty. We can't trust a thing that *witch* says. It was Donnie's fault that I couldn't kill her. He was a hazard."

"Don't blame the boy!" Aymie yelled back. Now, she was on her feet. Her gray eyes narrowed. "All he wants is to be happy again. Don't we all?"

Some members mumbled in agreement.

In the heat of the moment, I felt the urge to say that Shane *might* be alive, but I refrained. You gave me the order not to share, and I obeyed like the loyal Seer I am. However, that information might have helped. Shannon would've confirmed/denied your suspicions in an instant. But even if I wanted to, I couldn't get a chance to speak. The argument was white hot, and I would've gotten burned.

"Ladies, please!" Virginia Michaelson shrilled. Aymie and Shannon halted the argument; their breathing heavy and cheeks damp. "I understand you both are suffering from S. Hodgins' death," Michaelson continued, "but we can't let it hinder our sight. We have to look at the treaty for what it is. Not for what we hope it will be."

The two girls stared at each other and then slumped back into their seats. Shannon was doing her best to catch her breath, but I could tell it brought her discomfort. The poison inside her stirred violently like a tornado.

Michaelson exhaled sharply and continued. "The treaty states that we'll receive a truce plus our own country, supplies, and goods in exchange for the Bionics. To my understanding, this is what it offers," she paused and looked at the doubters, "it's offering a false happiness in exchange for the souls of our loved ones. They want to use the Bionics to overcome us in the end. That's plain to see."

I believed her, but not everyone else did. Whatever hold that Xenophonian had on Donnie grew stronger by the minute. His glare was so sharp it cut.

"Now, to wrap up this meeting," she turned to Shannon, "S. Hollinger, you said you had some things you wanted to report?"

The detective nodded, but didn't stand to speak. She managed to steady her breathing enough to report. "Dragonfly, L. Hollinger, and I encountered the Titan of Algeria: Munazam."

"And?" Aymie spat when Shannon stopped to think.

Shannon shot a look at her was-going-to-be sister-in-law. "He also offered us peace," she grumbled.

"And how long were you going to withhold that information from us?" Aymie replied, harshly.

"You're acting contradictory, Aymie," Shannon replied calmly. "First you worry about re-creating frequencies to free captives but now you'd rather sacrifice two of our own. Not to mention they're the most invaluable assets we have."

"I never said I agreed with the treaty," Aymie corrected. "I'm simply implying that your actions were too hasty and we should consider all options."

"Leave the girl alone. I don't see you doing anything to help in the field," Sonny mocked.

Aymie took that to heart. Her fists clenched, her face scrunched, her lips parted, and—

I shoved the table away and jumped to my feet. "You all know that Joshua made great progress, right?!" I bellowed.

The room fell silent. No one answered.

"Allow me to enlighten you," I growled through gritted teeth. I pulled up a copy of your letter onto my electronic clipboard. I looked at Aymie and Mark. I maintained eye contact as I delivered one of the most important messages of their lives: "Your father is alive. Joshua saw him."

Their eyes widened. "Wh-what?" Mark whispered, unbelieving.

"And you tell us this *now*?" Aymie chided, glaring at Shannon and me.

"We found out during the same time I encountered Sting and Donnie went into a coma," Shannon argued. "If you couldn't tell, things were a little complicated."

"Why hasn't he reached out to us?" Mark asked, still in shock.

"He said, and I quote," I scrolled through the letter, "'*If they are my children, they will find me on their own*'. He wants you to figure it out for yourself."

Mark chuckled. "Stubborn. Just like us."

I could've taken that opportunity to defy you and talk about Sinatra but I held back. I didn't want to get anyone's hopes up. I'm the only one who knows. I kept your previous letter from Shannon. I don't want her to be distracted.

"He's also getting closer to the Moirai," I said instead. "He identified one for certain and is ruling out another possibility. Their Division controls the computers. He'll succeed with his mission. I know he will."

That speech calmed the storm, but didn't stop it. Aymie was still flustered and Donnie, angry. Everyone else thought quietly.

"Thank you, Yared," Michaelson said and then added in a low voice, "Your father would be proud."

That came out of nowhere. *Wait, my father? What on earth is she talking about?* She gave no further hints. I think I was the only one to hear it. That's my own mystery.

The meeting was dismissed. Michaelson blew her tarnished whistle and we rose to our feet. After she left, Aymie shot Shannon a final glare and stormed out. One by one, the members dispersed. I let everyone go out ahead. I needed to speak with Blake. I caught his gaze and he understood. He waited until it was the two of us.

"Dude, you knew about all this, didn't you?" I stated.

Blake was quiet. "I told you before. RRPR will divide," he finally whispered.

"I thought you said we 'may' divide?"

He tugged on the gray beanie that covered his white hair. "I wish it was still a maybe. We're cracking now, but soon we will break."

My jaw clenched. I know the team had a little fight, but that doesn't mean we won't recover. *Right?* "Anything else we should know?" I asked.

Blake shrugged. "You know more than I do at this point. Hopefully you can share your and Joshua's secret with Shannon soon." He tried to smile, but couldn't. Saying nothing more, he left me alone.

I was taken aback. *He knows about Sinatra.*

I shook off the thought and marched out of the conference room. I needed to check on my fellow Isle members. I turned a corner to see Ethan, Lucas, and Axel waiting up for me.

"Thanks for hanging back, guys," I said, going over. I couldn't offer any words of sympathy. As you know, not my forte.

"Hey, Yared," Ethan greeted. "We were just talking about the meeting." Together, we made our way down the hall.

"I'm still in shock, mates," Lucas confessed.

Axel shook his head; his white curls bounced back and forth. "I can't believe Donnie feels so strongly about this," he muttered, keeping his eyes on his robotic feet as they clinked with every step against the cold ground. "What happened to him?"

"We're not sure what that woman did to him," Ethan said, fixing his white lab coat. "I want to monitor his brain waves and do a body scan, but he won't let me anywhere near him."

"The whole thing is bonkers," Lucas put in. "Also doesn't anyone remember I was bloody *stabbed* by Sting?" He rubbed the bandaged gash on his shoulder. "She isn't safe. I don't trust that Munazam fellow either."

"I don't think we should trust anybody," I stated. "Let's keep doing our thing and hope for Joshua to pull through."

"I hope he does so soon. Tell him *rápido*," Axel said with worry in his voice. "I don't want to be a puppet for the Xenophonians."

You heard the Bionic. Get a move on, Joshua.

Look, man, I know you're doing your best. You're trying to solve so many puzzles at once. I give you credit. I'm going to cover for you as much as I can. Just please figure out whether Sinatra is Shane. If you can get him to

us, maybe that will pre-occupy everyone while you solve the other mysteries.
Bravery and fidelity,

Yared Prinz

Yared Prinz
Seer Commander

LETTER 17

Joshua: IX

Hi Yared (and Shannon),

I can't believe those members feel that way... poor Axel and Alison. I promise to find answers quickly.

What I found today proves I'm a man of my word.

The latest poem from Marcellus needed to be deciphered. PH claimed I was too distracted watching Sinatra to focus. In order to have my full efforts, PH sent Sinatra away on a mission with a Supervising Officer. As much as I didn't want him to go, I had no choice but to obey.

It was early in the morning, far before the Strange Voices told the soldiers to arise. I sat across from PH at a clean table in the empty dining hall. To my right, Emel cursed and laughed as she prepared a luxurious breakfast with her subordinates. A faint melody floated from the kitchen. I was surprised to hear it was coming from a CD player. My heart panged when I recognized the artist. It was the Hollinger girls' favorite band whom they called *ABCD*.

Don't get emotional, Joshua. I shook off the memories and returned my attention to PH.

My Titan's eyes locked on the wrinkled paper. I found myself staring at him, defining all his features. (I swear, I'm not a creep.) At that moment, his different colored eyes weren't empty and heartless. Each iris told its own story. His green eye showed determination and vigor while there was a touch of sadness in the blue one. His brown curls seemed shorter today, but just as bouncy. Pulling his green scarf over his mouth and freckled cheeks, he breathed in the scent of the freshly washed fabric.

I know, a clean Titan. How about that?

As I watched him, I got a strange feeling in the pit of my stomach that I never felt about PH before.

It was a familiar sympathy.

Can I explain that? No. But something inside me claimed to know PH on a different level. I felt his pain and sorrow. What it was, I couldn't tell you. *Another mystery for me to solve.*

PH pulled his scarf down slightly so his round nose peeked over the fabric. "Wolf?"

"Yes, sir?"

"Any ideas?"

I shook my head. "Nothing. I've tried every black light, heating lamp, but no hidden messages. Nor can I decipher anything from the text."

"And I can't figure out what these bloody lines mean," PH whined, swatting the letter with the back of his hand.

I peered over the top of the paper. Surrounding the poem were broken wiggly lines. They tried to reach one another but failed to connect. "This must be important," I stated, referring to the strokes. "There was never anything like this on the other letters."

"You think there's another poem? One that explains what they mean?" PH turned the paper upside down. "Maybe it's a bloody code or somethin'."

I couldn't confirm nor deny his speculation, and there was a silence between us. Out of the corner of my eye I saw Emel walking over with a tray in each hand.

"Morning, boys," she called as she approached with heavy steps. "It's way too early to solve puzzles. You especially can't do it on an empty stomach." She slid us plates piled high with food. With a smirk, she added, "Let me grab you some coffee." Before I could thank her, she turned and left, singing her own version of the song's lyrics: "Hiiiiiighway to hades."

Starving, I dove right in. Normal Titans would've rebuked their subordinates if they ate before them. Thankfully, PH wasn't like a normal Titan.

He yanked his scarf down until it hung around his neck and chuckled. "Ah, Emel. The kindest of the Moirai."

I choked on a strip of bacon. The food stabbed the back of my throat as he casually dropped one of the most important pieces of information I could stumble across. I coughed ferociously while PH laughed.

"You all right, mate?" he chuckled and picked up his fork. "Yes, Emel is one of the Moirai. Couldn't tell, could ya?"

My face turned beet red. Unable to speak, I nodded.

"She's the charming Lachesis; the Moirai that measures the thread."

I stared at him, processing this secret he casually shared. *It's more than a name and symbolism*, I realized, *it's real*. I wriggled my nose to turn on my glasses. I wanted to record any information I could gather.

"Wow, that's incredible," I marveled, pausing before eating again. "Emel mentioned that she would've seen me at that last Titan Meeting, but she wasn't there."

"The Moirai rarely make real appearances." PH twirled his fork in his left hand. "And with you there? Forget it, mate. They prefer their ominous theatrical communication."

I paused. I knew for a fact that Arata was a Moirai. I guessed she was the first one: Clotho. From what I recall, Clotho spins the thread. Emel is the second, Lachesis, who measures it.

Who cuts it?

My heart thumped loud in my chest. I reached a point in my mission I thought I'd *never* see. I was convinced that I—Joshua Wolfrum—would've been dead by now. But Wolf held on and is getting more than he bargained for.

I must've spaced because PH whistled, bringing me back to Earth. "Sorry, sir," I apologized.

"Relax, mate. You're a subordinate with more information than allowed. I understand the shock."

I didn't know what else to say, so I smiled and we continued to eat.

"Here you go, boys," Emel called with a cheery tune. She returned with two cups. The nutty aroma of freshly brewed coffee hung in the air. I took the sturdy red mug from her calloused fingers, feeling its warmth on my palms. I turned the cup around, looking at its distressed design. One side had the black OX logo; on the other, the text "*Coffee before Chaos*" was written in a scrawled font.

"I brought you our special drinkware," Emel chuckled. "My sisters and I fought over these all the time growing up. It wasn't until we were inducted that we stopped arguing over petty things."

"What do you mean? You *only* fight over petty matters," PH smirked.

She grunted. "Yes, I know the lives of Mortals are silly things, but my sisters don't listen to me. Clotho keeps changing where I want some Mortals to go and Atropos wants to dispose of them before I say."

My heart continued to race. The information I sought was thrown on me all at once. *Did she forget I'm here? Or have I reached that level of trust?* I didn't want to push my luck. I quietly sipped my coffee and watched the two discuss.

"Well, Emel," PH began. "*I* know you're the most powerful of the three; don't tell the others," he quickly added. "You 'ave a lot of weight upon your shoulders. You're in charge of the Mortals' lives. The others don't understand."

She scoffed and crossed her burly arms. "Like hell they don't. And I hope the Big Man appreciates all I put up with."

"I know 'e does," PH reassured. He held up his mug. "You make 'is coffee every mornin' and it's the best bloody coffee I've ever 'ad. If he doesn't appreciate that then 'e's not the great god he cracks up to be."

I felt each individual bead of sweat dripping down my neck, slithering into the concave of my OX brand and out again. Every movement, every feeling, every heartbeat escalated ten times. PH's and Emel's voices were like a thousand drums sounding amidst a battle. I couldn't believe what I was learning over a simple meal.

Their god was real and I needed to destroy him.

"Yo, Wolf," Emel called, snapping her fat fingers in front of my face. I returned to reality and stared at her. "You all right there?"

PH answered for me: "It's the first time he's heard of the Big Man and your sisters."

Her thick eyebrows raised. "No kidding." She turned to me. "You didn't know any of that? Not even that I am Lachesis?"

Having no words, I shook my head.

Her dark eyes filled with surprise. "Well, then I suppose I should give you a more proper introduction." She picked up the tray and winked. "Meet me in the south-west corridor after the other Xenophonians get their breakfast." With that she turned and left.

Dazed, I sat in silence. PH chewed his final piece of toast while the rest of my breakfast went cold.

Is this really happening? Will I finally see the Moirai's Division? Will I finally escape this nightmare?

"Oi, Wolf!" PH exclaimed, causing me to jump. He snickered. "You should've seen my face when my supervisor first took me under his wing to be the next Titan."

"I apologize, sir," I replied, bowing.

"No sweat, like I said," he replied. "Now, finish your breakfast and then meet with Emel; I'll research the letter. I think it'll be good for ya to get acquainted. I 'ave big plans for you and the more you learn now, the easier my job will be." He rose to his feet, wiped the crumbs off his scarf and trench coat, and left with Marcellus' poem.

I finished my frozen breakfast in silence while the other Xenophonians swarmed in. I took the last sip of my coffee when I saw Goliath, Solomon, and Leprechaun. I jumped to my feet and quickly cleared my tray. I didn't want to stop and talk. I hurried towards the door.

Unfortunately, one of them noticed me. I was happy it wasn't the one to ask too many questions. Diego leapt off of his master's stick and crawled over several heads to latch onto my back as I ran out.

JOSHUA: IX

"You don't make any sense sometimes, you know that?" I said as the creature got comfortable on my shoulder.

Diego squeaked as if to mock me and started playing with the curls on the top of my head. He didn't approve of the bottom half being shaved, but I wasn't about to take fashion advice from a monkey.

I waited in the dark, damp south-west corridor for Emel. Nervous, I paced back and forth. *C'mon, Joshua, you've gotta relax*, I scolded myself. *This is what you've been searching for. You're getting so close. Don't screw it up.*

Diego hopped off my shoulder and paced with me. He cooed.

"I pace when I'm thinking," I told him. He made another noise. "No, I'm not scared. Why would you think that?" After three minutes of arguing, I stopped and sighed. "Now, I'm talking to a monkey," I grumbled, throwing out my arms in exasperation. "You can't understand a thing I'm saying. I must be losing my mind."

To my surprise, the creature looked offended. It tried to cross its arms it seemed, but he was probably just scratching himself.

Before I could bicker further, heavy footsteps grew louder down the corridor. "Hey, Wolf!" Emel called. I turned to see her marching towards me. She wasn't dressed in her usual lunch lady garb. She wore ripped jeans that were too tight around her thick thighs. Her leather jacket hung open over a red graphic t-shirt that had the OX symbol printed onto it. On her left arm was a patch with a new emblem: a ribbon covered in short horizontal lines. A measuring tape.

"Hello, ma'am," I greeted with a smile. Diego chirped.

She petted the monkey and smirked. "You know my name; call me Emel. Only in formal situations should you call me 'ma'am' or 'Lachesis'." She held her arm out. "Now, let me show you what I do outside of making the best damn food in the world."

She led me (and Diego) down the hall and began to share vital information. After seven years, I was spoon fed the intel I starved for.

"Not sure how much you know about our history," she began, "but Xenophon in the Ancient world was a Greek military general, philosopher, and mercenary. He wrote books and shared some wisdom, but nothing too significant. He was chosen as our founder because of one thing." She paused as we reached the end of the hall. She punched numbers into a hidden keypad and glanced over her shoulder. "Loyalty," she finished and the door slid open.

Going through, we strode along a cat walk enclosed by glass walls. It was similar to the corridor where I first met Arata; the Moirai Clotho. This room below was more gruesome than Arata's hall of seats, screens, and machines.

It was a torture chamber.

Each chair served a different purpose: electrocution, stretching, puncturing, and other horrific uses. Weapons hung along white walls stained red. Handprints streaked across the bottom part of the windows as if the victims tried to escape the unbearable pain.

I held in my horrified exclaims and expressions. Wolf was used to this, Joshua was not.

"I do more than 'measure the thread' as it goes," Emel explained as she stopped to admire the scene. "I handle the tests that each Ares member endures before they can truly become a Xenophonian. Hermes and Eros don't undergo such tests. Those Divisions are so fragile that they shatter on the battlefield. However, we have higher expectations for those of Ares." She gestured towards the door in the room below. It slid open as if on command. Pouring in were members dressed in combat uniforms with patches of the Ares Vulture on their arms. "Now you'll witness some of my handiwork."

Slowly yet mechanically, the members went to chairs in different sections of the room. They sat, and simultaneously, all their limbs were strapped down. A few took deep breaths while others looked ahead with a deadpan expression.

"What exactly are these tests?" I inquired.

Emel stood up straight and put her arms behind her back. "They are called the Tolerance Tests. Loyalty is critical in the Order of Xenophon. As you're aware, our Ares members aren't the lightest on their feet. Many of them get captured, but," she nodded to a technician below, "we make sure they don't talk."

The technician stood by the door and flipped down a large switch. Whirring and creaking emanated from every direction. I didn't understand what was going on until the screams began.

Ares members were electrocuted, burned, hit forcefully with metal prods, and other horrendous forms of torture. Some screamed and cried for mercy, others were content and still.

That's what Emel wanted.

"They undergo these tests either until their throats bleed or their mouths shut," Emel explained. She pointed to a few quiet members. "Them over there are pretty much done. They've passed every test we have from flogging to gun shots. The ones who stick it out are loyal." She turned and took a few steps toward the end of the hall, looking out the window behind us. "Those who don't make it fail their duties as an Ares member. Either they die during the tests or I give the orders to my sister."

My heart stuck in my throat. Diego screeched in horror and ran to hide. I wanted to join him, but I forced myself to watch. The men and women below me cried and shrieked. It was pitiful. They writhed in pain and tried to fight, but it was no use. The straps were tight and Emel never gave up. *This must be why all the Ares members' voices sound alike*, I realized as I tried to tolerate their blood curdling screams.

I didn't want to think about it, but I needed more information. "If you don't mind me asking, why were you put in charge of these tests?" She arched an eyebrow. I quickly added, "Not a question of your power, ma'am, I simply want to understand your responsibilities."

She chuckled. "Understood, Wolf. I know you have your questions." She cleared her throat and explained, "Each Moirai handles a different stage of the Xenophonians. Clotho handles birth, I—Lachesis—handle life, and Atropos handles death. Clotho takes Mortals and gives them a new purpose. She handles the Entrance Rituals and decides who becomes Xenophonian and who is thrown into our Reborn population.

"Being that I handle life, I have the most power. I decide the Division and Pandemonium of each Xenophonian. I choose how high they'll go and for how long. I decide if they're worthy enough for life after a screw up. I decide who lives and who doesn't." The corners of her mouth turned upward. A sinister smile crept across her round face; something I'd never seen before in Emel. "Ultimately, *I* pave the path for every Xenophonian and decide when they've reached the end of it."

I hope she paved my path miles longer than everyone else's.

As if reading my thoughts, she whispered, "Don't worry, you'll be around longer than you think."

I didn't even think I'd get this far. I faked a smile.

"Now, Atropos is the one who handles death as I said," she continued, "and she *hates* that I give her the orders." She scratched her hairy face and continued casually, "She should be grateful that she gets to decide how they die. It's a trickier business than you'd think. We don't go around and kill everyone where they stand. It's done according to habit, trait, and time."

I must've had a confused look because Emel laughed.

"Think of it this way," she explained, "You wouldn't have known it was us disposing of the other Xenophonians if I hadn't told you, right?"

"Right." Even though I *did*, but never knew how.

"We do it like that to keep our chaos organized. Some of them die slowly and painfully from internal diseases. Others have unexpected heart attacks or accidents. All are by Atropos' design." She waved her hand to the screaming people below. "Except for the ones who don't make it through my tests. Those are their own fault."

I nodded and tried to take in the information. Thankfully, I had turned my glasses on for documentation so I could review it later.

She finished her explanation, and we watched in silence. My heart ached as I gazed upon the suffering souls. The fact that they endured such horrors and still survived amazed and terrified me. They left with a deeper pain than gruff and raspy voices.

Finally, their session ended. Emel gave the signal for the technicians to turn the machines off. The switch was flipped and everything was quiet. The screams ceased. The suffering Xenophonians' sweaty chests heaved. The content Xenophonians sat as still as before; emotionless.

The straps released. Some members dropped to the floor out of their chairs, unable to move. Others jumped right to their feet, standing tall. When the technician blew the whistle, they marched out the door. Those on the ground were mercilessly dragged out. Once it was clear, men and women in all white entered to clean up the mess before the next session.

At last there was silence, but it was eerie and heart rending. I interrupted it: "Do they remain loyal after they endure this? The Supervising Ares, I mean."

Emel's eyes narrowed. A look of disgust crossed her face, but a pang of disappointment and sorrow shone in her dark eyes. "Usually. If not, they're eliminated. There was only one mishap," she grumbled.

Is she talking about who I think she's talking about?

Diego the Monkey came out of hiding and jumped up onto my back. He squeaked, wanting to hear the rest of the story.

"He was the son of one of the traitors," she continued, feeling like she needed to explain herself. "Not that fellow Marcellus. We're still looking for his kids." She sighed. "The father was the former Titan of the Russian Pandemonium. His Mortal name was Nikita Patya but his Godly name was The Headmaster."

No way... I thought. *Headmaster meant more than the Isle members realize.* Shannon, Yared, you guys have to tell those kids about this… actually, that might make them feel worse. Never mind.

"His son's Mortal name was Erik, but his Godly name was *Mars*," she spat as if it was a curse to say his name aloud. "He was the greatest assassin we ever had. The boy undertook everything we threw at him and exceeded with flying colors. A weapon of mass destruction. He was my best pupil and was set to take his father's place."

My mouth went dry. *Sonny Wilcox endured these tests when he was a child.* I imagined the slick haired boy sitting in a chair with his feet dangling, screaming for parents that'd never come. Nikita murdered Sonny's father and took his mother as his prize. No one was there to save him from the tortures that room brought him.

Emel's harsh exhale brought me back to the present. "But when The Headmaster—Patya—betrayed us," she continued, "he took his son with him. We found out later that Mars betrayed his father *and* the Order of Xenophon. He's now part of the Resistance and is a great threat." She turned; a serious and deadly look in her eyes. "You tell no one about this. Everyone believes

Mars died alongside his mother. No one must know. It'll wreak havoc like no one has seen."

Definitely going to tell everyone. Well, you tell everyone. I think we could use this knowledge to the Resistance's advantage.

"My lips are sealed, Emel," I lied.

"I appreciate your discretion, Wolf," she snickered. "No wonder our god is so fond of you. A normal Xenophonian like yourself would've never made it this far without his blessing. You're starting to exceed our Supervising Officers. Don't tell them that though," she added with a whisper.

Their leader favors me? Or does he just suspect me? Questions swirled in my head. However, I played it cool and added an extra dose of humility. "I won't tell," I replied calmly with my hand up. "It's an honor to be thought of so highly."

She grinned and patted my arm. "Glad you think so." She took a deep breath. "Well, I think that's enough for one day. Don't want your head to explode. Besides, PH probably needs your help figuring out that message from Marcellus." With that, she led me out of that horrendous hallway and back into the cold, damp, smelly, but somehow comforting corridor.

Diego and I bid farewell to Emel and went our separate ways. My head couldn't wrap around how much I learned. Emel has power and I'm on her good side. She must be the one in charge of the Division of the Children of Moirai.

I also know that they *must* fear Sonny. Use that to your advantage.

Finally, there is one person that rules over the entire Order. I believe once we find him and understand his position, then we can make a plan of attack against them.

Shannon, Yared, all this information is critical. Analyze it, figure it out, do whatever you can and fast. I have a feeling things are going downhill very soon.

With safety and secrecy,

Joshua Wolfrum

Joshua Wolfrum

THE UNDERGROUND

Letter 18

Shannon: V

Hello Joshua,

I can't believe what you've learned. Xenophon is more than an insane organization. It's a murderous cult. They worship some false god with hopes that he'll bring the world back to life. But when you call upon Satan, he'll drag you down to hell. OX is waiting for that day.

I brought this to the attention of the other members, praying it'd change their minds from thinking that living in "peace" with OX is the best option.

"I can't believe this 'Zeus' dude actually exists," Mark marveled as he typed away at his computer. I sat with him, Myles, and Aaron in one of RRPR's tech rooms. They were hard at work coding a frequency to cancel out the Strange Voices transmissions, but they made little progress.

"I believe he's nothing more than a Mortal man hiding behind lies," I told them confidently. "He is *no* god. He's simply someone with too much power."

"And too many toys," Myles put in. "Whoever this guy is, he must have access to all the computers and technology of OX."

"Blondie's right," Mark said. "He probably also has the final say."

"Which is why he's the one we need to go after," I decided. "Joshua found out so much yet I feel like we know less than before."

"Then, what do we do?" Aaron asked. He took a break from his research to think. His black glasses lay on top of his head, hidden in his spiky blond hair like a creature in tall grass. His blue eyes were tired and worried. The young Isles Geek had so much thrown on his plate. It aged him.

"We proceed with our initial plan," Mark responded. "We have to try before it's too late."

"When's too late?" Aaron cried.

His Isle Commander sighed. Mark's fingers hovered over the keys as if they were afraid to continue. "When the Annex is complete," he said softly. "When everyone experiences that false happiness."

"But to them it's real, isn't it?" Aaron asked. He was never a doubter, but his twin sister Sami is having a hard time coping with what Donnie shared.

"No, it's not real. Not even to them," Mark snapped. "Their minds are withering away. The effects of OX will wear them down over time. They'll become nothing but mindless wanderers, living out each day the same as before. They'll experience no emotion, no pain, nothing."

"Their humanity will be stripped from them," I whispered. "Their souls lost forever."

"Eesh, so dramatic," Myles butted in. "Whenever the two of you are in a room together, I feel like we're in some crazy movie or book."

Mark smiled and looked at me. Confidence shone in his blue eyes. I stared back. The creases in his face were a result of age and wisdom. His dark hair remained short and he never put his silver hoop earrings back in. His metal dog tag hung proudly around his neck. He let go of his former life and accepted his new one. He became a mentor, a caregiver, and a friend.

I felt myself staring for too long and my face reddened. I quickly looked away. Mark's new attitude and demeanor reminded me of his brother.

I miss you so much, Shane, I thought, biting my lip. I gripped the dog tag that hung around my neck. I felt its cold metal in my hand. I tried hard to feel the one it belonged to, but it was no use. *Shane is gone.*

My eyes burned as I held back tears. I couldn't let them see me like that: weak and pathetic.

I casually rose from my seat. "Well, boys, I'll leave you to work. Please keep Zeus in the back of your mind during our next mission. Now that we know what we're looking for, hopefully our eyes will help us see it."

The two blond boys nodded and went back to their work. Mark kept his eyes locked on mine. His expression said he wanted an explanation. Mine replied that he wasn't going to get one. He sighed and returned to his computer.

Hastily, I left to find Director Virginia Michaelson.

As I walked through the bright corridors of the Underground, I played with the silver engagement ring around my slender finger. It was beautifully crafted and portrayed the Celtic culture perfectly.

My mind flashed back to June 23rd. Though it was only a few months ago, my heart felt like it had been ages. I remembered Shane's nervous face as we stood on the hill top. Despite his anxiousness, his voice and speech was eloquent and romantic. Unlike Shane at all. I recalled the patterns of the stars as we sat and sang together. That was the last calm night.

Then, I left him the next day. I left for the Isles out of pride. I wanted to be the one to save Mark. I felt like it was my fault he left. I needed to forgive myself and I thought that was the way.

My heart couldn't believe I'd been so selfish. I worried Shane sick and I feel like that pushed us apart. I wanted him to be there for me, but my stubborn nature wouldn't let him.

Now, he's gone.

I froze mid-step in the Hall of Royals. My heavy gaze raised to Shane's oil painted portrait. His bright green eyes were lifelike as if he'd wink at any moment. His smile was happy and caring. I waited for his lips to part and for a song to escape.

Beneath his painting were smaller photographs; contributions from Blake when he was photographer for WHYP. They were Shane in action, his achievements, and times of fun. The largest photo was of him and me before we left the Isles. We were standing on a beach, overlooking the water.

One of the things he feared most.

It hit me like a crashing wave. Shane proved that he'd do *anything* for me. He'd face his biggest fears to keep me safe. To make me happy. And how did I repay him? By being selfish. Blind.

I doubted everything I'd done. Tying up Shane, almost killing myself for Nic, rescuing Mark, protecting my sisters, taking the arrow for the triplets, everything. I thought about my father and how all I wanted to do was grow up to be just like him. We were supposed to solve cases together. We were supposed to find my big brother Pietro together. All I wanted to do was help others. I thought I was succeeding, but maybe that wasn't the case.

Did I really do it out of love? What was it for? I looked down at the scars that striped my arms. They were permanent reminders of the pain caused when I left for the Isles. The blade didn't cut me alone.

It cut everyone that cared about me.

Those memories flooded back like a strong current. As the images flashed by, I felt knives stabbing through my chest. The scar where I'd been shot with the poisonous arrow burned and ached. I clutched my jacket and breathed heavily.

What's happening? I tried to steady my breathing.

Nothing worked. I didn't have my mask or inhaler. The pain increased and I felt my legs turning to jelly. My throat burned like fire.

The poison awoke in my lungs.

I dropped to the ground. My head rested against the wall and my chest heaved. Sweat dripped down my face. The burning in my lungs and neck grew hotter and hotter. My vision blurred. I needed to get help. Crawling on all fours, I dragged myself towards the door on the other end of the hall. There was a panel next to it with different commands. I entered the code and signaled Virginia Michaelson. I hoped she'd be nearby.

I tried to calm my body while I waited, but it was too difficult. Tingling travelled from my toes up to my thighs. Slowly, I was becoming paralyzed. Anxious, I signaled again. Nothing. This time I tried Johanna.

The panel pinged and a green light showed that the signal was received. *"Yo, Shannon! What's up? Why're you calling me from the HoR panel?"*

My lungs and throat were inflamed, but I made out one broken word: "An...ti...dote."

"Oh sh—." It silenced.

The numbness reached my torso. I lay on the ground and gasped for air. Every breath filled with agony.

My head spun and my eyelids grew heavy. My mind was ready to fade, but held on when it heard a faint humming of machinery. The sound grew louder and louder until the doors at the opposite end flung open.

Flying in at full speed was Alison the Bionic. She wore her full armor and clutched my mask in her left hand. She landed at my side and placed the mask on my face. The cold metal expanded to my ears and covered my mouth. I bit the tube inside and inhaled the antidote frantically. It painfully filled my lungs and combatted the poison that fought to take over.

As it was taking effect, Alison took me into her arms and flew back out of the room, along the tracks, and to the infirmary.

I weakly looked around at the other patients. It broke my heart to see how many rooms were full. Our team members go on missions constantly, but not everyone makes it.

Alison brought me to an empty bed in the back where Sonny, Johanna, Janelle, and Ethan stood. She carefully laid me down. Ethan administered IV while Janelle swapped out my metal mask for the infirmary's plastic one.

I pinched my eyes shut and breathed in the medicine. I was embarrassed, but I couldn't keep them closed forever. I popped open an eyelid and looked around.

Janelle kept her good eye locked on the screen. Her thick braids were pulled back and she wore red scrubs that nicely accented her dark chocolate skin. Even with her scars and wounds, she is a beautiful young woman; I hope she knows that.

Ethan held my hand while he watched my breathing. His dark eyes were sunken and full of pain. The seventeen-year-old doctor was well beyond his years, feeling such weight and sorrow.

Johanna sucked on the string of the sweatshirt Nic gave her. Her green eyes watched Janelle intently. Her golden hair was in a messy bun and she was more nervous than I'd like.

Alison stood quietly in the corner with her metal arms crossed. Her eyes were shut and her head hung down; her short silver hair falling over the nasty scar on her forehead.

Sonny's red eyes caught my gaze and we had a staring contest. His lips were tight. When it came to me, he always had something to say, but he refrained this time. I won the contest and he averted his eyes, casually fixing his short black hair. After PH slashed off his ponytail, he kept it at that length.

Janelle breathed heavily and announced, "She'll be all right. From here, I can't tell what caused it. She didn't do any sort of physical activity."

"Although," Ethan added, leaning closer to display, "her heart rate increased excessively, causing her body to panic."

"What'd you do?" Johanna asked, nervously. She pulled up a folding chair and sat beside my bed. We looked at each other for a while. "This never happens, Shannon."

"I think she was thinking too hard," a raspy voice put in.

"I always think too hard, Sonny," I replied through the mask.

He rolled his eyes. "Not in that way, Detective."

I paused. "Fine, so I was overthinking personal matters and upset myself. No harm done."

Johanna laughed sarcastically. "See, you're funny. Sure, 'no harm done'. Absolutely. You dying is no big deal."

"I didn't die, Johanna," I said coldly.

"But you could've."

"But I didn't."

"Enough!" Sonny snapped. "This could be more serious then we're making it out to be."

"Unfortunately, Sunshine is right," Janelle said. She stole that nickname from our deceased friend, Roxanne. Even though Sonny hated it, it brought back happy memories of our time at Wyght's Home for Young People. For everyone else's sake, he let her use it.

In the moment, it brought me sorrow. *Roxanne,* I thought. She was a friend we didn't have time to mourn. *Roxanne, Dylan, Alexandra, and the others. They're gone and I couldn't do anything.* I felt the poison try and fight the antidote, so I took a few more deep breaths. I gripped the sheets of the bed under the blanket, careful not to let anyone see.

"Why is he right?" Johanna growled, bringing me back to the conversation. She spat the wet string out of her mouth.

Janelle pointed to the screen. "I think these particles awoke by themselves."

THE UNDERGROUND

Johanna didn't need an explanation and neither did I. I had nightmares about the day where I'd battle my insides on my own, but I didn't think it'd be this soon.

A light rapping on the wall interrupted our sad silence. "Mind if I come in?" a sweet voice asked.

Everyone stood at attention. "Of course, Director Michaelson," Janelle said, stepping aside. She turned to Ethan who nodded. "We'll catch y'all later," she said to us. "Ethan, Prince, and I have other patients to attend." The medics saluted Michaelson and went out of sight.

The fair skinned woman leaned over me and brushed the brown curls out of my face. "How are you feeling, dear?"

"As good as I can, ma'am."

The sides of her mouth turned upward. "You gave me quite a scare. What caused this episode?"

"Unpleasant memories, ma'am," Sonny interjected, clasping his hands behind his back.

Michaelson looked to Alison and Johanna for confirmation. Alison's head still hung low and Johanna just shrugged.

"Well, I think I'll discuss that matter privately later," she said. "For right now, it's good that you three are also here. This concerns you as well."

Johanna pointed to herself. "Me too? I'm no fighter."

"You need to know what's going on in order to offer better counsel," she explained. "Unfortunately, things aren't going well. Young Donald has a terrible yet powerful influence on many other members. He's told stories to the survivors. There's false hope everywhere." She rested her hands on her blue utility belt and sighed. A glimmer of regret in her eyes. "I'm afraid we may have to remove Donnie for the time being."

Alison's head shot up. "What do you mean 'remove him'?"

"I simply mean keep him confined until we can find out what that Xenophonian woman did to him," she explained.

"You're going to lock him up like a prisoner? He's just a kid and all he wants to do is help," Alison stated. "He can't do any harm."

"But you can," Sonny interjected.

The Bionic paused before rebutting. She looked down at her metal fists, clenching and opening them again. So many fell at her hands during the Battle of the Isles. Deaths that haunted her at night. She'd never sleep if she was under OX's control.

"Wilcox is right, Miss Alexus," the Interpreter Director whispered. "The boy isn't Donnie right now. He's a puppet. Give us time to cut the strings."

Alison took a shaky breath. "After everything we've been through, I would've thought he'd be stronger," she croaked. "He was so brave battling for a cause he didn't understand." A tear streaked down her face. I didn't know Bionics could experience sadness. "He was so strong watching his best friends fall. He endured so much pain."

"Under all that weight, he may have collapsed," Michaelson said, softly. "His mind is fragile now; one tap and the glass shatters." She walked over to the Bionic and put a hand on her cold, metal shoulder. "Donnie's burden is heavy. We have to start taking the load away."

Alison bit her lip and cast her gray eyes to the ground. There was a silence before she answered in a low voice. "I understand. Take him away; I'll explain it to the others."

Michaelson managed a smile, attempting to comfort the broken hearted Bionic. "Thank you, dear. I promise he'll be in good hands." Standing erect, she looked at Sonny who gave a nod and left. She turned to Johanna. "Watterson, be prepared to defend our mission in every session. Help them through their problems with love and care, but discipline and a strong will must always be shown. Papa E can give you further counsel. Go to him now."

Johanna stood to her feet. Patting my arm, she whispered, "Don't think too hard anymore." With that, she left.

"I suppose I should be there when Donnie is put into confinement," Alison mumbled once Johanna was gone. Michaelson nodded. With a sigh, Alison made her way out; her metal feet clanked heavily with each step.

"Now, Miss Hollinger," my superior said, sitting beside me. "What caused your episode?"

I thought for a moment, collecting my thoughts. I was about to tell her everything but refrained. Something inside me still held on, and I wasn't going to let it go just yet. So, I told her what you shared in your last letter, Joshua.

Once I finished, Michaelson sat back and upright in the chair. She thoughtfully chewed the information. Her expression showed she knew I was hiding something, but she didn't probe. "So Joshua is close with the Moirai Emel, or Lachesis as is her purpose."

"Yes, and I believe he can get a meeting with the other Moirai, Zeus, and the Division of the Children of Moirai."

She paused. "And they're still afraid of Sonny Wilcox?"

"I assume so. They haven't picked a replacement for him yet. They must fear him."

"Or hope he'll return." Michaelson leaned forward in her chair and looked me in the eyes. Her question was one I didn't expect. "You are *certain* there is no chance of Wilcox reverting to his old way of life?"

Before the mission in Moscow, I would've said yes in a heartbeat. Now, I wasn't sure. When he revealed his marks, he showed he craved the power he once had. To be reduced to nothingness and watch your peers rise to the top is difficult to endure. *But Sonny sacrificed so much for us,* I immediately thought. *How could I even entertain such an idea?* Guilt washed over me and my chest burned once more. I gritted my teeth behind the mask.

Michaelson placed a soft hand on mine and gave it a tight squeeze. "Deep breaths, Shannon."

I did as she said and the pain receded. I looked at her and stated, "There is no chance Wilcox would return to OX. He took the oath as an RRPR member and with us he will stay."

Michaelson patted my hand. "Very good. Then, I have another plan of attack in addition to the frequencies." She unzipped her utility belt and pulled out a square piece of paper. It was torn around the edges and showed signs of age, but the blood red and black ink didn't fade.

The image was a Roman helmet: the Mark of Mars.

I stared at the symbol as if it'd come to life and attack me. "Wh-what are you saying, Michaelson?"

"I'm saying the boy has gifts and high potential." She turned the card over in her fingers delicately. "I know he desires power but also wants revenge. You know I hate those sort of vendettas, but we can turn bad to good. I've considered this for a while when Thyme," she paused, recalling the RV Combatant that we hadn't heard from since our return. Her eyes tried to fill with fear, but she wouldn't let them. She had to be strong. "When his superior informed me of his past," she went on. "Now, I'm convinced. Wilcox came to us for a reason." Her eyes locked with mine. "Let's help him fulfill his personal mission."

I understood immediately. Sonny mentioned that if he couldn't be in control, no one could. He wanted to avenge the murder of his parents. He wanted to strike fear into the hearts of the enemy as he once did.

We'd help him do that again.

"How will we go about this?" I asked, sitting up in the hospital bed. My arms shook under my weight, but I managed.

"We'll start by leaving his 'calling card' in one of the Temples where the Annex has been completed." She placed the paper back into her pocket. "Those Titans must remember him or at least the stories of his accomplishments. I'm sure PH will remind them when he sees Sonny's Mark." Rising to her feet, she prepared to take her leave. "This will at least give Joshua more time before the Annex takes full effect. We'll also continue our search for Marcellus in the meantime."

"Two ex-OX members threatening the Order," I said slowly. "Between them, the Bionics, and even the Mutants, we can round up more chaos than they ever imagined."

Michaelson nodded grimly. "I wish it didn't have to be this way, but until we shut it down from the inside out, I see no other choice. Let's turn their humanized weapons against them." She stepped towards the exit but stopped in the doorway like she forgot something. She looked back at me. Kindness and sympathy filled her light eyes. "Shannon, I want you to know that we are very proud of you. What you're doing now is more than anyone could ever ask of you."

I bit my lip. I didn't know what to say, so I nodded.

The woman smiled. "Shane would be proud of you, too." With that, she left.

I sat in silence. *No, I failed him.* I felt my eyes well up with tears and I lay back down. I took the mask off of my face and breathed the damp, infirmary air. *Shane, I'm sorry.* Then, I cried myself to sleep.

Sorry you had to suffer through all that, Joshua, but thank you for reading.

Godspeed and goodwill,

Shannon Hollinger

Shannon Hollinger
Royal Strategist of RRPR

LETTER 19

Joshua: X

Hi Shannon (well, Yared, actually. I see the pattern),

Yared, tell Shannon everything will be okay. Soon she'll know Shane was proud of her.

Because, Yared... I've got a mission for you.

Don't. Tell. Anyone.

But first, why I am 93.7% sure that Sinatra of the Hermes Division is Shane Hodgins the Royal Agricola of RRPR. I know you're convinced, but now I am.

I sat at the bar with PH. Lucky's was empty except for us and Leprechaun. PH ordered the pub cleared and no one was permitted entry for the rest of the night. I thought we'd discuss the letter and determine what the lines meant, but PH just needed a break.

"All this 'as been hurting my 'ead," he complained as he took a swig of beer. "Between Sting always buggin' me about Marcellus' kids, this letter, and everything else that's going on."

"Why won't Sting leave you alone?" I asked, wanting to know what she was up to.

He sighed and slid his glass from one hand to the other across the marble counter. "She can kill, but not hunt. One of her many faults."

I'd say her greatest strength, I thought, relieved. "You're just one man, sir. You can't handle everything on your own."

The corner of his mouth turned upward. "Thanks, mate. You're all right."

We sat in silence as Leprechaun refilled our glasses. The bartender's pitcher clanked against my cup, causing me to look up. I was surprised when he met my gaze. His eyes were serious and his face meant business.

He needed to tell me something.

I arched an eyebrow and he subtly shook his head. *Not here,* I realized. I gave a slow nod, and Leprechaun turned away.

PH was too focused on his beer to notice the exchange. He gulped down half of it before he stopped and slurred, "Since we're 'ere, let's take a look at this letter again." PH dropped his mug on a coaster and pulled the paper out of his trench coat pocket. "It's the strangest riddle yet." He held it upside down.

Leprechaun turned back from washing the dishes and saw the letter. He cocked his head to the side and his lips parted as if to say something but refrained.

Despite drunkness, PH noticed this small detail. "What is it, Leprechaun?"

"Beg your pardon, sir," he flung a towel over his shoulder, "but I couldn't help but notice the shape of those lines."

"What shape?" I asked.

"They're an outline of a sort," he explained. "I'm sure you already know that. But I believe I know someone who knows exactly what this is. He spoke about it before, I think. I'd tell you myself, but," he tapped his forehead, "I hear so many conversations an hour that my brain doesn't remember them all."

"What're you talking about?" PH asked impatiently.

"Sinatra spoke of something he found during the last mission," he explained. "I believe he said it was 'very cool'. He drew it on one of the napkins like a child. His juvenile artistic abilities seem to match those of the letter. It's a long shot, but he may know what you're looking for."

"I'll take it," the Titan spat. He slid off the stool and teetered, gripping the marble counter for support. He slung his sheathed sword over his shoulder and added, "Any idea is better than sitting around with nothin'. I 'ave no more time to waste. Come, Wolf." With that, he ran towards the door. He misjudged his path and smashed his elbow on the doorway. He yelped and cursed the men who built the "bloody exits". That sobered him up.

I was about to follow suit when Leprechaun grabbed my arm. I stopped and looked into eyes that shone with determination and secrecy. Without averting his gaze, he placed a leather wallet onto the counter.

Maintaining eye contact, I slid the wallet off the marble and shoved it into my pocket. I wanted to ask questions, but couldn't. There were ears everywhere. We stared in silence.

Leprechaun turned away first and returned to cleaning. All the while humming the tune that he and PH both knew. It was so familiar, and I didn't know why.

I didn't have time to think about any of it. Was it weird? Absolutely, but getting you the coordinates to Marcellus was my priority. I ran after PH, pushing everything else to the back of my mind.

I found him waiting outside one of the training halls, waving at me to hurry up. When I reached him, we entered together.

The place was damp, dark, and disgusting. It reeked of sweat, blood, and other nasty odors. Since no one could be at the pub, everyone was there. Men and women from all Divisions swarmed to the gyms to train. Even though no one said it, there was a mutual understanding that if you didn't improve you would get "bumped down".

Although I was the only one who knew it meant "be eliminated".

PH walked through the sea of sweating bodies with his head held high. The moment the Xenophonians saw him, they backed away and let him through. A few jumped off their equipment to stand and salute, but PH had no time to put them at ease.

We made our way to the back where we found Sinatra running on one of the treadmills. His skill and speed was so impressive that others around him paused to watch. He had the machine on the highest setting and raced like it was nothing. His focus was forward and his lips sang a joyful tune.

PH cleared his throat and Sinatra looked at us out of the corner of his eye. He did a double take and then smiled. "Hello, sir. Wolf." His attention was on us but his legs kept pumping. "What can I do for you?"

"There was a rumor that you could help us with somethin' important," PH said, crossing his arms.

"Ooh important you say? Is it a secret?"

The Titan nodded.

Sinatra slowed his pace until he came to a stop. He shut off the machine, grabbed the damp towel that hung on the handles, and wiped his bearded face. "Where to, sir? I'll help any way I can."

PH smirked and jerked his head, leading us through the sea of staring faces. We followed him down the hall and into Lucky's.

Rather than sitting at the bar, PH led us to one of the marble tables in the back. As we sat down, Leprechaun caught my gaze and gave a subtle nod. *Still don't know what that's about.*

"So, Sinatra," PH started, leaning his long sword against the table. "You will not share this with anyone. If you do, you'll be severely punished for betrayal and dishonesty. Understood?"

Sinatra leaned back casually. "Of course, man. I get the whole loyalty thing; I went through orientation."

PH pulled the letter out of his pocket and laid it on the table.

"Oh, this thing," Sinatra said. He rubbed the tape that held the letter together. "This guy was a great songwriter. Loving these verses."

"It's not just meant to be a poem," PH tapped the lines on the paper, "these are clues. Hints. Directions to lead us to a dangerous man."

Sinatra raised an eyebrow. "I'm guessing he doesn't want us to find him if he went through all the trouble. What do we want him for?"

"That ain't none of your business," PH stated. "We just need your 'elp figuring out what these lines mean." He traced his finger along the edges.

Sinatra leaned forward and took a closer look. He pondered it for a moment and then gently placed his hands on the edges of the paper. In a swift motion he turned it horizontally. "There's your problem," he chuckled, "you're looking at it the wrong way. Now I recognize it."

I didn't see anything different.

PH shrugged. "I still see nothin', mate. Whatcha got?"

Sinatra traced the lines with his finger. "I was telling Leprechaun about this; I saw it last week." He jerked a thumb over his shoulder. "I don't know why my Supervising Officer yelled at me for coming in here. Leprechaun's a pretty cool dude. I drew him what I saw and he thought I was a good artist."

Even though PH wasn't pleased that Sinatra interacted with Leprechaun, he couldn't help but stifle a chuckle. *Sinatra really is like a child,* I thought with a smile.

"The Supervising Officers were actin' under my orders," PH explained. "Now, what was it that you drew for Leprechaun?"

Sinatra looked at me. "I thought Wolf would've recognized it. It's that cool map we saw in Australia."

My memory received a jump start. Sinatra commented about a map on the floor, but I didn't have time to look. I was too focused on the mission. "I remember now. You mentioned it when we entered the library. Do you remember what it was a map of?" I asked.

Sinatra shook his head. "Nah, sorry, man. Probably some part of Australia. I'm the one fast on my feet, not the one with the photographic memory."

Hearing this, PH shot Sinatra a confused look. That comment triggered something. He wanted to speak but was at a loss for words.

Part of me knew exactly who he was talking about, so I quickly changed the subject: "I suppose we'll have to return and check it out. What do you think, sir?"

"I think it'd be wise," PH said, snapping out of it. "You two will go and finish what you started."

"A solo mission?" Sinatra replied; his green eyes lit up. "This is going to be epic."

"You're not to tell anyone, you understand?" PH ordered. "Don't even speak about it amongst yourselves. No drawing it out for Leprechaun either.

If I see fit, I may admit another into the party."

"Ooh, party," Sinatra beamed. "When does it start?"

"You leave some time this week. You won't know when," PH informed. "Be prepared every night when you go to sleep. You won't know where you'll wake up."

I always hated it, but Sinatra was thrilled: "Yes, love the suspense!"

"Is there anything else you want us to do while we're there, sir?" I inquired, ignoring Sinatra's enthusiasm.

"Nothin'. Just figure out what's on that bloody map and return back," PH stated. "Can't 'ave you both out there too long. I fear the enemy knows more than we'd like."

"What do you mean?" I asked. I felt my palms dampen with sweat. My body feared what he was about to say.

PH looked around the room. "The enemy's got some way of seein' the future, I'm tellin' ya," he explained in a low voice. "They know our next move before we do. Sting 'as encountered it numerous times with the Resistance's smaller teams. I know other Titans 'ave experienced the same."

That's not all me. It didn't take me long to realize who they were talking about:

Blake Bain.

"Surely it's entirely coincidental," I said, playing dumb. Blake's precognitive dreams kept the Resistance one step ahead, and I prayed it would stay that way.

Someone didn't have the same prayer.

"Wolf's wrong," Sinatra replied. "They've got someone who knows stuff."

My heart pounded. *Not now.*

"Who knows 'stuff'?" PH asked. His heterochromatic eyes widened.

Sinatra shrugged. "Dunno why I know, but I'm pretty sure they have a Weapon of some sort."

No, Sinatra, stop.

PH scratched his head of curly brown hair. "Interestin'. So I'm not the only one who heard of this 'Weapon'. I'll continue this pursuit. Thanks, mate."

Sinatra saluted him.

PH thought for a moment then stood up. "If that's the case, I'll send more men with ya. You won't know 'til the day. For now, rest and prepare to be swift." He slung his sword over his shoulder. "Stick together. Wolf, continue your training with Sinatra. Nothing physical; mental for now."

We rose and saluted our Titan. Saying nothing else, PH left us alone in the back of the pub.

Sinatra stretched and yawned. "What now, Wolf? I'm ready for a nap, but I hear we've got other things to do."

First, I wanted to slap that smile off his handsome face. Then, I wanted to interrogate him. He's said too many Shane-like things to not be Shane. *However, if he really was, wouldn't Sting have known that she caught one of the triplets already?* Things weren't adding up. "Yes, we have training," I told him.

As we walked out, Leprechaun shot me another glance. Subconsciously, I patted the leather wallet in my jacket pocket. *I need to know what this is.* But it'd have to wait. I led Sinatra out to train his brain to think like a Hermes member.

Hours later, our session ended and it was time to prepare for dinner. We were on our way to the bath house when a female voice called out, sending shivers up my spine. "*Todo bien*, boys?"

I turned to see Sting strutting towards us. "Hello, ma'am," I greeted as kindly as possible. "How may we help you?"

"'I'," she corrected. She turned to Sinatra, "Sorry, song boy, but I have important business with Wolf only."

"Of course." Sinatra turned to me and added, "If you need me, I'll be at the showers." He winked and went off.

This is not going to end well. Nevertheless, Wolf had to act charming and desirable. I needed to know what she was up to even though I—Joshua— hated her presence. "What can I do for you?" I repeated.

She rubbed her hand along my back and nudged me to walk with her. I mustered all my strength not to squirm away from her calloused touch. "I wanted to check in and see how you were doing with my prize?" she asked. She read the confusion on my face. Snickering, she added, "The new Hermes member, Sinatra. He is my trophy for my victory against that agitating RRPR group."

So, he was taken after RRPR attacked Madrid... when Shane died. "Oh, I was unaware," I replied. "I hope you can see he's in good hands."

As we walked, she took my hand and examined it. Her fingers traced the lines in my rough palm. "I do see," she purred.

My face turned bright red and I pulled away, clasping my hands behind my back.

She smirked. "You know, Wolf, I never met any low Xenophonian like you. So intelligent, yet so naive. So mature, yet so innocent."

I tightened my lips and nodded.

"That's why I am so fond of you," she professed. "You are different from the other low lifes. You have potential for greatness," she stopped mid step and grabbed my collar, jerking me close to her. Our noses touched, and I looked into her chocolate eyes. While I didn't know what would happen next, I acted content with whatever followed. She smiled and continued, "and

I desire nothing more than to come out on top." Her breath smelled of sweet wine.

We stood close for a few moments before I gently pushed her away. "I appreciate the high regard, ma'am. I fear that you may think too much of me."

"Humility," she observed, biting her lip. "A good trait but one I'll break you of. You've achieved much. You should wear your victories proudly. Don't let anyone view you as anything less than what you are." She ran her finger down my sternum, pressing my white shirt tight against my sweating chest. "You'll understand it one day." Leaving it at that, she spun on her heel and walked away.

When she was out of sight, I let out a long breath. *Now I know she'll never leave me alone.* If she keeps revealing important information, it could end in my favor. *Her last victory must've been when she killed Shane. So why is Sinatra a trophy?* I kept trying to think of ways for my brain to be wrong. It all seemed too good to be true.

I need to find out. Now.

Without another thought, I raced to the showers.

Not to my surprise, the bathroom was empty. The open, mold covered showers were dry; no sound of running water. *He hates water...* I tip-toed my way around. The bath house was gigantic with all sorts of nooks and crannies.

I was about to give up when I heard muffled singing. Quietly, I made my way to the source. I peered around the lockers to see Sinatra standing before a cracked mirror, fixing his perfect brown hair. He was barely wet and had only a towel around his waist. His muscular torso was covered in bruises and cuts. On his right side was a long red scar: a fresh stab wound.

As he did his hair, he sang a tune that made my heart race. The one I heard for years and didn't know why. The one that was familiar and held distant memories that were tucked away in the back of my mind. They were locked up until that very moment, because Sinatra had the key.

He was singing the lyrics.

Sinatra *knew* the lyrics.

My eyes widened, and my jaw dropped as I was able to pinpoint what the song was.

It was the Hollingers' Gaelic lullaby.

With a joyful heart and a beautiful voice, he sang the lullaby—*Codladh Mo Ghrá*. The first time I heard it was at my Royal Celebration. The Hollinger girls sang it for me and their sister, Shannon, whose birthday was the same day.

I listened in shock as Sinatra sang:

THE UNDERGROUND

Codladh mo ghrá	Sleep, my love
Tá Lá ag deireadh	Day is at an end
Heaven thuas	The Heavens above
Ag breathná thar tú arís	Watch over you again
Codladh mo daor	Sleep my dear
An chuid eile I mo glacadh	Rest in my embrace
Nuair Tarraingíonn maidin in aice le	When morn draws ever near
Céimnithe me le bánú an lae	I fade with break of day
Codladh mo ghrá	Sleep my love
Fiú nuair a théann i	Know even when I go
Tá mé fos an ceann	I'm still the one
Chun grá agat mar sin	That always loves you so

In the middle of the song my heart ached and my head throbbed. Memories came flooding back. The first time I met Shane and the girls at that gas station. When I returned Blake Bain to Aymie Hodgins. When Shane and those little girls sang on stage. All the moments with the Hodgins and Hollingers leading up to that last goodbye when the WHYP doors shut behind me as I left for the Order of Xenophon.

My heart was in my throat. *He is… wait.* I had to check one last thing. Leprechaun gave me a wallet, and I knew whose it was. I fumbled it out of my pocket and slowly opened it. There was no identification—only a few American dollars—but there was a folded paper and a cord.

I took out the former and opened it up. It was a photograph of a couple sitting in a library I knew all too well. The man had his arm around his sleeping girlfriend. A walker rested against their chair.

I carefully put it back and pulled out the latter: a leather cord. Dangling from it were eight silver rings and a Celtic key in the middle.

My eyes widened. *This is… this was… Shannon's.*

Now, there was no doubt in my mind.

Shane Thomas Hodgins was alive.

I put the necklace back into the wallet and shoved it into my pocket. I needed to tell Sinatra the truth. *He doesn't know he's in a nightmare. I need to wake him up.*

Taking a deep breath, I stood up straight and turned the corner to talk to him, but he was gone. My heart sank and I ran through the bathroom, calling his name, but he was out of sight.

I was afraid to search the base. *Shane's alive. Shane's alive. I need to save him. Where is he? What happened?* My mind was in such hysterics even Wolf wouldn't calm down. If I ran into any Titan or Supervising Officer I would crack and everything would've been for nought. Playing it safe, I returned to my room.

My brain is so overwhelmed. *What does this mean? Will this mend the tear within RRPR? How do PH and Leprechaun both know the Gaelic Lullaby?* These questions swirled in my head like a whirlpool that sucked me inside. I had to swim to the surface. I plopped on my bed, covering my face with my hands. I took deep breaths, calming my paranoid mind.

"One thing at a time, Joshua," I whispered aloud. "Shane is alive. Get him out of here before he is lost forever."

But how?

I slipped the electronic tablet out from the slit in my mattress; ready to write this letter. I checked the pattern and saw that it was Yared's (your) turn to write me back.

That's when it hit me. A plan formed in my mind and you, Yared, are at the center of it.

Don't tell anyone. Not even Shannon.

Go back and read Shannon's letter about the Mark of Mars. You'll know what to do. Shane and I will be in Australia within the week to figure out Marcellus' letter. Meet me there and take him home.

Save him from this hell.

With safety and secrecy,

Joshua Wolfrum

Joshua Wolfrum

THE UNDERGROUND

LETTER 20

Yared: V

Yo Joshua,

Let's do this. You can't imagine how excited I am. The fact that Shane's alive, and *I* will rescue him. I yearn for the heat of battle. There better be gunfire.

I hope you don't mind; I've gathered a little team. Shannon's not going to like it, but that's why it's a secret, right?

I sat on my bed, packing a bag. I tried to refrain from smiling as I thought over the situation. It all happened so fast, and yet I couldn't contain my exhilaration. I desired to leave as soon as possible, but I needed approval from Virginia Michaelson. I couldn't just *leave*. I have orders. There's protocol. I'm an obedient Seer, but could be sneaky if necessary. I planned to request permission to plant the Mark of Mars in the Australian temple. I'm not lying, but I'm not telling the whole truth. No need to cause a panic about Shane when we don't need to, right?

With a grunt, I flipped over my heavy pack and emptied out a hidden compartment that was underneath. Carefully, I slid in a syringe and bottled sedative.

I zipped it up and wondered how I'd do it alone. Shane is taller and (as much as I hate to admit) stronger than me. I didn't want to raise suspicion by asking for your help, Joshua. I knew Virginia Michaelson would send soldiers with me, but they had to be *my* soldiers. *I need those that I can trust,* I thought.

As I shoved the bag shut under my bed, there was a rapping at the door. "Yo," I answered.

The metal door slid open a crack. Worried brown eyes peered through. "Hey, Yared," the Saviors Commander greeted.

"Sup, Ethan?"

He opened the door wider, revealing his stained doctor's coat and tattered red t-shirt. "Have you seen Mark lately?" he asked anxiously.

I shook my head. "Isn't he usually with Aaron and that smart guy, Myles?"

"They haven't seen him for a few days," he sighed, stepping into my room. One hand hid behind his back. "I'm worried he's losing it."

I arched an eyebrow. "Why would you say that?"

He raised a brown glass bottle that he held behind him. The label was torn off and only a few drops were left inside. "I'm worried about him. I found more of these than I'd like."

I shrugged. "The man is allowed a few beers now and then."

"Twenty beers a day?" Ethan cried, shaking the bottle. "I'm afraid he's passed out on the tracks somewhere. He barely talks with us about what happened to Shane. What if this is how he's coping?"

I rose and pulled my navy Seers combat jacket over my black tank top. He was right. Mark never spoke to us about his brother's "death". *Even if he is depressed, Shane's return will fix that*, I thought. "This is Mark we're talking about. He's fine," I told him. "I'll help you look for him later, man. Right now—" I paused. I wanted to tell him about my plan (which I hoped he'd be a part of), but I needed approval from Virgina. Can't go against protocol. "Look, I gotta go. I have to meet with Michaelson," I added.

Ethan stifled a disappointed sigh. I know he's doing his job as a doctor, worrying about people's health and junk. As for me, I wasn't fazed. If Mark wanted to drink away his problems, let him.

Although, my thinking isn't always right. Don't trust me in that regard.

Brushing past him, I left the Savior in my quarters and went to find the Interpreter Director.

As I walked down the RRPR corridors, I heard shouting in one of the rooms. I loved a good fight. Curious, I stood outside the door, eavesdropping on the argument.

"I can't believe you let them do that!" I heard Sami the Cat yell; her voice cracked. "Donnie is one of us. Why would they take him away?"

"It's for the good of us all," Alison sternly replied. "I'm sorry, but this is how it has to be."

"Sami, please try to understand," Aaron said softly. "Donnie wants to get rid of Alison and Axel. We can't let that happen."

Sami was in hysterics. I heard the cat part of her growl and moan like she was in great anguish. Sami's nature was sweet and timid, but the Battle of the Isles took its toll on her. She was becoming a tired, angry feline.

Sami's sobs became quiet breaths. "But you're strong enough, Alison," she croaked. "What if you do go with them then take them down on the inside?"

There was a pause.

"Sami, it won't work like that," Alison choked. The disappointment in her voice was unbearable. "They'd manipulate me before I could do anything. Hasn't our family been broken apart enough?"

Even though I loved a heated argument, this sibling quarrel was not one I wanted to sit through. That final comment got the better of me. *Poor Jeremy Alexus. He died fighting for a cause he didn't understand.* My blood boiled thinking about how Mr. Nik showed barely any remorse after he shot ten-year-old Jeremy who sacrificed himself for Mark.

Mark... I thought about Ethan's worry for him. Our friend suffered so much. He lost his best friends and foster father from Fallout. He thought his brother Shane was dead. The blood of children is on his hands, and there's nothing he can do about it. *What if he is slipping into anguish?*

I snapped out of it when the Alexuses' argument got loud again. I needed to leave. I held my breath and ran to meet Michaelson.

Entering the conference room, I found her sitting at the table surrounded by papers. They were plans, requests, and death certificates that required her signature. Her golden hair draped across the back of the swivel chair as she leaned back with her hands on her face.

She was distressed.

She didn't notice me enter. Clearing my throat, I asked, "Permission to be in your presence, ma'am."

Startled, she sat upright and inhaled sharply. "Yared," she put her hand on her chest, "you gave me quite the scare. Please, sit."

I did as she asked. "Ma'am, permission to speak?"

A smile spread across her smooth face. "I understand you're used to military formalities, but with me it's quite all right."

"Thank you, ma'am, but I have a big favor to ask." I took a deep breath while she sat up straight with intent. "With your permission, I would like to lead a small mission to Australia to intercept a Hermes team, utilizing the Mark of Mars."

Her lips parted in surprise. That information was only told to Shannon and you, Joshua. It almost slipped her mind that I also exchanged letters with you, but she remembered. "Any particular reason?"

I paused. I wanted to tell her the truth about Shane, but you ordered me not to, so I refrained. Rather, I shared my selfish reasons. "I desire the thrill of combat," I confessed. "My assignments are few and far between. I need to be out there, fighting for what I believe in. I'm tired of cowering." I leaned forward, resting my forearms on the table. "Let's show those Xenophonians that RRPR is *not* afraid."

There was a silence as Michaelson thought. She looked over at the map on the wall. The red Xs peppered so far across that the map would soon be consumed like locusts swarming crops.

Turning back, she looked at me; a light of hope glimmered in her eyes. "I will grant you this assignment," she answered in a low voice. "But promise me this: no unnecessary bloodshed. Get the message across, intercept that mission, and return home. No casualties. Understood?"

The hair stood up on the back of my neck around my Isles brand. "Understood, ma'am." I rose to my feet and she copied. I firmly shook her hand. "You will not be disappointed."

She smiled. "I'm sure I won't be. Any other requests for this mission?"

"Yes, if I may. I'd like it to be classified at least until we return. The division within us Isle members is too great. The small team that should accompany me will be of my own choosing and be secret as well."

She granted this to me and sent me on my way to inform my soldiers. We were to leave by nightfall. As the door closed behind me, I did a victory dance and ran to assemble my team.

I snuck around the base searching for my three boys: Ethan, Axel, and Lucas. I didn't feel terrible about leaving Aaron out; I had no need for a Geek in my company. Besides, he needed to be there for his sisters.

I searched for a while, but they were nowhere to be found. I didn't want to ask for help, but I grew impatient. I was looking around the infirmary when I ran into Janelle Arends: Aymie's best friend who was kidnapped and tortured by the Xenophonians, Masdit and Gerrior. I knew Masdit was dead, but I never learned what happened to Gerrior and the other prisoners.

"What can I do for ya, Yared?" she asked as she wrote down patient information at the desk.

"I'm looking for Ethan. Is he here?"

She shook her head. "Haven't seen him. Prince might know where he is though. I remember he was talkin' to him." She pointed to a lean man with dark brown skin that conversed with a nurse down the hall.

I only remembered the stories of Prince that Shane told at the end of our journey to the Underground. He was the middle aged jeweler that gave Shane the engagement ring for Shannon.

As I approached, I got a weird feeling in the pit of my stomach. I wasn't sure why.

When he saw me, he did a double take and stared. "How may I help you, Seers Commander?" he asked slowly.

"I'm looking for Ethan Shaw, Saviors Commander. Have you seen him?"

He nodded awkwardly. "Y-yes, he was on his way to the dungeon, if I recall correctly."

"What?" I said, utterly confused.

"We have a containment area," Prince corrected. "If you go out to the tracks and travel north, you will find the sector."

I gave him my thanks and left. *What was that about?* I wondered as I raced down the corridor on a rackety wooden cart. I didn't have time to think about it; I needed to get everyone prepared to leave. I zipped down different sectors I didn't even know about until I came across a tunnel with "CONTAINMENT UNITS" stenciled in white above the opening.

I slowed my approach and parked the cart by the platform. As I got out, I heard a faint thumping. *Someone else must be down here.* That didn't matter. It wouldn't be unusual for me to explore, so I made my way down the dank long dark corridor.

Open rooms were along either side, and blackness consumed whatever was in them. I poked my head through a few doorways and called out Ethan's name. Nothing but my echo responded.

After searching for a while, I heard a faint flutter. Abruptly, I turned around with my guard up. Nothing but an empty hall. Scoffing, I shook it off and kept searching.

I came to the end of the corridor where I saw a dim light shining in the farthest room. Before going in, I heard the noise again. I didn't look this time. *Probably a bat or some nasty sewer beast...*

Entering, I found an open space with four doors along the far side of the wall. Scattered around the room was rusted training equipment. Tetanus city. I took one step and felt a crunch beneath my foot. Lifting my leg, I saw I stepped on the neck of a beer bottle. *Is this where Mark's been hiding?*

I took a deep breath to call his name when the fluttering grew louder and louder. A prickly arm flung around my waist and a small hand clamped over my mouth. I felt my feet lift off the ground as I was carried toward the mezzanine above the entryway.

When I realized it was Lucas, I didn't thrash. The Dragonfly put me down and landed next to Axel and Ethan who changed into his navy combat uniform. They were patiently waiting for something.

"What on earth—," I spat, frustrated. I wiped Lucas' palm sweat off my face. "What was that for?"

"*Cállate*," Axel hushed. "He'll be back any second."

"Who?"

He jerked his chin towards the center door on the far wall. I crouched beside them and watched.

A few moments passed before we heard footsteps and laughing. The door slid open and out stepped Mark. He was dressed in black jeans and a new green shirt. In his arms were an excessive amount of empty beer bottles.

To my surprise, he walked straight, tall, and sober, not swaying an inch. He beat boxed as he walked out of the room, his tune fading the further he went.

Doesn't seem depressed to me. When we could no longer hear him, I whispered, "Where was he?"

Ethan shook his head. "We're not sure. We think he was meeting with someone. We don't know who though."

An answer popped into my head. It was fate that I thought about him just before. Now, I was curious.

"Do we want to find out?" I jumped over the mezzanine railing and dangled until I was secure enough to drop to my feet. Ethan did the same while Axel and Lucas flew down. Quietly, we made our way to the door and down the winding steps. I didn't think of what dangers awaited us at the bottom of the dungeon. Not that I cared anyway.

We found ourselves in a corridor with jail cells on either side. The air reeked of urine and body odor. We sneaked down the hall and peered in all the rooms. They were empty.

We were about to turn around when a low voice hissed, "Yo, who's that?"

We halted. The others looked at me to respond. I took a quiet breath and said in a fake booming voice, "Friends of Mark Hodgins; code name *Bandit.*"

There was a throaty chuckle. "First rule of RRPR: never reveal the identity of any Officer with a code name especially to those in confinement."

I wanted to slap myself for being so careless, but I kept cool.

Before I took another step, a head peered out of a cell to the far end of the room. Two large yellow eyes glowed in the dim light. It smiled, revealing sharp pointy teeth. "Little Mark's kiddos," he chuckled. "We've been dying to meet ya."

Unafraid, I smirked and we went over. I looked in the two cells and was satisfied that my hunch was correct. They were the Mutants from Mark's old gang, Fallout.

"Theo, Jordan," I greeted, "A pleasure to meet you in person."

Jordan rose to his feet. He appeared sort of what I pictured from Mark's descriptions, only the real version was much older. The Slowloris Mutant was covered in dark hair with golden highlights. He had fangs and bright yellow eyes that were too big for his face. The Fallout symbol was burned into his bare chest. On his inner elbows were the glands that secreted deadly venom.

Theo the Shrew sat on the floor of his own cell, nibbling on a fresh loaf of bread. His pale skin shone through his blond body hair, and his tail tapped against the floor rhythmically. His nervous brown eyes darted across the ground, focusing on our boots.

YARED: V

Jordan raised his arm and leaned against the cell bars. His animalistic body odor floated down the hallway. "What brings you boys down here?"

"Curiosity," I stated. "The name's Yared Prinz: Seers Commander." I gestured toward my companions. "This is Ethan Shaw: Commander of Saviors. He's not wearing his garb, but he's a doctor who does all that fun stuff. The machine with the curly white hair is Axel Ramirez and that bug-freak is Lucas White."

Jordan looked at Lucas and did a double take. He tensed. "No freakin' way. You're—"

"A Mutant," Theo finished almost dropping his food. He was so focused on eating he didn't notice the massive Dragonfly staring down at him.

"Crikey," Lucas said softly. "This is incredible." He rubbed his hands through his blond hair. "You two are the originals. My heroes," he chuckled nervously, "just don't tell anyone."

"Who did that to you?" Jordan asked.

"Same as to you. Carl Mallory gets around. He was my Keeper."

The Mutants could barely believe it. "So he's still out there. Doing this to kids," Jordan muttered.

"Not right now," Lucas reassured. "After his facility was destroyed on my home island, he turned around."

Theo squatted and scooted closer to the bars. He squeezed his face between them and looked up at Lucas. He reached his arm out to grab Lucas' wing. The Dragonfly didn't refuse. Gently, Theo grabbed the delicate wing that lightly crunched beneath his fingertips.

Jordan shook his head. "I can't believe it. How many more monsters are there?"

Lucas shrugged. "Not sure, cobber. I heard he dialed down the serum after he left Manhattan. I don't know how many Half-Mutants there are. He ran those experiments for over ten years on the Isles. My Rank was the first to return to the method of experimentation you experienced."

Gripping the bars, Jordan snarled, "How long have you been like that? How many were in your 'Rank'?" Hatred for Mallory burned within him for many years. Lucas' existence was fuel for the flames.

Lucas thought for a moment. "I've been like this about six years. In my first Rank there were about a hundred of us. He's done heaps more experiments since. I'm unsure of how many were successful."

Jordan exhaled. He couldn't believe it. "He's always been making an army. Him, Devin Page, and those other guys Theo couldn't eat."

That was something I didn't want to think about, so I changed the subject. "What are you guys doing down here?"

"What does it look like?" A different voice growled. I turned to see a figure sitting against the back wall of his cell. He had dark skin, curly hair on his head and face, and three silver hoops on his right ear. "We're trapped here for life. Prisoners of war."

"Hey, it's not all bad, Brand," Theo replied, standing up. "We're alive, unlike those other guys down here that were from OX. Their big bad bosses killed them when they started talking." He stretched, scratching the ceiling with his sharp nails. "We said sorry, so we don't die! Now we get to run around, hang out, drink beer, and eat food." He cackled. "Food, food, food." Scurrying to the back of the cell, he opened a mini fridge that was hidden in the wall and took out another sandwich.

"Wait," Ethan started, "You're Brand? Mark's best friend from Fallout?"

Brand scoffed. "'Best friend?' Look, man, I ain't a six-year-old girl who went on play dates with Mark. We were acquaintances at best. I showed him the ropes and he held onto 'em." He leaned forward. "Then, he pulled them from me, leaving me empty handed."

"What is with everyone and holding grudges?" Axel muttered.

"Grudges make a man what he is," another voice said. This one was deep and gravelly. The cell across from Theo's hid another mysterious prisoner. "They make a man weak, undesirable, hateful, and prideful."

"Like you're any better without grudges, Gerrior," Brand retorted, rolling his eyes.

Ethan put his hands on his cheeks. "No. Way. Gerrior? Like *the* Gerrior? The one who was after the Hodgins triplets their entire lives?"

"No need to remind me, kid." He stepped forward and peered out at us. He was bigger than I thought: height and width. The Mark of Ares tattoo crawled up his neck and onto the side of his bald tan head. It was a double edged sword, marking his accomplishments as a murderer. "I don't mind doing my time," he confessed, "It's peaceful down here and they're good to us, despite what we've done. We've taken a lot from those RRPR Officers, and yet they still treat us like human beings."

"To each his own," a fifth voice growled. Behind Gerrior, a young man with tan skin and long slick hair sat on the floor with a brace around his leg. Zander. The nephew of Masdit (who was the sadistic killer and Hodgins' pursuer). Zander was the Combatant who betrayed the Hodgins triplets because of his love for Aymie. Blake predicted his plan, but no one acted in time. WHYP paid the price. "I wish they'd kill us already and get it over with," he mumbled, throwing a stone against the wall.

"Okay, let's change the subject," Brand interrupted, jumping to his feet and stepping forward. "What do you four want?"

To be honest, we didn't want anything; we wondered where Mark was. The others didn't speak, but their silence birthed a new idea. *I'd be breaking rules*, I thought, *but…*

"Well, I was going to keep this an Isles only thing," I began, "but I think I have room for a few more."

"Uh, Yared," Ethan put his hand on my shoulder, "can we talk for a minute?"

Rolling my eyes, I turned around and huddled with Ethan, Axel, and Lucas.

"I have no idea what you have in mind, but I can figure parts of it out," Ethan whispered, sounding worried. "You want to get these guys out of here? Are you *nuts*?"

"What makes you think I want to break them out?" I asked.

Axel chuckled and crossed his arms. "This is Yared we're talking to, right?"

"Fair point," I replied. "Guys, trust me. These guys will make this mission so much easier."

"What's bloody wrong with just us?" Lucas spat. "What's so difficult about this mission?"

My turn to be offended: "You didn't hear anything about it and you're already questioning my decisions as leader?"

"Considering how I was on your team for the Isles Challenge," Lucas reminded, "yes I'm always questioning your decisions, mate."

I wasn't going to get into that subject. "Look, this is a top-secret, highly dangerous mission. If we're not careful, we could not only blow an Officer's *and* our cover but also screw up our only chance to save an asset."

"What asset?" Ethan asked.

I paused. Turning around to the prisoners, I said aloud, "Do you want a chance at redemption? A possibility to get out and be seen as heroes?"

Theo jumped to his feet. "Ooh, heroes. Is food included in being a hero?"

"Food *and* other rewards are possible." I honestly had no idea, but I needed to sound compelling. "If we succeed, I'll personally speak on your behalf to cut your sentences."

Theo squealed with joy. "Yes! I'm in. I'll do whatever you want."

"What's the catch?" Brand asked firmly.

"I can't tell you that until after you accept or reject," I replied.

There was silence.

"I'd give anything to start over," Gerrior said in a low voice. "I'll do whatever I can."

"Same here," Jordan added. "I regret everything I've done. Mark knows that, but I haven't proven it to the others. Even though you're only offering us a chance, I'll take it."

"I'm out," Zander spat. "I'm not going to give back to those who've taken so much from me. I'll stay here and rot."

"Thanks for the dramatics, Zander," Brand scoffed.

"Are you going to be just as dramatic?" Jordan asked, looking at his fellow prisoner with wide yellow eyes.

We turned to Brand. He exhaled. "It'd be nice to get out of this cell for a bit." He threw his hands up. "Just make it interesting for me, all right?"

Zander muttered curses under his breath.

I pumped my fist. "Yes! Oh this is going to be great." I was too excited.

"Relax, man, what's the mission?" Axel asked.

"Oh right." I cleared my throat. "This mission is classified but approved by Virginia Michaelson. Only she and the eight—well, nine including Zander—of us know about it. Although, she doesn't know about you four joining us," I pointed to the prisoners. "We are breaking you out so do *exactly* as I say, when I say it. Don't pull any fast ones, understand?" They gave their word and then I continued, "We're traveling across the globe to intercept a Hermes mission, send a message, and retrieve a lost asset." I looked over my shoulder at my three friends who listened anxiously. I smiled and added, "We're going to get Shane Hodgins back."

After everyone soaked in the reality, I gave a quick explanation of what happened. The prisoners knew about Shane's supposed death and were just as shocked as my friends. Brand and Jordan weren't convinced, but the others believed it. Fine with me. As long as they obey orders, it doesn't matter what they think.

I went over the plan which I made up on the spot. In an instant, I mapped out the entire assignment. The beauty of being raised as a Seer. I laid everything out perfectly and no suspicion will be raised towards you, Joshua.

"Glad I'm out," Zander said when I finished, spitting on the floor. "You're all going to die for no reason. Have fun with that."

"At least we won't die alone!" Theo cackled. "Zander die on his lonesome. No girlfriend, no friends, no girlfriend, no friends."

Zander growled and screamed at the Mutant to shut up. The other prisoners sighed simultaneously. They were used to the childish behavior.

Not wanting to sit through another temper tantrum, I ordered Axel to break the men out of their cells. Once they were free (and we made sure Zander was secure), we headed out.

Sneaking around the base and to the hangar was a blast. I'm not even being sarcastic. Breaking the rules was such an adrenaline rush. *Why was I never a rebel before?* Like we could get in deep for doing it. While my friends went to pack supplies, I kept the prisoners in hiding. An intense game of hide and seek.

Somehow, I led the four prisoners to the hangar unseen.

There was a plane waiting for us. I ordered our four allies to find a new hiding spot. As I helped Ethan, Lucas, and Axel finish loading the plane, I kept a side eye on the prisoners. Thankfully, I couldn't find them. I forgot that the four of them were trained soldiers and killers.

Also the reason they were in confinement in the first place, but I kept telling myself they'd be great assets.

At last, the Drones finished fueling and headed out. Our mission was about to begin. I was going to signal to the prisoners when Blake Bain entered the hangar. I hoped he'd inspect some plane or cargo, but nope. He strolled right up to me.

"Hey, Yared," the white haired Officer began. His hands were shoved deep in his pockets. "What are you boys doing?" A large camera bag was slung over his shoulder... too big if you ask me.

"Classified," I stated, flinging another bag of sandwiches up to Ethan in the plane. "What are you doing?"

"Being bored, I guess," he chuckled. "The guys are busy and Aymie is on another mission. I thought I'd come see what you were up to."

Honestly, I wasn't surprised. We had a strange hidden connection, I guess. He did look right at me several times when he experienced his precognitive dreams. He's definitely a cool guy, but not cool enough for me to let in on our mission. "Well, unfortunately I can't let you hang with us either right now." I threw up another bag.

"You sure have a lot of food provisions," Blake noticed.

"Lucas' Dragonfly appetite's been out of control, lately." Out of the corner of my eye, I saw Theo's head shoot up from behind a crate, drool dripping from his mouth. Then, a dark hand shoved his blond head back down and out of sight.

He pointed to the coat hangers in the bay. "And you each have two jackets?"

"No, Lucas is also a diva. He can't choose just one."

"Are you planning to get hurt? You have a lot of medical supplies."

"Don't you have better things to do?" I retorted.

He ignored me. "What about that over there..." and continued asking questions.

So, yeah. He wouldn't shut up. I managed to get him to walk and talk with me around the hangar. While I distracted him, the others snuck on board. Do you know how hard it is for four very distinguishable prisoners to go unnoticed? I was lucky they're pros.

After talking for a half an hour, I informed Blake I had to leave. Then, he started asking questions again. He was persistent. Frustrated, I cut the conversation short and stormed onto the plane.

The problem is I don't remember Blake leaving the hangar.

He might be in the bay somewhere. Where? No idea; these planes are huge. However, I don't want to worry anyone yet. Hopefully, he stays hidden.

Ugh, it's such a pain. There are always last minute complications. We now have to make sure no Xenophonian sees Blake or learns anything about him. He is the Weapon that PH spoke of in your last letter. I hope the little Brit isn't with you.

And FYI, *you're* going to break all this to Shannon in your next letter. I ain't doing it; I have to deal with her in person. You face her written wrath.

We'll see you soon.

Bravery and fidelity,

Yared Prinz

Yared Prinz
Seer Commander

LETTER 21

Joshua: XI

Hi Shannon,

Soo… Hi, how are ya? I'm fine, thanks.

Heehee… you're probably wondering where your members and … uhm … prisoners went. Don't worry, no one traded the Bionic with OX. I'll tell you *exactly* what happened so when the boys return maybe their reprimand will be slightly less severe. To be fair, Virginia Michaelson did approve of the mission… just not the "breaking prisoners out of jail and putting the Weapon at risk" part.

When I awoke that morning, I was sitting upright in the back of a truck. I clung to my safety bar as the vehicle traversed at a high speed across the bumpy terrain. I blinked hard and looked around. Sinatra sat across from me. His head hung low and he was snoring loudly. Leprechaun slept to my left and Solomon across from him. Unfamiliar Soldiers occupied the remaining seats. Diego the Monkey was curled up between two rifles on the weapons rack.

I thought this was just going to be Sinatra and me? I wondered, worrying how I would hide his abduction from them. I had no way to warn Yared; he was going in this completely blind.

I cursed PH under my breath. He made things more complicated. After a moment, I realized he also contradicted himself. He said to keep Sinatra *away* from Leprechaun. Now there he was sleeping next to him. *I guess Sinatra sitting at the bar threw all caution to the wind*, I concluded.

The piercing buzzing and humming stung my ears. The Strange Voices murmured and crackled, *Arise… chosen Hermes members…*

THE UNDERGROUND

"Ready to heed," I growled, trying not to wince at the pain.

You have reached... your destination. The voice rang in my mind like a sharp, painful tune.

The noise was unbearable to the untrained mind. It startled Sinatra and woke him up. "What in the world," he cried, jamming his ear into his shoulder. "Why can I hear those freaky voices?"

"Shut up," I sneered as the others stirred awake.

Leprechaun yawned. "Morning everyone, whomever you may be. Not quite sure what's going on." He slipped his arm out of the seatbelt and rubbed his fingers through his reddish-brown hair. He smacked his lips and looked around. When his light eyes fell upon Sinatra, he stared longingly as if he'd seen the hills of Ireland he missed so dearly. The corner of his mouth twitched like he tried not to smile. After a moment, Leprechaun looked at me out of the corner of his eye.

I nodded. Somehow I knew what he was asking.

He returned his focus forward, not saying a word.

We traveled in silence until the truck jerked to a stop. The back opened and darkness pooled in. It was before dawn. PH stood outside, flaming torch in hand. He wore his black combat outfit under his trench coat. His green scarf was pulled up over his mouth and covered the freckles on his cheeks. His massive sword was in its sheath against his back.

He was ready for a fight.

Stepping out of the truck, I surveyed the area. We were parked behind a circular marble structure that stood in place of the ANZ Stadium. It was incomplete; only one side of it stood erect.

The Annex hasn't taken full effect here yet, I thought. *There's time to save Australia.* How? I don't know. That's up to you.

"Wolf!" a voice called. I turned to see PH waving me to their huddle. "There's been a slight alteration of plans," he started once I joined, "Sting gave word that she saw an enemy aircraft 'eaded this way. Someone is a clumsy pilot. She was able to intercept their landin' point."

I wanted to slap Yared across the face. You can tell him I said that too, Shannon.

"So that means we're gonna catch 'em by surprise." PH's blue and green eyes glowed in the crimson firelight. "I already 'ave a few Ares members waiting there. We are going to clean up the mess."

My heart dropped. *They're not going to make it.* Instantly, I scolded myself. Yared must be smarter than that. He'd prepare for such situations; he is basically a military general. *A teenage one.*

"You know your orders," PH concluded. "Get to your posts." Without another word, the other Hermes members departed leaving Leprechaun, Solomon, Sinatra, and me alone with our Titan.

I looked at each one speculatively. "Uh, sir? Permission to speak."

"Plans 'ave changed, Wolf," he informed, pulling his scarf down. "I know I said I didn't want more than two, but I fear that our mission searchin' for Marcellus might be compromised. I don't want anyone gettin' there before we do. These two," he pointed to Leprechaun and Solomon, "will keep watch while you and Sinatra get the information. They are now privy to our missions. The library is thirty-five minutes east of 'ere. You have three hours."

"What will you do, sir?" I asked, although I already knew the answer.

PH smirked. "I'm goin' to see what our enemies are up to, then use a few to send a message."

I held back a shudder. He wanted to leave his calling card: the pierced bodies. I prayed to God that he wouldn't succeed. Against my will, I smiled as he turned and left.

I took a deep breath. "All right. Let's get to it." The four of us (plus Diego) took one of the vehicles and made our way to the library.

I drove with Sinatra in the passenger seat who whistled the tune that convinced me he was Shane. The soothing melody of *Codladh Mo Ghrá* filled the cold truck. In the rearview, I caught a glimpse of Leprechaun's face. His eyes were wide and tears could've fallen any minute. He watched Sinatra with such care and… love, almost.

Okay, who is this guy, I thought, confused. *Once Shane is safe, he's next on my list.*

The shadows of the buildings grew smaller as the sun began to rise. I pulled alongside the library and parked. PH said we had three hours, but I wanted to do it in two. I needed to save Yared.

The four of us hopped out of the truck, weapons in hand. Stealthily, we made our way around the building. Diego hopped off Solomon's staff and climbed up the statue before the main entrance, surveying the area. Giving a screech, the creature determined the coast was clear, and we headed inside.

In the entryway of the ruined library was the map that Sinatra had remembered. I pulled the letter out of my jacket and examined it. Turning it landscape, I looked at the ground and chuckled. "What do you know? You were right, Sinatra."

He peered over my shoulder. "Of course I was right." He pointed to the outline of the map. "'Tasman Map'. Pretty cool. Now, let's figure out what this letter really means."

Solomon and Leprechaun kept watch while we tried to solve the puzzle. It was more complicated than the last ones we've seen. The bartender gave his two cents every now and then, which proved to be helpful. *He's smarter than he looks.*

It took almost an hour to decipher it and pull out all the clues. The map and letter cross related to some books in the library which Sinatra ran to get. We worked hard and were uninterrupted. The library was lifeless.

It worried me.

Filling in the final blank, my heart sank. We almost completed the coordinates. Only two numbers remained, but it could be figured out without another letter.

"We're almost there," I whispered.

"Almost there? I'd say we're pretty much done!" Sinatra explained.

Shannon can figure this out, I thought as I wriggled my nose to turn my glasses on. I recorded them to share with you later, but I got a weird feeling in my gut. Something told me my glasses would be unreliable. I tried to memorize them, but I didn't want to get a number wrong. So, I did the next best thing.

I tore a piece of paper out of one of the books and scribbled down the numbers. *Better safe than sorry,* I thought.

"What's that for?" Sinatra asked.

I folded the letter and handed it to him. "I want you to keep this safe," I ordered.

"Why?"

"PH is worried that there are enemies about," I lied. "If anything were to happen to me, I want you to complete our mission."

Sinatra took the letter, staring at it with amazement. He was honored to receive such a responsibility. Looking at me seriously with his green eyes, he promised, "I will guard it with my life."

I thanked him and placed the original decoded letter into my backpack. We were just about to head out when I heard a faint flapping. I stopped in my tracks to listen.

"What's wrong?" Sinatra asked.

My heart wanted to leap for joy, but I stopped it. "I don't think we're alone." Pulling out my pistol, I aimed it towards the hall on my right. The others did the same and followed me down.

As we walked, I listened, but the noise was gone. Leprechaun whispered, "I don't think there's anyone here, mate. Let's go." I didn't want to arouse suspicion, so I agreed and we headed back and out of the library.

I couldn't have been happier to go outside and find our vehicle on fire. In the billowing smoke above, I made out a strange glowing figure.

Dropping into a stance, I barked, "Weapons, now!" My three companions prepared for a fight. "Show yourself, coward!"

The figure descended and stood on the hood of the burning truck; the flames consumed its metal legs. It was some sort of half-human half-machine creature. He had gray mechanical eyes and curly white hair. I tried not to smirk when I remembered who he was: Axel Ramirez the Bionic.

"Drop your weapons, *amigos*," Axel ordered. "This doesn't have to get messy."

"I think it's a little late for that," Sinatra bellowed as he aimed his gun. "Get out of here before we turn you into scrap."

Axel didn't say anything. Silently, he hopped off the truck and took a few steps forward, but we held our ground.

Diego was not comfortable with the Bionic getting so close. Screeching, he leapt off of Solomon's staff and was about to attack when something flew past and snatched him. Startled, we dropped our guard to see what it was. Within that split second, Axel had lunged and grabbed Sinatra in a bear hug. Sinatra thrashed and kicked but the Bionic was too strong. Effortlessly, he leapt into the air and flew off.

"Sinatra!" I screamed. I started to chase after them when Leprechaun yelled behind me. I turned and he was gone.

Solomon's staff was on the ground, and he was staring at the sky.

"What happened?!" I bellowed.

"For the simple are killed by their turning away," he whispered.

"We don't know he's dead," I argued. "What took him?"

The wrinkles around Solomon's eyes grew deeper as his eyes widened. He was terrified.

Before I could comfort him, a cold hand was over my mouth and my feet were dangling. The crisp morning air rushed against my body as I held a metal arm for dear life. Closing my eyes, I felt my consciousness slipping and I passed out.

When I awoke, I was in an old, damp building. My hands were tied behind my back and my knees dug into the concrete ground. I yanked my arms to break free but it was no use. I looked around to see Solomon and Leprechaun chained at my sides. Their heads hung low, and they snored softly. In the corner, Diego the Monkey was fast asleep with ropes around his hairy ankles.

I heard a faint whirring and looked up. Across from me was Sinatra whose arms were stretched outwards and chained to walls opposite each other. Hovering over him was a figure wearing a navy combat uniform. His gloved hands held a sort of metal tool that was pressed into the back of Sinatra's neck.

He was trying to remove his OX brand.

"Ah, you're awake," a voice said from behind. A young man with dark brown skin stepped around and sat on the floor in front of me. His strong face had an expression that meant business but his eyes were friendly.

Yared, I thought.

"So, you're the one behind this," I growled, keeping the act going.

"Maybe I am, maybe I'm not. That's none of your concern." He held out his hand. He had my glasses.

I didn't even notice that I had lost them which I immediately scolded myself for. If anyone else had found them, seven years of secrecy would've been uncovered. They'd know I was a spy.

Chuckling, he shoved them on my face. The screens glitched and a message flashed across: *"Corrupted... Cleanse... past 24 hours."*

My glasses wouldn't have the coordinates. I wanted to swear, but I forced my aggravation back. *It's up to Sinatra to get them to Shannon.*

"Now you can look at the face of your enemies more clearly," Yared snarled, tapping my lenses with his dirty finger. "I want you to remember every detail, because I have a message to send."

I arched an eyebrow. "What is it?"

There was a thumping to my right and left. Leprechaun and Solomon were kicked awake by Axel the Bionic and Lucas the Dragonfly. My eyes widened as I looked upon them clearly for the first time. Their inhuman figures frightened me, but I wasn't the only one.

Leprechaun stared in shock and amazement while Solomon muttered prayers to send them away. Tears streaked down his wrinkled face especially whenever he looked upon Lucas and his massive compound eyes.

"Good, old man," Yared said, getting to his feet. "You've got the idea." He towered above me. Grabbing my dark curly hair, he yanked my head backwards. "Tell your Titans that *they're* the ones who should be cowering," he sneered. "We have no intentions of peace and will accept *no* negotiations." He leaned forward and breathed on my face. "Their reign is coming to an end." He threw my head forward and I used all my strength to keep from smashing into the ground.

Behind Yared, the whirring of a machine stopped abruptly and there was a whisper, "It's out."

Axel unchained the sleeping Sinatra. Lobbing him over his shoulder with ease, the Bionic revved up his rocket thrusters and was ready to take off through the hole in the roof.

The ground rumbled like thunder and he was thrown off balance almost dropping Sinatra.

Oh no...

An explosion tore through the far left wall. Rubble shot out, pegging us with the debris. Smoke clouded the air and the smell of gunpowder filled my nostrils. Cracking open an eye, I looked over to see a small figure gripping a large sword.

"What do you buggers think you're doing with my men?" PH growled. Stepping through the gray cloud, he pointed his sword towards Yared who was covered in blood and dirt. "You thought you could fool me, eh?" His eyes darted from the leader to Axel who had Sinatra over his shoulders.

Before the Titan could comment, Axel leapt out of the building, catching PH by surprise.

PH was still staring when Yared kicked him in the stomach, causing him to stagger backwards. During that time, Lucas grabbed the doctor (Ethan, I assumed) and was about to fly off with him.

The Titan looked over at the Dragonfly and gasped. "Impossible…" he muttered as he watched the two take off. Yared glared at PH before Lucas swooped back in and grabbed him, flying him out of the building.

PH jumped to his feet. He slashed our metal bonds with his sword, setting us (and Diego the Monkey) free. I shakily stood and held my throbbing head.

"AFTER THEM!" PH screamed and ran out of the building. Shaking my head, I was brought back to my senses and followed suit.

We almost reached the truck before PH skidded to a stop. He held out his arms for us to do the same. Standing still, I heard a faint ticking sound.

"RUN!" PH screamed.

We turned and bolted as the vehicle exploded behind us. The heat crawled up my back as we barely escaped the flames.

With no other choice, we chased our enemies on foot. PH yelled to me, "I know exactly where they are going. The other members are waitin' for them there!" With a menacing look in his eye, he added, "We're still one step ahead."

We raced across the ruined city. Warm air brushed against my face as we ran. The sun peaked midday but was becoming covered by gray cotton clouds. I looked over at my companions. For older fellows, I was surprised at how well they could keep up. Solomon had his staff over his shoulders with Diego clutching it tightly. The expression of horror still printed on his face. He couldn't fathom the Mutant. Leprechaun's light eyes were locked on the path before him, determined and focused.

My throbbing legs rejoiced when we reached the destination. The RRPR hideout was an abandoned building at the Sydney Olympic park; less than two miles from our camp.

We crept around the perimeter. The glass walls were shattered and the building was wrecked.

I looked around but the place seemed dead. No sign of RRPR *or* OX. "Sir?" I panted, clutching my burning chest. "Where are our men?"

PH wiped the sweat off his face and hands with his scarf. "Not sure, mate," he replied, sliding his sword out of its sheath. Stepping through the window, he made his way forward. I followed while Solomon and Leprechaun stayed behind.

We went past the stairwell and into a side room where we found remnants of food. PH crouched and felt the crumbs. He picked up a shiny wrapper and read the expiration date. "I was right, mate. This is where they've been 'iding. The Ares members and my other men must've captured them already." He scoffed, "They're bloody pigs... and eat as much as 'em too." He gestured to the variety of crumbs, spills, and wrappings that littered the ground.

Little did he know that was a good sign; a certain someone was satisfied.

I was about to comment when a crash and a screech resounded. We ran back outside to find no one but Solomon's staff laying in the yellow grass and a crying monkey.

"Bloody hell," PH exclaimed. "Where are my men?!" He called out the names of the other members that supposedly had the enemies in custody. I picked up my companion's stick and ran around the building.

I was appalled at what we found.

Five large Ares members lay dead on the ground covered in their own blood. They were littered with bullet holes and bite marks. All but one had lost the majority of their limbs. Their ambush failed and they paid the price.

PH couldn't believe his eyes. He walked around the carnage, trying to figure out what had happened. "This can't be," he whispered. He bent down and examined the teeth marks in one man's leg. "These don't belong to any normal animal. Wolf, look at this."

The stench of death filled my nostrils. My stomach bubbled and bile crawled up my throat. I swallowed and examined a mauled member. The bites were large, but the teeth marks were peculiar. The front teeth were long, sharp, and pointy like a rat but the far back molars were that of a human.

Then, I noticed something else. This Ares member's hand was untouched. Clean, scratch free, and closed. Carefully, I wrapped my fingers around his cold hand and forced it open. Inside was a folded piece of paper.

"What is that?" PH snatched it. As he read it, his jaw clenched. "Can't be..." He jumped to his feet and ran back to the main road with me and Diego following behind.

The sky rumbled as the storm chased us. The gray clouds turned black and the temperature dropped. The cold air filled my lungs, helping me forget the stink of decay.

When we reached our encampment, I skidded to a stop and gawked. Our tents were destroyed and our boxes of supplies were blown to bits. The other four Hermes members and the rest of the Ares lay dead. No sign of Solomon or Leprechaun.

With a growl, PH punted a box across the camp, cursing and swearing in different languages.

"Heyyy shortie!" a voice cackled. "I should put soap in your mouth! Soap, soap, soap!"

Whipping himself around, PH tore out his sword and his pistol. I turned to see a figure scurrying behind some debris. The Titan shouted and chased after it. We ran after this shadow of a creature for longer than we should've.

We found ourselves in the middle of the street before the marble structure. Huffing and puffing, we tried to catch our breath. I looked around to see a skinny, hairy man standing on top of an old sign. At his sides hovered Lucas the Dragonfly and Axel the Bionic.

PH screamed and aimed his gun as did I. Together, we fired every bullet. The two Mutants hid while Axel's hand shot out, deflecting each bullet with frightening speed and precision. Panting, PH threw his gun and gripped his sword with both hands.

"Relax, man, you're the lucky one today," a voice called. Yared stood to our left with two men at his sides. One had three earrings and dark eyes while the other was covered with hair and sucked on his inner elbows. "My friends are awfully kind," Yared explained with a smile. "Letting a Titan go free is no easy task."

PH scoffed. "You couldn't kill me if ya tried."

Yared laughed. "Who said anything about killing you?" He held his hand out to the large marble structure. The moment my eyes fell upon it, my jaw dropped.

The beautiful white marble was stained with red. Fresh paint (hopefully) dripped down the crevices of the structure. It was a symbol that no Xenophonian could ever forget. It was a red Galea—a Roman helmet.

It was the Mark of Mars.

PH growled, appalled to see the emblem once again. "That traitor no longer possesses that Godly name!" he bellowed. "You call 'im that because there are no other names for that monster."

"Monster is right." Yared pointed to the symbol once again.

Looking closer, I saw two figures suspended in mid air, clutching the ropes that were tied around their waists. Above them, two individuals stood atop the marble structure.

No, get out of the way, I thought, anxious. They were too distinguishable. One was a large bald man in all back and the other was a smaller, thinner fellow with a hair of all white.

PH didn't pay attention to his dangling men. His heterochromatic eyes were locked on the white haired man. When the two figures disappeared, PH snapped out of it and turned back to Yared. "A'ight, fine. So let's say Mars is back in play. Where is 'e then?"

Yared tapped the side of his face. "Can't say."

"And why not?" PH growled.

"No fun! No fun!" the creature perched on the sign cackled.

"Attaboy, Theo," Yared called. "PH, you just tell everyone he's back."
He turned and started walking away. "Oh, and you better get your men down
before those ropes slip. They aren't tied that tight."

Without another word, they slipped from our grasp. PH didn't move.
Vengeance wasn't his priority.

"Sir, shouldn't we chase after them?" I asked.

PH growled, "Leave 'em be. They don't concern us right now." He
pointed his sword towards the old stadium. "We 'ave to get these buggers
down."

"What about Sinatra?"

He sighed, "We'll 'ave to count 'im among the casualties. We don't
'ave the manpower to get him now. If they try to get him to talk, the Children
of Moirai will kill 'im."

I prayed it didn't come to that. "It's such a shame… I know he
would've been a valuable asset."

"Yeah, but at least 'e didn't know too much." PH slid his sword back in
its sheath. "Do you have the letter?"

Nodding, I pulled the crinkled paper out of my pocket. PH snatched it
and shoved it in his trench coat.

"Now let's crack on," he decided. "Gotta get Solomon and Leprechaun
before the 'eavens open up."

Without another word, we went to get our companions.

So, Shannon, that's what happened. I'd say it was a pretty well thought
out plan. Somehow RRPR knew PH's every move. Was that *all* Blake or did
Yared actually anticipate it? Either way, I'm impressed.

I just hope your fiancé is able to remember you. Note, I still have his
wallet. He'll probably need that when he comes to. Also, make sure you get
the paper with the coordinates from him before he wakes up. It'll be much
easier to take them when he's off guard.

Don't punish Yared and the others too severely. I think they did a pretty
good job, but let me know what actually happens.

With safety and secrecy,

Joshua Wolfrum

Joshua Wolfrum

LETTER 22

Shannon: VI

Hello Joshua,

Honestly, I don't know how to react. I want to thank you and slap you at the same time.

After Yared left for his mission, no one noticed anything was amiss. Mark was concerned, but Michaelson assured him that their mission was approved. Aaron was hurt that he wasn't invited, but his sisters needed him more. The only thing out of place was Blake. No one could find him, but Aymie claimed there was no cause for alarm. She assumed he was spending time alone on the surface, trying to interpret his dreams (which he often did). Despite forgiving him for Shane (even though he didn't do anything), she kept her distance.

As for her and my relationship, Aymie continues to reinforce the wall between us. Her only words to me are bitter ever since I withheld the treaty and Donnie was compromised. I hope I can break through the blockade soon.

It was about a week since Yared left, and I sat on my bed, going over notes. Normally I'd involve Sonny and Mark, but I needed to be alone. Aymie and I exchanged harsh words just before. My heart ached at her claims, but I'd never show it. When she spat fire, I returned the gesture.

I looked to the corner of my room where my viola lay on the table. Normally, I'd play it to aid my concentration, but etched into the smooth ebony wood were joyful memories turned sorrowful. When I played, there was always an accompaniment. Shane. His original guitar melodies would entwine with the strings of my viola. Our duets were happy and full of life. They brought joy to those the notes kissed.

Now, I'm left playing sad solos.

My head dropped to the mattress, scattering my research on Greek mythology and OX. I was depressed and distressed. Shane's death and Aymie's angry accusations clouded my deductive reasoning. Nothing made sense and I wanted nothing more than to slip into a long, uninterrupted sleep. My damp eyes grew heavy as the nightmares beckoned me.

A loud banging at the door jerked me back to consciousness. The knocks had a frantic rhythm, and a voice shouted for me. I stood up and wiped my tears with the back of my hand. Flinging open the door, I found Mark breathing heavily and dripping with sweat.

"Shannon," he panted. He held his hands out. "Look, I know this will sound crazy, but I lost some things I know I shouldn't have. I don't know how it happened, but it did."

Normally, I could guess the answer, but I was too out of sorts. "Calm down, what happened?"

He chuckled nervously. "The prisoners are gone."

My eyebrows raised. "Say it again?"

"Theo, Jordan, Brand, *and* Gerrior are missing. Zander stayed behind, but won't spill." Frustration and worry covered his strong face. "The prison bars were melted and the system was hacked."

"Impossible," I replied. "Those cells are reinforced and have high security. No tool outside of Myles' workshop is that advanced."

Mark took a deep breath. "It wasn't a tool."

My face fell. "Where are the Bionics?"

"Alison is here, but Axel is on that mission with Yared, Ethan, and Lucas. It's classified so no one knows where they are or when they'll be back."

I couldn't believe it. "You don't think..."

Mark nodded. "My theory is they took our prisoners with them to do something behind Virginia's back. Whatever it is won't end well."

Without another word, I put on my mask and the two of us raced out of the living quarters to find Director Michaelson.

She was in the infirmary speaking with Johanna, Janelle, and Prince. A look of surprise crossed her face when she saw us racing towards her. "What is the matter?"

"The prisoners were released," Mark answered. "We fear they are no longer in the Underground."

Michaelson's thin lips parted in surprise. "What do you mean 'released'?"

"We believe it was Yared and Axel," he answered.

Johanna scoffed. "Of course it was Yared. I'm not a fan of that kid."

"What did Yared do?" Prince asked, concerned. His dark eyes widened.

"Is he good?"

"For now," Michaelson said in a low voice. "I knew something was up when he didn't report back. He hasn't made contact since he left." Michaelson clenched her fists. "He better have a good explanation," she grumbled as she stormed out.

Janelle whistled. "Ooh that boy's gonna get it."

"I'm sure he has his reasons," Prince argued. There was a tone of worry in his voice. Why he cared about Yared so much, I wasn't sure.

Although from further observations, I can speculate an answer.

"Maybe he'll respond if I reach out," Mark thought aloud. "Hopefully, I can knock some sense into him and get him to return."

"Knock him out in person. They should be back now," Janelle put in. We stared at her.

"What are you hiding now, Janelle?" Johanna asked, shaking her head.

She shrugged. "Let's say that *maybe* I provided Ethan with med supplies and Myles' special tools. Let's also say that I *maybe* saw them leavin', and they *maybe* spilled the beans about the mission's details. The ones Director V. Michaelson doesn't know about anyway."

I wanted to interrogate her but Mark's electronic watch—BoMF, they call it—buzzed. He read the message and exhaled sharply. "Why that little—" Without another word, he ran out of the infirmary with me following quickly behind.

We made our way to the tracks and zipped down the tunnel towards the concrete city. Mark braked at the last second before we crashed into the platform. Jumping off, we headed towards the crowd of people surrounding the fountain.

"Out of my way! I'm going to kill him first," Mark yelled as he elbowed his way through the amazed citizens. He got to the front but stopped dead in his tracks.

I bumped into his back. "Hey! What happened?" I rubbed my cheeks and fixed my mask.

He didn't respond.

I stood on my tiptoes to try and see over him, but I was too short. I put my hand on his shoulder and onto the bystander next to me and shoved them to the side. "What's wrong, you've never seen rogue Mutants and soldiers before?" I looked up at the troublemakers and gasped.

Sitting on the edge of the fountain was a man with thick dark hair and a beard. His muscular arms were tied behind his back, but there were no other restraints. Curious green eyes jumped from face to face until they fell on mine. Our gazes locked, and a smile spread across his face. A smile I could never forget.

"Shane," I whispered slowly. My hands grew clammy and my heart raced. *This isn't real. Who is this?*

Yared hopped off the fountain and walked over to me. A grin spread across his face. "I have a present for you, Detective. Hopefully, he isn't too broken."

I looked at the "present" then back at Yared. I couldn't find what to say. I watched my fiancé die. He was dead. "Who is this?" I demanded.

The Seers Commander chuckled nervously. "Well... I sort of kept a few details from you that were in Joshua's letters." He placed his hand on my arm and gently pulled me towards their prisoner. "Detective, this is Sinatra. Sinatra, Detective."

This is Sinatra? All I gathered was that he was a new, naïve Hermes member that you were put in charge of. I couldn't have deduced that he was my dead fiancé.

"This is Detective?" Sinatra asked speculatively. "You didn't tell me she was this cute... or a she for that matter." His silvery voice matched my fiancé's.

I swallowed the fiery lump in my throat. *It still can't be,* I doubted.

"We didn't want to ruin the surprise," Yared smiled.

"She's the one who's supposed to help me?" he asked. Hope filled his familiar beautiful green eyes. "Apparently I'm broken, or so they keep telling me."

I blinked hard, holding back tears. I wanted to believe this bearded Xenophonian was Shane, but my logical brain refused to accept it. *I watched him die. He's dead. This is a trick of OX. Another Trojan Horse like Donnie.*

A Mutant screech interrupted my internal crisis. "Yep!" Theo the Shrew butted in. "You have a few screws loose. A few screws. A few screws."

Jordan elbowed him to shut up. Theo was about to fight when he was handed a sandwich. Joyfully, he plopped down on the dirty ground and munched away.

I tore my eyes off of Sinatra and looked at the Mutant. I shook my head hard, locking up my conflicting feelings for the moment. My mind returned to being Detective: the Royal Strategist of RRPR who is meant to keep everything in line. I grabbed my forehead and scolded, "Yared Prinz, bringing this Xenophonian will not divert from the fact that you released war prisoners from confinement."

Yared took a step back and held his hands up. "Please, Detective, I had to. Joshua said he'd tell you everything. His letter just came in. Didn't you see it?"

I was so caught up in my own emotions the last few days that I hadn't seen the message.

"Explanation or not, you guys are in hot water," Mark added, resting his elbow on my shoulder. Out of the corner of my eye, I noticed Sinatra glare with disapproval, but I dismissed the observation. "Just because I visit you guys doesn't mean we're on good terms."

"Look, stupid, we got your brother back," Brand spat, crossing his arms. "Cut us some slack."

"I am not the one in charge of cutting slack," Mark retorted. "Besides, I'm not the one charged for crimes against RRPR," he looked to Gerrior, "murder included." The ex-Xenophonian hung his head low.

Brand's posture stiffened and he stomped forward, stopping an inch away from Mark's face. He was now shorter than his old friend. "Your crimes are just as bad as mine," Brand growled. "You're a Fallout delinquent. Always have been, always will be."

Mark snarled and was ready to return fire, but I yanked him away. "You can't do this here," I interrupted. Brand's lip curled but Mark said nothing. I turned to the Isles members. "You three take Sinatra to the observation rooms." Looking at the four prisoners, I sternly commanded, "Cuffs must be worn at all times. If you behave and obey, maybe we can—" The words caught in my throat. My chest burned as I looked at the prisoners. Theo and Jordan were responsible for my disability. *They're* the reason poison stirred in my lungs. Brand was accomplice to the notorious Nikita Patya and Walter "Wally" Jarvis. And Gerrior? He's responsible for Shane's aquaphobia and the Hodginses internal suffering.

I gripped Mark's arm. I couldn't finish my sentence. He stepped away from Brand and completed my thought: "*Maybe* we'll negotiate some sort of reward."

Theo leapt up from the ground so high I thought he'd hit the angel on top of the fountain. He danced and held out his hairy hands. The others understood, but Brand was reluctant. After some cursing and complaining, he surrendered. Cuffed, they followed us to the conference room.

Inside we met the remaining RRPR Officers and the Isle Commanders. Their eyes widened when the prisoners scurried inside. A little later, Yared, Axel, Ethan, and Lucas returned from placing Sinatra in confinement. Their lips were sealed tight.

The room was quiet as we awaited Interpreter Director Virginia Michaelson. I sent her your last letter, Joshua. She was in her office reading it. I didn't get a chance to read it myself; I had no context.

A beep interrupted our silence. The door slid open and Michaelson stormed in. "What on earth were you thinking?!" she bellowed as she marched to the front of the room. "Where do I even begin. You disobeyed direct orders, failing to keep the mission quiet. You broke your promise of no bloodshed. Not to mention confronting a Titan and personally threatening him. He knows all of your faces now." She threw her hands out and pointed to the Mutants. "Oh, and you also broke prisoners out and abused them as your super weapons."

"No abuse!" Theo argued, scratching his blond hair. "Yared is a nice Commander. He gave me lots of food. Food I haven't had in a long time." He licked his lips and cackled.

I almost threw up.

Michaelson was appalled. She pressed her hands against the table, hung her head down, and took a deep breath. "I don't need to be reminded," she growled. She lifted her gaze and looked at each one of us. "Do any of you have any context? Not about that, I mean the mission in general," she quickly added.

Each Officer and Commander shook their heads.

"Okay, so here it is in brief." She stood up straight. "Yared was supposed to 'try out' a new tactic for us. We wanted to see what hold one of our Officer's has on the Order of Xenophon. From what I gathered, I'd say our grip is stronger than we thought." Turning to Sonny, she said, "Wilcox, I apologize for doing this without your knowledge. I should have informed you sooner."

Sonny tensed. "What did they do?"

Stepping forward, Yared slid a small card across the table until it stopped before the ex-Xenophonian.

Sonny glanced at it and then looked to the Seer. "What have you done?" he snarled.

"They're totally scared of you, bro," Jordan put in. "Like, when those Ares dudes saw it they totally freaked out."

"Panicked! Cried!" Theo added with a sinister grin.

Sonny looked to Gerrior who was also a former Ares member. "It's true, Wilcox," the big man said softly. "They still fear you. Your legend lives on."

Satisfaction shown in Sonny's red eyes. It pleased him that he was still feared within OX, but he didn't want to show it. "Was this a result of your AWOL?" he inquired, pushing aside his feelings.

"No, I authorized it," Michaelson explained. "S. Hollinger and I agreed that if we can threaten the Order of Xenophon with two former esteemed members, we may have a chance to cause disarray within their ranks."

"Yeah, and it worked great," Yared grinned. He was clearly thrilled at the fear and chaos it caused. "Imagine if we added your mark to a place where the Annex took full effect! The madness would be *insane*. I can't wait to try it."

Sonny nodded, but remained silent. He had no more words.

"Okay, can we back up a bit?" my best friend Johanna asked, growing impatient. "What exactly happened? Someone said they brought back something?"

Michaelson turned to me and smiled. I tried to smile back, but no emotions showed. I didn't know how I felt about the whole situation. Frankly, I still don't.

"Well," I started slowly, removing my mask, "they brought back a Xenophonian who goes by the name 'Sinatra'." I took a deep breath and looked to Aymie who stared at me with wide gray eyes. "They and Joshua claim him to be Royal Veteran Agricola Shane Hodgins."

The room was quiet. No comments, no gasps, nothing.

"I know it's crazy," Yared put in after the silence was too much to bear. "But I'm telling you. This guy *is* Shane. He looks like him, talks like him, acts like him. However, there's only one problem," he added under his breath.

"What's the problem?" Aymie asked desperately. She wanted to believe him, but it was too good to be true.

Yared exhaled sharply. "While Sintra may think and act like Shane, he doesn't know he is Shane."

Aymie's face paled. Her heart sank as did mine. I knew he didn't remember, but I didn't want to be reminded.

"Have you said his name?" Sami asked hopefully, playing with her black cat tail. "That's how we remembered our past for the first time. Sure things are incomplete, but it's a start."

Yared and Ethan looked at each other. "We haven't tried yet," Ethan confessed. "But I'm afraid it might not work."

"How can you be so sure?" Sami cried.

"The new Process is different from what you endured, Sami," Sonny interjected as kindly as possible. "Mortal Names mean close to nothing now." His red eyes became serious, yet there was a pool of sadness behind them. "Trying to recover a low Xenophonian's memory is near impossible."

The uncomfortable silence returned. No one knew what to say.

I didn't believe Sonny. I couldn't believe him. There are many ways of tapping into the recesses of the human mind. The Order of Xenophon can't completely cut off all memories.

Right?

"That won't stop us from trying," Michaelson declared. She stood up straight and faced the war criminals. "Now, what is the consensus on Yared breaking out prisoners to exploit them for his own gain?"

"Whoa, slow down, ma'am," Axel interrupted with his metal arms up. He still wore his battle armor. "My *amigos* had no intent of 'exploiting' prisoners. Yared believed they'd benefit from this mission as much as we did."

Theo nodded frantically. "Yep! Yep! He said maybe I could get more food. Positive things. Good things!"

Mark crossed his arms and glared at Yared who shot, "Hey, man. I said they *might* have a chance for better things if they did something good. Second chances are for everyone, aren't they? I wanted to offer that even to the lowliest."

"Hey! Who you calling lowly?" Brand protested.

"Look, man, I get you," Mark replied. "But this defied all rules. You shouldn't have been down there in the first place."

"To be fair we were worried about you, mate," Lucas butted in. "You're the one walking around with heaps of bloody beer bottles. We followed you but found them instead."

Mark sighed. "I guess I haven't been the best influence."

"Yeah, take better care of your kids, Mark," Johanna joked.

"Can we *please* get back to my brother?" Aymie cried. "You just said he is *not* dead and there is no way we can get his memory back." She put her hands on her head in despair. "What do we do?"

Seeing her in anguish was like being shot by the arrow all over again. The pain in my chest was unbearable. I clutched my shirt and swallowed the fiery lump in my throat. I loved her like a sister and I'd do anything for her. *But right now, I can't.*

"I promise you, Aymie, we'll do all we can," Michaelson reassured. "I ordered Prince and Janelle to place Shane aka Sinatra into one of our special care units. As long as he cooperates, he'll be put under *no* restraints." She paused. "Know upfront that while we don't want to, we may have to handle him in a forceful manner. Technically speaking, he *is* an enemy and we might have to treat him as such."

Aymie wanted to protest, but Mark put his hand on hers and shook his head. She took a deep breath and nodded.

"Now, to wrap up the meeting." Michaelson tapped a few things on the electronic tablet in front of her. "We know OX is afraid of the Mark of Mars. We plan to use the Mark of Marcellus against them as well, but have to find him first." She scrolled down on her device. "Joshua Wolfrum gave Sinatra the almost-completed coordinates that will lead us to Marcellus' location. He was ordered to guard it, so it may not be easy to obtain. I will assign certain members the task of retrieving the coordinates as well as recovering his memory."

A few communication devices beeped including mine which meant I was assigned to helping my fiancé remember who he is.

"In the interim, I'll reach out to my Australia Interpreters," Michaelson continued. "After Yared's performance, I don't think the Annex will be carried out on that continent anytime soon." She shut down her device. "Any comments?"

Mark's and Yared's hands shot up simultaneously. They glared at each other jokingly. "Seniority first, Yared," Mark joked.

Yared nodded. "Yes, sir."

The RV Nerd turned to Michaelson. "Ma'am, I have a comment about the Mark of Marcellus. Why wait to use it? *You* have Marcellus' kids. They're afraid of us too. From what I heard, the Order already knows Aymie's and my faces. We can strike fear just as well as our father."

Michaelson paused thoughtfully. "Do you have an idea of what your tactic may be?"

"Just wreaking havoc," Mark put simply. "The Mark of Marcellus will become the Mark of the Hodginses. We'll cause a discord like they've never experienced."

"Shouldn't we have been doing that already?" Johanna asked flatly.

"Yes, but this has an entirely new effect," Mark explained. "If Aymie agrees, we can travel to separate locations, leave calling cards, and mess with the lower Xenophonians until they freak out. My theory is they'll grow so paranoid that their defenses will be spread thin, leaving an opening for RRPR and the Interpreters to make a powerful move."

"What about your responsibilities trying to develop the frequencies to cancel out the Xenophonians' chips?" Sami asked.

Mark smiled. "Your brother and Myles are capable of handling that without me. They're the smarter ones anyhow."

"That's not true, Mark! You're smart too," Myles protested. The blond boy genius always hated it when others put themselves down. "But I can spearhead the operation while you are away."

"I feel like we have too many plans in play," Sami mumbled.

Michaelson smiled. "I apologize, Sami, if it gets confusing. We're a big operation and this happens often. M. Hodgins, I authorize your request as long as A. Hodgins consents," she concluded.

Aymie was quiet, pondering the situation. She took a shaky breath before replying, "I accept this mission." Her eyes narrowed and fire burned in her voice. "Anything to get back at what they've done to our family."

Michaelson managed a tight smile. "Thank you. Now," she held her hand out, gesturing towards Yared, "what was your comment?"

Yared smacked his lips nervously. "Well, do you want to hear good or bad first?"

"Good, I suppose," Michaelson winced.

"The good news is the Xenophonians fear more than just Mars and Marcellus," he explained. He threw his arms around Lucas and Axel. "They practically crap their pants every time they see a Mutant or a Bionic. I suggest they travel in groups on Mark's and Aymie's sabotage missions." Axel and Lucas agreed.

The Interpreter Director chewed on the thought. "I'll consider it. Now the bad news?"

Axel and Lucas stepped away from the Seers Commander. Yared shoved his hands in the pockets of his navy combat pants and mumbled, "There may have been another Officer on the mission." He chuckled nervously and gave a cheesy smile. "REM was a stowaway on our mission, ma'am. While he saved our lives multiple times, I fear it was not wise of him to expose himself."

Aymie jumped out of her seat. "Where is Blake?!" she cried.

Yared, his men, and the prisoners simultaneously spoke aloud in their defense. I couldn't understand a word of what they were saying. "Shut up, guys!" Yared shouted finally. Exasperated, he answered, "He's fine. He's taking a nap in the bay of the plane. He was exhausted from the mission, so we let him sleep."

"What do you mean he saved your lives?" Michaelson asked, curious. Her expression remained neutral.

Standing up straight, the Seer replied, "If it wasn't for Officer Bain's dreams exposing PH's plans of ambush, we never would've survived. PH knew we were coming the entire time. We'd be dead right now if it wasn't for Blake."

"In that case, I am glad he joined you." Michaelson managed a smile, but I knew it was forced. Fear hid behind her eyes. "Yared, check in with him when he awakes. We need to know how he's feeling." Michaelson blew a tarnished silver whistle, and we stood at attention. "This meeting is drawing to a close. M. Hodgins, A. Hodgins, prepare teams for your first sabotage missions as Marcellus' Offspring. Those assigned to Sinatra will begin your assignments in the morning. Powell, work with Aaron and finish that frequency. Yared," she paused to take a deep breath, "while I do not agree with the actions you took, I say your mission was more than a success. My comment is to monitor Wolfrum's letters for feedback and see if PH learns anything else. You are also in charge of watching Bain."

Everyone saluted as she walked around the table and towards the door. "Wilcox, please follow me out with the prisoners," she ordered finally and left.

Sonny rose and commanded the four to exit and followed her out.

I slumped back in my chair. I couldn't grasp what was happening. My intelligence was failing and my problem solving inaccurate. My brain lacked an explanation for everything.

I felt an arm on my shoulder. I looked up to see the blue eyes of Mark staring at me kindly. I stood up and threw my arms around him. He was taken aback, but returned the gesture a few moments later. I buried my face into his lean shoulder and cried.

SHANNON: VI

There were only a few glances, but no prolonged gazes, thank goodness. I didn't want to start a scene. I just wanted to be comforted. I'm confused, overwhelmed, and doubtful. I'm carrying too many weights, but the heaviest one I fear I'll never find a solution for.

I'm scared my fiancé won't remember me.

Anyway, so that's how we reacted, Joshua. Like I said, I still don't know how to respond. My input remains neutral until I return to my senses. In the meantime, get me more information on how PH addresses the previous situation to the Moirai as well as your other duties. For now, I have one thing to say:

Thank you.

Godspeed and goodwill,

Shannon Hollinger
Royal Strategist of RRPR

THE UNDERGROUND

LETTER 23

Joshua: XII

Hello Shannon (well, Yared again),

Yared, tell Shannon not to thank me yet. The war isn't over and Shane isn't cured.

But, I do have some better news. After 7 years, I finally did it. I've reached the highest point. The tricky part is not to fall.

The return journey from Australia was a mixed drink of emotions. Throughout the plane ride, I was nervous. PH was furious and yet his eyes showed a sort of sinister satisfaction. Solomon was traumatized. He clutched his monkey, Diego, as if the moment it left his side it would turn into a hideous Mutant. The fourth and final survivor was Leprechaun. His emotional response to the whole thing made me uneasy. He wasn't appalled, frustrated, or even frightened. He was happy. Our men were dead, Mars has come back to torture us, and Sinatra was abducted. Among all the despair, Leprechaun was struggling to contain his joy.

Why is he as giddy as a school boy after being dangled by a rope from a stadium? No clue.

A low hissing filled my ears, and I felt a light breeze on my sweaty neck. Vents above our heads opened up and gas poured out. In seconds, we were sound asleep.

The moment I awoke in my bed, PH summoned me. *Wolf...* he said directly into my head. *Titan meeting... final letter... New Greece... now.* I grabbed my jacket and fumbled my way out the door. I was confused. *PH has the letter already, so why does he need me?*

On the way, I heard the patter of small feet racing behind me. I turned to see the monkey Diego tailing me. Solomon must've still been asleep. "Diego, what are you doing?" I whispered.

The creature stood on its hind legs and pointed to the hidden entrance of New Greece.

"No, you're not allowed."

It put its hands together and cooed, pleading for it to accompany me. I ignored him and proceeded to enter my identification number into the panel. As the door slid open, I felt tiny fingers jab into my shoulder. Diego had leapt onto me and clung to my back. Unable to shake him, I sighed and entered the clean white city.

I crossed through the plaza and examined Zeus' statue for a moment. His toned figure expressed his strength and power. His staff, royalty; his flowing beard, wisdom. While the carving's eyes lacked irises, they were watchful and shone with determination. I stared with wonder and speculated as to which mortal man took the name of this false god.

Who is the man behind these horrors? I'm growing impatient.

Frustration and anxiety stirred inside of me. I wanted to tear down the statue where it stood, but I had to contain myself. Wolf is the perfect servant. He has no thoughts or feelings of his own; only questions.

Joshua, you'll get your chance.

I took a deep breath. Diego slapped the side of my face, urging me forward. I scolded him and made my way up the marble steps and down the hall to PH who was already seated on his throne.

"You're late," my Titan whispered through the green scarf he pulled over his freckled nose.

"My sincerest apologies, sir. I tried to shake the creature," I jerked a thumb towards Diego who swatted it, "but that proved to be impossible."

PH chuckled. "Understood, mate. This one's a persistent little bugger."

Diego squeaked, tapped his lips, and pointed forward. I peered around the Hermes' throne to see three women standing before the statue of the Moirai.

My face paled and my heart sank into my shoes. I wriggled my nose to turn my glasses on.

The three Moirai were before me. The seven years it took were worth it. They showed themselves freely and without suspecting a thing.

The first Moirai is Clotho who we know as Arata. The slender woman looked around with kind yet serious almond eyes. She stood tall in her black dress suit; her hands behind her back. She is the one who spins the thread of life.

The second Moirai is Lachesis who we know as Emel. I used to see her as a server in the kitchen. Now, I see her as the boss. Her larger stature, half shaved hair, and rough tough attitude are a testament to her powerful role in the Order of Xenophon. She is the one who measures its length.

The third Moirai is the one I haven't met in person. She is a gorgeous devil. Her cheekbones were high on her fair square face. Blonde hair draped over her shoulders, covering her white flowing dress. Her angular brows were furrowed and her thin red lips were pursed with disapproval. To my surprise, the only thing ugly about her was the image hiding behind her light eyes. It was something dreadful and evil.

She was Atropos. The one who cuts the thread.

PH elbowed me to stop my staring. I shook it off and stood at attention.

Clotho/Arata stepped forward and cleared her throat. "Greetings, Titans. It is a pleasure to stand before you once again. It saddens me, however, that these are the circumstances." She raised her hand, and the flame in the center pit rose to the ceiling. The image of the stained stadium flickered in the flames, but the mark was easy to distinguish. The moment the other Titans laid their eyes on it, they gasped.

They feared Mars as they had before.

Sting leapt to her feet and swore in Spanish. "This is all a ruse!" she finally spat. "Mars doesn't even exist anymore. He perished along with his father."

"I thought that too," PH replied, standing from his throne. "The Headmaster—I mean Patya and Jarvis died at the 'ands of those Bionics you adore. Mars lives on in the embodiment of his former self, Sonny Wilcox. He kept 'is mother's name."

Sting grumbled and paced around the fire pit, staring at the symbol. "No one has even seen Mars since his dismissal."

PH made a quiet noise as if he stopped a secret from spilling out.

Unfortunately, Sting's hearing is sharper than her aim. "Something you mean to share, PH?"

All the Titans stared at PH in surprise.

He sighed. "About that," he pulled his scarf down slowly. "Remember the Resistance base I blew up 'alf a year ago? Well," he paused, "'e was there."

Sting stared at him as if she was trying to melt him with her eyes. She swore some more and stomped towards PH, reaching for her knife.

When she was less than a foot away, Lachesis/Emel held up her hand, causing the Ares Titan to halt. "Look, missy, I know you hate Mars' guts because he showed you up as an Ares," Lachesis/Emel chuckled, "but that's no reason to take it out on PH. Mars was always better than you. Just face it and move on."

Sting took a few heavy breaths and stormed back over to her throne, grumbling the whole way.

Lachesis/Emel shook her head and stepped forward. "We have

many enemies in play: Marcellus, his kids, the Resistance, and now Mars. This means we need to take extreme measures and move things a little more quickly." She looked at each Titan. "No more negotiations for peace especially Sting and Munazam. I know that you both approached the one called Detective in order to trade sanctuary for their weapons."

Munazam and Sting made no reply, but shifted quietly on their thrones.

Lachesis/Emel rolled her eyes. "Anyway, my sisters and I have decided to take the offensive course of action. We've waited too long for them to come up with a way to defeat us. Let's make the first move." Her dark eyes scanned the room until they locked with mine, making me queasy. Diego felt the burn of her gaze and hid his face in my hair. She smiled sinisterly and explained, "We will bring the fight to us."

"How do you propose we do that, Lachesis?" Munazam asked timidly, stroking his mustache.

With eyes still on me, she replied, "We're going to piss Mars off. His pride won't back down from the fight. Then," she turned to Sting, "we will abduct your precious metal people."

"We do enough to agonize the Resistance. Mars is ill tempered, but excels at containing his emotions," Sting argued. "What else could we do to anger him?"

Lachesis/Emel smirked. "We'll get under Mars' skin by finally filling the throne originally chosen for him." She gestured to the empty marble chair with a blank emblem.

The Titans murmured quietly. "Ma'am, no one 'as ever been able to fill Mars' shoes," PH objected. "His accomplishments were *almost* unmatched." Proudly, he flung his scarf over his shoulder.

"Listen, Shorty, I know that," she retorted, growing impatient with her doubtful subordinates. She composed herself. "But I found someone who has achieved much in a short amount of time, especially for working from nothing." She raised her arm and pointed to me. "I think Wolf should take his place."

My heart stopped as the eyes turned to stare. I felt the gaze of each Titan piercing through me like dozens of knives. Sweat dripped down my neck, but I didn't show intimidation. Wolf was stronger than Joshua.

This isn't real, I told myself. *It's a ploy. A lie. A scare factor.*

Clotho/Arata, the first Moirai, lifted her slender arm. "I second the motion. I have watched Wolf closely and he has not once faltered since he was reborn."

The third Moirai agreed. "I, Morana, the Moirai Atropos also declare that Wolf should take the place of Mars as Titan of the Russian Pandemonium. His thread is still long and my shears have not been sharpened for him."

Shears? Sharp? Me? Questions swirled in my head. I felt as if I'd topple over. There was a silence and I didn't know what to do. I didn't know what to say.

"Well, Wolf?" Lachesis/Emel said, crossing her burly arms. "Do you accept?"

Diego the Monkey slapped my face and squeaked. He leapt off my shoulder and crawled to the fire pit in the center of the room. He screeched and waved me over.

He wanted me to take the position.

This monkey has officially freaked me out, I thought, staring at the little capuchin. Slowly, I walked towards the bowl.

Arata/Clotho came forward. Taking my hand, she placed a small mound of dust in my palm. She whispered in Greek and breathed into it. Then, she took a thread out of her pocket and wrapped it around my arm. Once the knot was tight, she stepped back and stood beside her "sisters".

I clenched my fist, feeling the smooth dust beneath my calloused fingers. I turned to PH who nodded his head. His heterochromatic eyes looked at me with pride.

He wanted me to take the position, also.

I closed my eyes, taking a deep breath. I wasn't confident, but Wolf was. *Wolf deserves this. He is a loyal Xenophonian. He is powerful. He will fill the empty throne.*

My eyelids shot open. I stood at attention and raised my chin. "Clotho, Lachesis, and Atropos," I started, loud and confident. "I am highly honored with this offer. If it is your will, so be it." I bowed slowly. "I will take on the burden of becoming the Titan of the Russian Pandemonium in order that the Order of Xenophon will triumph." I threw my hand into the air and immediately thrust it downwards, casting the dust into the bowl of fire. There was a crackle and explosion as green flames roared to the ceiling. I stepped back, escaping from the heat. I marveled at the sight as an emblem began to form within. It was the profile image of a wolf baring its sharp teeth.

That was my emblem. My new identity. The Mark of Wolf.

The marble room filled with booming acclaims. The Titans jumped from their thrones to applaud me. The Moirai stood tall with pleased looks and clapped as well. PH ran to me and clasped a hand on my shoulder. His smile was one that will forever surprise me. He was happy. He was glad that I was becoming a peer rather than a subordinate.

Sting, on the other hand, had a look of displeasure across her face. Despite how much she wanted me, she desired to keep me in check. Now, I couldn't do her bidding.

I know her bitterness won't last long. She'll think of a way and will approach me more. I need to be ready for that.

Clotho/Arata stepped forward and held her hands aloft. "We met out of pain but are leaving with joy. The final throne has been filled. The Order of Xenophon is complete. Once the Annex is finished, the world will be whole again. It will be perfect."

"Yes, it will be," a deep voice boomed. Startled, I stepped back. The statue of Zeus was illuminated with a blinding white light. Smoke billowed around the sitting god-figure. "The world will be free of impurities," the voice continued. "Perfect as it once was. It has taken thousands of years, but the time is now."

Oh my gosh, oh my gosh, oh my gosh, I panicked internally. *It's Zeus.*

"But before we can do that, we have to eliminate one final group," Lachesis/Emel interrupted. "I apologize, my lord, but we still have some dirt that needs cleaning."

"Of course, Lachesis," Zeus replied. "The time has come to unleash the final stage of the Cleanse. Those we have been preparing are ready now."

PH slid his hand off my shoulder and stood erect. "Permission to speak, my lord."

"Granted, PH."

The short Xenophonian cleared his throat. "I tried to speak about this before the joyful tunes, but never got a solo."

"You're always singing," Sting mocked.

"Anyway," he continued, annoyed, "I believe the first course of action should be to remove the enhanced from the side of the enemy. I ain't only talking about the Bionics that Sting wants so desperately." PH raised his arm and the image in the flame changed.

I held back a gasp as the image of Lucas the Dragonfly, Theo the Shrew, and Jordan the Slow loris flickered in the light.

"They've got these little buggers, too," PH sighed. "They and one of the Bionics took out my men with such ease. They are stronger, faster, and smarter than we thought. However, they 'ad some help." He flicked his wrist and the image changed.

My heart fell into my shoes. It was a blurry image of a young man with white hair.

Blake Bain.

"This is the Weapon we've been warned about," PH stated with conviction. "Each enemy we've captured swears that there is only one person who knows our plans. They usually die before we can get anything else out of 'em," he clenched his fist, "Sinatra knew something about 'im, but we lost that information in the fight. It's a miracle that we still 'ave the coordinates." He paused as if remembering the capture of his subordinate but shook it off. "This white haired fella is their key," he went on, "he knows our every move. Time and time again they've outsmarted us. They're always one step ahead.

He's the reason why."

The room was silent. All eyes found their way to the statue of Zeus. It was dark for a moment. Finally, it illuminated and spoke, "Yes, the Mutants and Bionics must either be captured or eliminated at all costs. And I also believe your outlandish story, PH, about this man being a Weapon. There was a prophecy of one who had this Gift of Apollo. I do not doubt it is him."

"My lord," Sting interjected. "Our forces will be spread thin if we go after Marcellus, the enhanced, *and* this Weapon. We need to focus on capturing the enhanced."

"*No*," he snapped; thunder crashed and resounded off the Temple walls. "Leave them be for now. Marcellus is first. That is our plan; we are remaining on course. The rest of these problems will be dealt with in time. We have to be patient. The Resistance will tear itself apart. For now, Titans PH and Wolf will prepare immediately for their mission of eliminating former Titan *Marcellus*," he spat his name like a curse. "He gives the impurities hope. He is their strength. He has been a thorn in our side for years. Time to pluck it out. You, Sting, must continue chasing his children. They are starting to follow in their father's footsteps. You have failed me repeatedly; start making up for it. The rest of you have your orders."

The Spanish Titan shut up and bowed low as did everyone. The three Moirai stood tall and raised their arms. The fire crawled to the sky and smoke filled the room, making it hard to see. When it dissipated, the three were gone and Zeus' statue was dark.

I let out a deep breath. Diego the Monkey jumped on my shoulder and patted my face, telling me everything would be all right.

After so long, it's now going by too quickly. I don't know how I can stop this.

PH put a hand on my back and led me out of the temple, speaking as we walked. "You should be proud of ya'self, Wolf. You've worked 'ard to get 'ere."

You have no idea, I thought.

We stopped in the center plaza surrounded by the statues. PH looked up at the sculpture of Hermes and back at me. A smile crossed his freckled face. "I'm proud of you, mate. I never thought I'd have another close companion after Mars betrayed us. Originally, I suspected you for something else, but you turned out a'ight in the end." He patted my back, rubbed the head of Diego the Monkey, and went away humming the Gaelic lullaby that Sinatra/ Shane knew the lyrics to.

I stood in shock and stared blankly. *All this time... he suspected I was a spy? What really changed his mind?* I wondered. *PH is smart... he wouldn't be swayed so easily. No, something didn't change his mind.*

Someone.

Yared, Shannon, whoever is reading this. You have to do many things. Warn the enhanced, find Marcellus, and get Shane Hodgins back. I think Shane might've said something to PH. I just don't know what.

With safety and secrecy,

Joshua Wolfrum

Joshua Wolfrum
Titan of the Russian Pandemonium

LETTER 24

Yared: VI

Joshua, Wolf, my man!

I can't believe it! You're a *Titan*? That's incredible! I won't tell Sonny you stole his thunder. Even if he does find out, it might not have the angering affect the Moirai hope for.

Don't worry, the Bionics and Mutants are aware of the attempts against their lives. They've encountered many enemies that targeted them specifically. Right now, Axel and Alison are taking a break from the front lines. Good thing too, they need some alone time.

Not that I'm into romance or anything. Axel just keeps complaining. He finally asked Alison out before we came here, but hasn't taken her on proper dates or what not. I don't know what he means. I barely listen when he rants.

Anyway, I told Virginia Michaelson that OX knows about Bain. She said there is nothing we can do but keep him hidden. His precognitive dreams have been constant which is awesome. We've been able to do some epic planning. Mark, Aymie, and Sonny have been busy leaving their Marks where OX is about to attack. Dude, you should watch the Xenophonians' faces when they see the '*H*' and Roman helmet. It is *hilarious* how scared they are. You'll be hearing about those complaints soon enough.

On a more important note, the transmission to free the survivors is almost ready. We are worried though. Aaron and Myles have some doubts. We need a chance to do a short wave experiment. I just hope it won't get messy...

So, I covered all the good stuff; time for the not-so-good:

Donnie.

The little puppet boy has been mischievous even in confinement. However, you gave us some information that proved useful. We know what happened to him.

It was a slow Sunday afternoon, and we returned from Papa E's weekly service with Mark. Not sure how I feel about it yet, but I promised Mark I'd give it a try. He also bribed us. If we go, he promises to treat us to something afterwards. This week was my pick.

In the lounge, the Isle guys and I played poker while Mark mixed drinks at the kitchenette behind us. I convinced him to make us wonderful alcoholic beverages as our treat. On top of going to the service, we deserved a thanks for our heroic mission. Sure we broke some rules, but we still did good. We got his brother back. I figured a few drinks as a thank you wouldn't hurt anyone.

"Here you go, boys," Mark said, sliding five glasses across the island for me, Axel, Ethan, Lucas, and Aaron (even though he wasn't invited to the mission. I'm still mad he shared in the glory.).

Lucas flew over and snatched the cold drinks for us.

"Hey, no flying in the base," Mark scolded.

"Yes, Dad," Lucas mocked as he handed us our rewards.

Axel rubbed his organic hand through his white curls and chuckled. "You've really been taking care of us, haven't you, *amigo*."

"More than we could ever repay you for," Ethan said sincerely.

Mark smiled, and his blue eyes lit up. "You don't have to repay me. You all helped me, too. Taking care of you all has made me take care of myself."

"Good. Your other haircut was hideous anyway," I teased as I sipped my drink.

Mark ruffled his short brown hair. "I'm not gonna lie. I *don't* miss the bang."

"Yeah, I'm not sure if the ladies of R&D would've gone for that hair style," Aaron joked, playing with his own spiky blond hair. "Although no girl could resist *my* locks."

Lucas snickered. "Listen, cobber, girls like blond hair like *mine*. Not yours." The Dragonfly flipped his longer hair.

"Hate to break it to you guys," Axel interrupted. "I'm the only one who's been successful with the girls. Which means," he paused, "white curly hair rules all." He slammed his cup down. The room filled with jesting arguments and *ooooooohhhhs*. (Mostly from me.)

While we bickered, his white-hair-loving-lady entered the room. Alison's solemn manner and serious face caused us to shut up instantly. Axel stood and went over to her. They whispered for a few moments before she finally spoke.

"Have any of you spoken to Donnie lately?" she asked softly.

"Johanna and I went in to see him the other day," Ethan said, "but he said nothing to us. He sat in his corner and stared; same as always."

"Alison," Mark started, walking towards her slowly. "What's wrong?"

Her gray eyes glanced at him, then to the rest of us. "He's missing."

I jumped up from my seat. "What? Where could he have gone?"

"I don't know," she cried, and the blue lights in her arm flickered. That was something I'd never seen before. "We don't know when he escaped, but that's not all." She looked at Aaron and said, "Sami is missing too."

"She can't be, I saw her early this morning before we all left," Aaron replied, shifting uncomfortably on the leather couch.

"What did she say?" Mark asked. He threw his black combat jacket over his green t-shirt.

The Geek paused for a moment. "She didn't say anything. She seemed more timid than usual though. She was looking for things around my work bench. She—" he trailed off as the objects popped into his mind. His face fell and sadness pooled in his sapphire eyes. "She could break door locks with the equipment she borrowed."

"Why would Sami want to break the little ankle biter out?" Lucas questioned; his wings fluttered anxiously. "She'd never do something against the rules."

"Sami and I haven't been seeing eye to eye lately," Alison confessed. "I'm afraid Donnie might have convinced her that Sting and Munazam could offer us a better life."

Mark clenched his fists. "Then, I know who he's talking to next." He raced out of the room and we all followed.

He led us back out to the plaza, calling the names of the Hollinger girls: Peggy, Lucy, Carol-Ann, Rebecca, Agnes, and Rachel. "If these girls turn, so will half of the city," Mark called back as we ran. "My theory is that Donnie knows the girls are vulnerable *and* are the most influential amongst the survivors. If he can corrupt all six, the city is his."

We raced along the tracks until we made it to the concrete city. Lucas flew ahead while the rest of us trudged on foot (even the Bionics). I watched the Dragonfly's cape flap as he soared above the huts, searching for the six girls.

"Let's split up!" Mark ordered. Without hesitation, the six of us dispersed. Ethan ran alongside me as we wove in and out of the streets, calling the girls' names.

It didn't take me long to spot a bright yellow shirt and brown braids. Lucy was in front of a fruit stand and talking with a bunch of young girls. Her chocolate eyes gleamed in the dim light. Whatever she was discussing made her happy.

Too happy.

"Lucy!" I yelled as Ethan and I made our way forward. She didn't notice us coming until we pushed our way through the crowd, instructing everyone to go back about their day.

"What is your problem?" she complained. "Aren't I allowed to talk with friends anymore?"

"Not with the lies you're spreading," I snapped.

Her brow furrowed and her nose scrunched. "They aren't lies," she spat. "I've seen the temples and the result of the Annex. Those people are happy. Prosperous. We can be like them."

"Yes, you're right. We can be mindless zombies with no purpose," Ethan retorted.

"Lucy, you have to stop this," I begged. "Filling these people with false hope and lies is wrong."

"It's better than having no hope at all," she cried. "We have been suffering for years. No family, no freedom. You say we won't have a purpose? Well, what is our purpose right now?! You tell me." Tears filled her eyes. The rough, tough, Lucy Hodgins was fragile and cracked. Something tapped her and now she was breaking.

I didn't know how to reply. I am no comforter. I had no words. Unfortunately, neither did Ethan.

Mark would know what to say. Where is he?

"Ya know she's right, Yared and Ethan," a little voice said. Turning around, I saw the little monster himself. This eleven year old boy had become a toy for the devil. Donnie's light hair grew down to his shoulders and was a disheveled mess. His overalls were ripped and dirty as if he'd been dragged through the playground. His freckled face and gap tooth smile were no longer charming and cute. He had the menacing look and eyes of a troublemaker who wouldn't stop until he got what he wanted.

"Donnie, man, you know this is wrong," I tried to reason.

"What do ya know about wrong? Either of ya? You're both *murderers*," he spat. "The Seers are mindless. They do what they're told. You spy, lie, and kill. And the Saviors?" He turned to Ethan and shook his head. "Y'all are even *worse*. You kill children and sweet old folks. You seek only perfection. Y'all decide who lives and who dies the moment they step into your cold facility. Those who ain't perfect?" he slid his finger across his throat and dropped his head.

Ethan trembled. His eyes shook and became sorrowful. He knew Donnie was right.

As for me, I wasn't fazed. That's what Seers are supposed to do. I knew that, I accepted it. It made me who I am, and I wouldn't have changed a thing.

"The past is the past, Donald," I declared, taking a step towards him. "Put yours behind. We all have to."

"Yeah?!" he cried. "I lost my best friends. I lost everything I love. Marlene and Ava are *gone*. 'Cause o' war. 'Cause o' hatred. 'Cause o' chaos." Tears tore through the dirt on his freckled cheeks. "We may not be able to have real peace, but I'd rather take the fake stuff than be sad my whole life. Don't we deserve to be happy?"

"Not like this!" I bellowed. I was growing impatient. I didn't care that he was a scared little boy. He was being used. "You are being fed lies. The Moirai have done something to your head. Tell them to get out of your brain."

"NO!" he screamed. He held his head as if I was going to tear it off him. "They're the only ones who've been nice to me! They showed me joy, they showed me happiness. It didn't cost much."

"What did it cost?"

Donnie thought for a moment. He glanced at his hand like he should be holding something. "I… I don't remember."

I tried to recall it for him. I stared at him for clues, but he gave me none. Until I noticed a little bulge in the pocket on his chest. I walked towards him, but he didn't budge. Without permission, I shoved my hand in his denim pocket and pulled it out.

The Best Family heirloom: Marlene's pocket watch.

"Hey! What do ya think you're doin'?" he cried, jumping up and scratching my arm.

I clicked open the watch and stared at its face. It wasn't moving. I held it to my ear. Nothing.

It was broken.

I looked down at the boy as he tugged violently on my navy combat jacket. Harshly, I grabbed his shoulder and turned him around. I examined his neck and his number brand. The scar from where the Isles chip was removed remained, but there were no other incisions.

He pulled away from me. "What are you lookin' for?" He tried to hit me but I grabbed his wrist.

I looked speculatively at his hand in my grasp when it caught my eye. There were three incisions on his wrist. Perfect size for an OX chip. "Is that your dominant hand?"

"If you mean I write and fight with this hand then yeah," he replied coldly. "Now give me back the watch!" He leapt for it again, but I cruelly threw him to the ground, and he scraped his arms on the jagged concrete.

You fight with that hand… I replayed.

Then, it clicked. I loomed over him and stated, "If those Moirai ladies of yours are so nice, then why did they steal Marlene's shears from you?"

"To end the pain," he hissed. Slowly, he sat up and held his bleeding forearms. "I told ya it didn't cost much. Sure, I loved her shears, but the lady said she needed them. They're gonna serve a higher purpose with her. She's going to use 'em to end it all."

Shears, end, purpose, all...

The answer hit me like a train and I staggered backwards. "You met Atropos," I whispered. "By it all, she didn't mean the war you idiot." I spun around and ordered Ethan: "Take Donnie and get him to the lab, now!" Without another word, I ran through the city to find Mark.

I raced through the crowded streets, calling his name. From what I could tell, Donnie and the girls had spoken to a lot of people. There were arguments and threats buzzed throughout the city. Things were starting to heat up, and I fear it will boil over.

I found Mark trying to reason with Rachel. Her pale face was red and she stomped her feet. Well, foot. She couldn't do much with the leg that was paralyzed.

Mark saw me running and did a double take. "Yared! What's wrong?"

"It's Donnie," I panted. "We found him and I know what happened to him." I handed Mark the pocket watch. "I know this sounds crazy, but just hear me out." I took a deep breath. "The Moirai Atropos was the one who spoke with Donnie, not Clotho. She took Marlene's shears and stopped the watch. There are also incisions on Donnie's wrist," I demonstrated. I tried to explain it as best as I could but I was internally panicking. No words made sense. I was never good with the 'revealing villains' plans' stuff.

Somehow, Mark caught on to my rambling. "Atropos is the one who cuts the thread," he whispered slowly. "Are you saying that?"

"Donnie's thread is running short," I replied. "I think that she hypnotized him or something. He says they still talk to him. She is in his head somehow and when she gets what she wants, she'll cut his thread."

"But why would she take the shears or stop the watch?" Mark wondered.

"He must've lost his memory, too," I said. "I don't know maybe they're like charms or something that could've been used for triggers."

Mark's face lit up. He grabbed my shoulders and shook them. "Yared, you are a genius! That is *exactly* what they are. Sonny said they removed trigger words regarding a human's memory. That explains Sh—" he stopped himself. "Nevermind about him right now. Let's get Donnie. I hope he hasn't fulfilled his purpose yet."

"Mates! Up here!" a voice shouted above us. Lucas was hovering with an unconscious Sami in his arms. Her tail dangled and her whiskers fell flat across her face.

"What happened?" Mark asked as Lucas carefully put the cat girl down.

"I don't know," Lucas confessed, pulling the goggles back over his massive compound eyes. "I tried to stop her from talking to a group of people and she just passed out. I didn't touch her; I swear."

"Let's get them to the infirmary," Mark commanded. Saying nothing else, we picked up Sami and left the city, hoping the Hollinger girls developed some sense.

We entered the hospital to find Donnie passed out in a bed with the remaining Isle members around him. Ethan looked distraught as he was going over something on the computer. Axel, Alison, and Aaron watched. Once they saw us rolling Sami in on a gurney, the Alexuses jumped to their feet and ran over.

"What happened to her?!" Alison cried, stroking her sister's furry face.

"We don't know," Lucas confessed. "I was talking with her, trying to convince her to stop and then she just collapsed. Bloody oath, I tell you."

"We believe you, Lucas," Aaron replied as he nervously cleaned his black glasses. "But what did she say?"

The Dragonfly shook his head. "She was just babbling. She kept crying on about how mean we were to Donnie and how we should try and help him, not hurt him." He thought hard. "She was really scared. Something spooked her. I know she's timid as a Cat-Mutant but I mean something *really* freaked her out."

I stepped back and stood next to Mark. "Do you think Atropos could be speaking to Sami as well?" I whispered.

The RV Nerd shook his head. "I don't know. Maybe she can sense Atropos in Donnie. She is a cat after all. Alison said that Sami begged her to turn herself and Axel into OX. That is *not* like Sami. She would never do anything to hurt her siblings."

"So we've got another puppet to worry about," I grumbled.

"Not a puppet," Mark disagreed. "A scared soul." With tight lips and sad eyes, Mark gently put Marlene's watch back in Donnie's pocket. The little devil slept with a bitter expression on his face.

As of today, the two are still in the infirmary. Donnie aroused a few times but didn't fight. He's become exhausted. As for Sami, she woke up but won't answer any questions. I don't know what's going on. She's scared, and we don't know how to comfort her.

All I know is that the Hollinger girls were busy at work. Half the city is disturbed, and we don't know how to fix it. The nights have lost their peace. There are fights, arguments, and discord. They've lost all hope. They need something, *someone*, to convince them everything will be all right.

We're dividing rapidly. First the citizens, next will be the Officers and

Isle members. Please, Joshua, hurry up. We're almost there. I can feel it.

Bravery and fidelity,

Yared Prinz
Seer Commander

LETTER 25

Joshua: XIII

Hello Shannon,

I hope Yared caught you up. Everything is starting to make sense now. The Moirai Atropos—Morana—is always depicted with shears. She kills slowly and everything happens in *her* time. From what I know, Donnie's mission isn't complete. RRPR is not entirely torn apart. Atropos/Morana is resourceful; she won't throw things away before they're expired. Donnie is safe for now.

Things are happening so rapidly. Today, I finally saw what I've been dying to see. I know how they send messages to Donnie and all the Xenophonians.

My first week as Titan of the Russian Pandemonium ended. I was anxious throughout the induction. My first order of business was to get marked.

Yes. I now have a tattoo of a wolf's head in the center of my back.

It hurt so bad, and I barely had time to recover. They slapped some ointment on it and then immediately introduced me to all the Xenophonians under my "reign". If I didn't have my glasses to translate, I don't know how I would've made it. Everyone believes I'm multilingual, but it's all part of the act. I'm relieved I can keep it up.

After the ceremony, I sat in one of our meeting rooms while a Hermes member embroidered the Wolf emblem into my combat jacket. I sat quietly listening to the hum of the sewing machine. I thought of the chaos ensuing in the Underground and the pain you're enduring. I feel helpless. I want to help save the day, but I feel like nothing I do is good enough.

When will this nightmare end?

PH burst through the door, snapping me back to Wolf's reality. "Wolf, mate! Are ya ready for today?"

"I guess that depends what today entails," I replied smirking.

He chuckled. "Once your emblem is stitched, you and I are goin' to be working as peers to end the Marcellus mission."

"That's great, sir," I lied confidently. A bead of sweat dripped down my neck. "I'm getting tired of chasing a ghost."

"Bah, I told you: PH. I'm not 'sir' any longer," he corrected. "Grab your uniform and let's head out. You'll like where we're goin'."

The woman tied off the last stitch and handed me my jacket. I took the heavy leather in my hands and rubbed my fingers over the embroidery. It was the first time I saw my Mark up close (I can't really see my back tattoo). The white wolf looked menacing against the green background. It's black eye was cold and dark as it bared its sharp teeth; ready to tear apart any prey.

I can't believe this. I can't believe how far I've come.

PH walked over and peered at the newly stitched design. "Incredible, ain't it? Your Godly name is more than what we call you. It's a mark of intimidation and power. It is now your legacy."

Which is pretty cool, I thought, but quickly scolded myself. I don't want to die and be remembered as a hero in the Order of Xenophon. Honestly, don't remember me. I don't care. Just don't know me as a Xenophonian.

I stood up and pulled on my jacket. It felt different. It seemed heavier and thicker as it hung on my lean frame. It was like the weight of being a Titan was embroidered within the emblem. It was a test to see if I was strong enough to carry it.

"Looking good, mate," PH grinned. "Now, let's crack on." He led me out, explaining more of my Titan duties along the way. From what I gathered, they simply follow orders from the Moirai and execute them accordingly. While they have some freedom, Titans are mostly delegators who instruct the mindless Xenophonians.

I was baffled when we arrived at our destination: the kitchen. I walked around the clean marble establishment. To my surprise, everything was pristine and shining. Not a crumb to be seen.

Emel takes her role as head cook and Lachesis very seriously, I admired, running my finger across the counter top.

"Hungry, mate?" PH asked. He jumped and snatched an apple off a high shelf. "I'm bloody starvin'." He tossed the fruit up in his left hand, caught it, and took a bite. "We might be in the meetin' for a while," he added with his mouthful.

I held up my hand. "I appreciate the offer, but I'll be all right. I'm not used to the mealtime luxuries of a Titan yet."

PH swallowed and threw the unfinished apple aside. "Suit yourself." He spun on his heel and headed toward the fridge. Opening it, he stepped inside. I stood surprised. A moment passed and he poked his head out. His brown curly locks dusted with white snow. "You coming? I can't stand 'ere all day. It's freezing." PH shivered and pulled his green scarf up over his nose.

Hesitantly, I stepped through the large metal door and shut it behind me.

I looked around to see crates and cartons of food supplies. They were stacked high and overflowing with meats, cheeses, vegetables, and more. *Where do they find all this food?* I wondered.

PH shuffled towards the back, pulling his trench coat tighter around his body. Gently tugging aside some hanging sausages, he bent over and spoke his name into a panel on the wall. Nothing happened. "Your turn," he instructed. "You're in the system already."

I went over to the wall and saw a microphone the size of a dime.

Voice recognition is the main security of the Order of Xenophon. Hence your voice-copying breathing apparatus, Shannon. But you already knew that. I was clarifying for my own brain.

I let out a deep breath which formed a small cloud of fog that touched my lips. "Wolf. Titan of the Russian Pandemonium."

A small light turned green and I heard a whirring to my left. A door behind some hefty crates was revealed and PH was already walking through it. Hastily, I followed.

We exited the chilly chamber, down a long dark corridor, and finally through another door on the other side. The moment my foot stepped through and I raised my gaze, my body froze and my jaw dropped.

The vast dark room was filled with thousands of busy Xenophonians sitting at desks. They clacked away at their keyboards, staring intently at computer screens. I looked down from the mezzanine, trying to comprehend what I was seeing. Seven massive blue holograms illuminated the hundreds of Xenophonians circling them. The setup was similar to the bases in Guadalajara and Madrid. Although, this is a grander scale.

"PH, Wolf, welcome!" a deep female voice called. Releasing my clutching hands from the railing, I turned to see Emel wearing her "lunch lady" garb. "You ready to nail that dastard?"

"I've been ready since he betrayed us," PH smirked.

We followed her along the mezzanine and into an office on our right. "Now, let's get started," Emel said as she sat down in a marble chair. She typed a few things on the keyboard before her. A mini hologram projected from the center of her desk to the air above it. It illuminated her round face in its blue glow. "PH, give me the letter with all the coordinates you found."

Gingerly, PH pulled the letter out of his trench coat pocket and handed it over to Emel who snatched it. "Let's see where the traitor's been hiding all these years," she muttered as she entered the numbers. It took a few moments to run through the algorithms. Finally, it beeped, indicating that it found a match. "Gotcha," she added with a smirk.

"Where is he?" I asked eagerly.

"Can't tell you that yet, Wolf," she sighed. "It's not that we don't trust you or PH. We've got a bad feeling about those around you."

"Better to be safe than sorry anyway, mate," PH chimed in. "I don't trust a couple blokes. We suspect two spies within your old rank."

Two? I thought, amazed. *I thought I was the only one.* "What makes you so sure?" I asked inquisitively.

"Marcellus has avoided us too easily," Emel explained. "We know that RRPR has an omniscient weapon, but Marcellus can't possibly have one, too. Besides, some members have rubbed me the wrong way." She stood up and walked out of the room. Gesturing to the members seated around the holograms, she continued, "These are the Children of Moirai. They control and connect with every member of the Order of Xenophon: soldier and survivor. We monitor brain waves, actions, thoughts, everything." She tapped the railing three times and the blue hologram in front of us changed its image.

To be honest, I wasn't surprised.

It was a picture of our Irish bartender: Leprechaun. On the right side were his vitals, recent activity, and other information.

"What's funny with this one is that he is a little too normal," Emel said, pointing. "He does exactly as he's told. No irregularities. He's the perfect Xenophonian."

"What's wrong with that?" I inquired.

"He's too perfect," PH put in. "This Mick knows every Titan's and Xenophonian's drink as if it was his own name. He shows up punctual to every meetin', asks no questions, and executes everything as we ask."

"He has no flaws, and that's the issue," Emel added. "Every Xenophonian has some sort of irregularity. The Rebirthing Process does not entirely change the mind of a person. They'll still have their shortcomings and their doubts." She looked at me and smirked. "Hence why you ask so many questions." The happy expression faded. "Leprechaun hides nothing, asks nothing, and appears to know nothing. That's what makes us suspect him."

Strange, but I'll buy it for now. "So, what do we do?" I asked.

"You keep an eye on 'im," PH explained. "Stay his friend. Get him to slip up somehow. Also, get him to *stop* hummin' my tune, a'ight?"

I nodded, remembering that PH and Leprechaun both know the Gaelic Lullaby that belongs to the Hollingers. "But what about this other suspect?"

"Pretty sure they're harmless," Emel dismissed. "Focus on Leprechaun; I think he might cause some trouble on your next mission."

PH and I bowed to Emel as she left for her office. Standing upright, I looked out towards the Children of Moirai. I couldn't fathom what I was seeing. Hundreds of thousands of people were being monitored all in this one room. After seven years, I finally saw the control hub with my own eyes.

"Impressive, ain't it?" PH interrupted my gawking. "To think that years ago we didn't 'ave all of this. It was just me and a few guys. We got 'em going." His eyes became distant as he mentioned it. He shook the feeling off. "But that was mere child's play, right mate?"

"Did you help launch this program?" I asked.

PH chuckled. "Yeah, I did. With Marcellus, actually." He sighed. "That traitor was like a father to me. Taught me everything I know. He was the best with these computers."

"I knew Marcellus was involved as a Titan, but I never suspected that he was so important," I marveled.

"No one did. He was so humble 'bout it. When he betrayed us, everyone thought his worst crime was setting us back." PH clicked his tongue. "It was much worse than that, mate. His knowledge of the Order of Xenophon is great. If he got in 'ere, 'e could stop everything like that," he snapped his fingers. "We've sent a couple spies to try and befriend with intent to betray, but he's much smarter than that. He shakes our tail every time and now we haven't seen 'im for years. That's why he's left letters. 'E wants to be found, but not by us."

"But we're going to find him anyway," I added with a smirk.

"Yes," PH managed a smile, "we'll find him and kill the bloody traitor."

We spoke a few more minutes before we left the home of the Children of Moirai. Reaching the kitchen, we parted ways.

My heart was pounding as I walked through the corridors of the base. I needed to find Leprechaun. I went to "Lucky's", but he wasn't behind the bar. Questions and doubts filled my mind. *He can't be a spy... could he? Is that why he's been so nice to me? But yet it's not a surprise.* I didn't want to appear like I was frantically searching for him, so I played cool. I went about my Titan duties, checking on my new subordinates while looking for Leprechaun.

After hours of walking around, he was nowhere to be found.

I plopped down on a tattered sofa in one of the side rooms to rest. I lobbed my tired legs in the air and dropped them onto the chipped coffee table before me. I leaned my head back, closed my eyes, and let out a sigh.

I was still for a moment, trying to ignore my swirling thoughts and exhausted spirit. My attempt at relaxation was interrupted when my nostrils were filled by the unpleasant scent of foul odor and berries. Cracking an eye open, I found two black beads surrounded by a mane of white hair staring down at me.

Diego the Monkey cooed and smacked my forehead, trying to get me out of my chair.

"Where have you been? And where's Solomon?" I asked the creature.

It stood up on his hind legs and threw his arms into the air, squeaking with the gestures.

"As long as he's all right; I haven't seen him for a while." I rubbed the back of my neck and leaned forward.

Diego leapt off of the couch and onto the coffee table. His little face looked frustrated. He squeaked and motioned to something behind me.

I didn't have time to ask who it was. The moment he spoke, a chill went up my spine.

"Always amazing you can understand Diego. I feel like he's always acting the maggot," Leprechaun laughed.

I jumped up from the couch to face him. The bartender's light eyes shone kindly from beneath curled reddish-brown bangs. The creases in his face grew deeper than last I saw him. Something was going on inside.

"What's up, Lep?" I asked as casually as I could.

I heard a metal door sliding shut. Out of the corner of my eye, I saw Diego jump down from a shelf that gave him access to the keypad.

"Wolf, we need to talk," Leprechaun demanded, his voice serious, but not sinister.

I took a step back and clenched my sweating fists. "What is this about?"

"You know what this is about. If you haven't discovered it, you're not as bright of a lad as I took you for."

I was silent for a moment. I stared hard at him. "You *are* a spy, aren't you?"

He smirked. "As are you," he whispered.

My heart leapt in my chest. *Oh no, oh no. Don't give it away. He could be lying.*

"What makes you say that?" I replied.

He took a step towards me, but I didn't back up. Even though he was a half an inch shorter than me, he was still intimidating. Suddenly, he snatched the glasses off my face.

I stifled a gasp and restrained myself from tearing them out of his hands like a child whose toy was stolen by a bully.

"First off, you don't use these to see. Well, in a sense." Leprechaun held them up and stared through them. They were off. "I know you turn them on with your nose. Your twitch is more than nerves." He put them on his face and tried it, but nothing worked.

They don't turn on unless they're on my face: an advancement of Myles at Powell Enterprises. However, if they fall off me and are functioning then we'd have a problem. One of the machine's flaws.

Leprechaun chuckled and adjusted the frames to fit his smaller face. "Never thought I'd see technology like this in my time."

"They're just eyeglasses, man, what are you getting at?" I lied.

His smile faded and he pulled the spectacles off his nose. "Mate, I know who you are," he whispered. He held out my glasses. "You're from RRPR. A close friend of the Hodgins triplets and some others I know. Your mission is to tear down OX from the inside."

My face paled and my legs almost gave way.

Leprechaun smirked. "To the untrained eye, many would think of your screw ups as flaws, but not for a detective like me." He walked me over to a chair and sat me down.

I could barely focus. My hands were trembling as I clutched the armrests. *After all these years. I thought I was doing so well...*

"Look, mate. I'm not going to turn you in," Leprechaun promised, snapping me back into reality. "I've been trapped here for years; finding someone to trust is like hen's teeth. You're the second person I've met that I can rely on."

"How are you a friend of the Hollingers?" I snapped. "Who else do you know? How did you have Sinatra's wallet?"

"Telling you is a danger. Just know this," he leaned in. I smelled the tobacco on his breath. "I am on your side. I've been in this fight just as long as you have. I'm sorry I didn't tell you sooner but I feared the worst. Now that it's nearing the end, I thought you should know." He stood up and began walking towards the door.

"What do you mean near the end?" I asked as he reached for the code panel.

Leprechaun entered the numbers with his left hand. "You're a Titan now and we will be going after Marcellus within the next week." He smirked. "I have something planned that will push you forward. *You* just need to provide the opportunity." The metal door slid open and he slipped into the dark corridor.

Diego climbed up my back and perched on my shoulder.

I sat dumbfounded with a monkey cooing in my ear. *Is he actually going to help me? Who is he really?* Subconsciously, I rubbed Diego's head, stood, and left to continue about my day, dreading the mission to come.

Better hurry up and get those coordinates from Sinatra—Shane—guys.

You have to get to Marcellus before we do.
    With safety and secrecy,

Joshua Wolfrum

Joshua Wolfrum
Titan of the Russian Pandemonium

LETTER 26

Shannon: VII

Joshua,

I wouldn't trust Leprechaun yet. His words appear sincere, but his actions will tell a different story. Take precautions. He sounds eerily familiar, but I can't figure it out. I can't think straight. I'm too preoccupied with Shane—err Sinatra.

Yared and his "boys" (as he calls them) have been busy trying to undo the mess that Donnie, Sami, and my sisters made: spreading lies throughout the Underground. Unfortunately, the weed was planted and it's growing rapidly.

The only way to change their minds is to prove peace is impossible, and we *will* win this war. We must show the survivors that we're stronger than they realize. We have many steps to reach that goal, but the first was getting my fiancé's memories back.

I visited Sinatra/Shane's containment quarters every day, but never went in to see him. The other Officers didn't want to take unnecessary risks. PH and the other Titans don't know my identity, and we want to keep it that way. The less they know the better.

Standing behind one-way glass, I watched Mark speak with Sinatra in his cell. The Nerd sat cowboy style in a chair facing his chained brother. Sinatra kneeled on the cold ground with his arms extended to either side; wrists shackled and chained tightly to the wall. His bare chest was covered in wires that monitored his heartbeat, reactions, etc. Green eyes stared inquisitively out from beneath a mess of brown hair, and his thick beard was bushy and untamed.

I need to go in there with a razor, I thought. Sinatra/Shane was just as handsome, but I prefer clean shaven men.

I quickly shook my head. I remembered why he was chained up in the first place. We had to take drastic measures after Sinatra went after Aymie, clawing at her like an animal. Something inside him snapped. He wanted something from her, but she wouldn't give it to him. If Nic wasn't there, she would've been scarred and mauled by her own brother.

After that, Mark and Aymie went in at set times every day with at least four people in the observation room in case of an emergency. The siblings talked with Sinatra/Shane about different memories or pieces of his past. I watched intently as they shared stories with their amnesiac brother.

However, they never *ever* mentioned their own names. They went by their codenames: Mark, *Bandit* and Aymie, *Princess*. If Shane remembered their real names that meant he was making progress.

Unfortunately, he continued to call them "Little Nerd" and "Bald Beauty". Not very original, but then again Shane never really was.

During each session, Sinatra/Shane's expressions would range drastically. One moment he'd look surprised or excited and the next he'd appear disappointed or enraged (like when he attacked Aymie). From my observations, Shane and Sinatra were having an internal battle, and something prevented Shane from surfacing. A weight keeping him down.

I needed to figure out how to release it.

The conversation lulled and Mark ended the session. He stood, looked at his brother one last time, and left the chamber without another word.

A moment passed before the door slid open to my right and Mark entered the observation room to speak with me, Sonny, Aaron, Johanna, and Nic.

"Get anything good?" Mark asked, trying to sound hopeful.

Aaron leaned closer to his computer screen and sighed. "Nope. Same as last time."

"And the time before that, and the time before that…" Nic mumbled.

Johanna elbowed him. "He'll get there. We just need to find the right trigger."

"I mean we could use the siblings' names, but you guys keep saying no," Nic replied. "We've tried his name, his songs, all his belongings," he counted on his large fingers, "what else is there?"

Sonny coughed and waved a pale hand towards me.

Mark shook his head. "No, we can't yet. It's too dangerous."

"What makes it dangerous?" Sonny snapped. "You've said that every time." He pinched his red eyes shut and rubbed his temples. "Look, I know the Order of Xenophon's Rebirthing Process got more complicated, but the principles are the same. She could be the trigger we're waiting for."

"But what if she's not? She and Shane could be put in more danger," Mark snapped. He was desperate to keep me out of harm's way. "If Shane says the wrong thing, he could get killed or trigger himself to do something to her."

"We removed the chip, though," Aaron interrupted, hoping to prevent a fight. "How could either of them get hurt?"

"The chip may be gone, but OX has a deeper hold," Sonny replied. "Their new technology connects with his nervous system."

"But wouldn't that mean it's still in *your* nervous system?" Aaron asked.

Sonny shook his head. "I never had a 'controlling chip' if you will." He subconsciously rubbed his neck where the OX brand was burned into his skin. "Like many of the Titans, I was born into the Order so I never needed it. I only had the chip for tracking and communication."

"It's what Joshua has," Mark added. "It's the nervous system connection that worries me. Joshua's reports indicate their systems advanced significantly. Anything that can happen, will happen."

Sonny groaned. "Fine. I understand. Makes perfect sense." He wanted the bickering to end, but he had one more point: "But if she doesn't go in to talk to him now, how are we supposed to get the coordinates?"

Mark was about to argue, but stopped himself. Sonny had him cornered.

"Wait, I thought Joshua put a note in Shane's pocket?" Johanna asked, confused.

Mark went to a cluttered counter and pushed some papers out of the way. He rummaged for a moment until he found it. "Even though he calls himself Sinatra, he's still my pain-in-the-butt brother," he grumbled, handing Johanna a torn piece of parchment.

Amused, she read, "'*Want our enemy's coordinates? Good luck getting them now.*'" She peered closer and laughed. "He can't draw to save his life. What is that? A flat beach ball?"

Nic leaned in. "I think it's supposed to be a brain."

"You and Shane would make a great game-show team because I *never* would've guessed that," Johanna replied with sincerity.

Nic tugged dramatically on his red collared shirt and joked, "I recognize the work of a fellow artist when I see one."

"Sorry to ruin your critiquing session, but what does it mean?" Aaron asked, adjusting his black glasses.

"It means two things," Mark held up his first finger, "one, as said before, my brother is still in there somewhere. We just have to find him. Two," he sighed, "it means he memorized the coordinates and destroyed the original copy. Now we have to convince him to tell us what they are."

"Which is why we need Shannon to get in there and talk to him," Sonny added. "Remember, code names only. He won't know anything else about her. It's up to him to remember who she is." He looked at me, then back to Mark.

I remained silent. I didn't want a say. My heart was torn. I was beyond making wise decisions. Someone needed to choose for me.

I turned to Mark for an answer. His blue eyed gaze gripped me hard. It wasn't violent or hurtful. It was firm and caring like a brother holding back his sibling before they fell to the ground. He was genuinely concerned for my safety.

The Royal Veteran Nerd sighed. Defeated, he shoved his hands into his dark jean pockets. "Fine. She goes in once," Mark grumbled. "Only because we're running out of time."

Saying nothing, I exited the observation area and walked five paces to my left, stopping before the confinement door.

As I was about to enter my code, I felt strong yet slender fingers grab my forearm. "Shannon, please be careful," Mark begged.

"Why are you so worried?" I asked, looking up at him. "He's chained up; there's nothing he could do to hurt me."

"You know what I mean," he whispered.

I looked down at the glimmering ring that found its home on my finger for several months. "I understand," I muttered.

Mark wanted to say more but refrained. He gave my arm a tight squeeze then backed away.

It was time. Taking a deep breath, I entered my code and closed my eyes. When I heard the *woosh* of the door, my eyes shot open and I was no longer the "fragile" Shannon Hollinger. I was Detective: the Royal Strategist and the one who'd crack the case. Straight and tall, I marched through the confinement area and up to our prisoner.

This isn't my fiancé, I told myself as I dragged the chair noisefully across the concrete floor. *This is our OX prisoner, Sinatra.*

Sinatra's dangling head lifted when he heard me enter. His green eyes followed closely as I sat down. "Finally, it's Detective," he slurred. He fell asleep within those few moments Mark was away. "I thought you'd never come. Yared promised you'd help me, but you were never there."

"I've always been here," I corrected. "I've been observing you from the outside."

He scoffed. "Why, because you're a coward?"

"No, because I needed to get a grasp on the situation," I disagreed. "I wasn't going to come in here and waste my time having a staring contest. I needed to understand."

"How is this understanding the situation?" Sinatra flicked his wrists, trying to regain feeling. I'll admit the setup was cruel but it had to be done. "If you really wanted to help me you wouldn't keep me chained to the walls like an animal and wired like a lab rat." He kneeled up straight; each vertebrae cracked individually. He was stiff, uncomfortable, hungry, and exhausted.

He had a point, but this was for the best. *He did this to himself.* Clearing my throat, I started our session. I decided to take a different approach. While Aymie and Mark focused on triggering Shane, I wanted to trigger Sinatra whom I was talking to.

At first, he was reluctant to answer. He almost didn't share the name of his Pandemonium Titan (which we know is PH) or his Division. However, when I started asking about his personal likes/dislikes and skills, he perked up like an up-and-coming celebrity during an interview. He showed off and sang a few oldies that stuck in his memory bank after the Rebirthing Process. He never lost his pipes.

"All the ladies love it," he added smugly after singing the final tune in his brief repertoire. "Is it safe to assume you're one of them?" He eyed me up and down.

He's flirting. I thought of a new plan. It might hurt, but I gave it a shot. "That depends."

Concern spread across his face. "Depends on what?"

"Depends if you *want* me to be one of them." I leaned back in my chair and crossed my arms. "What do you think of me?" I asked.

Sinatra cocked his head. "What do you mean?"

"Oh you know," I shrugged, "a lady needs an honest opinion once in a while."

Sinatra cleared his throat. "Well, I don't have any good lines."

"Just say what's on your mind."

He raised his bushy eyebrows in disbelief. "Freedom of speech? Didn't know I had that privilege."

"I encourage truth and openness always."

"Well," he chewed his thoughts for a moment, "you're definitely different than any woman I've ever met. Mysterious, strong, beautiful in so many ways." He proceeded to praise and compliment me in more ways than one. He used cheesy similes and metaphors, trying to be that mediocre poet of love I was used to. It was simple, innocent, and sweet.

These are things Shane would say, I thought. My heart thumped in my chest; I felt like I was bringing my fiancé back.

Unfortunately, the Order of Xenophon had a tighter hold. Green eyes that were wide with puppy love narrowed. The moment I saw that, I knew it'd go downhill. Everything got out of hand. The kind words of a man in love turned to the vulgar, disgusting comments of a boy overtaken by lust.

Sinatra's seductiveness horrified me. His expressions, his words, his actions. I wanted to throw up. The hopefulness disappeared. Blood rushed to my face out of embarrassment for myself and my fiancé who was trapped inside that villainous mind.

That was the hurt Mark worried about. Sinatra was too strong. *Please, Shane. Prove to be stronger.*

When he tried to approach me was when I had enough. I abruptly jumped from my chair and stepped back.

"What's a matter, *Detective*?" he mocked. "Don't you need to question me through a little more," he paused and posed provocatively, "thorough analysis?"

Shaking my head out of disgust, I turned and tried to run out of the door, but Mark blocked the entryway.

"Detective, I think it's time to work on your next case," he said, eyeing Sinatra.

"Awe, you've got the Nerd to save you? Isn't this a true underdog story," Sinatra cackled.

"I think we better wash your mouth out with soap, man," Mark replied. He took a step into the room and stood beside me... a little too closely.

Sinatra watched him like a hawk. His menacing and lustful smile turned into a scowl. He glared at Mark and gritted his teeth.

"What's the matter, *Sinatra*?" Mark lifted his hand, waved it, then placed it on my shoulder. "It's time for Detective to get away from you. She doesn't even want to be here anyway." He gave my shoulder a squeeze.

"Get off of her," our prisoner growled.

The blue eyed Nerd smirked at Sinatra's anger. I stood frozen while Mark tapped his fingers on my shoulder. Sinatra winced with every gentle touch. I felt Mark's other hand gripping mine. He lifted our clasping palms into the air. Mark touched my back and pulled me close. He nudged me towards him. A few steps forward, a few steps back. Before I knew it, we were dancing across Sinatra's prison cell. In the moment, I couldn't tell what it'd accomplish other than make Sinatra bitter.

Mark hummed and we waltzed back and forth and then out the door. He spun me beneath the archway. He stopped me gingerly, pressing my body against his. My hands still rested on his lean shoulders from our dance number. He combed my short curly hair with his fingers. I looked up at his strong face and our blue eyes locked. My face reddened as I stared into irises as mysterious and beautiful as the sea.

Mark's gaze left me and met his brother's. He smirked and teased, "Sorry, Sinatra. I have to take her away for a while."

Before anyone could respond, something I never would've guessed happened.

SHANNON: VII

In a split second, I felt one of Mark's hands cupping my cheek and the other lifting me off the ground. He leaned in and pressed his warm lips firmly against mine.

I was kissing my fiancé's brother.

My entire being tingled as my hands gripped his shoulders to prevent myself from falling. My heart raced in my chest. Blood rushed to my cheeks. I couldn't hear a thing. I didn't know how we got there, why we got there, or how I felt about it.

Frankly, I still don't.

Mark pulled away, almost reluctantly, brushing his nose up against mine. He wanted to go in for another kiss, but pulled away. As he gently placed me down my senses started to come back and I heard a loud and violent shouting.

Sinatra cursed, swore, and yelled bloody murder. Out of the corner of my eye I saw him trying to break free. He tore and pulled at the chains as he ran in place, trying to tear the metal out of the walls. His face was bright red and spit flew as he screamed, "MARK! YOU KEEP YOUR HANDS OFF OF HER! I SWEAR I WILL KILL YOU, MARK! I WILL—" his threats were cut off by the shutting of the door.

Mark chuckled. "I think we better let him cool down before we move onto the next phase."

I stared at him dumbfounded. I had no words.

"Uh, Shannon?" he waved his hand in front of my face.

I snapped out of it. My face got hot and my lips burned. I realized what happened. I opened my hand and slapped Mark so hard his smug smile should've fallen off.

His jaw dropped and he scoffed. "Uh, ouch!" he shook his head and rubbed his red cheek. "Geez, sweetheart! What was that for?"

"What do you think?!" I yelled. "Why'd you do that?" My heart raced and my chest burned and stung. A million tiny knives poked holes in the sides of my lungs, filling it with liquid to drown me. It became harder to breathe.

Oh no, I better calm down.

"To be fair, I wanted to do that since I met you," he muttered. I raised my hand to slap him again, but he flinched so I refrained. "Look, look, I get it. I'm sorry, I shouldn't have done that. But first of all, I got you out of an awkward situation."

"And got me into a more awkward one!"

The poison beat against the sides of my lungs. *Calm down, calm down.*

"Which is thanks to me," he added smugly. "Listen again." He jerked towards the door with his head.

I let my anger recede for a moment to try and understand. I pressed my ear against the cold metal. All I could make out was muffled screaming and cursing. "He's just yelling at you, Mark."

A bright smile spread across the Hodgins brother's face. "Exactly."

The lightbulb went off. "Wait, he's yelling at you." The frustration dissipated and so did the pain in my chest. I wanted to burst into tears out of sheer happiness. "He's yelling at *you!*" I exclaimed. I ran into the observation room and Mark followed.

We entered to see four surprised members. "Mark, I swear I'm going to punch you right in the schnoz," Johanna threatened as she marched forward, rolling her sleeves up.

"Johanna, wait! It was a genius plan," I explained, stepping between her and a cowering Mark. "Don't you hear Shane? He's yelling at Mark."

"Yeah, and I'm about to join him," my best friend growled.

"No, no, no, Johanna." I grabbed her arms and shook her gently. "Shane is yelling at *Mark*."

It clicked. "Shane remembered his brother's name," Johanna whispered. "He remembered his name."

"Shane remembers who his brother is," I exclaimed. Tears streamed down my face.

My best friend embraced me as I cried for joy.

Shane is in there. He's in there.

Sonny clapped, not entirely sarcastically. "Well done, Mark. Painful memories are five times stronger than happy ones. OX usually leaves the pain. Builds character."

Nic whistled. "But man, kissing your brother's fiancée right in front of him? That took guts."

"Nah, just years worth of temptation," Mark joked with a wink. I wanted to slap him again but couldn't. He brought back part of my fiancé's memories and that's what mattered. I'd let this instance slide... for now.

"I hate to be the raincloud, but pain won't be enough," Aaron put in. "We still need a trigger to bring Shane back. Mark can't kiss her all the time just to make Shane mad."

Mark made a face, indicating he disagreed.

Sonny rolled his eyes. "I fear that if Shannon shows affection it'd only bring out Sinatra's lustful nature from OX," he put in. "We know his tie to Shannon is stronger than anything else. We'll focus on her. What object or memory means more to Shane than anything?"

We stood in silence as we thought. I couldn't think. My lips burned and my head was swimming. I looked to my friends, hoping they'd know me better than myself.

Nic scratched his neck thoughtfully but stopped mid itch. His violet eyes lit up as he gripped a cord around his neck. "Guys, I know what we need." He lifted a necklace with a heart shaped key and two silver rings attached.

It was Johanna's promise necklace.

"That's it!" Johanna exclaimed. "Shannon, *your* necklace! That memory of Shane receiving it, the box, the letters, everything. Those are a bundle of memories of you both: happy and sad. That has to do the trick."

"It better. We have no other options," Sonny replied. "Where is it?"

I thought hard. "Joshua has it," I replied, defeated.

"Don't give up yet," Mark said, putting his hand on my back and I flinched. He chuckled. "I've got another idea that'll work for the interim. Aaron, buzz me in." He leapt off the platform, down the hall, and was back in the confinement room.

Sinatra was still on his feet. His chest was sweating and he breathed heavily. He stared at Mark and growled, "Back to face me like a man?"

"Nah," Mark replied.

"What did you do to her?" Sinatra scowled.

"Wouldn't you like to know?" Mark provoked. "Actually, I think you don't."

Sinatra snarled and charged. The chains jerked him back before he could take two steps. Aaron tightened and loosened them as needed.

Mark must've enjoyed seeing Sinatra frustrated because he continued to tease. "Look, man, it's obvious you have some sort of...'thing' for my girl."

"'*YOUR GIRL*'?" Sinatra bellowed. "She is far from it!"

"Prove it," Mark said, crossing his arms. "I have a challenge for you."

Sinatra stopped struggling to advance and stood up straight. He steadied his breathing. "What do you want?"

"The coordinates," Mark demanded. "If you give me the coordinates to Marcellus Hodgins, I'll leave Detective alone."

Sinatra chewed on the deal for a moment. "I feel like I'm getting the shorter end of the stick."

"We're not going to beat you with the longer one if that's what you're getting at."

"I don't trust you," our prisoner snarled.

"Fine, how about I throw something else in the pot." Mark paused to make sure Sinatra was listening intently. "We discovered a cure for fixing you. On top of Detective being left alone, she'll give you back something you've lost, curing you from your brokenness."

Sinatra's face lit up. We told him he was broken, but up until now I don't think he ever believed it. At that moment, I saw he wanted the truth more than ever. He let out a deep breath and locked eyes with Mark. "Deal."

Within a few moments, we got the coordinates to Marcellus Hodgins hidden in Sinatra's mind. When Mark returned to the observation room, Aaron entered the numbers.

"Okay, so they aren't complete which means we have to find the right one through hundreds of possibilities," Aaron said.

Mark exhaled sharply. "Lots of pressure."

We waited eagerly as the information processed. The machine beeped and a long list came up.

"This will be fun," Nic grumbled.

Johanna wanted to scold him, but she was just as nervous. We only had one chance.

"All right, Aaron," Mark said after a moment. "Let's go through this list."

The Isle member nodded. "We can categorize it in two ways: geographically or alphabetically."

"Shannon, any thoughts?" Mark asked.

"Do geographically and then alphabetically. Search mostly in North America," I answered without thinking. I went with my gut. Something told me Marcellus wouldn't travel far from home.

Mark clapped his hands together. "All right, man. Let's do this."

We hovered over Aaron's and Mark's shoulders as they went through the names. They started in Canada and ventured through the states and cities of the USA. Alphabetically they went: *A, B, C, D...*

"Wait a second," Mark exclaimed as we went down the list. "Scroll back up to the *A*s of *C*; California specifically." Aaron obeyed. Mark ran his finger down the screen until it froze. We couldn't see the name and his finger wouldn't budge for a few moments. He zoned out.

"Mark?" Aaron asked. He waved his hand in front of his Commander's face.

"This is it," Mark whispered softly. "The home of the Hodginses. My parents met here. This is it."

Pushing his glasses up the bridge of his nose, Aaron leaned in and read, "'Anaheim, California'?" He tapped a few buttons. "500 N Dwyer Dr, Anaheim, California; 33.836353, -117.9289022."

"That's it," Mark declared. "It has to be. I don't know why, but I feel it."

"You don't want to look at any of the other ones?" Johanna suggested. "We barely got through half of the list."

"Remember we're sending out major resources on this mission," Nic added. "We have one shot."

"I understand, but I won't look any more. This is it." Mark had his heart set. He believed that was it.

Frankly, I did too. "I trust him," I admitted. "When Gerrior confessed, he mentioned Marcellus met a street musician in California."

Sonny sighed. "I sure hope your instincts are right; California's a big state. We better nail this guy before the opponents do."

"Trust me; if they're there it'll be even better," Aaron said smugly. He winked at Mark who nodded, but neither of them offered an explanation.

"We better get to our positions," Nic ordered, standing upright. "I'll order my men to prepare to depart in 48 hours. Who knows when Joshua and OX will leave."

"Oh, that reminds me," Mark exclaimed. "Shannon, not only should you tell Joshua we're coming, but don't forget to remind him to bring Shane's wallet. We're going to need it."

That meeting ended and we went our separate ways.

After seven years, we were finally getting Mr. Hodgins back.

"Seven years," I mumbled to myself. As I walked away, I thought I was happy but sadness panged me. I spent seven years working this case and it was finally coming to a close, but I never found a *single lead* on my own family. I had no information on my father, mother, or my brother, Pietro. *I gave everything for this Mr. Hodgins. He better be grateful.*

Thoughts of my parents flooded my mind. I missed my mom dearly. It's been years since I saw her beautiful face and dark long curly hair. I longed for her to sing to my sisters and me. She was always there for me when I needed her.

If she were here, she'd be able to snap my sisters out of their fantasy. She'd convince them and the entire community that Donnie is wrong.

My eyes burned as I thought of the pain my lonely, confused, hormonal sisters caused. They're young; they don't know any better, but they refuse to learn the truth.

Dad would be able to teach them.

The reputable Detective Quinn Hollinger. I missed him. I wanted nothing more than to sit with my dad in the library, going over case files or learning the ways of the police force or more importantly, working together to find my big brother Pietro. But the final memory I have is of his blood on the walls after he bought us time to escape.

I stopped dead in my tracks. They gave us everything. They always did. I haven't been able to do anything to give back.

My face reddened and my lungs stung. Breathing heavily, I tried to rid my mind of the sorrowful, painful thoughts. I tried to think positively: I solved a case. But failure blocked any happiness from seeping through.

I should've searched harder. Tears streamed down my face. *I could've done both. I should've solved all of them by now. They're not here and it's my fault.*

My chest heaved and I felt myself crashing to the ground. My breathing became shallow and my legs tingled. *No, no, no, don't be weak. Not now, Shannon. Not now.* I tried to move. I needed to get my mask, but couldn't. I felt myself going numb.

My vision blurred and my breathing slowed. I closed my eyes and was ready to slip into the sweet realm of the unconscious. Not forever, just for a while.

But someone pulled me out of the darkness.

I felt the cold metal of my mask press around my face. It expanded and I inhaled the antidote. Strong hands gently lifted my head and shoulders, resting them on his lap.

I cracked open an eyelid and looked up to see a pale face with slick black hair. Concern filled Sonny's red eyes. "What've I told you about thinking too hard?" he said softly.

I couldn't deny it this time. He was right. "So...rry."

"Don't apologize to me," he scolded. "You have nothing to be sorry for. That's your problem. I know what's going on inside your head. You need to stop it."

We didn't say another word. I lay there on Sonny's lap recovering until I fell asleep.

I woke up a few hours later in my bedroom. I glanced over at my nightstand to see that most of this letter was written. Sonny started it for me to save time which was very sweet of him. I went back in and filled in the blanks and my feelings.

And now you finished reading our collaborative effort, Joshua. You must be ready for your mission in Anaheim. We'll meet you there, but stay on your toes. Find a way to get Shane's wallet to me, but don't give yourself away. You don't know us; we don't know you.

Godspeed and goodwill,

Shannon Hollinger

Shannon Hollinger
Royal Strategist of RRPR

LETTER 27
Joshua: XIV

Yared,

Shannon was at this battle, so I'm going to catch you up.

Several days after my encounter with Leprechaun, I awoke in a soft cot. *This is new*, I thought. I sat up, slid out of the clean linens, and explored my spacious quarters. A pristine marble dining set was positioned in the center of the room. Scattered across the table were old papers and clippings related to our target: traitor Titan Marcellus. To the far right was a firm throne that faced a wall of computer monitors. I saw vital signs, surveillance, and other data. Not of the enemy, but of our own men.

"Good morning, Wolf," a rustic British voice greeted. I turned to see PH standing in the tent's entryway. His heterochromatic eyes glimmered in the early light. Something about PH was different this morning. His curly brown hair frizzed from the humidity, but that couldn't be it. The freckles on his face danced when he smiled.

Wait, that was it. *Why is he so happy?*

"You better get dressed properly," he advised, interrupting my thoughts. He was decked out in his adorned combat jacket rather than his long trench coat. Despite the warmer climate, he still wore his green flowing scarf around his neck. Against his back hung his trusty double edged sword that pierced and slaughtered so many. I espied crusted red along its blade...

PH was busy that morning.

I held back a shudder. "Yes, sir," I replied mechanically.

"What 'ave I told ya," he reached into his pocket and pulled out his pipe, "next time you call me sir, Imma give you a severe beatin'." He lit it, clenched it between his teeth, and puffed a perfect smoke ring. It rose and dissipated as it crashed into the roof of the tent. "C'mon, off you pop."

"Sorry, *PH*," I replied, enunciating his godly name. I went into the bedroom section and changed.

I heard PH seat himself at the marble dining table and rifle through the papers. "Can you believe it, mate? After twenty-five years we're finally going to nail that dastard; makin' 'im pay for what he's done."

I paused before pulling on my new jacket. *Wait, twenty-five years?*

"PH, might I ask you a sort of personal question?" I asked timidly.

I heard a chuckle. "Depends what it is."

"How old are you?"

PH hesitated before responding. "Uh, five and twenty I think. Why?"

But he said Marcellus was a father figure to him, I thought, confused. *He would've been a baby when Marcellus betrayed everyone and started causing trouble. He's the same age as the triplets.*

"Just curious," I answered finally. "Just amazed that someone at such a young age became a Titan and is spearheading a mission that is as old as he is."

Unfortunately, PH catches onto things quickly. "Look, mate, if you're implyin' something just spit it out," he chided. "It's too early in the morning to be solvin' riddles. I haven't 'ad my tea."

I stifled an exhale. *Joshua, you have power now. You're a Titan.*

Peeling away the curtain, I stepped back into the open room and started to explain, but was interrupted by a piercing screech in my head followed by static and a booming voice: *Titans... PH and Wolf... mission start... forty eight hours max... capture Marcellus alive if possible... kill if necessary... start now.*

"Aight, you heard the Big Man." PH rose from his seat. "Let's get to work." My interrogation would have to wait. Perhaps Marcellus would tell me himself.

Wait, I don't want him to tell me, I remembered. *I want him to tell his children.* Letting out a deep breath, I followed PH out.

I looked around at the barren land. The once green grass was a scorched yellow. Dead and fallen palm trees lined the pathways. OX tents encircled the remains of a park. Our equipment and weapons sat atop the old restroom buildings. Our setup was amidst a broken rusted playground and cracked basketball courts. I watched as Xenophonians chaotically scurried about, manning their posts.

"Ah, beautiful California," PH said, inhaling the muggy air. "We're in Pearson Park, I believe."

"Anaheim," I whispered. I ascertained that from Shannon's letter of course, but PH thought I was smart.

"Very good, mate. Now, let's get to business." As if on cue, a mob of soldiers rushed before us and halted, waiting for instructions. PH led me to his truck. Taking a step back, he leapt up onto the hood and then climbed to the roof, waving for me to follow him.

Once I was at his side, he began, "Xenophonians! For years we 'ave been chasing a traitor. For years we 'ave been fooled, lied to, and set back. For years we 'ave put up with this treachery. No more!" His arms shot up and the crowd roared with approval and determination. "My predecessor, the former Titan Marcellus of the English Pandemonium, will no longer pose a threat. Once we have him in our custody, the Order of Xenophon can proceed with the Annex. We will not be defeated! The world will be cleansed and only the righteous shall live!"

The crowd screamed and shouted its agreements like a hoard of animals. As the sounds erupted, we jumped down from the truck and walked through the boisterous soldiers. "I gotta explain what happens next," PH yelled over the noise. "You 'ave several Russian Pandemonium soldiers to lead. I'm also going to give ya a few that you're familiar with to 'elp ya out."

I nodded and we exited the sea of mindless monsters. PH shouted some orders and his Supervising Officers dispersed the crowd. In seconds, the swarm chaotically went about their duties.

PH jerked his head and led me to a rusted swing set that was out of earshot.

"Do you have a gameplan?" I asked.

"Somewhat, yeah," PH replied, pushing an empty swing. He was nostalgic as he did so like a distant memory returned.

As I watched this simple act of boredom, my heart tore in two. I wondered how many children that sat in that swing have perished. How many died at PH's hands… he was in charge of America after all. How many had he pierced and hung for public display?

I shook off the feeling. Sometimes horrific thoughts like this are good reminders of whom I am dealing with. But as I watched him play with the swing, I… pitied him. He grew up in the Order of Xenophon. Everyday was filled with violence and hatred. I wondered if he ever felt joy or love… other than when he was with his Challenger II tank.

"Wolf?" PH asked again, snapping me back into reality. "What's the matter?"

"Sorry, sir—I mean PH," I quickly corrected, "I just can't believe that after so long we're finally going to have him."

PH managed a half smile. "Let's not screw it up. Basically, my plan is we storm 'im out. He's familiar with me, if I 'ave to talk to 'im I will. We 'ave to be wary. 'Is home is probably a stronghold. He's smart as a whip and sly as a fox. My soldiers will cause the distraction as will my beloved girl and I. You and your team will be on stealth and exterminate 'im if he doesn't surrender. The Big Man wants him captured as leverage but," PH shrugged, "if it were up to me, I'd say just kill 'im."

"Seems simple enough. Any backup plans?"

He cocked his head. "What do ya mean?"

"If something goes wrong?"

"Nothing will go wrong," he insisted. "His bloody kids don't know we're 'ere. If they do, all the better. We'll use 'em as bait. And trust me, Marcellus *will* be here."

I thought for a moment and then said in a low voice, "But what if Mars returns?"

PH let the swing hit into him; the chains rattled. "What about 'im?"

"Our soldiers are terrified of him. It's bad enough that they fear Marcellus, but both of their Marks were sighted across the globe. Our men *know* the two of them and Marcellus' kids have actively slaughtered and sabotaged us. Not only that, but I took the position Mars left vacant for years." I looked around. "What if his wrath will be like nothing we've ever seen?"

PH chewed on this for a moment. "I believe his anger will be that of 'ell, but I know we can 'andle him. Also, Marcellus 'asn't been the one leaving those Marks." He offered no other explanation, but I knew. Now, so did PH.

Before another conversation could start, my team approached. Among the unfamiliar faces were three I knew well: Goliath of Ares, Solomon of Hermes, and Leprechaun of Hermes. Oh, and Diego the Monkey.

I eyed Leprechaun carefully but he displayed no sign that he even remembered telling me he was a spy. In fact, he was so relaxed and ready for the mission it was a surprise.

Emel was right. He's too normal.

"Aight, Wolf, this is your crew. You know what to do," PH said. He patted my back. "Good luck." He left to get his tank and soldiers.

"All right, boss," Goliath said. His voice was deeper and more gravelly than normal. "What's the plan?"

I scrunched my nose, turning my glasses on. As I did, I saw the corner of Leprechaun's mouth twitch. He knew what I was up to. I needed to translate my thoughts into Russian. I wasn't really multilingual like all the other Titans. "All right, boys, you ready?" I said in English. Quickly, I went over the plan with my three acquaintances.

My Russian subordinates seemed frustrated that I didn't speak to them first. Very short tempered, my Pandemonium. They had no leader for so long. The Headmaster was the perfect Titan, apparently. They cursed and mumbled amongst themselves, stating I wasn't fit to fill his throne.

I became intimidated as they doubted and cursed me.

Show power, Joshua, a voice inside me said.

I needed to put them in their place. I froze mid conversation and turned to them, my eyes narrow. I took a deep breath and bellowed, «Хватит! Я твой Титан,независимо от моей первоначальной дивизии. Обращай меня хорошо или жестоко бы наказывайся.» I told them I was their Titan and they must treat me as such or be punished.

My Russian subordinates' eyes widened and their lips tightened. They stood at attention and waited for orders. After I explained the plan to them in their tongue, they were willing to serve. Out of respect or fear? Not sure. Either works for me.

I ordered them to retrieve our supplies while my men from the English Pandemonium remained behind.

"So, Titan Wolf," Goliath said, "How's it feel?"

"Heavy," I replied honestly, rubbing the shaved part of my head. "There is a lot of pressure."

"Believe it. And having to know more than one language?" He chuckled and smacked my back… quite hard. "Couldn't do it. In fact, I didn't even know you could."

"I pick up things fast," I winced.

Diego the Monkey squeaked and crawled to the top of Solomon's wooden staff. *"Do you see someone skilled in their work?"* the old man said. *"They will serve before kings; they will not serve before officials of low rank."*

"I agree, Solomon," Leprechaun chimed in, understanding his verse. "Wolf, you have the potential to rise even higher than us. Who knows? Someday you may govern alongside our leader."

"Bah, I wouldn't go that far," Goliath dismissed. "Anyway, let's get to it. I'm ready to see the guy that's killed so many of my acquaintances. If that Mars guy is there too, even better."

Without another word, we regrouped with my Russian subordinates. Time to begin.

Stealthily, we made our way down ruined West Cypress Street. I looked around and noticed fresh bodies pierced within red Xs against the broken buildings. *PH, no…* I averted my eyes and remained focused.

We took the long way around the back while PH's clattering tank and army marched down West Sycamore Street. We were to circle back to 500 North Dwyer Drive where Marcellus supposedly was hiding. We went down the street and through the wide grounds of an old High School, steering clear of PH's men.

Once we were away from the school, we stopped for a moment in the backyard of an old historic house at 400 North West Street. As I caught my breath, I looked around at the site. It was an American Territorial style cottage with a tall tower that peaked over its top. Its white shingles were discolored with dirt, and ivy crept up to the brown roof like long snakes. A few windows were boarded up, but other than that it was beautifully preserved.

I turned my glasses on to identify what the home used to be called. *Mother Colony House. Cool,* I thought. Out of curiosity, I switched to "thermal vision" to see if anything was inside.

The moment the mode changed, my heart stopped.

Inside was highly advanced machinery; powered and working. Sitting at the helm was one lonely male figure.

"Leprechaun, come with me," I whispered. "The rest of you, stay put." I turned to my Russian subordinates and ordered the same: «Ждите за приказов!» All were confused, but obeyed.

Quietly, Leprechaun and I snuck around the side of the Mother Colony House to search for a point of entry. We found a low window that was cracked open.

Suspicious… but that never usually stops anyone. We went in.

The old pioneer house was gorgeous. The furniture, carpeting, and walls were intact. We entered through a sitting room with colonial style couches, mahogany end tables, and other old furnishings.

I dragged my finger across one of the tables. I lifted it and looked closely. Not a speck of dust. "Whoever lives here keeps up with the place."

Leprechaun said nothing. He walked about purposefully and searched intently. Turning on my glasses, I did the same, but Leprechaun was faster even without enhanced vision. "Wolf, I found what you're looking for," he called.

My heart rate quickened as I joined him. There was a floor cabinet against the wall in one of the foyers. Several images, knick knacks, and statues were organized across its top. The bartender pointed to a small porcelain statue towards the back. It was of three children standing shoulder to shoulder. Music notes covered the little book split between them. The kids were singing.

Gingerly, I lifted the trinket. Hidden beneath it was an etching in the wood: a beautiful illuminated letter *H*. "The Mark of Marcellus," I whispered. I rubbed my fingers along the engraving. I traced each groove as if I was writing out the letter myself.

That's when I heard the click.

Machine gears turned and creaked as a contraption was set off beneath our feet. The shelf slid away with a low rumble, revealing a staircase. Without another word, we descended.

The basement was sectioned off by a long wall with four doors. I scanned each one and detected one sign of life.

"This one," I whispered, reaching for the third door handle. I pulled out my pistol and raised it beside my face. Leprechaun did the same and nodded.

Holding my breath, I swung open the door, aimed my weapon, and bellowed, "Move and you die!"

Frightened, a tall teen jumped 6 feet out of his swivel chair and faced us. His arms shot up, and he backed against the wall. Scared blue eyes stared out from behind black-rimmed glasses. All his hair stood up with fear... either that or his blond locks were just spiky.

Unnaturally spiky, I thought, eyeing him up and down. I lowered my weapon and Leprechaun followed without question. "State your name," I ordered.

"A-aron A-a-a-lexus," the teen stuttered.

I knew it. I was thrilled to meet him in person, but I couldn't show it. "Where is the man who lives in this house?"

The ground above us shook; dust falling like snow. I heard the clamor of tracks traversing along the terrain above. PH was getting into position. "Leprechaun, stay with him," I ordered as I ran out of the room.

If Leprechaun was a spy like he said, he'd make sure the boy got out of there safely.

I stormed out of the Mother Colony House and back to where my men should have been. They were gone. «Солдаты! Перегруппировывайтесь!» I bellowed. "Men! Regroup!" I repeated in English. No reply.

There was shouting, screaming, and a hissing.

Things started to get heated. Literally.

Across the street, 500 North Dwyer Drive was up in flames. PH and his soldiers had invaded and started burning it to the ground. PH's tank was positioned right in front. Thankfully, it hadn't fired yet. Chaos and shouting roared louder than the fire.

I watched as PH's men ran frantically about, firing blindly into the smoky sky. Looking up, I caught a brief glimpse of what they were shooting at: a quick flash of blue light.

It was a Bionic.

I raced to the rear of the formation, cocking my weapon on the way. I wove through the screaming men and made my way to the base of the tank. "PH!" I shouted. "What's going on?"

"Exactly what we want!" he yelled back. "Our enemy is 'ere. Marcellus will slither out of his 'ole at some point or burn. I don't care which!"

I wasn't going to tell him the little civilian house they set aflame was innocent. I didn't want to over-complicate things. Well... not yet anyway.

PH hopped down from his tank. "Where are your men?"

"I came to ask you that," I replied as I shielded my face from the heat of the burning house.

"Ya mean they're gone?"

I nodded. "I took a small group to scout out one of the houses because I sensed movement. When I returned they weren't there."

"This just means the fight is going to be a little tougher than we thought," he growled. He was unhappy which was not good. He looked out into the chaos for a second before his eyes widened and he screamed, "COVER!" He grabbed my shoulder and jumped, dragging us both to the ground.

There was a loud *CRASH* and the creaking and sparking of metal being dragged against the asphalt. Lifting my head, I turned to see PH's beloved Challenger II shoved back several hundred feet. The side armor was crushed inwards and smoke billowed out of the hatch. The once beautiful shiny silver was damaged and covered in soot.

Standing on its hull were two metal figures glowing blue. They had silver hair and piercing eyes. Staggering to my feet, I faced them and raised my weapon.

Axel saw me before Alison. He smiled and elbowed his girlfriend. Before she could shoot me down, she realized who I was. Then, they leapt off of the tank and disappeared into the smoke above.

PH leapt to his feet and cried, "NO! Not my baby! Not again!" He wanted to run towards her but was infuriated. Gritting his teeth, he ripped his sword out of his sheath and screamed, "THEY WILL PAY!" No plan went through his mind. He raced into the chaos with his men.

Before he could get very far, a familiar hairy blond fiend side tackled him to the ground. "Hi shorty! Hi shorty!" Theo cackled. His teeth dripped with drool and... something else.

PH kicked the Shrew in the stomach, sending him flying. He leapt to his feet as Jordan the Slow-loris sucked venom of his inner elbows and charged. Patiently, PH waited. As Jordan was about to strike, PH sidestepped and struck Jordan in the back of the neck with the hilt of his sword. The Slow loris rolled across the ground and jumped back up. They were about to duel when another Xenophonian engaged.

With the Mutant busy, PH ran alongside the flames and shouted, "Wolf! Let's go!" PH wasn't sure where he was going, but he was determined to get there.

I followed him. I didn't know what to do so I told him the truth. "PH! This is the wrong house anyway!"

The Titan skidded to a stop. "What?!"

"I was trying to tell you! We found machinery in the house across the way!"

He swore and took off for the Mother Colony House. I had no choice but to follow suit.

We raced through the scorched backyard. We were about to reach the front of the house when two figures blocked our path. A large brawny man was hunched over; his hairy fists dug into the ground. The smaller figure beside him raised a weapon. They had a machine over their mouth that glowed white. It was Kong/Nic and Detective/Shannon.

We skidded to a stop and PH looked at them for a moment. "*YOU!*" he bellowed. "You're the Gorilla-man that hurt my baby first. And," he peered closely, "if it isn't Detective. I've longed to see you again, mate. How's that little girl's leg doin', eh?"

Detective growled and charged, screaming. PH smirked and side stepped, hoping to trip his opponent. However, Detective was smarter. She spun on her heel and kicked PH as he stepped, causing him to stagger backwards.

Impressed, he stood up straight and put his sword in its sheath. "I'm going to enjoy this." He raised his guard.

"Bring it on," Detective growled in her electronic voice as she did the same.

Together, they charged and started a life or death match.

I thought Nic would intervene but he ran off to combat some other men who tried to shoot Detective while she was brawling.

In the midst of that, the Mutants (Lucas was there, too, but not Sami) and Bionics charged the enemy from all sides. Seeing all of them together caused the Xenophonians to falter. They were scared out of their wits.

I looked a little closer. *No, they're confused.* They shot at the Bionics but not the Mutants. *Why?* Their hesitation was their doom. In no time, the RRPR enhanced members had all of the Xenophonians corralled like cattle.

No sign of my subordinates among them. To be honest, I stood in the midst of the battlefield dumbfounded. I was surprised I didn't get shot. I wasn't sure what to do. The men I was responsible for were missing or in the "pen", PH was occupied, I lost Leprechaun, and Marcellus was nowhere to be found.

The chaos and fighting began to dwindle. All of PH's men were captured or dead in RRPR's circle, and the Titan was still fighting Detective, but they both grew weary.

I was about to intervene when a chill went up my spine. I felt a cold gaze stab me in the back. Slowly, I turned to see a figure coming down the steps of the Mother Colony House.

He was a strong, tall man wearing a ratty trench coat over an old OX combat jacket. His sharp jaw was clenched. Gray eyes glared out from beneath a black baseball cap.

"Marcellus," I whispered, taking a step backwards.

His gaze softened and his mouth turned upward when he saw me. He knew who I was, but wasn't interested in me. He marched past me and stopped before PH and Detective as they were about to give their final blows.

What happened next shook my soul.

A loud piercing noise caused all the Xenophonians to stagger. Even PH fell to the ground in the middle of his fight. I felt it, too. It was unbearable. It was like needle thin knives were driven into each ear and then up throughout each curve of my cerebrum. I clutched my head, but tried not to cave. I needed to watch.

Shoving their palms into their ears, the mindless Xenophonains groaned and hissed at the pain. Their bodies quaked. Blood trickled down the sides of their faces.

"*PH!*" a deep voice bellowed. Marcellus strode forward with his chin held high.

"Marcellus," PH groaned. I turned to see him staggering to his feet, taking his hands off his ears. No blood.

I looked at my own hands. No blood either.

"Surrender or face the consequences," Marcellus demanded.

PH chuckled and shook off the pain. "It took me forever to find you, mate. You think I'm going to let you go that easily?"

The former Titan sighed. Lifting his hand, he snapped his fingers.

The piercing noises' pitch rose higher and higher until we couldn't hear it anymore. I watched as the Xenophonians shook with pain and fear. Their faces paled and their teeth chattered. After an agonizing moment, their eyes rolled back in their heads. One by one, they dropped to the ground.

Never to stand up again.

PH stared; his mouth agape. "What did you bloody do…" he whispered.

It must've been the frequency Mark, Aaron, and Myles were working on, I speculated. *That's why Aaron was at Marcellus' controls.*

Marcellus shook his head. "We'll have to keep trying," he whispered over his shoulder. He brought his attention back to PH, "Surrender and no harm shall come to you."

Ripping his sword out his sheath, PH gritted his teeth. "Go to the crows," he sneered. "You will pay for what you've done!" He raised his arm, aiming the tip at his foe. "Every. Last. Deed." He was about to charge but he hesitated. His gaze fell upon a figure in the background.

From where I stood, I couldn't see who it was, but PH knew. A smirk crossed his face and he lowered his hand. "Aight, mate, I know you're never one to shy away from a wager. You let me and my fellow Titan go and we'll report what 'appened. You know, to scare our men and such."

"What's the catch?" Marcellus asked, raising a scarred eyebrow.

"You return with Mars and we have our final showdown," he explained. "Predecessor against successor. No enhanced. No tricks."

Marcellus thought for a moment. "All right, PH. Just because you're you, I'll make an exception. You tell no one of this, you understand?"

"Titan's honor," PH promised, bowing. "I'll send word of time and place soon. For now, we bid adieu." Without another word, PH spun on his heel and headed back to camp.

I took in the scene one last time before departing. The Mutants and Bionics circled around the dead Xenophonians; a result of their failed experiment. I looked to Marcellus who nodded.

Letting out a deep breath, I turned to follow my fellow Titan, but was stopped by Detective. I peered closely and could see Shannon's blue eyes through her goggles. Their gaze touched my soul. For the first time in years we stood face to face. I wanted to embrace her; tell her everything in person, but I couldn't.

She held out her hand. I looked over her shoulder to make sure no one was watching. Then, I slipped the wallet out of my jacket, placed it gently into her palm, and left.

After so much work, we let Marcellus escape, lost so many men, and practically admitted defeat.

And for some reason, PH was fine with it.

Just tell me how things are going on your end. Also, tell Mars—I mean Sonny not to kill me at our next meeting.

With safety and secrecy,

Joshua Wolfrum

Joshua Wolfrum
Titan of the Russian Pandemonium

THE UNDERGROUND

LETTER 28

Yared: VII

Joshua,

Man, let me tell you. Things are heated down here. People are arguing, fighting, screaming, and even trying to escape the Underground. All this is thanks to Donnie, Sami, and the Hollinger girls. Sami and Donnie are in confinement but the sisters are loose. The boys and I have been trying to keep the Hollingers quiet but it's no use. Shannon doesn't know the severity yet. She's too wrapped up in the return of Marcellus.

Thankfully, he was our saving grace.

I was in the village plaza, trying to prevent a riot. Lucas and Axel were out having fun on your Marcellus mission while Ethan and I were on another assignment. When we returned, angry survivors were our welcome home party.

"Everyone, you have to trust us!" I yelled as I dodged the shoe that was hurled towards my head. "The Order of Xenophon is failing. We have mostly halted the progression of the Annex."

"They're still winning!" one cried as he searched for something to throw.

"'*Mostly*' halted? What does that even mean?!" screamed another as she chased after Ethan with a shovel.

"All you do is take our resources and trust on one man's stupid dreams! You have no skills yourself to win this fight!"

"Leave REM out of this," I commanded. Blake was the most hated person in the Underground because of his slip up with Shane. I don't know who spread that detail around. (My bets are on Lucy.). Frankly, I didn't even know the citizens *knew* about him and his gift.

But as much as it panged me, I felt they had a point.

We relied too much on his dreams and your information, Joshua. Shannon's too wrapped up with Shane to figure things out for the team, but even then… she shouldn't have to do it alone.

Thankfully, I didn't have to say anything else. The mob stopped tearing Ethan limb from limb when a little girl shouted, "LOOK! IT'S MARCELLUS!" Everyone dropped their weapons—pots, pans, shoes, whatever. Their eyes widened when they saw him.

I turned to see a tall man with a strong jawline leading the returning RRPR members through the plaza with his son and daughter by his side.

The crowd parted like the red sea as he marched through them. They froze and gawked. No murmurs, no whispers, just utter admiration.

Stopping by the fountain, Marcellus turned to address them. "Hello, everyone. I'm glad you found your way here safely."

They stared dumbfounded.

"I know you're probably wondering what I've been up to or where I was," he smiled, "but I don't want you to worry. The brave men and women of Resist, Rescue, Protect, Retake are more capable than I ever was alone." He looked at Mark and Aymie. "They've already done more good in these short years than I have in a lifetime." Without another word, he marched through the village with the others following close behind.

The crowd was silent as they watched him disappear into the concrete city.

"Yeah, what he said!" I shouted, wanting to get the last word in. A woman gripped a sandal and raised her arm to attack. Flinching, I grabbed Ethan, and we chased after our friends.

We caught up to everyone in the Hall of Royals. Virginia Michaelson greeted Marcellus with a firm handshake. "It's a pleasure to see you again, Mr. Hodgins."

"Likewise, Ms. Michaelson, but you know my name."

She smiled sweetly and said, "Of course, Thomas."

"Thomas?" Mark said, amazed. "That's Shane's middle name."

"Now he doesn't have to be jealous about you being named after Marcellus," Nic chuckled.

Marcellus smiled. "Yes, Mark. I feel like I should properly introduce myself." He faced us. "Please forgive my secrecy and the dangers you encountered searching for me. You know I had to take all the necessary precautions. My full name is Thomas Mark Hodgins but am known as Marcellus: the former Titan of the English Pandemonium," he looked at Mark and Aymie, "and the father to three of your closest friends." He glanced around; a look of concern crossed his face. "Where is Shane? You said he survived his capture."

"He did, but we've had some trouble," Shannon spoke up. She pulled a brown tattered wallet out of her jacket pocket and shook it. "We hope this trigger may help."

"It should if they haven't drastically changed my methods," Marcellus replied.

"Wait, you invented the Entrance Ritual?" I asked without requesting permission. "Just how big were you with OX?"

"I was pretty 'big' as you say," he answered. His gleeful expression faded. "To much of my sorrow, I progressed the Order further than anyone. Before I joined as a teenager, the Order of Xenophon was very old fashioned. They were a hidden cult, encouraging individuals to give up everything and become followers. Back then, they poisoned the world through word of mouth and silent deeds, but it was never enough. They needed something more."

"How did you get wrapped up in all this?" Aymie asked her father. Her voice shook as she held back tears. She didn't want to believe that the family she searched for was the cause of so much pain and anguish.

Marcellus sighed, casting his gray eyes to the ground. Everyone watched him, waiting for the truth. "The Hodginses have been loyal to the Order of Xenophon for generations," he began. He pulled out the dog tag that hung around his neck. It was identical to the triplets': his name on one side and the illuminated letter *H* on the other. "Like my father and grandfather, I was born into it through the Eros division. I never knew my mother." He chuckled. "And yet, I somehow was given a normal life for fifteen years. I dabbled with my share of computers and got into plenty of trouble, but I wanted more. My father offered to take me under his wing in the Order and so it happened. With my skills and youthful mind, I developed and designed the most effective tools for the Order of Xenophon in history. I studied the human brain in such depth that I could manipulate it and transform it. That was my greatest gift to them."

The group was silent for a moment as he finished. It was amazing that the man who was *supposedly* going to save us was the one who started it all in the first place.

"You Hodginses always have to show off, don't you?" I said in jest, trying to make the mood light. I got a smirk, but nothing more. So, I decided to ask a pressing question that you wanted answered, Joshua. "Okay, let me try again." I cleared my throat. "Hi, I'm Yared Prinz: Commander of the Seers. I've been communicating with Joshua Wolfrum, the new Titan of the Russian Pandemonium, and he told me something that hasn't been sitting right."

Marcellus cocked his head. "If it's about my standings, I assure you

I'm on your side."

"Nah, man, it's not totally about you. It's actually about PH."

He stood up straight. "I think I understand."

"Cool, so why is it that PH said he worked under you?" I asked. "Gerrior claims you left the Order around the time the triplets were born. PH is the same age as them. If you left, how could he know you?"

Mark and Aymie looked at their father in surprise.

"After mom abandoned us, you left the Order, didn't you?" Mark asked. He tried to sound convincing, but he faltered.

Marcellus breathed out through his nose. He was disappointed with himself. "I lost control," he confessed to his son. "I thought you three and your mother were dead. I roamed alone for two years. I didn't know what to do with myself. I needed someone I could trust."

"So you chose a kid?" I asked. "PH must've been a toddler when you started 'trusting him'. Instead of looking for your own kids, you returned to the Order to play 'dad'?"

Marcellus' eyes narrowed. "I've *always* searched for my children. It was during my search that this instance occurred. I *never* returned to the Order."

"Well what happened then?" Mark demanded, growing impatient. "What does PH mean to you?"

Marcellus sighed. He put a hand on his son's shoulder. "I lost hope," he started. "If I couldn't get my family back, I'd work hard to take down those who took them from me, but I knew I couldn't do it alone." His eyes became distant, recalling a life-changing memory. "One day, I saw a little boy on a playground. I watched from afar and studied his every little movement. He reminded me of you and your brother, Shane. I saw potential. I knew that small child could give me the revenge I desired." He paused and looked away from his children. "So, I took him."

Jaws dropped. The Hodgins triplets stared at their father. Out of the corner of my eye, I saw something in Shannon's face. She wasn't as horrified as we were. There was something else… a curiosity?

"Hold up, man," Mark spat, pulling away from his dad. "You kidnapped a two-year-old kid and threw him to the wolves hoping he'd do your bidding?"

"I never abandoned PH," Marcellus snapped. "I kept him until he was five, then sent him to the Order's London base where he was overlooked by a trusted Xenophonian from Burmingham. I visited PH every two weeks until he turned eighteen. I taught him everything I know. I raised someone who knew the Order back to front; the one who could take it down from the inside. He was going to undo my horrors."

"Let me guess, it backfired?" Mark scoffed. "Either he felt betrayed or he fell in love with the Order? Either way he does OX's bidding."

"PH can be saved," Marcellus declared. "Does he skewer people to buildings? Yes. Is he uncontrollable? Yes. Is he too obsessed with that hunk of metal I gave him?"

"Whoa, you gave him the Challenger II?" I smirked.

"Yes," Marcellus growled. "The point is, he is absolutely a sinner. I am too. Aren't we all? However, within us is a little spark of redemption. We can change, we can be forgiven. We just need to ignite the fire within us and let it roar."

"So, you're saying there is still good in him?" I asked like the insolent Seer that I am.

Marcellus grew impatient—as easily as Shane does. "Yes, that's what I was saying. He's confused; that's why he didn't kill me when he could've."

"We believe you," Aymie put in, placing a hand on her father's shoulder. "But how can we stop him?"

"Remind him of who he really is," Marcellus stated. "Remind him of his purpose. Remind him to stand up and fight back against the Order like he was taught." He tugged down on his combat jacket. "Now, it's time to prepare. PH will keep his word and challenge us again. Where is the one formerly known as Mars?"

"Right this way, sir," Virginia Michaelson said as she gestured towards the door. Together they and most of the RRPR Officers followed. Mark left to put Jordan, Theo, Brand, and Gerrior back into confinement.

I know; they got to help with the fun mission and not me.

The Hall of Royals grew quiet with only the Isles members and me... oh and Blake.

"How are you four holding up?" Ethan asked Axel, Alison, Lucas, and Aaron.

"Well, I was held at gunpoint by our RRPR spy so that was fun," Aaron mumbled. "He didn't even hint at who he was."

"That's right; he left Leprechaun with you," I put in. "How was that by the way?"

Aaron shrugged. "It was fine, I guess. I did my work, he didn't speak. When the commotion started, he bolted," he thought for a moment. "In fact, he didn't stop me from working at all. Wasn't he supposed to?"

"Leprechaun is a spy, too," I spilled. "We don't know who he is yet, but Joshua's working on it."

"That makes me feel better I guess," Aaron sighed. "Although, there was definitely something familiar about him."

"We'll let Joshua worry about that part," I said, brushing it aside.

"Yeah, he has to worry about a lot of things," Axel added, "like Alison accidentally blowing him to bits for starters." She elbowed him, but he laughed and put his arm around her. "It's okay, appearances can be deceiving."

Lucas, who was quiet in thought, finally spoke up. "Speaking of looks, why were they so shocked to see me, Theo, and Jordan? PH's men have seen Mutants before. Remember the triplets' story about when PH hurt Rachel?"

"That's been troubling me too," Blake said quietly. He came over from admiring the photos he took. "I fear there is another card that hasn't been in play yet."

"I barely know how to play Go Fish," Aaron replied. "What game are we playing?"

Blake pulled his beanie tighter over his white hair. "A dangerous one. One with liars, cheaters, and bribery. The Order of Xenophon has one more trick up their sleeve to push the Annex forward. I just don't know what it is."

"Joshua mentioned they have their own 'secret weapon' or something," I replied. "He doesn't know what yet."

"After this battle, he'll know everything," Blake stated. Fear shone in his light blue eyes. Something bothered him, but he said nothing.

I opened my mouth to speak but there was an urgent announcement over the speaker: "*EMERGENCY. ALL ISLE MEMBERS REPORT TO CONFINEMENT IMMEDIATELY. EMERGENCY.*"

We looked at one another and then raced to the tracks with Blake tailing. Once we were piled in a cart, Axel and Alison sped us down the corridor, taking us to Donnie's room.

Johanna stood outside his cell. Her hand was over her mouth. Wide green eyes stared through the open door. She was shaking.

Ethan ran over to her. "Johanna, what happened?"

Her eyes quaked as she pointed.

Entering the room, we found Janelle and Prince pinning Donnie to the floor. There was silver tape across his mouth. His disheveled long hair draped across the cold ground. Tremors shook his entire body. What worried me the most were his eyes. You could only see white; they rolled back.

"What's going on?" Ethan demanded.

"He's havin' some weird seizure," Janelle explained as she repositioned her hand on Donnie's legs.

"Why does he have tape over his mouth?" I questioned.

"You don't want to hear his words," Prince cried. He locked eyes with me. "You really don't."

"Well, man, just because you said that now I want to hear," I stated as I walked over.

"Yared Prinz, don't you dare," Prince ordered.

Hearing my name come from him was strange. The way he said it was way too familiar... *If this guy is my dad, then God has a weird sense of humor.* Even if it was true, I didn't care. I was still going to disobey. I've been an obedient Seer for so long. *Even if Prince is my dad, who actually listens to their parents at my age?*

Kneeling down, I tore the duct tape off of the little boy's mouth, ripping hair off his face. Despite the pain, Donnie was unfazed. His chapped lips moved like they never stopped. He was whispering and muttering things in a different language—Greek, I guessed—like he was possessed.

"What is happening?" Alison whispered.

Donnie cackled. "You know what's happening, don't ya?" He tried to shake himself free but couldn't. "The one known as REM knows *exactly* what's happening. He always does, right?"

No one said anything. Janelle looked up at us and shook her head. She didn't want us to answer.

"Well?!" Donnie screamed. "Does he have the gift of the gods or no?"

"There's only one God, first of all," I answered, "and second, you're acting insane, Donnie."

He gritted his teeth and screeched, "NOOO! This war is insane. Peace is possible. Just surrender." He tilted his chin upwards. The veins in his neck bulged and sweat dripped off his dry skin. "The Order of Xenophon will rise. We, the Moirai, will rise. Zeus will triumph and reign once again." Donnie strained to raise his head. The whites of his eyes fell upon Blake who stood in the doorway. A smirk crossed the boy's face.

Donnie's smug expression disappeared as he screamed at the top of his lungs. He gave one final effort to push himself off the ground, causing Axel and Alison to jump in and help hold him down. Abruptly, his screeching ceased as if someone had turned him off and his body dropped to the floor.

He slipped into another dreamless sleep.

They released him and let him lie on the cold ground, breathing heavily.

"What just happened?" Aaron asked timidly, standing behind Johanna.

"He knows…" Blake muttered. "They know." Without another word, he ran out of the room.

Alison gently put her metal arms under Donnie's fragile body and carried him to the bed in the corner. As she placed him, she knelt down and hung her head low. "Why are they doing this to him?" she choked. Axel went over and knelt beside her, but had no words to say.

"They want to weaken us, make us afraid, but it won't work," I stated. "We can fix Donnie, I promise. We will make him better."

"And Sami?" Aaron asked.

"She'll be all right, too." I didn't know on what grounds I was making these promises, but I did it anyway. *Totally out of character for me, that's for sure.*

"So, what do we do now?" Ethan asked.

I sighed. "Wait until PH calls on us. I have a feeling we aren't going to honor Marcellus and Sonny going alone."

I would ask you not to tell PH but it seems he already knows. Blake had a dream two nights after that incident. He saw your Titan meeting. It was so vivid it frightened me (if you can believe that).

I must relay it; please tell me if it's true. Everything that Donnie was saying makes sense after this. Here is what Blake told me he dreamt of:

"What happened out there, Titan PH?" a woman asked. The deep voice came from a lit statue in the center of the room.

"Marcellus escaped because I let 'im go," PH replied smugly.

"You ambushed the wrong house and were destroyed, idiota," another Titan said. She had black hair tied into a long braid. The emblem above her throne was a wasp. Sting.

PH wagged his finger in the air. "That's why I let 'im go. Our enemies somehow got ahold of the same clues we did but managed to get the address correct."

"What are you saying?"

"You know what I'm sayin'. Moirai, I think you should finally let me act upon this." He turned to the statues. "Their weapon is the man with white hair. He has the Gift of Apollo. He foresees all. I've told you this countless times; this is 'ow the enemy 'as infiltrated our missions."

"Listen to yourself, PH," Sting whined. "It's impossible."

"They said we were impossible," a booming voice answered. The largest statue was lit. Zeus spoke. "They said we were hopeless; that our goals were unachievable. They called us chaos. Look at us now. We are organized chaos. We will fix humanity. Have faith, child."

PH bowed his head. "My lord, you know I speak truth. Once my mission succeeds, we can proceed with our final stage. The Annex must be completed." He gestured towards a man with a monkey on his shoulder sitting on a marble throne. Above him was the emblem of a wolf. "We need your permission to unleash our own weapons," PH continued. "Wolf and I can 'andle this. We just need your permission to use them."

The voices were silent. "I deny your request," Zeus said finally. "Only in the sense of the Unleashing. I have an alternative for you."

"Your will be done, lord," PH said finally.

And that was the end of Blake's dream. He's terrified. I've been told to stay close to him, and I have. He confided in me.

"Yared, I'm sorry I'm placing these burdens on you," Blake whispered the night he told me. Sweat dripped from his pale forehead. "You have great weights on your shoulders. You don't need any more."

"It's my job, I can handle it," I reassured him. "Are you sure that's all you dreamt of?"

Blake nodded but kept his blue eyes to the ground. "It's all that's relevant. We'll report to Michaelson first thing in the morning."

All that's relevant... He's hiding something. I don't know what.

I haven't gotten a chance to speak with anyone about his dreams. All the RRPR Officers are too preoccupied with Marcellus. They are too busy for us Isle members and poor Sinatra/Shane. They haven't had time to work on bringing his memories back.

I went to check on him once with the boys. Franky, his condition worries me. He's unresponsive. Sinatra and Shane both have something on their mind. I tried to get the others to check on him, but Marcellus forbade himself, Shannon, Mark, and Aymie to see him. He doesn't want them to get distracted until the battle with PH is finished.

Joshua, everyone is falling apart. Can we end this soon, please? Shannon will be receiving your next letter; please give her good news.

Bravery and fidelity,

Yared Prinz

Yared Prinz
Seer Commander

THE UNDERGROUND

LETTER 29

Joshua: XV

Shannon,

I'm sorry.

I'm sorry, I'm sorry, I'm sorry. I don't know what to say. Tell Yared I couldn't deliver good news, but please know I had *no* idea. I'll share my side of the story so you know I was in the dark.

But don't all good things come at a price?

I hadn't slept for days. I lay in my bed, staring at the white ceiling. After the Marcellus mission—my first mission as a Titan—I was surprised with an upgraded living quarters in New Greece. I had my own "mini temple" off the courtyard next to PH's. It was comfortable and homey, but I got no rest.

The meeting Blake saw happened the moment we returned. Everything you dictated was accurate, but Blake was right. There was something else.

Sadly, I didn't know what it was.

The clock hit 0300 when I decided to get up and walk around. I knew PH sent out the battle invitation to you several days ago. No idea how he got it to you. I still don't even know my own location...

Going out of my temple, I walked the pristine streets of the dim-lit city. Despite being underground, New Greece had the illusion of night and day. The concrete ceiling was peppered with glowing speckles: our stars. No constellations; only a chaotic sparkling painting.

Just the way they like it.

Strolling along, I made my way to the plaza that was encircled by the gods' temples. I stood by the fountain, watching the clear water flow down the marble tower and into a glimmering pool below.

I bent over and looked at my reflection. It had been a while, and I didn't recognize myself. Staring back from behind rimmed glasses were serious dark eyes that weren't mine. My tan face aged and was blemished with scars. My hair was shaved on the bottom and curly atop; a look I despised. That man in the water wasn't Joshua.

I only saw Wolf.

"What're you staring at?" a female voice purred, causing me to jump. Sting laughed. "Scared of your own reflection?"

"No," I replied mechanically. I didn't want to speak with her. I know you all want revenge for her taking Shane and stabbing Lucas, but I had no intention of gathering intel at that moment.

She sat down on the edge of the fountain and looked up at me. "While I may not be your superior anymore, I'm still a lady. Show some respect. Ask me how I'm doing."

I chuckled. Something about her was different that night. She wasn't trying to seduce me, fight me, *or* kill me. She appeared… pleasant.

"How are you this evening, ma'am?" I asked.

"*Bien, gracias*," she replied with a pretty smile that quickly turned into a frown. "Are you all right, Wolf? You seem different after the mission."

"Well," I hesitated, thinking of a lie. "My first assignment as Titan failed. My men perished and we didn't capture our target."

"Failure is how you learn," she stated; kindness in her brown eyes. "Each moment is a teaching moment. From there we decide what we are going to do to improve."

"You're wise beyond your years, ma'am, but I think I decided *not* to fail before the mission," I replied sarcastically.

Punching my arm, she added, "You will have your chance of glory, I promise you. For now, continue to learn." As she stood, her hand rubbed up my arm until it rested on the side of my face. Her calloused palms were somehow soft to the touch. Their warmth comforted my restless spirit. "As I said before, you have potential. That's why I like you," she cooed. I felt my cheeks getting hot as she took her hand away. "Now get some rest, we fight tomorrow." With that, she departed.

Butterflies panicked in my stomach as she left. *No, Joshua, no. She is evil and has had it out for you since the beginning.* I splashed fountain water on myself, trying to snap out of it. All I could think of was her brown eyes and smooth accented voice. For some reason, I wasn't angry.

The thought of her brought me contentment.

I sauntered to my quarters and lay down. My mind thought about Sting as I drifted to sleep, unknowing I'd be escorted away.

The next morning I awoke on the floor of a metal building. I was dressed in my combat uniform with my holster at my side. A large monitor covered the wall at my feet and weapon racks lined the perimeter. Propping myself up on my elbow, I looked around. I saw PH at the door slipping his sheath over his head.

The battle was about to begin.

I jumped up. "Sir, what's happening?"

"It's time, Wolf," he said solemnly. "Time for Marcellus and Mars to die." The tone of his voice was sorrowful. Mars was his best friend; Marcellus was like a father.

Now, he'd kill them both.

Despite how his ways disgusted me, I pitied who he was as a person. Maybe what Marcellus told you guys got me thinking. "What's troubling you?" I asked.

PH took his pipe out of his pocket. "Nothin' about this seems right. Normally, I can execute a showdown without any hesitation, but this time feels… strange."

"You said that Marcellus was close to you," I suggested.

He shook his head. "That's not it. I have a hunch and I'm usually never wrong." His heterochromatic eyes looked at me with care like I was an old friend. "If anything 'appens to me today, I want you to continue my work. Promise?"

I couldn't believe my ears. *Is PH admitting defeat? Death? What's going on?* "Sir, you are going to continue your work."

Before he could say anything, static and piercing rang in my head. *They… are… here*, a female voice said through the crackling. It was familiar, but I couldn't put my finger on it.

PH clenched the pipe between his teeth and left the tent.

I was about to follow suit when something nagged me. PH was unsettled and it unnerved me. I needed to be ready for *anything*. I went over to the weapon's rack. I snatched more magazines, a tranquilizer pistol, a dagger, a mask, and several grenades. I was able to shove them all into my uniform's pockets and backpack. *Can't be too prepared.* Ready, I rushed out after PH.

The cracked pavement was white with freshly fallen snow. Flakes fluttered down to the earth in brisk wind that nipped my skin. I pulled my jacket tighter around me. I've lost track of time and seasons; I wasn't sure if we were in a place of colder climate or if it was winter.

We trekked along ruined city streets until we reached a wide intersection. Waiting on the other side were two figures in all black.

"Glad to see you found it all right," PH called.

"Took us a while to find your message, but we did it," Marcellus replied. His salt and peppered hair brushed in the wind. His baseball cap was gone. He had nothing to hide; nothing to fear.

"I wanted to make it hard for ya," PH answered. "Like you've done to *me* all my life."

"You just couldn't handle the challenges," Sonny scoffed, taking a few steps closer.

That hit a nerve. It sliced PH's heart and the blood poured out. PH whipped his sword out with a *shing*. "Don't you tell me about challenges!" he snapped. His gloved hand gripped the sword's hilt so hard I thought it'd break. "You abandoned the mission, Mars. When things got difficult, you *bailed*. You *betrayed* me!" His heterochromatic eyes darted back and forth to the two ex-Xenophonians. "Both of you! You left me!"

His voice wasn't solely angry. Within the rage hid tones of sorrow. PH was distraught that the two people he trusted most left him behind.

"I was going to come back for you, PH," Marcellus said as kindly as he could. He put a foot forward. When PH flinched, Marcellus froze. "I *swear* to you."

"No, you lie," PH swore through gritted teeth. "All you cared about were some kids you never knew. Kids you were never there for. What use are you to them anyway, huh?"

Marcellus paused. He let out a deep breath. "PH, please don't make us do this. There is another way."

PH's lips were sealed tight. He didn't grace him with an answer.

A cold moment passed then Marcellus stated, "We are sorry." He looked up at PH kindly with his gray eyes, "*I* am sorry."

"IT'S TOO LATE!" PH screamed; his voice cracked. "Now you both will pay for your betrayal of the Order... and ME!" He raised his arm over his head and charged. He knew they wouldn't pull a gun. The two leapt to either side, letting PH slide between them. He spun around; his green scarf whipped behind him. His expression transformed from rage to surprise in an instant. He gasped. Something changed.

And it wasn't good.

I didn't heed the sign fast enough. I looked over my shoulder to see a hunk of metal charging at me. The wind escaped my lungs as cold arms crashed into my chest and wrapped around my body. I became light headed and wanted to drift into sleep, but I held on, figuratively and literally.

I clenched my eyes shut until the brisk wind wasn't stabbing my back. I cracked open an eyelid to find myself miles away. I lay in an open space formerly known as the Kremlin. I wriggled but couldn't get free. Cold metal pressed against my back. Out of the corner of my eye, I saw the white curls of Axel the Bionic.

"*¿Qué tal?*" he said with a smirk. "Play along, please. I won't hurt you." He held up coarse rope.

Saying nothing, I nodded. The metal teen yanked me to my feet. He stripped me of my weapons. He looked at two of my guns and shoved them down the back of my pants. "Protection only," he whispered. With a quiet apology, the Bionic tied me tight and shoved me down to the concrete. I heard his metal feet clanking away.

Carefully, I looked around. I didn't dare move. I was unaware of your plan, Shannon.

Shannon...

I saw you.

Behind a pillar stood a soldier in all black with a glowing mask and head covering. Another was with you. Someone much taller with a distinguishable feminine figure.

Aymie.

One by one, I picked out several members. Friends I hadn't seen in what seemed like ages.

Nic.

Myles.

Johanna.

Mark.

Blake.

Wait... no. I realized and my heart dropped. *Blake is here. He shouldn't be here.* How could you have exposed him like that?

In the distance was shouting followed by several gunshots. Running footsteps echoed off the broken buildings.

As they approached, you—Shannon—came to my side. You said nothing, but your presence was comforting.

And yet, it filled me with dread.

PH barreled into the clearing. His scarf was gone and his freckled face was splattered with blood. He skidded to a halt when he saw you in front of me. "Detective," he snarled. "We meet again."

"Let's make this the last time," Detective growled.

He slipped his sword back in its sheath and charged with no preparation. I thought you were going to duel like the last encounter, but I was surprised. PH sidestepped and tripped you. He was coming to save me.

"Wolf, we don't 'ave much time," he whispered as he helped me up.

There was the hum of rockets. Axel flew forward, knocking PH to the ground. The Titan tumbled and lay face up. Nic ran out of hiding to grab him. PH felt the vibration of his footsteps and leapt to his feet. He dodged Nic's long arms and looked to me for help.

I needed to play my part.

I struggled to stand and shimmied out of the ropes PH loosened. I reached down my pants and tore out one of the weapon's Axel left me.

Gripping a pistol, I whispered, "I'm sorry, Nic." I aimed at the Beast's shoulder and fired. It struck its mark and Nic wailed in agony. *Hope your Mutant genes heal you fast.*

PH dove under Nic and ran towards me.

You wouldn't let him. All the Officers emerged from hiding and rushed to encircle us; their weapons fired at our feet. Debris flew into our faces. We were blind. We were stuck. I held my glasses so they wouldn't get damaged; not caring about the cuts and bruises on the rest of my body.

The firing ceased, the dust settled, and the two of us were surrounded by Marcellus, Axel, and the eight RRPR Officers.

No...

Blake was there, too. He stood beside you, Shannon. His bright blue eyes shone in the daylight. White hair poked out of his beanie. Only four wore a head covering: you, Aymie, Mark, and Blake, but Blake's dressing was sloppy. He forgot his goggles and his hair could be seen.

Marcellus gripped his handgun tighter. "Surrender, PH," he commanded. "Come quietly and this can all be over."

PH kept his eyes to the ground. He said nothing, but was nervous. He tapped his foot anxiously.

I listened again. It wasn't anxiety.

PH's mouth turned upward ever so slightly.

KABOOOOOM. The building before us was blown to bits, causing the Officers to stagger. My ears rang and my head spun. I struggled to watch Axel fly into the air to see what happened. He was no higher than six-feet when he started convulsing. The lights in his armor turned on and off like power during a thunderstorm. His thrusters spat fire and smoke. Suddenly, he stopped moving.

As he fell to the ground, Nic went to catch him, but a strong shadowy figure ran through the smoke, smashing into him. Nic was knocked over and Axel fell to the ground with a crack.

I looked over to see a familiar Ares member pushing himself to his feet.

"Goliath," I gasped.

He didn't look back, but charged the Mutant-Gorilla again who gripped his bleeding shoulder.

I turned to see Marcellus and the Officers of RRPR fighting for their lives. They scattered. Most hid behind crates and pieces of buildings. Somehow, I was behind a line of Xenophonians; their guns hot. Shots flew like an angry swarm of bees protecting a nest.

Sting... I thought.

I heard a familiar cackle that chilled me to the bone more than the snow on the ground. I turned to see the Spanish Titan hovering over the unconscious Bionic. "Finally, I have my prize," she hissed. "I lost my first trophy, but you'll make an even better one." I watched as she and a familiar Hermes member lift the metal teen onto the back of a truck.

"Leprechaun?" I said, sounding almost disappointed.

He was quiet, but Sting commented, "Surprised to see us? Don't be. You should have known. I wasn't about to let anything happen to you." She winked and jumped on the back of the truck.

Leprechaun patted the side and it drove off with one of the Bionics Sting wanted so desperately.

"Snap out of it, Wolf," Leprechaun ordered through gritted teeth. I stopped my staring. "You have bigger problems." I turned to see that PH halted the fire that pushed RRPR back. Goliath managed to inject Nic with something, causing him to crash to the ground. Blood dripped from the shoulder I shot.

To my relief, he was snoring. *Please don't bleed to death...*

"Ya know what I want!" PH declared, taking a step towards the hiding Officers. "Hand 'im over!"

There was a distant murmuring. A few painful moments passed before a pale hand shot up. The murmurings became angry whispers. "If I obey, will you let the others live?" a nervous voice called out.

PH paused and answered, "Only for the moment."

"You must send the Ares members away," the voice demanded.

PH growled. "You're demandin' too much."

"That or death," the voice stated.

With a sigh, PH dismissed the Ares members—Goliath included—with a flick of his wrist. "They're gone. Only Hermes with me now."

A man stood up, raising his arms. Slowly, he removed his mask, revealing a head of white hair.

Blake.

The Officer had his hands behind his head. He shook with every step. He didn't know what he was doing, but he knew he had to do it. He knew it was the only way.

He dreamt it.

PH aimed his gun and motioned for Leprechaun to get restraints. He handcuffed Blake and ordered another Hermes member to take him away. The Officer was shoved into the back of a truck.

PH turned his back and patted the side of the vehicle to take off. While the Titan was distracted for that split second, a woman cried, jumped up, and ran.

PH quickly turned and fired.

The female figure—Aymie—went down, screaming in agony and clutching her leg. Mark (I assumed) rushed out of the debris to his sister's side. The truck carrying Blake drove away.

The Order had the Weapon.

When Mark was in view, PH raised his gun to shoot again. In an instant, Detective jumped out of hiding and shoved the gun out of his hand. Before you, Shannon, had time to react, PH threw a left hook to your temple, causing you to go crashing to the ground. Bending over, he grabbed you by the back of the head and pulled a knife out of his boot. PH pressed it up against your throat and—

"PIETRO HOLLINGER!"

Someone screamed... no, someone scolded. This person's voice echoed in everyone's ears. The name flew through the air like an arrow towards a target. This one hit the bullseye.

PH froze. The knife hovered above a conscious Detective's throat. The heterochromatic eyes of the Titan shook. His knees wobbled; his hands trembled. Sweat dripped down his forehead.

PH looked over at me. No, he was looking behind me.

I turned.

It was Leprechaun.

"Put that knife down, *now, Pietro*," he ordered.

For some reason, PH obeyed. He threw the knife and you, Shannon, to the ground. Immediately, you jumped to your feet and tore off your metal mask and head covering. Your curly brown hair flowed in the cold wind. Confusion and horror spread across your freckled face as you looked at PH then at Leprechaun then back again. Tears struck the snow beneath your boots.

PH saw your face for the first time. Gasping, he took a step back. The curls, the freckles, the eyes. He didn't know whose face he was seeing. Was it a reflection? A trick? A hologram?

No, a Hollinger.

"Who are you?" he whispered. He turned to Leprechaun. "Who are you?!" he repeated.

Leprechaun smiled; his own freckles danced on his cheeks. His lips parted, but he didn't speak.

He sang.

"*Codladh, mo ghra.*"

"No," PH cried. His eyes widened and his face fell. Those first three words stabbed his heart.

"*Fiú nuair a théann i.*"

"I order you to cease!" PH commanded, staggering backwards as Leprechaun stepped forward. Another stab.

"*Tá mé fos an ceann.*"

"Stop it!" PH cried, jamming his palms into his ears. Struck again.

"*Chun grá agat mar sin.*"

"ENOUGH!" he screamed, sinking to the ground. The final blade pierced through. Four invisible knives impaled his heart and distant memories poured out. Memories PH didn't know he had.

Leprechaun finished the final verse to the Gaelic lullaby. The Lullaby that was taught to the bartender's daughters. That was taught to Shane. That was taught to those he loved most.

His family.

"Pietro," Mr. Quinn Hollinger said softly. He turned to you, Shannon. His eyes sparkled. "My darling, Shannon. I missed you dearly."

Your eyes welled up with tears. You were about to embrace your father when PH sprang to his feet. He whipped out his pistol and—

A shot rang out, but it wasn't an Officer's.

It was mine.

I found myself gripping the tranquil gun: the second weapon Axel let me hold on to. I looked down its barrel to see PH staring at me with disappointment and sadness. His heterochromatic eyes welled up with tears.

He was betrayed, again.

The Titan dropped to his knees and fell on his face.

I glanced at Leprechaun/Quinn Hollinger then at you, Shannon. I looked upon your real face for the first time in seven years. Your expression was blank. You are feeling nothing. You don't understand.

Leprechaun/Quinn turned to me. "You need to get back now, Wolf," he declared. "This is the advantage I promised you. Seize it."

I looked at him and then at Marcellus… who was now at Quinn's side. The two nodded.

I had no words. I looked one last time at you and the Officers at RRPR. Frankly, none of you had anything to say either.

I spun on my heel and ran back to my tent.

Inside, I threw my jacket to the floor. My chest heaved; my head spun. *What advantage?... PH is Pietro?... Why didn't Leprechaun tell me?... Were Marcellus and Leprechaun in contact all along?... We have Blake and Axel. How did that happen? No one told me anything...*

My heart dropped. *I betrayed PH. My best friend.*

I sank to the floor, digging my nails into my skull. The lies, the confusion, the sorrow. Wolf hurt. Joshua hurt. I am two men in one body. Two men with different feelings, likes, dislikes, purposes.

And both were thrown into despair.

Tears dripped down my tan nose and cleaned my muddy pants. I took several deep breaths, trying to calm down. Somehow, it was working. My muscles relaxed. My mind was drifting. All I wanted to do was sleep.

But it wasn't my own doing. Amidst my screaming mind, I heard a hissing. The sleeping gas filled my nostrils. It was time to go back to New Greece.

Both Wolf and Joshua succumbed and we slipped into unconsciousness.

Joshua's final thought: *I must save Axel and Blake.*

Wolf's: *I must fulfill PH's promise.*

I'm sorry, Shannon. I have no words. I pray Aymie and Nic recover from their wounds. I pray you all heal mentally.

Also, Shannon, please, help PH—Pietro. Help your brother—if you accept him to become so. There is good in him. Convince him. Let him know that I knew that.

Let him know that… Joshua *and* Wolf are his friend.

With safety and secrecy,

Joshua Wolfrum

Joshua Wolfrum
Titan of the Russian Pandemonium

LETTER 30

Shannon: VIII

Joshua,

The devil is a thief on the prowl. Whatever good that's given, two times is ripped away.

Please offer us comfort with Axel and Blake. We received information that might help you, too.

I stood in the conference room, staring at the figures conversing before me. My eyes were focused, but my mind was distant. I couldn't believe my father was back. I couldn't believe he was a part of the Order of Xenophon and was now conversing with my would-be father-in-law, Marcellus. They spoke in Latin while Virginia Michaelson discussed the matter of Axel and Blake's capture with the other RRPR Officers.

I should've been up there trying to console Aymie and the others, but I was weak. They couldn't see me like that.

But saying nothing made it worse.

Aymie's gray eyes narrowed, glaring at me. Her bandaged leg was red with fresh blood. Her pale cheeks were damp with tears. Her pain was caused by a Hollinger.

No, *Hollingers*. She blamed me just as much as Pietro.

Pietro... My heart thumped every time I heard the word. The big brother I've been searching for. The one that caused many sleepless nights and sorrowful days. The one I desperately sought for was the *monster* I hated all along.

It made me sick.

I shut my eyes as my memory flashed back to the first meeting of PH.

The day he disabled Rachel. My little sister—his little sister. He slaughtered so many and wasn't afraid of killing his own.

My heart raced, my breathing quickened, my chest burned, my lungs ached. I wanted to sleep...

"Shannon, darling?"

My eyes popped open to see my father's freckled face staring back at me. Looking closely, nothing had changed. A few wrinkles, a fuller beard, but still the same soul.

Then why did I feel nothing?

"Yes, dad?" I replied mechanically. My breathing steadied for the time being.

He noted the tone, but said nothing about it. "It is time to go see him."

My stomach churned, but I nodded. I followed my father, Marcellus, and Sonny out to see my brother. Silently, we made our way to the observation units.

The rusty door slid open and the four of us went in to see our two Xenophonians. Sinatra/Shane's head popped up and a grin spread across his bearded face. I've been meaning to shave it and trim his long hair.

"Hey, you guys are back!" Sinatra/Shane's chains rattled as he pointed and added, "PH said you wouldn't come. He also said I wasn't fixable and I'll die here, but I don't want to talk about that."

PH was silent. His arms were outstretched and chained against the wall perpendicular to Sinatra. We stripped him of his beloved trench coat and scarf, leaving him in nothing but combat pants. His chest and arms were inked with tattoos. Markings of his killings and achievements in OX. His curly hair was unkempt and his face, dirty. The scuffs on his freckled cheeks reminded me of my little sisters' after they played outside...

"Of course, we'd be back," Marcellus smiled. "How could I stay away from my son for so long?" He finally visited Sinatra/Shane after a previous mission. Shane was responsive, but confused. He still didn't understand.

"Nor I mine?" my father added.

PH spat at our feet. "You're not my dad, Mick," he growled.

My dad didn't flinch. "Pietro, if I wasn't then why are you here?"

"Honestly, I don't know why I'm 'ere. Why 'aven't you killed me already, *Leprechaun*?"

Dad shook his head. "If you're not going to accept who you are, then at least accept that you're a hostage."

"Wait, then what am I?" Sinatra/Shane asked, confused.

"You're just a pest," Sonny retorted with a hint of sarcasm.

"Enough," PH snarled. "What do you want to know?"

"Everything," my father answered. "From the beginning of your life until now. Fill in the blanks for us."

PH dropped his ear to his shoulder. "Why would I do that? Anything in it for me?"

Marcellus stepped forward. "A chance at a better life," he told him. "I know you won't help us for my sake. Do it for your own."

PH laughed. "Why would you ever think I would do it for *you*?! From what I've been hearing from this one," he jerked his head towards Shane, "you lost your own kids so you kidnapped another one to make up for it."

"I regret the pain I caused the Hollinger family, believe me," Marcellus stated—more to my dad and me than PH. "But I raised you with purpose. Don't tell me you've forgotten."

"You. Abandoned. ME!" PH roared, jumping to his feet. "I will tell you NOTHING!" He tried to lunge, but the chains retracted in the walls, pulling him back. His head hit the concrete with a crack, causing everyone to wince. He sank to the ground, ignoring his pain.

Sonny squatted, looking PH in the face. "PH, you don't have to listen to them," he stated. "You know what the Order did to us." Sonny rubbed his side where his own tattoos hid beneath his shirt. "You said you wanted to avenge the friends we lost. You swore with me to get *revenge* on the suffering they have caused us."

PH breathed heavily, sweat dripping off his freckled cheeks. "You abandoned me, too," he growled. "You betrayed me." His heterochromatic eyes darted around. "You all did. Now," he gritted his teeth, "my only mate turned against me." He squeezed his eyes shut and hugged his knees.

The room fell silent as PH choked back tears.

I looked at the young man on the floor. The door of my emotions opened a crack. I wasn't going to accept him as my brother. I wasn't going to accept him as my ally.

I was first going to accept him as a human being.

I knelt down and looked to Sonny who nodded and backed away. "Pietro," I whispered. "I feel it's only fair I show you something." I pulled a tablet out of my backpack. Powering it up, I decoded a message I received.

The last letter you sent, Joshua.

"I want you to read this, and maybe you'll understand," I said softly.

He took the tablet in his hands and placed it in his lap. PH quickly scanned the pages, but every word was processed. I watched his expression change. It softened, hardened, and blanked in a matter of minutes. He didn't know what to believe.

Gently, he returned the device. "Put me in my own cell," he whispered. "Please. Put me there and *leave me*."

I slipped the tablet back in my bag. It didn't fit. It got caught on something. I reached in and felt leather. My eyes widened. *I almost forgot...*

"Wolf wants us to treat you well," Sonny interrupted. "He wants us to believe there is still good in you. However, if you don't cooperate in three days time, we may have to break our promise."

PH stood up weakly. With a glare as cold as ice, he spat, "Wouldn't be the first time."

Saying nothing else, Sonny, Marcellus, and my dad unchained PH and escorted him into his new holding chambers.

"Bye, boss!" Sinatra called out as the doors shut. It was just he and me in that cold cell. "He seems rather cranky today."

"I suppose so," I muttered.

Sinatra sighed. "Yeah... so what are we doing today? More questions?"

I looked at my fiancé. He was hairy and unkempt. Mark let him shower today, thankfully, but refuses to do anything about his hair. "How about a haircut?" I asked.

He happily consented. I fetched the tools for the job and returned, kneeling before him. As I picked up the scissors, he genuinely asked, "You're not gonna stab me, are you?"

"Why would I do that?" I cut a long lock of hair.

"I don't know," he confessed. He paused and added, "I feel like you hate me."

I froze as I snipped. "What makes you say that?"

"You always look at me like you're depressed or going to cry. I may not remember or know much, but I know that look in your eyes." He sighed. "There's something about you, Detective. I don't know what it is."

I said nothing, but continued my work in silence. I trimmed his hair and styled it. I did my best to make it the way Shane likes it. Grabbing the razor, I was ready to tackle the beard.

Sinatra stared at the humming blades with wide eyes like a child. "That's not going to hurt, is it?"

I couldn't help but smile. "Of course not."

His face lit up. "You... you smiled."

"I guess I did," I replied.

A grin spread across his face as I gently pressed the razor to his cheek. "Stop smiling or it might hurt," I warned.

"I can't help it, I'm sorry," he laughed. "I don't know why that made me so happy."

Gently, I shaved the thick brown beard off of his face. The hairs fell into the towel I laid across his lap. When I finished, I averted my gaze. I placed the razor down gently and moved the towel away. I took a quiet breath and looked up.

Shane was staring back at me.

A bright smile across his face. Familiar emerald eyes shone with love and care.

SHANNON: VIII

My eyes burned and my stomach tied in knots. The man before me was my fiancé. I felt that Sinatra was gone. It was Shane. It *had* to be Shane.

"Detective," he started, "I need you to know something."

"I need to know something first," I interrupted. I reached into my bag and pulled out a leather wallet. Sinatra looked at it with wide eyes. "I need to know, if you remember," I whispered. Gently, I opened it and wrapped my fingers around a necklace inside. I lifted it out and dangled it in front of his face. The celtic key glistened in the cell lights. Reaching behind my neck, I lifted up the dog tag he had given me when he asked for my hand in marriage.

"Shane Thomas Hodgins," I began, rubbing the illuminated *H* on the dog tag, "do you remember your fiancée, Shannon Veronica Hollinger?"

His eyes stared, his lips parted, but his expression was blank. So blank that he didn't move. He didn't speak. He didn't even blink. He was so still that one touch would knock him over.

PH claimed he wasn't fixable… Sonny was afraid that his memories would kill him.

No. I wasn't going to believe that.

While he was in this state, I slipped the necklace over his head, letting my Celtic knot key dangle around his neck. I rubbed it between my fingers and remembered the night I gave it to him.

I thought about it all. I thought about the time I was selfish. The time I was prideful and left him because I felt like I had to fix Mark's problems. Shane was always there for me… well, he always wanted to be.

I just never let him.

Tears streamed down my face as Shane's frozen expression stared ahead. He wasn't looking at me anymore. His eyes were distant. His face was relaxing. The color was draining from his cheeks.

He was fading.

No, no, no, no. I pressed my forehead against his. "Shane," I whispered. "Please, please come back to me." No response. "Please, wake up." I rested my hand over his heart.

One…

two…

No third beat.

"No, no, no," I cried. "Shane, please wake up. Please, please, please." He wasn't listening. I felt his body losing its temperature. "No, this *cannot* happen." I placed my nose beside his, resting my face on his cheeks. "I'm here now. I'm not going to leave you again."

His body dropped another degree.

"Shane." Tears dripped down my face and onto his. He hates water, and yet he'd let me cry on him.

He'd do anything for me.

"Shane, I'm sorry. I'm sorry. I'm sorry," I sobbed. I clutched his chest and pressed my face hard against his.

He was going cold.

I didn't know what to do. Time was running out. My patience was going; something I always tested Shane for...

"I wouldn't even kiss you because I said I liked to test you. How stupid and selfish am I?" I cried through gritted teeth. "You did so much for me, and I gave you practically *nothing* in return." Closing my eyes, I leaned in closer with my hand still firmly over Shane's heart.

I kissed my fiancé's dead body.

Pulling my lips away, I rested my forehead against his. "No, no, please." I pecked his cheeks with kisses, hoping they'd strike a nerve. Wake him up. Something.

My heart stopped and my gut twisted. I clutched his shirt and smacked my hand against his chest. I screamed, praying to God for him to wake up.

There was a burning in my chest, and a slight sensation under my palm. I tried to calm my breathing, wondering if the feeling was all in my head. I held my breath and pushed my fingers against his chest. I felt it. The slightest thump. I pressed my palm harder. There were rapid beats.

He was still alive and knew who I was.

"Shane, wake up!" I shook his shoulders. His body was still cold. I peeled off my little jacket and laid it across his lap, hoping to warm him up. "C'mon, Shane."

He wasn't coming to.

I stood up and announced, "I need a bigger shock." I tried signaling Alison, but it was no use. She turned off all communications when Axel was captured...

Shane is out of time.

I ran into the observation room and looked around for something. A tazer, a fork and an outlet, anything. I scanned the control panel to see a thin metal cylinder in a cup of pens. It didn't belong there; it belonged to Aaron's best friend, Cecil.

It was his weapon.

Cecil presented it to the Officers before we invaded the Isles. Sonny was impressed by it. The Geek could control a blue "fireball": a powerful charge of electricity. Aaron kept it in remembrance and normally carried it with him everywhere. By the grace of God, he forgot it among the pens.

Snatching it, I returned to Shane. "Scientists have said electricity improves memory," I said aloud, trying to convince myself. "It also shocks the heart back to life." I twisted the cap. It warmed up with a purr. I pressed my thumb and forefinger to it gently. I took a step back and aimed at Shane.

His eyes were glassy. "God, let this work," I prayed and activated the machine.

The metal grew hot and a blue light emanated like a flashlight. Electricity cracked and shot out the end like lightning. It crawled through the air until it made contact with Shane's chest, blue sparks flying.

In an instant, Shane's pupils dilated, his body shook, his mouth opened and he screamed, "CERCOPES!" He slumped back against the wall and breathed heavily. "Cercopes, Shannon. Cercopes."

I let out the breath that was caught in my lungs. It was stinging, painful, and unbearable, but it didn't matter. Mouth agape, I whispered, "You said my name."

He panted, "Shannon... no time... Cercopes."

Shane was back.

He was back. God returned him to me.

Filled with joy, I laughed, cried, and flung my arms around Shane's neck. "I'm so sorry, I'm so sorry," I said through sobs. The poison scratched at the inside of my lungs.

It took Shane a second to realize what happened. I felt him wrap his arms around my small shaking body and pull me close. "Shannon," he whispered. "I've missed you."

I pressed my wet face against his. "I missed you too." When I realized I was dampening his face with my tears, I pulled away and immediately apologized again.

He chuckled softly. Leaning forward, he pressed his face against me, letting the tears fall over his nose. "When I'm with you, I'm not afraid of anything." He pressed his wet yet warm lips against mine. I cupped his face with my hands. I felt a shock, but I didn't care. It meant life.

I pulled away and he brought me close to his chest. I lay in his embrace for a while, softly sobbing. The pain in my lungs stirred from getting hysterical, but I didn't care. If Shane isn't afraid of anything when we're together, neither am I.

When I calmed down and the poison in my lungs subsided, Shane repeated, "Shannon, you know I love you, but we both know the war isn't over and we're losing time. I learned something I shouldn't have. Something Sting slipped up about." He carefully pushed me away. His green eyes looked into mine with all seriousness. "You need to write your letter to Joshua, right now. Tell him, Cercopes."

So, I did.

Shane sat with me as I wrote, and he needs you to add Cercopes to your list.

This could be leverage or a hint at something. Get close to Sting and find out.

Report your findings on Blake, Axel, and Cercopes.
Godspeed and goodwill,

Shannon Hollinger
Royal Strategist of RRPR

LETTER 31

Joshua: XVI

Shannon and Yared,

It brings me joy to hear Shane is back. When he was Sinatra, I always felt like he knew something more from Sting as if they gossiped like school girls. Glad to see the pain wasn't for naught.

I awoke in my Titan quarters the morning after receiving your letter. I slid off my bed and wandered down the stairs to the plaza of New Greece. No one was around. I heard no orders; no voices in my head. I wasn't sure what to do.

Cercopes.

I needed to learn what that meant. Snapping back to reality, I headed into the Hermes Temple. I made my way to the computer and sat down in the marble chair. I typed the word *CHALLENGER* and the screens lit up.

As I searched, I heard a rustling behind me. Looking over my shoulder, I saw no one there. *Must be Munazam,* I assumed and resumed my work. Then, I heard a scampering followed by a faint footfall.

"There you are, *mi amor*," a sweet raspy voice called.

My heart sank to my stomach. Out of the corner of my eye I saw Sting with the monkey Diego sitting at her feet.

The creature looked at me quizzically. Screeching, he hopped up onto the console and tapped some buttons that closed out my search.

"Hey!" I shoved him off. He growled at my touch.

"Oh, don't worry, Wolf, he won't break anything," Sting said, picking up the monkey. It cooed as she pet its fluffy head.

I sighed. "I'm sorry. I've been under some pressure."

She bit her lip. "I'm sorry about PH." Her tone was sincere. "He's strong, though. He'll pull through."

Slumping back into my chair, I sighed, "I know, it's just…" I rubbed my hand across my face. "He knew something would happen."

Sting rubbed my arm gently with her calloused hands. Butterflies fluttered in my gut. "Not all is lost," she said. "We have an advantage. They took one, we have two." She bent over, looking intently at me with her caramel eyes. "They've lost so much more. Now, let's take the rest." Grabbing my hand, she pulled me to my feet and didn't let go until we were standing outside the Temple of Zeus. Diego leapt out of Sting's arms and climbed up onto my shoulder.

She giggled at the monkey. I never heard her laugh before… "I feel he abandoned Solomon for you," she beamed then headed inside.

I pondered that. "Why have you?" I asked the creature.

Diego squeaked and slapped my lips. Shutting me up? Maybe. Being an annoying monkey? More likely.

Entering the temple, I saw two figures sprawled across the floor around the bowl of fire. They were unconscious and breathing heavily.

Oh no…

Axel the Bionic was wrapped in tight chains that bent his biomechatronic body. The blue lights in his armor flickered and creaked like a ship suffering the tension of a storm. Blake was naked and shivering. His white hair shone in the marble's reflection and his pale skin was almost translucent. Slender arms wrapped around his quaking body, trying to keep itself warm.

Sitting down on my throne, I tried not to stare. Diego hopped off my shoulder to take a closer look at the prisoners. He gently tapped the face of Blake, but the white haired man didn't wake. The monkey shuffled to the Bionic. Diego gently rubbed Axel's cheeks. Slowly, the cyborg's eyes fluttered open. His pupils dilated and contracted frantically as if they were damaged.

My heart broke at their condition.

But they were breathing. That's what mattered.

Smoke rose from the three statues of the Moirai. The three female figures stepped through, attending the meeting in person.

Diego screeched and ran back to me, hopping up on my shoulder.

The Moirai Clotho (Arata) raised her arms and proclaimed, "Praise to Zeus, honor to Xenophon! Today is the day to rejoice. The man with the Gift of Apollo dropped to his knees. The Man of Metal and Fire has fallen from the sky, destroying all he left behind."

The Titans roared and cheered. I joined them.

"While we have our victory," Moirai Lachesis (Emel) stated, "we *still* have sacrificed. PH was betrayed by a spy within his ranks. However, the enemy is stupid enough to keep him alive. Our brother will return to us soon with greater knowledge and strength." She turned to me. "Wolf, please come forward."

Obediently, I went with Diego clinging to my back. "Yes, ma'am?"

Emel smiled. "You did all you could to help PH. You were always at his side and never let him down. You've pleased him, us, and Zeus." She held her hand out and stepped to the side. Emerging from the shadows was a man.

Zeus.

My jaw dropped as I laid eyes on him for the first time. He was a proper man with a tall stature and strong build. The flames of the fire reflected off his red suit and black tie. His tan face was one no one could ever forget.

"Wolf," he greeted. His voice rang with authority. "I've watched you for many years. Your strength and will has impressed me and the Moirai. I wanted to personally thank you for all you have sacrificed." Determination and gratification shone in his eyes.

I didn't know what to say. I bowed. "Sir, it is an honor—"

"Save your words," he interrupted. "There is much to be done." I looked up to see him waving at the Titans behind me.

Turning, I watched half of them approach Blake and Axel. They violently jerked Blake to his feet and dragged away. Where? I wasn't sure. They prodded Axel with a weapon, sending a shock that jolted him to consciousness. The Bionic screamed and started swearing in Spanish. Sting retorted and kicked him in the side.

"You are going to be in charge of this one," Zeus informed. "Once his will is reworked, he will be your subordinate. For now, you must plan." He bid me to go with him.

Taking a deep breath, I followed Zeus through a door within his statue.

We walked in silence down a dark corridor. The air smelled so putrid; I almost threw up. Holding my breath, I followed quietly, feeling Diego's tiny heartbeat against my shoulder like gentle taps.

My eyes strained as the room became pitch black. I struggled to stay upright as our pathway declined. Going down, I heard strange noises bounce off the walls. Hissing, grunting, groaning, crying.

Cercopes.

The word slipped back into my consciousness. *Is that what I'm going to see?*

I didn't realize Zeus stopped until I bumped into him. Blood rushed to my face. *You're dead, Joshua.* "My lord, please forgive me," I begged frantically.

Surprisingly, he laughed and my anxiety calmed. "Wolf, no apology is necessary. Without a light, no one can see." I watched a match flicker to life before me. It illuminated Zeus' face. Creases formed by his eyes from a menacing smile. "Without *our* light, the world cannot live." He turned and dropped the match.

Flames roared high before me. Red light raced out from the center and to the walls, lighting a trail of coal. The fire spread across the perimeter and kindled the torches and pits along the path.

As the room lit up, the noises grew louder and louder until they pierced my ears. I looked around to see hundreds of cell doors lining the walls. Rows and columns of prisoners screaming bloody murder... but their screams were unfamiliar. Peering closer, my face paled at what I saw.

Inside these cages were Mutants. Thousands of Mutants. Their animal eyes glowed in the dark and stared at me with malice. They screamed, thrashed, bit, and tore at each other and the cell doors before them.

This isn't possible... only Carl Mallory had the power to create the Mutants. What are these?

Zeus thrust his arms out. "These are the bringers of light," he announced. "Those impurities still roaming our world will be snuffed out and rekindled by the fires of Hades. This is the final stage of the Cleanse. The start to the Annex. These will help make our world pure again." He turned to me. The malevolence in his eyes sparked in the firelight. "This is the final Unleashing."

They're going to send Mutants after everyone... These creatures are the epitome of the Order of Xenophon. They are pure Chaos. They have no rhyme, no reason, no order, no direction. They are monsters, beasts, demons.

And I had to be proud.

"Sir, what are they?" I asked in awe.

"Their creator called them Mutants. I call them the Children of Hades."

Mallory did create them...

He pointed to a cage in front of us. "Notice the *arkoúda, nychterída,* and *alepoú?*"

I saw three Mutants. They were calm and different from the others. It was strange. What was more peculiar was they stared at me as if they knew me.

Looking closer, I realized I knew them, too.

The *arkoúda* was a chubby boy I knew a long time ago: Umbrella Dylan Cheatle from Wyght's Home for Young People. The one who was stolen in the raid and Spliced with a bear by Carl Mallory. This bear was old, tired, and worn. He had scratches and scars from many battles. He gripped the iron bars and panted.

The *nychterída* was the Royal Veteran Polymath that supervised Aymie: Adeline Zarra. Her beautiful face and slender arms were hideously transformed, matching that of a fruit bat. She was my age, but her wrinkles and beady eyes made her look older than fifty.

Finally, the *alepoú*. I'd recognize that creepy smile anywhere. Clive Foxwood. The one who took the animal of his own name. His orange and white tail wagged back and forth. His glowing eyes stared menacingly at me. I felt he wanted to betray me; tell Zeus who I was. But he refrained.

My heart raced as I stared upon their faces. The last time I saw these Mutants was five years ago when Carl Mallory came to RRPR's aid. *How did they fall into OX's possession?*

"These Children of Hades are traitors of their people," Zeus continued. "They were part of the Resistance, but we stole them from their homes. We changed them to be the heroes of Xenophon that they are today. These three have done more damage than all the other Children of Hades combined." He looked around. "But now the others will have their chance to prove themselves. With REM in our possession and his Gift of Apollo, we will be unstoppable." His eyes met mine. "I shall personally lead the Unleashing. I shall watch the Resistance as their flesh is torn and their souls crushed." Menace and evil spread across his face. "I am going to enjoy every moment of their fall. With you at my side, we will watch our traitors die." He put a firm hand on my shoulder. "We will watch when the world becomes pure again."

Out of fear, I nodded.

Zeus patted my back and walked me away from the Mutants. Away from the demons that will be unleashed upon the world.

"Wolf, first you will lead the Bionic," Zeus instructed after we exited the temple. "He will give us an advantage against the enemy. Even after REM gives us their location and their plan of attack, we'll need another way to weaken their defenses. The Resistance has one Bionic. She alone could take out our army with ease. He will be the one to stop her." We stopped and stood in the plaza. "You will ensure that the Bionic's mind gets reworked to do your bidding. This task is yours and yours alone." He leaned in. "Sting had her eye on these Bionics and I know she would do anything to get him to be hers," he whispered. "This is why we are leaving Arata out of this process. You are on your own with this." He stood up straight and cleared his throat. "Once we are given the location and the Bionic is yours, then we Unleash. After that, there is no going back."

Lowering my head, I thanked him for everything. Diego the Monkey squeaked and bowed as well.

Zeus smiled and pet its furry head. "I'm pleased that we allow this creature to live. Such a good, *Cercopes*."

I blinked. I thought I was slapped, but Zeus had uttered just one word. *Cercopes*. I didn't notice Zeus left me alone with the monkey until Diego patted my cheek. I wrapped my hands around the monkey's torso and held him out in front of me. He didn't protest. "What are you?" I asked.

He squeaked. His beady eyes confused.

I stifled a gasp. "You've *actually* been understanding me?"

He slapped his forehead and screeched.

I held him closer to my face. I smelled its foul breath. "Are you some sort of Mutant?"

Diego smiled.

My grip loosened and the monkey fell, landing on its feet. I was dumbfounded and confused. Shane swore that *Cercopes* was important. A reverse Mutant monkey shouldn't surprise me, but why was it special? Why was Diego so significant?

I felt a tugging on my pant leg as Diego cooed and pointed behind me. I turned to see Sting approaching.

"*Hola*, Wolf!" She slipped her arm through mine and bid me to walk with her. "What an honor, you going along with Zeus."

"Yeah, an honor," I said nonchalantly. My mind was all over the place. *Zeus, the Children of Hades, the Cercopes…*

She laughed. "I know you're probably in shock, but snap out of it. There's work to be done. But for now," she clutched my arm tighter, "let's take some time."

My face reddened. I felt her soft touch around my bicep. *No, this can't happen now. I need to stay focused*, I thought. There were too many things happening at once I couldn't possibly—

Avenge them.

I took a deep breath. I promised Shannon. I promised the Hodginses. I promised you all.

"You always know what's best, ma'am." I held her hand and squeezed it gently.

The start of her betrayal.

So, Yared, warn everyone. Zeus is a real dude and he has Mutants. Don't worry about Axel and Blake; they're okay for now. Axel more so. I'll keep him safe. I'll play Sting to find out where Blake is and why Diego being *Cercopes* is so important.

With safety and secrecy,

Joshua Wolfrum

Joshua Wolfrum
Titan of the Russian Pandemonium

LETTER 32

Yared: VIII

Joshua,

I have to say, I almost crapped my pants reading your letter. I wasn't the only one. I kept this from Shannon, but I had to tell someone.

"Where the bloody hell did he get all those Mutants?" Lucas fumed after I read it aloud.

"Carl Mallory," I growled. "He made the Order of Xenophon all their little monsters."

Ethan shook his head and clutched the stethoscope around his neck. "Who'd do such a thing? Who could perform that procedure so many times?"

"Mallory, apparently, but he must've had help," I replied.

Aaron was quiet. His blue eyes looked down as he cleaned his black glasses. Something was bugging him.

"You wanna speak up man or just clean that dust for the fiftieth time?" I snapped. I don't know why I was short with him.

He sighed. "We know the three Mutants Joshua saw were created before Mallory left the Mainland for the Isles."

"Probably most of them were. What's your point?" I spat.

Aaron glared. "If that's the case, Mark had a hand in creating those Mutants. He was gathering ingredients for more than Fallout. Fallout only provided the boys for experimentation, so," he paused, "where did the Mutants go?"

We were silent.

"Are you saying," Ethan began, "Mark knows who Mallory was working with for OX?"

Aaron nodded. "He has to. I think—"

"Mark knows Zeus," I finished. The quiet of the room hurt my ears like the screeches of the Mutants Mark helped create.

"If we can show him a picture or describe his appearance," Aaron continued, putting his glasses back on, "Mark may be able to identify him. Once we know his name, we can search for information."

"Mark deleted all OX's digital presence, remember?" Lucas put in.

"He deleted who they are now," Aaron replied, standing up straight. "He didn't delete who they once were."

I clapped my hands together. "Aight, man, let's do it. How do we get a picture of this dude? Joshua can't send photos with his letters despite his 'fancy' glasses."

Aaron thought for a moment. "Did you say Axel was in the room when Zeus appeared?"

"Yeah, but we have no way of contacting him," I added. "Otherwise all our problems would be solved."

"We may not be able to reach him, but we can get inside his head," Aaron explained. "We won't get the location or anything else of use, but we can use him as a security camera." Without another word, we followed the Geek out.

We made our way to the confinement chambers where Alison was waiting in the hallway. Her white hair was a mess and her gray electronic eyes were damp with tears. She stared through a door window, watching her Mutant sister sleep uncomfortably.

Sami was breaking. She still hadn't recovered after Donnie's episode. We aren't sure what he did to her.

Speaking of the little cretin, he was in the room behind Alison. I could hear his small fists banging on the wall and muffled screams which he did whenever he was awake.

"Alison," Aaron greeted.

His sister turned slightly, barely acknowledging her brother's presence.

"Alison, we need your help," Aaron said softly.

"There is nothing I can do," she choked. "I should've been the one to go with the Officers. Not Axel. And now," she lifted her Bionic hand, "he's gone, Donnie is going, and Sami is breaking, and I can't fix it."

"Axel wouldn't have had it any other way," Aaron told her. "He's strong. You know that. He loves you and wouldn't want you to cry for him." He put an arm around Alison. "Our sister is the same way. We have to keep fighting for their sake."

Alison took a shaky breath. "I know… I promised them."

"Then let's fulfill that promise," he whispered.

Closing her eyes, she sniffled, "All right. What do we need to do?"

"We need to access Axel's mind," the Geek explained. "What was the last thing he saw? I know we can reach him no matter how far away he is."

She slipped the drawstring bag with the Roman numeral *I* off her shoulder and slid out her electronic clipboard. Both were given to her by Keeper Cameron Allaway when we were made Commanders of our Isles. Powering it up, Alison searched through the short list of names: her Bionic Buddies. Finding Axel, she held her breath as she tapped it, and the rest of us gathered around.

There was nothing. The screen was blank. Alison exited the program and returned. Still nothing.

"Anyway to access previous footage?" Aaron asked.

Alison scrubbed the bar at the top. Hours and hours of blackness. She continued to rewind until it started to glitch.

"Whoa, what's that?" Aaron exclaimed, grabbing his sister's organic hand.

Slowly, she moved forward. Pictures and images cut in and out. At first, all was white. Then we realized it was a marble ceiling. Axel was laying flat on his back.

"This is it," I told them. "This is when he and Blake were laying in the Temple of Zeus."

"What are we looking for?" Alison asked.

"I'll let you know when I see him," I said.

Alison's finger jerked along the screen, moving frame by frame. Then, an image startled us. Two beady black eyes and a white furry face stared into the screen.

"That's Diego the Monkey," I blurted. "Man, is he ugly."

"He woke Axel up," Ethan marveled.

With hope, Alison scrubbed a little more. The image cut in and out, but all we needed was one frame. We watched as three women emerged through smoke; the first one with her hands aloft.

"Almost there," I whispered.

We watched as a man in all black with a creature on his back stepped towards them. He had curly hair on the top of his head and wore black rimmed glasses.

"Joshua," Ethan recognized.

The image cut and jumped until I saw a flash of red. "Wait, go back!" I exclaimed.

Alison obeyed and after three tries, we found it. A man in a red suit stood in the middle of the frame.

Zeus.

"Are we sure this is him?" Alison asked, doubtfully.

"This is the guy Joshua described," I replied.

"I know, but what if he's just a decoy? A pawn," Alison stated.

I hadn't thought of that. *No, he can't be. We're so close.*

"I know how we can find out," Lucas stated as he snatched the clipboard from Alison. He ran to the door behind us and flung it open.

"Lucas, wait!" Alison called. We ran in after him.

Lucas cornered Donnie. His arm was across the boy's chest. Bug eyes stared him in the face. Donnie squirmed, screamed, and kicked but it was no use. Lucas fluttered his wings to keep adding pressure.

"Are you crazy?!" Ethan shouted.

"All right, Donnie, you're going to listen to me," Lucas demanded as the boy tried to bite his nose. "You have one chance to tell me truthfully who this is otherwise you'll never see him again."

The boy growled and made inhuman noises. Sweat dripped down his face. He was losing all sanity.

With one hand, Lucas turned the clipboard around and shoved the image in the boy's face. "Give us this man's name, *now!*"

Donnie tried not to look, but he saw something out of the corner of his eye. He gazed upon the image and relaxed as if its sight was a pleasant memory of his beloved farm. Something about the man gave him comfort.

"Master," Donnie whispered. His gray eyes widened and a smile was upon his lips.

Disturbed, Lucas jumped back. "Blimey. What did you say?"

"My lord," Donnie gasped. Regaining his senses, he jumped to his feet and tried to tackle the Dragonfly. "SEND ME BACK TO HIM! SEND ME BACK!" He clawed at Lucas' legs. Lucas took off to the sky, but Donnie grabbed his cape, trying to strangle him.

I ran forward and wrapped my arms tight around the boy.

He screamed bloody murder and tried biting my arms.

I felt a lean body crash into my back. Long arms wrapped around me, helping steady the thrashing Donnie. "Hold on, Yared!" Mark yelled. I watched as he stabbed a syringe into Donnie's neck. Mark pulled away and I clutched tighter.

Donnie writhed and screamed, "MASTER, MASTER, MASTER..." he started to fade, "master... master... ma...st..er." He fell silent.

Panting, I lay the boy gently down on the bed. "Thanks," I grumbled.

"What are you guys doing in here?" Mark demanded. He wiped the sweat from his forehead. "I thought I told you to stay away from him. Atropos could cut his thread if he keeps acting up like this."

"Sorry, Dad, but it was an emergency," Lucas explained. He went over to Mark, hiding the clipboard behind his back. "We'll only explain why if you can identify someone for us."

Mark was hesitant. "What is this about?"

"Everything," I stated.

Determination crossed Mark's face. "Okay, lay it on me."

With a deep breath, Lucas turned the clipboard around to show Mark. Taking it in his hands, the R&D Commander looked at it closely. His head cocked. He was thinking hard, but failed to find an answer. He closed his eyes and continued to search his memory.

Lucas fluttered his wings, trying to straighten them out.

Mark's eyes popped open as if the wings' soft crinkle was a scream in his ear. "I know this guy." He looked again. "He has a face I could *never* forget." He tapped the screen and looked around at us. "He was the buyer of Couch's concoction. Carl Mallory presented him to us when I was in Fallout." He scoffed. "This guy is Mr. Devin Page."

My jaw dropped. "The guy you stole ingredients for? The one who initially hired you and Mallory to create the Mutants for him?"

"Yes. Now he's part of the Order of Xenophon?" Mark asked, amazed.

"I think he always was," Lucas explained. "Who you are looking at, mate, is the one Joshua has been chasing for seven years."

Mark's blue eyes widened. His brain searched for words but found none.

"That's right," I chimed in. "This is Zeus. The leader of the Order of Xenophon."

A moment passed before it hit him. Mark's memories, crimes, lies, all of it rushed back to him like a river. He staggered and the clipboard slipped from his hands. I caught it before it crashed against the cold floor.

"I can't... no... why," meaningless words fell from his lips. He didn't know what to say.

"Mark, it doesn't matter that you helped him," I stated. "What matters more is that you know him."

Mark put a hand to his forehead. "There is something else you're not telling me."

I exhaled. "Yes. He has an army."

"Of what?"

The words wouldn't come out. My eyes looked to Lucas.

Mark understood. "When can we expect them?"

"Whenever Blake has a dream," I sighed. "They're going to force him to provide intel on our location and then use the Mutants to attack. They call it—"

"The Unleashing," Mark finished. "Are these Mutants sane? Do they have consciousness?"

"I think we'll have to reach out to someone for that information," I replied.

Mark nodded. "Let me brief Shannon and the others. Then we'll schedule a meeting to speak with Carl Mallory."

That's where we are now, Joshua. When we figure out more about the Mutant army from Mallory, we'll let you know.

Bravery and fidelity,

Yared Prinz

Yared Prinz
Seer Commander

LETTER 33

Joshua: XVII

Yared and Shannon,

I can't believe you know Zeus' identity. This whole situation makes my stomach churn. Before I throw up, I'm going to change the subject.

I went on a date.

Don't worry; nothing happened, but I learned a lot. I know how you can fix Donnie... along with some other things.

I sat on a bench in my corner of the hangar, tapping my foot frantically. To my left machines whirred and buzzed as they worked on Axel the Bionic. He was damaged and bent during his capture. Since he was now my possession, I ordered his repairs.

He sat upright with his organic arms chained to the chair. They removed the top part of his armor that enhanced his upper body and laid it across a work bench behind him. Robotic arms hung down from the ceiling to work on his Bionic legs. Axel kept his eyes shut as the sparks flew up and burned his bare skin. He hissed as his torso was peppered with hot fragments. Without his full armor, he was vulnerable.

Realizing his discomfort, I stood up to lay a shop towel across his bare chest and place work goggles over his gray mechanical eyes.

"*Gracias*," he said on an exhale.

"Don't mention it," I whispered. We were silent for a moment, hearing only the servos and welding of the machines. "How are you holding up?" I finally asked.

"I'm good, I'm good," he replied too quickly to be genuine. "I'm tougher than I look."

"I sure hope so." As I sat back down, I felt Axel's eyes follow me through the goggles. "You're going to help end this, I hope you know that."

He smirked. "Have a plan already?"

I managed a smile. "Of some sort. We need to find Blake before we do anything stupid."

"I'm at your command, Titan," he replied monotonously like a robot.

I laughed. "That's good. Do whatever you can to pretend I'm reworking your brain."

"Man, my brain was already messed with." He shook his head to move his curly bangs out of the way. I saw the scar left from the surgery that made him Bionic. "I don't need anything else put in there."

"I promise *no one* will touch you," I stated as I stood. "If someone else but me tries to work on you, fight back with everything you have. Say I'm your only Master and you'll only heed to me." I leaned over and whispered in his ear, "If you have to, use the magic words."

"Which are?"

"In the name of Xenophon."

Axel nodded and leaned back. "I won't forget that."

There was an ear piercing screech in my head. I winced for a moment.

Axel chuckled. "Getting a message?"

I rubbed my ear. "How'd you know?"

"I get them across my eyes," he grinned. "Freaks me out from time to time, too."

"I wish I got messages across my eyes." I tapped the side of my glasses. "That would mean you guys knew where I was."

"Whoa, wait, those glasses are like Optic Transmitters, right?" Axel asked, amazed.

I recalled from Alison's record log that their mechanical eyeballs were referred to as Optic Transmitters. It let them see messages, code, translate, and all sorts of things.

Exactly like my glasses.

"Yeah, they are," I replied, taking them off. "Honestly, it frightens me how much the Isles and WHYP were alike."

"Mr. Nik and Wally stole a lot from you guys—especially Powell Enterprises," Axel explained. "Our eyes must be Myles' design." A light bulb went off. "Dude, maybe I can send you messages through your glasses. Put them on."

I obeyed and waited. He stared into space then I received a message before my eyes: *Testing 1-2-3. Axel's really hun-ge-ry.*

I chuckled. "I'll get you something to eat." As I said it outloud, it typed my response and sent it back.

"Yes, this is awesome," the Bionic exclaimed. "I'll let you know if I hear, see, or learn anything."

"And I to you." I smiled. "I'll send an old friend, Solomon, in with some food for you. For now," I straightened my jacket, "I have to go on a date."

"I hope your date goes bad so betraying her will be more fun," Axel said with a wink.

I forced a smile. For some reason, I wasn't happy about that last part. Saying nothing else, I left the Bionic at the mercy of the repair machines.

I walked down the halls and first headed to the pub: Lucky's. Looking inside, I saw Solomon and Goliath sitting at the counter. Diego the Monkey was perched on his master's staff. A new bartender was chosen to replace Leprechaun/Quinn immediately. No questions asked.

"Goliath, Solomon," I greeted.

They smiled when they saw me and Diego chirped.

"There you are, sir," Goliath beamed. "We heard the news."

"There was a lot of news. What are you referring to?"

"*Love is strong as death, jealousy is fierce as the grave,*" Solomon smirked.

"It's nothing, Solomon," I assured. My face turned red. *I hope.*

Goliath took a swig of his Long Island Iced Tea. "You know you could always take the easy way out and spend time with the Eros members like she does."

"Pass." *Hard pass. Super hard pass.*

He shrugged. "Suit yourself." He took another sip. "Also heard you're in charge of the metal man. Nice job."

"Thank you, but it wasn't without a price," I replied, solemnly.

"PH will bounce back, you know that," Goliath stated.

"It still is troublesome." The buzzing noise in my head resounded again. I was going to be late. "Might I ask you both a favor?"

Goliath laughed. "You're our superior now; we do anything you say."

"Thank you," I said, genuinely. "Would you be able to keep an eye on my metal prisoner and bring him sustenance?"

The two nodded. "Anything you need, sir." Goliath winked.

Thanking them again, I turned to leave when I felt a body cling to my shoulder. Diego wanted to come with me again. I looked at Solomon who nodded. Something in his wrinkled face told me he wanted Diego to join.

Shane is convinced that Cercopes is important, but does Solomon know what it means?

I nodded and left Lucky's with the mystery of a monkey on my shoulder.

I met Sting by the plaza in New Greece. Her braided hair was clean and her uniform was spotless. She wore her combat jacket around her waist, revealing her Ares tattoos for the first time. Greek designs crawled up her toned arms and disappeared beneath a white shirt that hugged her beautifully curvy frame. The pristine marble reflected sparkles in her eyes.

My heart thumped when she caught my gaze. *Why does she look beautiful*, I wondered nervously as I approached her. Today was the day to demand answers. I couldn't be distracted.

But it was already too late.

"*Hola*, Wolf," she greeted with a smile. Diego chirped, and she added, "Hello to you too, Diego."

"You don't mind if he comes along?" I asked, petting the creature's fuzzy head.

"Not at all." She held out her hand.

I took it without hesitation, and we strolled around New Greece.

"This seems out of character for you," I confessed as we passed through the city's garden. The trees' pink leaves cast shadows over us as we walked. Flowers of all colors lined the marble path. Wolf wanted to pick one and give it to her, but Joshua refused.

"I'm tired of the Eros men," Sting replied with a shrug. "Fake. Lifeless. Always doing what I wanted when I wanted it. It became… meaningless." Her eyes caught mine. "You're different, Wolf. Your will is strong and you only do things because it suits *you*."

"How do you mean?"

"You don't do things because you have to," she explained, "you do things because you want to. I watch other Xenophonians and see their hesitation as they rush into battles. They don't want to fight, but they're forced. You? You do it because you *want* to. You believe in the mission. There is no hesitation in your step." We turned a corner in the garden. Sting ran her fingers along the green hedges as we walked. Diego hopped off my shoulder to mimic her. "That's why you ask questions," she continued. "You want to make sure whatever you're getting into suits you."

"Is that a bad thing?" I asked.

She shook her head. "I only wish I had the willpower to do that."

"You don't?"

She bit her lip. "I may act like the big, tough girl who shows no mercy which I totally am as an Ares Titan," she added quickly. "However, there are days where I don't want to be. I don't want to fight." Her tone softened again. "Some days, I don't want to kill, but I do it because it's my duty."

"That's what you should be doing, though," I said, squeezing her hand tighter. "You're the best example to your subordinates."

She managed a smile. "I hope you're right." Her happiness dissipated. "However, then why don't my subordinates respect me for who I am and not out of fear of what I might do to them? That's what I'm getting at."

She's jealous.

"You do things because you want to, not because you have to," Sting continued. "You ask questions to determine that. Now, your Russian subordinates have a higher respect," she rambled on and on.

I guess I'm a better actor than I thought, I realized as I listened to her babble.

But, she's right. Everything I do is out of the sheer will that I want to do it. I want to do it so that RRPR can succeed, nothing more.

The fact that I plan to betray everyone is what she was missing out on.

After a few minutes of nonsense, she sighed, "I'm sorry, Wolf. It's good to let it all out. I feel like Atropos is out to get me."

I was disturbed. "What makes you say that?"

"The way she's been looking at me lately." I felt her palm get clammy. "I sense my thread is running short. They cut ours too, you know."

I didn't want to think about it. "Why would your thread be short?"

"Because of my failure," she blurted and stopped midstep. Her voice shook and her hand slipped out of mine. "I led her to that boy and Detective in order that they might accept a peace treaty. That boy became her puppet and he still *failed* us," she spat. "I approached her with these ideas because I wanted to capture the Bionics. We managed to get one, but I had nothing to do with it. It was all PH's idea." She let out a long exhale. "Now my failure will cost me my life." She covered her face with her hands.

Gently, I wrapped my fingers around her palms and moved them away. I leaned my face closer to hers. Her caramel eyes watered; the tears glistened in the white light of the city. *She's scared.*

"Sting," I started, "I will help however I can to prevent your thread from being cut by Atropos." I stroked her chin with my thumb. "Just tell me how to do so."

She pulled my hand away. Ashamed of her weakness. "Wolf, there is no way…"

"Yes, there is," I declared. "You just need to tell me how."

She bit her lip. "We really shouldn't…"

"Your life's on the line." I put my hands on her strong arms, shaking her gently. "What do we need to do?"

Her mouth turned upward slightly. "Atropos and her Children keep a record of all the threads. If I could determine how my thread will be cut, perhaps I can prevent it."

"What about the child who failed as a puppet? If we fix him, could that help you also?"

She thought for a moment. "I think he is long gone. He may not have much time to live. Without the token of his memories, he will fade into madness."

Token of his memories, token of his memories, token of his memories, I repeated, trying not to forget. I needed to find that to save Donnie.

"All right, how do we find this out?" I asked.

She turned to Diego the Monkey who was chewing on a bright flower. The creature paused and looked up at us. He squeaked with annoyance that we were staring and continued to eat.

"Diego?" I asked, shocked.

She nodded. "It might sound crazy, but he's more than just a monkey." *Now somebody tells me.*

She bent down and clicked her tongue. Diego listened and went to her. "You know your subordinate, Solomon?" she began.

"Of course."

"You know how he only speaks in verses?"

"Yes, it's annoying when I can't figure them out."

"Well, he wasn't always like that." She tried to pick up the monkey, but he snarled and pointed towards a hedge. She nodded, and he ran off into the bushes to do his business. Quite polite, if you ask me.

"Solomon wasn't initially a Hermes member," Sting continued. "Believe it or not, he was a part of the Children of Moirai."

My jaw dropped. "Is that even possible?"

"Solomon was a rare case," Sting went on. "Normally those who fail in the Children of Moirai have their threads cut immediately. Something happened to Solomon that made them refrain." She jerked her head and we continued our walk. "From what I know, Solomon has been with the Order for many years. He was a faithful one. Odd, but faithful. He did his Children of Moirai duties with diligence and excellence. Emel—Lachesis—noticed this and developed a liking towards him. She rose him through the ranks, giving him much responsibility."

We stopped in the center of the garden. We watched as Diego chased a mechanical butterfly around a beautiful marble gazebo with tall corinthian pillars connecting to a domed covering.

"Then, something happened," Sting continued in a low voice. "One January day, our entire recruitment system was shut down. Gone in an instant." She snapped her fingers. "Everything we were working on to gather more troops was erased. Someone sent a virus through our systems. Solomon was distraught. He worked so hard perfecting Titan Marcellus' designs, but he didn't give up. He helped code the system and was determined to do it again."

She went over to sit down on the steps of the gazebo. I followed and sat beside her; our thighs touched.

"However, he couldn't remember everything he'd created," Sting went on. "He needed to jog his memory. He needed to reach into the deepest recesses of his mind and pull out *every piece* of information. So, we ran some tests. Tried to use whatever we could to get into his head. Lachesis/ Emel was against it, but the other Moirai were sure it would work. It was two against one and the procedure went on, but," she clicked her tongue, "Emel was right. Solomon's mind was fried. He should have *died*, but his spirit is strong. He had to be taught how to walk, eat, and even breathe again. Emel was moved with pity so she transferred him to Hermes where a Xenophonian named Leprechaun nursed him back to health."

Leprechaun changed his will, I thought. After a moment, I asked, "What does that have to do with Diego? It seems like Solomon should be the one we should talk to, not the monkey."

"That's the thing," she explained. "Diego came around when this happened to Solomon. It was because the Children of Hades Division was formed around that time." She chuckled. "I think Diego escaped the transformation chambers. They always brought in live animals to help with the procedure." Hearing his name, the monkey cooed and jumped up onto Sting's lap. "This creature found his way to Solomon one day and the two became inseparable instantly. That's why the Moirai keep him alive. The monkey and Solomon formed a bond." She rubbed his furry head. "A bond that's stronger than meets the eye."

"What are you saying?" I asked, genuinely confused.

She took a deep breath and looked me in the face. Whatever she was about to say was going to be hard to take. "This monkey is more Solomon than Solomon is," she stated. "Whatever he was exposed to from the Children of Hades intermingled with what Solomon was subjected to. I don't know much about the procedure, but from what I've seen and heard, it's the only logical explanation. I think Diego understands and knows more than we realize."

I was right, I thought. *A human Mutant monkey.*

"He can get us the information from the Children of Moirai?" I whispered.

She nodded. "He is called Cercopes for a reason. The Cercopes were monkey-like thieves in the olden days. Now, we have one of our own."

Diego chirped and jumped down the stairs to chase another butterfly.

I didn't know what to say, so Sting admitted, "Look, I know it sounds crazy. Hades, everything sounds crazy, but I'm willing to believe anything when my life is on the line." Her voice was desperate and her tone was terrified.

I gently pressed my hand to her face. She nuzzled her cheek into my palm, embracing its touch. "I believe you, Sting," I said sincerely. "If you think Diego can get us to your thread, then that's what he will do."

She smiled and kissed my hand. Her warm lips sent a tingling sensation that spread throughout my body. "Thank you, *mi amor*," she purred.

My heart raced, my head pounded, and I knew what I had to do next. I cupped her face with my other hand and pulled her towards me. I closed my eyes and pressed my mouth against hers. She didn't hit me. She didn't pull away. She brought herself closer and returned the gesture.

Before I knew it, I was kissing the woman I planned to betray.

And I loved every minute of it.

So… yeah. Uh, I have nothing else to say.

Ahem.

So… Donnie needs a Token of Memories for the link between him and Atropos to be broken. Tell me what it is and if you have it, awesome. If it's here, I'll get it for you and send it back when Axel and Blake are released.

With safety and secrecy,

Joshua Wolfrum

Joshua Wolfrum
Titan of the Russian Pandemonium

LETTER 34

Shannon: IX

Dear Joshua,

Be careful where you lend your heart. Not all hands handle with care.

Speaking of hearts: Shane continues to recover. Pieces of him are still missing, but we're patching him up.

I brought him into the conference room with Mark and Aymie immediately after I wrote you my last letter. The two rejoiced like you'd never seen before. They've lost one another too many times. Tears flowed, arms hugged, and words of love floated through the air.

But none landed on me; from Aymie, anyway. Even though I brought Shane back, her grudge was a strong concrete wall. Nothing I did broke it down. Despite her satisfaction at her brother's return, Blake's capture leaves her full of sorrow.

The day after Mark identified Zeus to be Mr. Devin Page, I sat in the conference room with Aymie. We both arrived early for the call with Mr. Mallory. I had some notes and papers with me about Cercopes and Zeus. I quietly read while Aymie played with Blake's ring around her dog tag.

I was deep in thought when she spoke; her voice cracked and fragile. "How does it feel?"

I looked up at her. "Excuse me?"

"To accomplish your goals." She lost me. I cocked my head to the side. She sighed and rolled her eyes. "You brought us Hodginses back together: my siblings and my father. You found your brother *and* your dad." She scoffed and gestured to my notes. "You've even helped find Zeus. How does that make you feel?"

I didn't like her tone. She wasn't asking out of support. She wanted to mock me. *Why?* "I feel like I haven't done anything," I confessed. "Everyone's contributed evenly to these cases. I'm not the only one to solve them."

She laughed sarcastically. "Are you trying to act humble, is that it? Be the better saint than I am?"

I was taken aback. "Aymie, clarify. I don't understand."

She scowled. "You're always the one to make the tough decisions. The 'Royal Strategist' has the final say. The final choice. You decide how the story ends."

Something is wrong. This was out of character for her. Normally, she's the sweetest, kindest woman. Always wanting to help and do what's right.

My silence angered her. "You don't care, do you?!" she screamed, smashing her fists on the mahogany table. "You've done *NOTHING*. You let this happen!"

I know now.

"You could've prevented so much pain," she spat. "If you were just brave enough to end it at the source, none of this would've happened. You should've killed Sting."

"I have no control of the past," I explained kindly, "but I promise I will make the future right."

She growled and put her head in her hands. I felt the angry energy emanating from her like a roaring fire. The flames were ready to climb higher.

A knock at the door threw sand on her fire, but the embers were still hot. Johanna poked her head in. "Hey ladies, you're here early." She looked to Aymie then back at me. The Royal Veteran Umbrella knew something was up (as a psychologist and counselor, she always did). However, she knew to keep quiet when Aymie and I fought. She sat down at my side, swiveling in the leather chair. She opened her mouth to say something, but shut it again.

One by one the rest of the members pooled in—Isle members included. Shane sat on the other side of me. Once we were all present, Virginia Michaelson entered and went to the front of the room.

"Let's get to the point," she began. "We know now that Zeus is Devin Page: a former associate of M. Hodgins." Mark hung his head low. "We also know," Michaelson continued, "that the next attack against us will be fierce. Bain will keep awake for a while, but even the sun needs to set. Hopefully, his will and strength are strong enough to resist, but we cannot bet on it. We must be prepared."

Aymie shifted in her chair and crossed her arms, filling the room with tension.

"I understand this is a difficult time for all of us. We've lost two dear members, but we were given gifts in their stead," she gestured to Shane. "S. Hodgins has regained his memories. We couldn't be more grateful for their return."

"Happy to be mostly back, ma'am," my fiancé confessed. He squeezed my hand under the table.

Aymie noticed and shifted again.

Virginia Michaelson nodded. "I am sorry your welcome back cannot be great. There's much to do." She turned on the television. A video icon appeared in the center of the screen. The visual glitched until a mirrored representation of our conference room was in the corner.

We dialed the Isles.

It rang and rang and rang. Nothing. We tried again. Nothing.

"I hope all is okay," Ethan mumbled.

The third time was the charm. After a few seconds, the call was answered and we saw a familiar chocolate colored face staring back at us.

"Hello, Dr. Damian I presume?" Michaelson greeted with a smile.

The Keeper of Isle II—Dr. Damian Agro—smiled and nodded. "Yes it is, my dear. Such a pleasure to meet you." He peered closer. His wide nose filled most of the screen. "And so wonderful to see so many familiar faces again!" He paused as if counting us. His gleeful expression faded. "Although, there seem to be a few missing."

"Not gone forever, I assure you," Michaelson added quickly. "I promise, we'll send a full update soon. Is Carl Mallory around?"

Dr. Agro looked up and around. I heard waves crashing and saw palm tree leaves rustle in the wind. "We just finished breakfast so he shouldn't have gone too far." I watched amused as Dr. Agro ran with the camera facing him. He almost dropped it a few times. "I don't see Mallory, but here are Brian and Yuki!"

The look on Michaelson's face expressed that she needed Mallory immediately, but she couldn't bring herself to demand it. It had been so long since the Isle members looked upon the faces of their Keepers: the people that raised them.

Dr. Damian Agro put the camera into the lap of an older man with a breathing tube stuck up his nose. The wrinkles in his face were deeper, but he was still full of life. "Hello, children!" he greeted with a nasally voice.

"Hey, Mr. Bamber!" Aaron called, waving to the camera.

"Aaron, my boy! You look marvelous," he beamed. "Oh, Mrs. Pieper says hi as well!"

He pointed the camera to a beautiful woman with almond eyes. Yuki Pieper—Aaron's old homeroom teacher—waved back.

Mr. Bamber pointed the camera back to his face—a little too closely. "Dr. Damian had to run, but he told me to wheel around and find Mr. Allaway for you."

"Apologies sir, we need Mr. *Mallory*," Michaelson corrected.

Mr. Bamber shot a quizzical look. "What?"

"*Mallory!*" she repeated louder.

Mr. Bamber still didn't get it. His eyes darted to his left and he smiled. "Here's Cameron now!"

"Wait, sir!" Michaelson protested, but it was too late. The red hair and crooked nose of the Scottish inventor was in frame.

Mr. Allaway smiled; his kind cerulean eyes glistened in the Hawaiian sun. "Hey, kiddos! What's going on?"

"Hi Cameron!" Myles waved. I forgot the child prodigy *knew* two of the Keepers prior to the Isles. From what I recall, both Bamber and Allaway tutored (and even worked with) Myles when he was young before they left to work for Nikita.

The Keeper chuckled. "Young Mr. Powell! Looking as sharp as last I saw you. How's the inventing been?"

"Good, but nothing will ever surpass the biomechatronics prototypes you let me help you with when I was a kid," Myles replied, humbly.

"Well, they're only unsurpassable because of *whom* they've helped. The person in the metal is what makes an incredible Bionic," Allaway stated.

The Biomechatronics Commander managed a smile through her pain. She loved her Keeper, but her sorrow was unbearable. "We need your help, Mr. Allaway," Alison said aloud.

"My dear, Alison!" he exclaimed. "Still just as lovely as when I saw you last. Speaking of love," he scanned the room, "where is my other Bionic Buddy, Axel?"

Alison's smile disappeared. "He was taken by the Order of Xenophon. We have some troubling news. We need Mr. Mallory's help."

Mr. Allaway's face fell. "Right away. I believe Carl's in the kitchen with Stanley." He tucked the electronic clipboard under his arm and ran. We saw the blur of the ocean front as he raced by.

They were on the shore of Hawaii in the vacation home that belonged to Mr. Nik where Bionics Axel and Alison were operated on over eight years ago.

Mr. Allaway steadied the camera. He panted and beads of sweat dripped from his forehead. "Carl, Stanley," he called off screen. "It's the kids. Something happened."

Immediately the camera whipped around. Another wrinkled face looked back at us. Mr. Stanley Wyght—the Director of RRPR and Wyght's Home for Young People—aged, but still had a look of strength and authority. His gray hair was now white, but his skin was tan and smooth from the sun. "What happened, Virginia?" he asked frantically. "Something not told in your last report?"

"I'm afraid so, sir," she sighed and quickly explained everything. We watched Mr. Wyght's face fall during the conversation. He didn't know what to say. When Michaelson was done, the camera was stolen by the last Keeper: Mr. Carl Mallory.

The crazy scientist's blond hair was still long but looked washed. He was clean shaven and wore a new tie-dye shirt. I hoped he improved his body odor problem, but thankfully, we didn't have to determine that.

"Whoa, man, that *is* crazy," he said honestly. "Look, I'm telling you. I knew there was something weird about that Page guy from the first moment I met Mark and the gang. The time I made Theo and Jordan Mutants."

"Does this mean you have no information for us?" Michaelson snapped.

I don't blame her. Every moment to pass is an opportunity wasted.

"Chill, I'm getting there," he retorted. He rested the device on a salt shaker to keep us steady. "So they're talking about the Unleashing. The only way to 'unleash'," he made air quotes with his fingers, "those kind of mindless Mutants is to have a leader who isn't a Mutant. Mark will clearly remember the day my beautiful creations saved him. They didn't tear apart those police officers on their own." He shook his head and pointed to himself. "This means someone trained will have to be their master. If he says jump, the Mutants ask 'how high'. Well… not literally but you get what I mean."

"Who's the Master?" Mark asked. "It'd be Page, wouldn't it?"

Mallory nodded. "This means he'll have to be present at *every* attack."

We all looked at each other. "Cut off the head, the body will crumble around it," I said.

"Unless you're a Hydra," Johanna pointed out. "Then two more will take its place."

"The counselor broad makes a good point," Mallory said. "However, from what I've seen and heard, the Order of Xenophon adores their god, Zeus. They also freak out when they can't hear the Strange Voices anymore."

"The frequency," Mark stated. "We need to keep pursuing that. We can't let our one failure get us down. Mallory, can you have Mr. Allaway and Mr. Bamber contact us about that matter? We need an extra pair of hands. It's more delicate than we first anticipated."

"Already on it, Mark!" Allaway yelled from off screen.

"Do whatever you gotta do, man, but listen," Mallory paused to think. "It may not always be Zeus leading the Unleashing," he said finally. "It probably will be, but maybe not."

"Do you think he's the kind of person who'd share power?" I asked.

"From my notes, it seems like he wouldn't be. He seems very full of himself."

Mallory wagged a finger. "Right you are, my dear Detective, but there is one thing Devin Page is good at." He leaned in and whispered, "listening." He slumped back into his chair and twirled his hair around his finger. "Get him to listen to someone you trust. Give him a good reason why *one* other person should be trained to lead the attacks."

"Joshua," I said aloud.

"Bingo." Mr. Mallory smiled. "Honestly, that's the best advice I can give. The training process is mostly getting the Mutants to like their master. If they end up liking Joshua more, then who knows what'll happen."

"It is most helpful," Michaelson said sincerely. "Thank you very much, Carl."

The scientist bowed. "My pleasure. Just don't hurt too many of my babies, will ya? Bring them back to me if anything. I worked on most of those kids."

"We'll do our best," Michaelson added. She was about to bid farewell when Mr. Wyght grabbed the camera again.

"I know you have work to do, but I need to ask," Director Wyght began. "How is the boy doing? How are the Hollinger girls? How is Sami Alexus?"

Michaelson let out a deep breath. "Donald McArthur needs a Token of Memories. From there he should unlock who he once was. After that, we hope he can convince the girls, Sami, and the whole city that he was a liar."

"Even with Marcellus back, do they rebel?" Stanley asked.

"Not all, thank goodness. He's actually with them now, trying to ease their suffering souls. The citizens are content with what we have shared but grow restless." Michaelson shook her head. "I can't say I blame them."

"But don't blame yourself," Mr. Wyght added. "Find Donnie's Token. The pain is cutting me straight to the heart."

His words went in one ear and got stuck in the middle of my brain. *Cutting. Heart. Cutting. Heart.*

Michaelson thanked her boss, signed off, and powered down the television. The room was silent, and the Interpreter Director let out a deep sigh.

"Once again, we're at the mercy of Joshua," Aymie grumbled.

"Not necessarily, A. Hodgins," Michaelson replied. "There is still much to be done on our part." She turned to Mark, Myles, and Aaron. "Hop on a call with Allaway right away to see what was wrong with the frequency. Interrogate PH—Pietro Hollinger—for insight as well."

Myles shot up like a rocket. "Yes, ma'am! I have a few ideas about using Axel's Optic Transmitter to get the right levels. With Allaway's help, we should be able to succeed."

"Don't tell us, just go!" Aymie snapped.

Myles' face turned red and he ran out with Aaron close behind. Mark looked at me over his shoulder before disappearing. I gave him a nod, and he left.

"While they work, we will prepare to return to the Temple of Munazam in Algeria," Michaelson continued. "Munazam's defenses appear to be on the light side compared to the others. My Interpreters confirmed that while the Annex has taken full effect, all is quiet. Not many transmissions from the Order to these folks."

"Makes me wonder if we even should attack this place," Aymie mumbled.

Johanna—who has no patience outside of her office—jumped to her feet, startling everyone. Her green eyes narrowed at Aymie. When Aymie looked away, Johanna turned to Michaelson and stated, "I agree with this plan. May I go now? I have soldiers that need me."

Michaelson dismissed Johanna who glared at the Hodgins sister as she left.

The tension rose.

"We'll discuss details in another meeting," Michaelson added. "I think this was enough information to take in. Isle members," she pointed down the table, "please try and think of what Donnie's 'Token of Memories' may be."

Cutting. Heart. Cutting. Heart. Cut...

Those words played over and over in my mind. *What is it, what is it?*

One by one the Isle members rose. "Of course, ma'am," Alison said. "We're still trying to think of what it may mean."

"Like is it a physical token, words, or an object?" Lucas asked, fixing the goggles over his bug eyes.

Yared shook his head. "No idea, man. Joshua just said we need a 'Token of Memories'. It could be the kid's sheer will power for all we know."

Sheer. Cut. Heart. Sheer. Cut.

"Shears!" I exclaimed. My eureka moment surprised the Officers. "Marlene Best's shears. Her sheep shears. The ones Atropos plans to use to cut the thread."

"You mean the ones she stole from him?" Ethan asked.

"It has to be. Why else would she take them?" I stated.

"Because the Atropos Moirai is always seen with shears and she lost hers?" Lucas put in.

Heart. Cut. Heart. Cut.

"There's one other thing," I thought aloud. "The shears and something else. It has to do with *heart*."

"All I know is the little guy doesn't have a heart right now," Yared said; his face crestfallen. "We'll go with shears for now but need to get them back."

"Yared, that will be your and the Isle members' assignment. Coordinate retrieving those from Joshua," Michaelson directed. "Also figure out what else Hollinger is thinking of." She turned to me with a smile. "Hopefully it works."

Out of the corner of my eye, I saw Aymie's lip curl.

"Finally," Michaelson looked at Ethan the Savior. "Mix more of the antidote for Sting's wasp venom. You may need it."

"Hopefully, it's just a precaution," Ethan replied.

"Hopefully… " A sad look was in Michaelson's eyes, but she said nothing more.

With that, we had a plan. We'd invade the Algerian temple, lure Zeus and the Mutant army, release the frequency, and have a fight to the death.

Something tells me it won't be that straightforward.

Michaelson released us and we went our separate ways except for Aymie and me. She convinced Shane to go ahead so she could get the final word in.

She cornered me before I could leave. She was taller than me, but I wasn't intimidated. Still… her tone was sharper than knives. "I want you to know that since you didn't act when you saw Sting that day, Donnie's life is on *you*," she growled. "Shane's amnesia is on *you*. Sami's health is on *you*. Your sisters' peace is on *you*. Axel's kidnapping is on *you*," she glowered down at me with her gray eyes. "If Blake dies it's on *you*."

I was silent. After a moment, I said something. Something I didn't think about before I said it. I wish I could take it back. "Well, I'm sorry *you* feel that way."

Aymie's expression turned to bitter hatred. She snarled; her gray eyes burned. I heard a *smack*. Next thing I knew, I saw stars and my cheek stung. She slapped me so hard I staggered, grabbing the wall for support. I breathed heavily and touched my red hot face. With a grunt, she stormed out.

As I stood, I struggled to breathe. My chest burned. The poison in my lungs was aggravated. I felt it stirring. My mouth could barely open; no air would come in. *Why couldn't I just have apologized?* But I knew why.

I didn't want her to be right.

I felt my consciousness slipping from me as I slid down the wall. My papers scattered around me, gliding to the ground like leaves in the wind. My eyes fluttered as I tried to stay awake.

I felt a strong hand behind my head and another forcing my mask over my face. It opened and I bit the tube inside, breathing in the antidote. It was Shane. His green eyes were filled with worry. I felt guilty that I scared him. I hung my head low. I wanted to tell him why. I wanted to tell him the reason for all my sorrows, but I was engulfed in pride.

Saying nothing, he wrapped his arms around me and pulled me close, silently listening to my rapid electronic breathing.

This was a long letter, Joshua. I'm sorry. I just figured you'd want in on the girl drama.

Also, I think it's good for you to see how much damage Sting has actually done.

She needs to be taken out of the equation before she causes any more pain. It is not wrong to do so. We are at war.

Stay strong.

Godspeed and goodwill,

Shannon Hollinger
Royal Strategist of RRPR

THE UNDERGROUND

LETTER 35
Joshua: XVIII

Yared and Shannon,

I will put an end to Sting's terror, but not yet. She led me to something important today.

Sorry, yes, we did go on another date. I promise I'm handling my heart with care… I hope.

"Now, you know where to meet me tonight, right?" Sting asked as we left New Greece.

I grabbed her hand. "Of course I do. You need to have more faith in me."

"You know who to bring with you?"

Diego the Monkey chirped from his perch on my shoulder. "I don't think I can get rid of him," I smiled.

Sting laughed. "All right. Good luck today." She kissed me on the cheek. "*Hasta luego.*" She marched off to fulfill her daily duties.

I didn't realize I was staring until Diego the Monkey wiped my face where her sweet lips touched. I recoiled, and he screeched in frustration.

"I know, I know, don't worry. It's not affecting me," I lied. I tugged on my jacket and walked down the corridor. I tried not to think about Sting… but I couldn't help it. Her caramel eyes, her silky hair, her soft touch, her—

"OUCH!" I yelped at a burning sensation in my ear. Diego *bit* me. He squeaked, indicating that I was walking too slow. "I'm sorry," I grumbled and jogged the rest of the way.

I met Zeus on the skywalk overlooking the chamber where the Entrance Rituals took place. Today all the white seats were vacant except for one. Poor Blake Bain was strapped down. Headphones sat atop his white hair, whispering into his ears. His light blue eyes were bloodshot.

He hadn't slept.

I went to Zeus. "My lord. You summoned me?"

"Yes, Wolf," he replied and pointed to Blake. "He has yet to provide us any intel. He is good at fighting fatigue."

"So it seems. Is this the only way we can gather information? How do we know he'll even tell us when he awakes?"

"He won't need to tell us," Zeus explained, fixing his black tie. "We'll watch his dreams while he sleeps."

My eyes widened. "How is that possible?"

He tapped the back of his neck. "You'd be surprised what else that thing inside of you can do."

How advanced have they become?

"I understand it must be a shock, but our technology is far superior than anything else in the world," he explained. "We can't read thoughts, but we can project dreams. The subconscious mind more specifically. Scientists have worked on this ability for ages; we've simply accomplished it."

"Has it been tested?"

His lips formed a straight line. "Once before," he answered hesitantly.

"Did it succeed?"

He let out a chuckle. "Not as well as we hoped, but this Weapon that they call REM is a different case."

"What happened the first time?"

"Let's just say during the process, a brilliant Xenophonian of the Children of Moirai forgot basic human functionality. It caused his mind to slip into his subconscious."

Solomon.

"We were able to read his dreams," Zeus continued, "but we lost the Xenophonian in the process. Without him, we couldn't interpret what his dreams meant." He jerked a chin to Blake below. "From what PH has said, this one's dreams need *no* interpreting."

I looked down at the figure. Blake was weak, and his will was fading. His eyelids started to droop. All was quiet as we watched him fall into a deep sleep.

His body gave in. In a matter of hours, the Order would know everything.

"What makes us think his dreams will give us what we need?" I whispered as if Blake might be able to hear me.

"It will," Zeus replied confidently. "While his mind is strong, his subconscious fears for the Resistance. That's all he's thinking about now. In time, he will tell us where they are." Zeus spun on his heel and marched away. Diego chirped and I followed suit.

"Do we have a plan for when we get the location?" I asked as we walked back to New Greece.

"Of course, Wolf, but that remains classified until necessary. You know the drill."

I was afraid of that. We walked in silence until I mustered up the courage to ask, "Sir, what if something happens to you?"

Zeus' polished shoes scuffed against the ground. "Are you insinuating something will?" he demanded, offended.

"Not at all sir," I responded immediately. "I look at all angles. What happens if you fall?"

Zeus' dark eyes returned forward. "Another must take my place as the Order arranges," he said simply.

"Understood, sir." I was quiet.

I felt Zeus' eyes on me. "Are you worried for me, Titan Wolf?"

Not really, I thought. "Of course, sir," I told him. "You said you want to be the face of these battles. What if the Resistance comes up with something unexpected?"

"The Resistance stands no chance against us. They never did," he stated. "With REM, the Children of Hades, and the Children of Moirai working harmoniously, we are unstoppable." He quietly sighed. "Still, I understand the concern. Someone should be prepared if I were to fall."

"Someone needs to take your place immediately, sir, for our fight to be won," I put in.

Zeus nodded thoughtfully. "Duly noted, Wolf." We reached the entrance for New Greece. It slid open with ease and Zeus stepped one foot inside then paused. He turned and said, "Thank you, Wolf, for your loyalty to me, the Moirai, and the Order."

I bowed. "In the name of Xenophon." Zeus disappeared into New Greece; the door shut behind him.

I let out a deep breath as Diego ruffled my curly hair. "Now, let's go get those shears," I told him.

As I made my way to the kitchen, a message flashed before my eyes. It was Axel. "Amigo, *get over here. Your girlfriend is tampering with some equipment.*"

I cursed aloud, turned around, and bolted towards the hangar. I got another message as I ran: "*Hurry up, dude, the big guy is getting feisty with her.*" I pumped my legs harder. "*She's crazy, man. Why do you like this chica?*" Sweat dripped down my neck. "*She's pulled a knife! It's the one with the Wasp venom. The big guy put his dukes up. Dude, I need to stop this. I can get our revenge here and now.*"

"Wait, Axel, I command you!" I yelled too loudly. I turned a corner, raced through the hangar door, and headed straight for the Bionic. I skidded to a stop before the scene.

Goliath was knocked down; a large black and blue mark streaked across his forehead. Solomon stood in the corner with his staff out in defense. Axel's organic hands gripped Sting's throat. His armor laid half finished on the table behind him. The Bionic hovered in the air with her dangling in his grasp. She was scratching and clawing at his arms, leaving marks and cuts. He didn't care. He squeezed harder. His mechanical eyes narrowed on his prey. Sting's face was turning white.

Let him finish, I thought. *The pain can end now.* But Wolf wouldn't let Joshua win.

"MAN OF METAL! IN THE NAME OF XENOPHON, I ORDER YOU TO HEED," I bellowed.

Axel snapped back into reality. Shock and horror fell upon his face when his eyes met mine. Having no other choice, he obeyed. He let go of Sting and she fell to the ground, gasping for air. He glared as he flew back to his chair and sat down. He knew how to play the part. He closed his eyes and remained motionless like a puppet without its puppeteer.

I ran to Sting and grabbed her arm. "What happened?" I demanded as I pulled her up. I gently rubbed my fingers over the red markings on her neck.

The look in her eyes said she wanted to tear herself away from me, but her body said otherwise. She collapsed on me, burying her face into my jacket. "The Bionic awoke and started attacking. He knocked out Goliath and came after me," she cried.

I heard a moan and a grunt behind me. "Li...ar," a deep, raspy voice panted. Goliath staggered to his feet, holding his bruised head in his hands. "Wolf gave us orders. We were following them."

Solomon nodded and Diego the Monkey did the same. I understood, but I wasn't going to explain. "Thank you, both. Please continue. I will send my subordinates to relieve you soon." I gripped Sting's arm and dragged her away.

We were in the hallway when she tore herself from me and cursed aloud. "Wolf, what was that?! The Hermes and Ares tried to kill me," she rubbed her throat, "and the Bionic almost did."

"The Bionic was placed under my care; you know this," I said sternly. Wolf wasn't afraid of her anymore. She would listen to *him* now. "They were ordered to keep my prisoner safe. You posed a threat to be stopped." I stepped towards her. "Why were you there in the first place?" I whispered.

Sting let out a sigh. "I was after the Bionics first, Wolf," she stated. "I desired them more than anything. You know that."

"But *you* know orders are orders," I replied. "Obey them as you should."

Taken aback, her brown eyes looked at me with shock and… sadness. It surprised me. I never made Sting upset before. This moved me almost to pity, but not quite.

"Understood, sir," she mumbled finally.

I slipped my hand in hers and massaged her rough palm. "Good. Now, let's go find your thread."

We made our way to the dining hall where Emel was preparing dinner with her team. She waved when she saw us. "Wolf, Sting! You hungry?"

Diego the Monkey chirped, leaping off my shoulder and onto the counter.

"Hey, down!" Emel yelled, smacking the creature with a wooden spoon. Diego yelped and dove behind a sack of potatoes.

As we entered the kitchen, I inhaled through my nose. The buttery aroma of scalloped potatoes floated in the air. My stomach grumbled at the sight of Emel's famous meatloaf, but we had a schedule to keep. "Emel, what you're cooking smells delicious, but we'll wait to get our fill," I told her.

"Wanting to head downstairs?" she asked as she chopped vegetables.

"Yes, ma'am, if it's all right," I said. "I'd like to ask the Children of Moirai some questions regarding my prisoner."

She thought for a moment. Her eyes darted back and forth before she waved me forward with her knife, but not Sting. Emel ordered the Ares Titan to about-face. Sting turned the other way, and I went to the Moirai.

"Do this for me after," Emel started. "My sisters and I are having a debate. Remember how we said there was another spy in addition to Leprechaun?" She peered over my shoulder to make sure Sting wasn't listening. "He's starting to cause trouble now. I need you to confirm some details so we can make the right call. We need to cut a thread, but you need to tell us whose it is."

"Of course, ma'am," I replied as calmly as possible. "Where do I need to go?"

"Any Child of mine can help with what you need; they're expecting you." She winked and went back to cutting her onions.

I bowed once more. I whistled for Diego to return, and he jumped off the counter with a small potato in his mouth. With him on my shoulder, I led Sting to the fridge where we descended to see the Children of Moirai. All the while Sting asked no questions.

We walked along the metal mezzanine, overlooking the Children of Moirai at their desks. I didn't know where to begin. "Sting, what exactly are we looking for?"

"I don't know. I know Atropos keeps records and progress of her threads here somewhere." She turned to Diego and rubbed his fuzzy head. "Hey, little guy. You knew the Moirai the best. Where is Atropos' console?"

THE UNDERGROUND

Diego nibbled on the potato and squeaked. Vegetable in hand, he hopped off my shoulder and waddled on his hind legs. We followed him into Emel's office. He turned right where a wall of shelving held Ancient Greek artifacts and books on cooking. In the middle were three mini statues of the Moirai like in the plaza of New Greece. Diego leapt up onto a shelf and patted the statue of Atropos.

With a rumble, the floor behind us slid away, revealing a hidden spiral staircase.

Just like Nikita Patya — The Headmaster, I thought.

We looked over our shoulders to see if anyone was following. Alone, we quietly descended.

The room was dark and cold. Stepping onto the floor, an unnerving feeling shot through my body. I felt a paranormal presence like the ghosts of Atropos' victims floated around me. It made me shiver. Rubbing my arms, I wriggled my nose to turn my night vision on. What I saw was even more disturbing.

Ancient Greek weaponry lined the walls: *dori, kopis, xiphos, gastraphetes.* (Sorry, spears, swords, crossbows, and stuff.) The tables were lined with surgical equipment, poisons, and medications. The back wall was covered in photographs and handwritten notes; all connected by different colored strings.

On the table below sat a lonely laptop and one gleaming weapon: Marlene's sheep shears.

I gasped quietly when I saw them, but in the silence, it was a scream. "What is it, Wolf? Do you see something?" Sting asked.

"Barely, my vision is coming slowly," I lied. "Find anything that can help yet?" I tiptoed forward, trying to get to them before she found a light.

"Not yet. I can see the glint of weapons on the walls otherwise my fingers would've been gone."

Diego squeaked and went to Sting. I had a moment. I went over to the desk and snatched the shears. I stuffed them in my inner jacket pocket and zipped it tight. I glanced down at the computer and papers scattered across her wooden desk. There were documents for each Temple where the Annex was complete. I gently wriggled the mouse of the computer and the screen powered on. Its glow cut through the dark like moonlight.

Diego squeaked and leapt up onto the desk. He tapped the keyboard a few times and danced across it.

"Diego, stop!" I yelled.

Sting grabbed my arm. "Wait, look." Diego unlocked Atropos' computer.

Right. Mutant Monkey.

He chirped and scrolled down. There were dates followed by names.

"How does this help? We don't even know what day it is," Sting grumbled. Diego's tiny fingers rubbed against the track pad until Sting pointed to the screen and exclaimed in Spanish.

"What is it?" I asked.

She stared closely. It was all in Greek. My glasses translated to these startling words: *A Titan failed once more. The thread has gotten much shorter. Elimination ... ?*

Sting winced.

"We don't know for certain it's you," I put in. "We don't know what the other Titans' duties are."

Saying nothing, she sluggishly made her way to the stairs. When she was gone, I checked one more thing. I scrolled through the dates. A lump caught in my throat when I found it.

Donnie was running out of time.

Diego shut down the computer and hopped on my back. Clutching the shears in my pocket, I ran up the stairs.

Sting leaned against the mezzanine railing, overlooking the workers below. Their blue holograms illuminated her beautiful face. I watched the water in her eyes glisten as she held back tears.

I placed my hand on her back. "We don't know for sure."

She scoffed. "You only say that because it's not you."

I pulled her close, resting my face against her head. She let out a deep breath and leaned her cheek against my chest. Quietly, she wept.

The heartless Ares Titan turned soft.

A few moments passed before she pulled herself together. With a deep breath, she stood up tall and said, "You complete whatever Emel requested of you. I will see you later." She leaned in and pressed her lips to mine. Regretfully, I kissed her back.

Pulling away, she turned and went up the stairs.

Once she was gone, Diego wiped his potato across my lips. I spat on the ground. "Dude, what is your problem?!"

He hit me on the head with his snack.

"I'm sorry, okay? Let's just get this over with," I grumbled as I went down the stairs to one of the consoles. This monkey was like an angry ex-who wanted to destroy my happiness.

I approached a mindless Xenophonian that sat staring at his screen. He didn't type; he didn't speak. His sunken eyes were glued to his monitor.

"Lachesis requested I look into something," I announced.

Silently, he raised his hands and placed them on the keys. His fingers typed and a set of instructions appeared on the screen: *Hey, Wolf. Out of the people you're close to, who goes to the pub the most?*

"Uh..." *She said she wanted to know about the spy... how would this help?* I wondered. "Ares Titan Sting, Hermes Titan PH, Ares Goliath, Hermes Solomon, and myself," I said aloud. The Xenophonian entered my answer.

The next: *Which of these frighten you the most?*

"Ares Titan Sting and Ares Goliath," I said without thinking.

Who quarrels with you the most?

"Ares Goliath." I recalled the day he strangled Rachel Hollinger.

Out of your former Hermes Division members, whom have you grown close to?

"Hermes Solomon and Hermes Titan PH."

Which low Xenophonian is the most intelligent?

I paused. I had no choice but to answer truthfully. "Hermes Solomon," I answered.

The Xenophonian typed the final answer and Emel's final message popped up: *Thanks, man! We've got ourselves a spy... hopefully. If not we've just lost a good soldier, but better to be safe than sorry! Keep an eye on this one, will you?* An image of the so-called traitor appeared.

It was Goliath.

I wanted to let out a sigh of relief, but confusion washed over me. *Why do they think it's Goliath? What has he done?*

A million questions swirled in my mind.

Is there... anything else... Titan Wolf? a voice said in my head amidst static. It was the Xenophonian I was working with. His mouth didn't move, but his mind spoke to me.

"What access to research do I have?" I asked kindly yet firmly.

Lachesis... has trusted you... Other Moirai... do not. You must... gain approval... from our lord.

"Are you always here?"

Not always... rotation. Mind... rest. His eyes fluttered as the words banged against my ear drums.

I thanked him and was about to leave when the large hologram in the center transformed into a map. There was a loud beeping and a location was pinpointed in Africa.

Oh no...

There was a piercing and buzzing in my head even louder than before. I winced. *Wolf... this is Zeus. We got them... sleep in uniform... we leave tomorrow.*

With a pain in the pit of my stomach, Diego and I left the Children of Moirai. I told him to run to his master. He hopped off my shoulder and left me alone. As I walked to my room, I messaged Axel about the situation.

"*Don't worry, man,*" Axel replied. "*We got this. My armor is ready. Make sure they take me with you.*"

"No, I still need you here," I answered. "We have to save REM."

A moment passed before I received a reply: "*As you wish, Titan.*"

I wish I could take you and get this over with, I thought, but didn't say. I couldn't. I can't guarantee anything, so I am going to sleep with false hope.

I have Donnie's shears. Get them from me somehow, Yared.

Also, tell Shannon to be careful and I know this sounds crazy, but please trust me.

Don't kill Zeus.

With safety and secrecy,

Joshua Wolfrum

Joshua Wolfrum
Titan of the Russian Pandemonium

THE UNDERGROUND

LETTER 36
Yared: IX

Joshua,

Why?

Why didn't you let us do it? Why didn't you let *me* do it? You're making the team doubt you. You're making the team doubt itself.

A week after we called Carl Mallory about Devin Page's Mutant army, we planned our attack. We knew the Unleashing would be upon us, but we were ready for it.

Well, we thought so at least.

I sat on the plane with a few RRPR Officers and the remaining sane Isle members: Alison, Aaron, Ethan, and Lucas. Sami refused to join us. She couldn't bear to leave let alone face other Mutants. Donnie... well, we're hoping he's still in there somewhere.

I clutched the straps of my seatbelt, pondering the little boy's situation. "We better get those shears," I mumbled.

Ethan overheard me. "You said Joshua has them. He'll get them to us somehow."

I chose not to dwell on it. My eyes kept straight ahead. I watched Alison open and close her metal fists, testing the strength of her Bionic arm compared to her armor. Her gray eyes were lost in thought. She was usually the strong one, but with her sister out of her wits, her boyfriend gone, and Donnie falling apart, she didn't know what to make of anything anymore.

I looked at Lucas. Goggles and a cape covered his bug features. His foot tapped rapidly and his head twitched nervously. He quietly scarfed down a few protein bars, trying to cure his appetite. As a Dragonfly, he already ate more than normal. An anxious Dragonfly was impossible to satisfy.

I glanced over at Aaron who sat close to Mark, whispering. They discussed their plans for the mission. Four blue eyes locked on the clipboard before them. The colorful code reflected in Aaron's glasses.

I hope they get it right this time, I prayed.

I let out a deep sigh. My friends were nervous, anxious, and dreading what was to come. I wanted to offer words of encouragement, but that wasn't my forte. That's Mark or Alison, not me.

Shannon would also know what to say, but she remained behind. The poison in her lungs caused her to collapse after our meeting with the Keepers. I think her and Aymie got into a fight. Despite her protests, she was ordered to stay back. She'd be our eyes from base.

We were a small group. Our RRPR overseers were Mark, Nic, Sonny, and Myles. The girls and Shane remained behind. How the eight of us and a small group of Interpreters were going to handle an army of Mutants was beyond me, but we had to try.

Sonny cleared his throat and unstrapped his seatbelt. "I met with PH before our departure." He stood up. "He barely spoke, but his silence was more informative than words." He walked down the aisle. "As we discovered, the Temples of the Titans are created as bases for supplies. Without the Temple, the Reborn can't survive. However, PH neither confirmed nor denied the Temple being used for communication." He displayed a map on the electronic board near the cockpit. He circled the Titan Munazam's emblem with his forefinger. "While the Order of Xenophonian is quite symbolic, everything is done for a reason. Inside this marble plate has to be where the communication beacon resides. We need to connect to that frequency to reach the minds of the Xenophonians in its region."

"If we can't do it wirelessly," Mark put in, "we'll have to get into the emblem and resort to Plan B."

"For now, stick with A," Sonny ordered. "You know your positions. Do not falter, and note," his red eyes scanned the rooms, meeting each of us individually, "the Mutants you encounter are *not* your friends. Shoot to kill. Have one another's backs and never give up. Remember," he paused, "Zeus will be there. We got word to let him live for now, but I say if you have your chance," his teeth clenched and he growled, "take it." Returning to his place, Sonny sat and strapped in. I felt a strong turbulence as the pilot brought us down. The aircraft landed with a bump and eased to a stop. There was a soft whirring and the hatch opened.

It was time.

Grabbing my weapon, I jumped off the bay of the plane and ran to action.

I raced to the Temple in the middle of the city. *Get the shears, protect the Geeks. Get the shears, protect the Geeks*, I repeated to myself. Those were my two missions. I scaled the wall of an unfinished marble building, sprawled onto the roof, and lay there. I set up my rifle and looked down its scope. Waiting.

Minutes went by like water dripping from a leaky faucet. My patience thinned. I watched as civilians passed in and out of my sight. Each body lined up perfectly with my crosshairs, but none of them were who I wanted. They shuffled by too peacefully, too happily.

But I knew it was a lie. It always was, wasn't it?

I felt a vibration on my wrist coming from my BoMF—Bracelet of Many Functions. It was Ethan. *"Seer, see anything yet?"*

"Negative," I sent back.

I heard a scuffling behind me. *"Hold on, something is here,"* I sent. I pulled out my pistol and held it up to my face. I rolled over and got into a crouch. I held my breath as I inched my way forward. I heard tiny feet patting against the marble.

Mutants are much bigger than that, I thought. I lowered my guard for a moment to whisper, "Diego?"

I heard a squeak. The kind of noise I expected to hear when I read your letters, Joshua. A white and brown haired capuchin jumped up onto the roof. He had a little backpack flung over his shoulder.

"Whatcha got there?" I asked, holding my hand out. It was rough and uninviting, but Diego wasn't afraid. He went to it and slid the bag off his shoulders. Carefully, I unwrapped the gift that was in my calloused dark hand. I gasped.

Marlene's sheep shears.

"Diego," I began. "I don't know what to say."

He flicked his little wrist as if to say, *Don't mention it.*

I rubbed his furry head. "Wolf is here? Where is he?"

The monkey put a finger to his lips. He pointed to one of the buildings below. It was the restaurant where Shannon, Lucas, and Lucy encountered the Titan with the second peace treaty.

"Are they in there?"

Diego squeaked.

"Savior, meet me at the restaurant," I ordered Ethan.

"What's going on?"

"We'll find out when we get there." I flung my rifle over my shoulder and jumped off the roof. I waited in an alley, watching the civilians pass by. From what Shannon mentioned, the Titan of Algeria had OCD and all his subjects were on a tight schedule. *They are due for a shift change any second now.*

I saw Ethan across the street, ducking behind a food cart. Strapped across his chest was his med bag. His tan face was covered in sweat and his brown eyes darted back and forth.

Something spooked him.

I felt a tug on my leg. Diego wanted to climb onto my back. Reluctantly, I clicked my tongue and the creature hopped up and sat on my shoulder. He was light, hairy, and smelly. I don't know how you let him sit all over you, Joshua. It's disgusting.

The footfall of civilians ceased and the streets were clear. I gave a nod and Ethan and I ran to the restaurant. I watched him whisper something into his bracelet. Not too long after, I heard the fluttering of wings, and Lucas followed us in.

All was quiet. Too quiet. The tables were clean; no workers were around. The faint aroma of meat and spices hung in the air.

Lucas' stomach growled, echoing off the marble walls. "Crikey, I'm starving. That food was bloody amazing last time." He took off his goggles, placing them atop his head. His bug eyes glistened in the fire light and noticed something in the corner. "Mates, hold up. Do you see that?" He pointed. "Something moved over there."

I tightened my grip on my gun and Ethan did the same. "Should we call for backup?" the Savior asked.

"Not sure yet," I replied. "They need to protect the Geeks."

There was a rattling of metal and a grunt. I looked to Lucas and signaled for him to check it out. He fluttered his wings and flew into a room off to the left. Once he was gone, someone cleared their throat behind us.

Ethan and I spun around and aimed our weapons. Before us was a man wearing an outfit of all black with the emblem of an open book on his arm. He had brown skin and thick dark hair pulled back into a bun. Calmly, he raised his hands. "I see the Detective has not accepted our treaty of peace."

"Never will, Munazam," I spat.

He looked at me quizzically. "You know my name."

"You seem surprised."

Munazam shrugged. "I don't meet many outsiders. And I know I haven't been introduced to you two. Your names?"

"Call me Seer. This is Savior," I jerked my head towards Ethan. "No more questions. Where is he?"

He cocked his head. "Who are you searching for?"

"Yo cobbers!" Lucas called. The flapping of his wings grew louder. He landed beside us carrying a young girl knocked unconscious. She wasn't a civilian. She was covered in black and white hair with a long tail. Her button nose was wet, and her eyes were the color of coal.

"A Mutant," Ethan gasped.

I took a step closer to Munazam. "Where is he?!" I bellowed.

A sinister smile spread across the Titan's face. "You will be purified. The world you know is gone." His eyes narrowed. "Give. In."

I growled. I wasn't holding back anymore. I felt my finger pull back and that was the end. The bullet left the barrel with a *bang*. Munazam staggered backwards. Blood seeped from his chest and dripped to the ground like a light rain. The corner of his mouth turned upward.

He laughed.

He laughed and laughed and laughed. Clutching his chest, he dropped to his knees, spitting out blood and saliva. "You've just... killed... yourself," he choked. His eyes rolled back and he dropped to the floor.

His words meant nothing to me. I had no regrets. It was time. Time to end it all. "Lucas, get rid of the girl. We have to find the rest of them."

He looked at me with desperation. "C'mon, man. She's a little kid."

"NOT ANYMORE!" I bellowed, startling my friends and Diego. My voice rang through the marble building, bouncing off the walls, down the halls, and into the darkness.

A rumbling answered my echo, and the floor shook. Screeches, grunts, and screams rang through our ears like gunshots.

"We have to get out of here," Ethan whispered. He grabbed my arm and pulled me towards the door. "NOW!"

I ran with him and looked over my shoulder. Emerging from the grand halls were hundreds of shadows with glowing eyes.

Lucas dropped the girl and flew behind us. We ran out of the building and headed away from the city. We needed them to follow us.

My heart raced as my legs pumped. Diego the Monkey clutched onto the strap of my rifle for dear life. Ethan struggled to keep up and Lucas flew above us. Every once in a while I looked over my shoulder. Mutants of all shapes, sizes, and species were on our tail. They leapt on top of buildings, destroyed civilian carts, and trampled each other. They weren't keen on working together.

They were out for blood and wanted ours.

"MARS! KONG! Hope you're ready!" I screamed into my BoMF. The three of us turned a corner to where we hoped our defenses were set up. They were, but we had an unexpected guest.

Standing in front of the row of weapons was Sting. She wore her combat uniform; the wasp emblem on her arm screamed death. Around her waist was a towel and small spheres filled with poison. Calloused hands gripped and twisted the hilt of a knife we knew too well... Lucas knew too well. The Dragonfly rubbed his shoulder as if the pain of her venom still ran through his veins.

Her dark eyes scanned our faces and then at the monkey on my shoulder. A look of confusion crossed her face.

Thankfully, I was quick. *Sorry, Diego*, I mentally apologized as I grabbed the monkey by the neck. "Is this your pet?" I glowered.

Normally, she wouldn't have cared. Today, she showed concern.

That was our chance. Lucas whipped out his pistol and shot at Sting. She dove out of the way and hid behind one of our mounted weapons.

Behind us, the Mutants were closing in. Ethan, Diego, and I ran for cover while Lucas flew above. With us Isle members out of the way, our line of weapons fired.

The first line of Mutants went down, but that didn't stop them. They scrambled over one another, trying to get at the source. Some were smarter than that and fell back. The majority of them kept coming like moths to a flame.

Ethan and I ducked between buildings and covered our ears. Ethan cradled Diego the Monkey like a child, rubbing its neck where I strangled him. Understanding the situation, the creature kept quiet. The shots rang, the Mutants roared, and I could barely hear my own thoughts.

"MARS, KONG! WHERE ARE YOU?!" I screamed into my BoMF.

One word appeared on the screen. "*Temple.*" Saying nothing else, Ethan and I scaled the building and ran across the rooftops with Mutants tailing us.

We shot them down as they came. They scratched, screeched, and bit, but none of them got too close. Lucas protected us from behind. Below us the civilians were out and about. They weren't afraid or angry. They were confused. They watched the Mutants attacking us with sheer and utter amazement.

In the distance I could see the temple. On the roof were four figures: Mark, Aaron, Nic, and Sonny. Alison flew about, defending them from the sky. The team had to connect directly to the communications beacon inside Munazam's emblem. Plan A failed. We were on Plan B.

Rushing up the stairs of the Temple was a stampede of Mutants. Nic, Sonny, and Alison shot at the flying Mutants, but more kept coming.

They weren't going to make it.

We need to find Zeus and stop him. That was the only way. He needed to die. "ETHAN! LUCAS! GO HELP THEM," I ordered. I jumped across a rooftop and headed back to the restaurant. I needed to end this.

Lucas nodded and whistled at the Mutants to chase him. The mindless animals played his games and followed the Dragonfly. Ethan disobeyed and tailed me. I didn't have time to yell at him.

I slid down the side of a building, bounced off an awning, and landed on the street below. Heaving and panting, I ran back into the restaurant.

Civilians swarmed inside. They calmly sat at tables, whispering to each other. All heads turned when we barged in. Ethan slammed the door shut, locked it, and barricaded it while I shot at the ceiling. The civilians dropped to the floor and cowered. The only one who didn't was the one I wanted to find.

Zeus.

He wore a red combat uniform with the OX symbol on both arms and a lightning bolt over his heart. He opened his arms wide. "Welcome, young ones." Menace was in his eyes.

Don't kill Zeus. Don't kill Zeus, I repeated as I marched towards him. I raised my gun and aimed. "Tell your men to call off the attack," I demanded.

He took a step forward. "Why would I do that?" he asked. "You're the trespassers. I should be commanding *you* to call yours off."

I cocked my gun. "Call them off or I'll shoot."

"What good will it do if you kill me?" he asked. "You won't be able to stop the Unleashing without me."

Lies.

I stopped a few feet away from him. Zeus had his hands out and was standing tall. He was unarmed.

I felt Ethan stop behind me; his nervous breath on my neck. "Yared," he whispered, "something isn't right."

He didn't have to tell me twice.

Zeus lifted his right hand. All eyes followed. Then, he snapped his fingers.

The heavy breathing of the civilians ceased and all was quiet. Their eyes glazed over and they rose to their feet, lurching towards us like zombies.

The ground rumbled and we could hear the screeching of Mutants outside. The Children of Hades chose to come after us.

"What do we do?! We can't kill the civilians," Ethan cried, pressing his back up against mine as the numb survivors encircled us.

"They're still Zeus' puppets," I growled. I aimed my gun again. I wasn't afraid to fire. My conscience wouldn't like it, but I wasn't going to die. Diego the Monkey screeched and leapt off of Ethan's shoulder. He clambered over the heads of the mindless civilians.

"Coward!" I yelled.

The screaming of the Mutants roared outside. They banged and slammed on the heavy wooden doors, trying to get inside.

"You won't kill these survivors to escape," Zeus taunted. "You think they're still savable."

I gripped my gun and aimed. *If I shoot down one line of them, Ethan and I can slip down the corridor and escape.* I didn't see another choice. I put my finger on the trigger and—

My BoMF vibrated. Ethan's did too. They continued to vibrate and vibrate until I finally glanced down. I held my breath.

The survivors trembled where they stood. Tremors shook their bodies and their mouths drooled. Quiet groans fell from their lips. Their eyes rolled back into their heads. One by one, the hundreds of civilians collapsed to the ground. No screaming. No blood dripped from their ears.

The Mutants outside were quiet. *Were they affected or just confused?* I couldn't be sure.

Ethan ran over to a young woman and checked her pulse. From his facial expressions, I could tell all was well. A smile spread across his tan face. His brown eyes sparkled.

The Geeks did it.

The frequency worked. The civilians no longer were hearing the Strange Voices.

Zeus watched in amazement. He couldn't understand it. He didn't know how to take it.

Now's my chance. I was done listening to orders. It was time. I aimed my gun while Zeus had his guard down and pulled the trigger.

The bullet hit a body, but it wasn't Zeus'. He was shoved out of the way by another Xenophonian whom my bullet grazed. They were both on the ground, but I couldn't see where.

"YARED!" Ethan yelled.

I looked over my shoulder to see a blade gleaming in the fire light. I jumped to the side, but not far enough. I felt metal rip through my flesh. A stinging, burning sensation like one I've never felt. It sliced the lower right quadrant of my abdomen. It wasn't deep, but it didn't have to be. I knew what happened.

Sting's venom was inside me.

I clutched the wound and dropped the ground on one knee. Blood dripped through my fingertips. I could barely move. My muscles tightened, my body tingled, and my vision blurred.

Sting raised her arm again to finish me off. Ethan screamed and lunged at her with his own dagger. She jumped away, causing him to fall off balance.

Get your gun, I thought as I watched helplessly.

She tightened her grip around the hilt of her weapon. Sting walked Ethan in circles.

Get your gun.

The two of them kept their eyes locked. While they paced, Ethan slipped his hand into the medical bag across his back. He pulled out a syringe.

The antidote.

I needed it desperately and Ethan knew that. He'd do anything to get it to me. With a scream he whipped his knife at Sting. She jumped back as it cut through the air, but lost her balance.

While she was distracted, Ethan turned, dropped beside me, and stuck my thigh with the needle. The antidote decanted into me, saving me from Sting's venom.

"It's okay, man, I've got—" There was a squelch and Ethan stopped with his mouth agape. I looked over his shoulder to see Sting hovering over him.

Her dagger lodged in Ethan's back.

"NO!" I screamed. I tore the syringe out of my leg and pierced her arm with it. She howled and tore the knife out of his back. Red pooled to the white tile floor.

I caught Ethan in my arms as he fell forward. He gasped and panted as I lay him down. His eyes fluttered and his breathing became rapid. He was fading.

Ethan, no.

I looked over to see Sting tear the syringe out of her bleeding arm. Maniacal rage consumed her like darkness.

I needed to *kill* her.

Screaming, I leapt to my feet with my fists flying. I couldn't see, but didn't have to. I hooked her across the face and then to the body. She staggered backwards, but kept up her guard. I heard Ethan moan and groan.

I need a gun.

With blurred vision, I assessed the scene and noticed Ethan's weapon lying beside one of the civilians. I ran to it, but Sting was quicker. She jumped in my way. She slashed at me with her knife, but I dove to the side, grabbed her arm, and threw her to the ground. I snatched Ethan's gun and pointed it at her. My finger was on the trigger and—

A shot rang out, but it wasn't mine. It felt like an iron fist had punched through my shoulder. I looked over to see blood seeping from a fresh hole in my jacket.

I raised my eyes and saw Zeus holding a smoking gun. A look of malice across his face.

He meant to miss.

With the pain in my shoulder, I couldn't raise my arm to shoot. I could've tried a lefty shot, but if I let go of my wound, I'd bleed out.

Either way, I was a goner.

I staggered then dropped to my knees. I watched as Sting laughed, not caring about the wound in her forearm. She walked over and knelt next to Ethan who coughed and spat blood.

Sting gently stroked his tan face, moving his dark hair out of his eyes. He tried to speak, but only gurgled the blood in his throat.

"Shhh, shhh, *buenas noches, guapo,*" Sting purred. She grabbed the hilt of her knife with both hands. Raising it over her head, she whispered,

THE UNDERGROUND

"Sweet dreams." With all her strength, she plunged her knife of venom into Ethan's heart.

I screamed. I screamed so hard my throat bled, and my voice pierced through every person present. My heart stopped as Ethan's body went limp. Sting tore her red knife out of his body like an ax stuck in wood. She stood to her feet and caught my gaze. With a wicked look in her caramel eyes, she blew me a kiss. Walking over the unconscious civilians, she rejoined Zeus. Together they lifted the bandaged Xenophonian that saved Zeus from my bullet.

That Xenophonian was you, Joshua.

I couldn't believe my eyes, but I didn't have time to try. I clutched my wet shoulder tighter and staggered over to Ethan.

His brown eyes were open and staring upward. His cold limp body lay in a red halo.

Ethan was dead.

The last Savior was gone and he died doing what he was raised to do. He saved my life but gave his own.

I knelt over his body. My blood pooled through my fingers, dripping down and mixing with Ethan's on the cold marble floor. We had grown so close. We both lost our second- and third-in-commands. We were the sole survivors. We stuck together. We bled together. We were supposed to *die* together, but I never would've admitted I considered him my best friend.

Now, I wish I did.

With bloody fingers, I closed Ethan's eyes, letting him sleep in peace.

My eyes burned and the tears flowed. I wept until I felt my lights fading. As the free civilians finally began to rise to their feet, I lay down next to Ethan, staring at the ceiling. My blood pooled around me. I was growing tired.

So... tired...

I heard the doors break down and soldiers rush in. The screams of my Isle members sounded like they were underwater.

"ETHANN! YAAREEDDD!"

Then, I fell asleep.

But unlike Ethan, I knew I'd wake up.

I'm back at base. I'm in the infirmary. Janelle, Prince, and Johanna are tending to my wounds. Normally, it's Ethan, but now, the Savior has saved his last patient.

And it's all *your* fault, Joshua.

Why didn't you let me kill Zeus? Ethan could've lived. I could've distributed the antidote to him and stopped Sting. Now he's gone. Your *girlfriend* took him from us.

You took him from *me*.

YARED: IX

I hope it keeps you up at night. Knowing what you've done.
Bravery and fidelity,

Yared Prinz
Seer Commander

THE UNDERGROUND

Letter 37

Joshua: XIX

Yared, Shannon,

Please know I am *sorry*. My heart is filled with anguish. My conscience filled with regret. Things I wish I'd done. Things I wish I hadn't. Things I wish never happened.

My reason for not killing Zeus is because—as I've said—I don't know who'll take his place.

Now, I do.

New Greece was dark and quiet. The marble structures glistened in the chaotic sparkling lights above. I hobbled on a crutch up the stairs of the Temple of Zeus. My thigh throbbed. The bullet grazed me, but it still stung.

I entered the Temple to find Zeus alone by the center fire pit. He smiled when he saw me. "Wolf. How are you holding up?"

"Fine, sir," I replied, limping over to him.

"That was quite an act of bravery," he admitted. "Self sacrifice is not often seen in the Order of Xenophon."

"It was loyalty, sir. Nothing more."

Zeus nodded and turned back to watching the flames. "Wolf, I've been pondering what you said."

"What was that, sir?"

"About what happens if I fall," he said almost in a whisper. "I didn't want to think about it. I feared it."

To hear Zeus was afraid of anything shocked me. "Death frightens even the bravest of warriors," I replied.

"And yet you have no fear." Zeus' dark eyes met mine. "That's what the Order needs."

My brow furrowed. "What are you saying sir?"

Zeus put his hand on my shoulder. "A better man must take my place if I fall." He shook me gently. "That man is you, Wolf."

His words were a punch in the face. My head throbbed as the statement sunk in.

"Wolf," he began, standing up straight, "do you accept the responsibility of taking on the name of Zeus if I die? The responsibility of becoming the god-head to the Order?"

"Sir, I... I don't even know what to say." Truly, I didn't.

He held up a finger. "You only need to say one word: yes or no."

"*It's your fault, Joshua,*" Yared's words repeated over and over in my mind. I thought of all the pain I caused. All the suffering. All the lies. All the death.

No more. I wanted to be in control.

I inhaled. "Yes, sir. I accept this high honor," I declared.

Zeus held out his hand. I shook it firmly, but he didn't let go. He turned my hand palm up. He slid a small knife out of his red jacket pocket. Without protesting, I let him slice my palm and watched as he slit his own. We grasped hands again, letting our blood entwine and drip on the edge of the fire pit.

"Titan Wolf of the Russian Pandemonium," Zeus began. "I hereby name you my predecessor. The day I fall, you will take up a new Godly name. That name will be," he gripped my hand tighter, "Zeus." The flames roared at the name, changing colors to match the Divisions'. The blaze was so bright I thought I'd burn.

"Sir, I will not let you down," I stated as the flames shrank.

Zeus pulled his bleeding hand away and gave me a cloth to bandage my wound. "I know you won't," he said as he wrapped his own. "I've much to teach you. For now, rest and be well. We have accomplished much."

"Might I ask what the next step is?"

"I appreciate your zeal, but your personal preparation will come in time. As for the Order, while that last fight may have seemed like a loss, we achieved a victory." A maniacal look shone in his eyes. "We caused chaos within their hearts."

Not wanting to think about the last part, I bowed, bid farewell, and left the temple.

I couldn't believe what happened. *I will be the leader of OX,* I realized. *I'll become their god.* I thought of all the things I could do as the most powerful ruler in the world.

My imagination was interrupted when words flashed before my eyes. It was Axel. "Amigo, *where are you? I've been trying to contact you for days.*"

"Sorry, I've been preoccupied," I said aloud as my glasses typed and sent.

"Tell me about what happened with Zeus and the Mutants."

"I'd rather tell you in person."

"Nah, man. That big guy is still here."

"Goliath?"

"Yeah, he hasn't left my side. Even after you sent soldiers to relieve him. The old dude left, but he's remained. Pretty chill Ares member if you ask me."

Strange... I thought. I recalled Emel's message about how Goliath was a suspected spy and not me. *What is up with him?* I went to check it out myself.

Hobbling into the hangar, I saw Goliath talking with Axel while Diego the Monkey examined equipment on the workbench. The two chatted like friends. Goliath saw me and to my surprise, smiled.

"Titan Wolf, sir, there you are!" He waved. "How did the big fight go?"

"We lost," I stated.

Goliath clicked his tongue. "That's too bad. Glad you and the Big Man are okay. What happened to those survivors? Rumor has it our Mortals fell asleep."

"They were released from their State of Peace," I told him.

Goliath's eyes widened. "No kidding." He scratched at the double edged sword tattoo on his neck. "How do you think they did that?"

"No idea," I lied. I pointed to Axel then back at him. "Is everything okay here?"

"Yes, sir. The Hermes finished and I thought he could use company." Goliath stood up, towering over me. "Loneliness does strange things to a man." He saluted me and departed.

I called his name before he got too far. The Ares member turned and raised an eyebrow.

"Is everything all right?" I asked.

Goliath chuckled. "You tell me, Titan Wolf. Am I going to be okay?"

He knows something. "I don't know yet," I replied honestly.

With nothing else to say, the Ares member left the hangar. I heard him mumble something to a soldier in the hallway as the door shut with a bang.

"Dude, who is that guy?" Axel asked.

"Honestly, I don't know," I sighed. Diego jumped up onto the chair and unstrapped Axel. "Someone thinks he's a spy."

Axel stepped down. "What do you think?"

"I don't know what to think anymore." I plopped myself down in a seat beside the workbench. I laid my crutches against the wall and solemnly said, "Axel, there's something you should know."

My tone made him nervous. "What happened? I see you're injured, but what's wrong?"

I let out a shaky breath.

"Is it Donnie?" Axel asked desperately. "Did they not get the shears to him in time?"

"That I don't know," I replied. "They have the shears, but I'm waiting to hear what they did with them. They don't have much time left."

"Then what *do* you know." Fear filled his gray eyes.

I motioned for him to sit down. "Sting was sent on the mission with us."

Axel's lip curled.

"We were in a hall with civilians that passed out after Mark and the others successfully set off the frequency to cancel out the Strange Voices. Their sleeping bodies surrounded two soldiers. They couldn't kill innocents, so your men were trapped. " I tousled my curly hair nervously. "Sting tailed them and caught them by surprise. The two fought hard. Both were struck."

Axel's face fell and his breathing became heavy. "Who were they?"

"One survived."

"Who *were* they?" he demanded again.

I let out a deep breath. "Yared was slit by Sting's venom, but was injected with the antidote." I cast my eyes down. "Ethan wasn't as lucky."

Axel exhaled sharply. He didn't want to believe it. He couldn't believe it. He leaned his back against the workbench. "I should have been there…" The blue lights in his legs flickered. "Couldn't anyone stop her?" he croaked.

"Yared tried, but Zeus shot him," I explained.

He glared. "Where were you?"

I grabbed my crutch and stood up. "Doing what I had to." I paused. "Axel, I'm sorry. Truly, I am. Know that Ethan did *not* die in vain. His sacrifice has led us closer to victory."

Axel pinched his eyes shut. "How?" he choked.

I held out my bandaged hand. Axel looked then our gazes met. "I am now Zeus' successor," I whispered.

Axel gasped. His mechanical eyes watered from sorrow but his lip snarled out of hatred. "Then hurry up and let's make you god," he growled.

I smirked and added, "We'll plan Blake's rescue over the next few days. You're permitted to roam around the base. See what you find. Stick with Goliath if you need protection, but do *not* bring attention to yourself. Understand?" Axel nodded. I took my crutch and whistled for Diego. He dropped the weapon he was fixing and hopped off the counter. "Now I must complete something I started a long time ago," I declared as I hobbled out of the hangar and headed to the kitchen with Diego.

The lights were off. It was the dead of night and Emel was nowhere to be seen. Diego and I went to the fridge and opened the door. As I stepped in, I heard a piercing screech in my ears. *"Wolf... where are... you?"* Sting asked through static.

I ignored her and continued my mission. I spoke into the panel, opening the hidden door with a *swish*. We descended the stairs to the Children of Moirai.

I limped across the metal mezzanine, looking at the workers below. *Will they even obey me?* I went down the stairs with Diego the Monkey close behind. I went to one of the computers a few rows in. A young woman with long curly black hair sat at the keyboard.

"In the name of Xenophon, I order you to rest," I commanded.

The woman stopped typing. *"Come vuoi,"* she replied. Standing up, she walked past the other workers and disappeared into a side room.

"All you, Diego," I said to the creature.

The monkey jumped onto the console and started smacking the keyboard. The computer came to life. I didn't know how he had the coordination, but I didn't care as long as he could do it. I sat down in the marble seat and let the monkey do his thing. I pulled out my tablet and started writing this letter. I wanted to be able to document my findings immediately.

As I wrote the greeting, a voice behind me caused me to jump. "Wolf, what are you doing?"

I turned to see Sting. Her beautiful face had been cleaned of the blood from the previous battle, but she still wore the uniform. The dagger hanging from her belt gleamed.

"Sting, I might ask you the same thing," I replied, sliding the tablet out of sight.

"You haven't been answering me."

"Can't you see I'm busy?"

"Doing what?"

"Looking deeper into the matter Lachesis requested," I lied.

"Why do you need Diego?"

"The other soldier was inefficient."

"Uh huh," she clicked her tongue and crossed her arms. "I spoke with Goliath in the hall. He told me you were with the prisoner."

"My prisoner," I corrected.

"Your prisoner, right," she nodded. "Well, I went in to see you and he didn't look like a prisoner."

I arched an eyebrow. "What makes you say so?"

"Friendly conversation. How you were telling him about our last battle." Putting her hands on her knees, she bent forward and whispered, "You called my victims by name."

Oh, no, oh no, my mind panicked, but Wolf was cool and collected. I stood up straight and tall. "What are you accusing me of, Titan Sting?"

Her brown eyes stared into mine without blinking. "You're not who you say you are, Titan Wolf," she growled.

I scoffed. "You know *nothing.*"

She broke my gaze and snatched the tablet I had behind the monitor. I wanted to tear it from her, but held back.

"Then what is *this?*" She turned it over in her hand, tapping it several times. Nothing appeared. She didn't know how to use it or what it was. All she knew is it wasn't of the Order.

"That is contraband I took from a survivor," I lied, trying to stay calm. "Return it to me at once."

"No," she stated, tucking it under her arm. "I'm going to turn it in. Then we'll see what the truth is." She turned to leave.

I wasn't going to let almost eight years of my life be thrown away. I promised my friends I'd do anything to end this war.

Anything.

I raised my crutch over my head and swung it at Sting. Seeing its shadow, she ducked, spun, and swept my leg. I hissed and caught myself on the console. She grabbed my jacket collar and threw me to the ground. I landed on my wounded thigh.

Wincing, I rolled over and jumped up before she threw her foot at me. She attacked with multiple kicks which I dodged and blocked. I returned the favor with a punch to the face. She turned in time, but I nicked her nose. Infuriated, she wasn't going to stand for it anymore.

We sparred. We fought hard and long. I tried to keep her from hitting the soldiers at their desks, but it couldn't be helped.

The goal was to let Diego work. If they got hit, so be it.

I grew weary and wanted to give up. She struck my wounded leg several times. It throbbed and burned. When she hit it the third time, I noticed the pattern. The pattern Shannon saw every time Sting fought her. It was killing you, Shannon, but I figured it out.

Sting never protected her head.

Her punches were always low. She relied on kicks.

This is my chance. I faint kicked her to the shin. She dropped her guard to block it. I threw two rapid upper target punches. My fists made contact with her head. Her neck snapped back and she staggered. Hissing at the pain, she brought a hand to her nose to stop the bleeding. She was done playing games. She growled and put the other hand on the hilt of her knife.

She wants to kill me. This is it.

"Sting, don't do this!" I bellowed, putting my hands out.

"You are a LIAR!" she whipped out her dagger and lunged. I dodged.

"I trusted you!" She swung again and missed. "I believed you!" She jabbed again and missed. "I LOVED YOU!" she screamed; tears streaked down her face. She made another attempt to stab me.

I sidestepped, grabbed her wrist with one hand, and shoved her to the ground with the other. I sat on her back and tore the knife out of her grasp. She squirmed and wriggled out from under me. She jumped up and tried to run.

I stood, snatched her jacket, and threw her to the wall, pushing myself against her. Our noses touched. The scent of fresh blood—her blood—filled my nostrils. I pressed her against the cold concrete with one hand around her throat. The other gripped her venomous knife.

She scratched at my hand, trying to loosen my grasp. Her sweet caramel eyes looked at me desperately. It wasn't hatred.

It was fear.

"W...olf," she croaked.

I closed my eyes; Wolf couldn't watch.

But she didn't give up. Sting shoved my hand off her throat and spun me around. That was it. I couldn't stall anymore.

With the knife in my grip, I thrust it behind me. I felt resistance and pushed until it wouldn't go any further. A squelch and gasp reached my ears. Yanking out the blade, I thrust it back again. My hand was wet. I tore the dagger out and held it up. Sting fell against my back. I could feel and hear her raspy breathing.

I glanced over my shoulder to see terror in her eyes. Blood dripped from her mouth.

I threw the knife to the side and turned to catch her. Gently, I lay her on the ground. She shook and coughed as her blood pooled beneath her. Her flowing black hair stuck to her face and her eyes widened. "Who… are… you?" she croaked.

I put my face next to hers. Her body tremored. I pressed my lips to her ear. "My name," I started in a silky voice, "is Joshua Wolfrum of Resist Rescue Protect Retake." I pulled away to see the fear in her eyes turn to sorrow. Tears streamed down her cheeks and she tried to speak.

But her heart stopped. She'd never speak again.

My eyes burned. I pinched them shut, trying to hold back the tears. A lump caught in my throat. I kept telling myself the love wasn't real. Wolf loved Sting, not Joshua. Joshua was the RRPR member who would do anything for the good of humanity.

Yet, his heart still ached.

With a shaky breath, I closed Sting's eyelids. I pressed my lips against her forehead, kissing her until she went cold.

I got revenge, but the sweetness died with it.

I know Sting was a horrible human being. She caused you excruciating pain, but at times, she brought me joy.

I destroyed my own happiness with my bare hands.

Diego squeaked and motioned for me to come over. I snapped out of my sorrow for a moment and ordered the Children of Moirai to clean up the mess. None of them had moved an inch during the fight. Their brains were truly wired for one task.

Wiping Sting's blood on my jacket, I sat down. I took a closer look at what Diego had found.

It was a map.

He scrolled closer to where a red marking was located. In and in he zoomed until I could clearly see its name.

I gasped quietly. "How is that possible?"

I found the location of the Order of Xenophon. I'm surprised I'm still alive. The Order of Xenophon resides in one place no one has dared to go for centuries:

Chernobyl.

With safety and secrecy,

Joshua Wolfrum

Joshua Wolfrum
Titan of the Russian Pandemonium

LETTER 38

Shannon: X

Joshua,

You followed your *orders*.

I wish I could feel sorry for you. I wish I could sympathize, but I can't. Forgive me.

Sting ruined all of our lives.

All I can do is pray for you and her soul. Let that be enough.

I sat alone in the observation room, overlooking PH in his cell. I twirled Marlene's sheep shears in my hands. Yared entrusted them to me. He was afraid. He lost his best friend; he couldn't bear to watch Donnie slip away too.

I snipped the shears in the air. I remembered the girl's beautiful face. The one that matched her sister, Marian. *Marian and Marlene*, I thought with a smile. They would've been the best of friends. *Like mine and I once were.* I thought about my sisters. They didn't handle things well. They're confused, disheartened. I never told them PH was our brother. They knew our father was back, but didn't believe me. Half of them refused to see him.

My chest stung as I exhaled. The poison never rested. My eyes burned as I squeezed them shut, trying not to cry.

"Joshua Wolfrum finally did it, eh darling?"

My eyes popped open to see my father and Marcellus. They never left each other's sides. They constantly planned with Michaelson, discerning the next course of action. They have something in mind, but keep it from the rest of us.

I cleared my throat. "Yes, sir. They're in Chernobyl."

"No wonder no one could find them," Marcellus said, removing his black baseball cap. "Chernobyl's still radioactive and who knows what else OX did to it."

"From Joshua's descriptions it seems like they're underground," I said.

"Or in a facility to make it look that way," Marcellus added. He pointed to PH through the glass. "Talk to him about it yet?"

I shook my head. "Haven't thought of what to say."

He smiled. "I'll break the ice." Placing his cap next to me, Marcellus went out and into PH's holding cell.

I watched as the two conversed. While PH was upset, it was apparent he trusted Marcellus. He was the young Titan's father figure. Despite PH's claims of hatred, I know he still loved Marcellus.

"Isn't it strange, darling?" my father began, sitting down. "All my life, I prayed for my son to return. Marcellus, prayed for the same. In the end, I raised and protected his son while he did the same for me." He chuckled. "I know Marcellus. There's good in Pietro."

I hoped he was right. The memories of the horrendous encounters flooded my mind. The times he and I fought hand-to-hand. The times he killed my comrades, destroyed our base, and disabled *our* sister.

My stomach churned. The thought of it made me sick. I couldn't do anything. I didn't stop him. I can't fix it.

PH is a monster. Unfixable, unchangeable.

The thought of it caused my chest to heave. I clutched my jacket and tried to steady my breathing. Calmly, my father took my mask out of my bag and placed it over my face. I shut my eyes and let the tears drip onto the cold metal.

"Shannon," my father started quietly. "These episodes occur frequently, Shane tells me. What's the story horse?"

I took deep breaths. "It's nothing, Dad," I replied in my electronic voice.

He shot me a look. Tapping the side of my breathing apparatus, he asked again, "What is going through your head, little one? You know you can trust me. I'm your parent."

My eyes burned as the tears fell. "You were once," I croaked in my own voice. My mind couldn't take it. My heart tightened. For years I held it in. I only screamed at the sky, hoping no one would hear me but God. I looked into my father's light eyes for the first time in years. His familiar gaze was something I longed for. My mother's too.

But she was still gone.

The dam burst. The tears flooded faster, and I let go of everything.

"I have the responsibility of parent, detective, girlfriend, sister, friend, and soldier," I bawled. "I've tried to keep things pleasant for my sisters, but now they won't see me. I've failed every Officer and things keep getting worse." I rubbed my eyes with the back of my hand. "I've… failed… Shane," I confessed through sobs. I could barely say it aloud. "He does everything for me. I thought *I* needed to be the hero. I deserted him and put it all on myself. I don't know what it is. I don't know why I can't let go." My cheeks were wet, and I put my head in my hands. I bit the tube inside my machine and breathed in the antidote. I tried to battle the poison in my lungs, but my hysterics made it worse. "I hate being so *weak*," I spat.

My father sat silently with his hands folded on his lap. Shaking his head, he stated, "You're *not* weak. You're far from it. You placed a heavy burden on your shoulders. You're only twenty-three, love." He put a finger under my chin and lifted my head. "I'm sorry I couldn't have been there for you." His eyes shook. "Mum misses you, too. I wish she was with us right now." He chuckled softly. "She could phrase this better."

My dad tried anyway. "You are enough," he stated, staring into my eyes. "You're doing everything you're supposed to. You can't solve every case on your own. Sometimes, it takes two. Sometimes," he tilted his head towards PH, "it takes eight. You need to know something, but it'll hurt your ego." He took my hands and squeezed them gently. "You. Are. Going. To. Fail," he stated, enunciating each word. "You must learn to live with that, but don't go beat yourself up over it. You won't get anywhere if that's all you do." He pulled me to my feet. "Now, repeat after me: I failed and it's okay."

A lump caught in my throat. I didn't want to do it. I couldn't admit it. "I—" I choked.

"Do it."

I let out a deep breath. "I failed and it's okay."

"I'm stronger than I know."

"I'm stronger than I know."

"But I cannot do this on my own."

I paused. *But I have to.*

"No you don't," my father snapped, reading my mind.

My eyes widened. "But I cannot do this on my own."

He leaned forward and kissed my head. I never realized how much I longed for his sweet touch. "You've done enough, my dear, let it go," he said.

"Let it go," I whispered. *God, I let it go.* My silent prayer unlocked my heart. The suffering, the fights, the sorrows, emptied. My cheeks dampened. I let the tears roll like stones I dropped from a hillside. My soul was slowly becoming at peace.

"That's my girl," he smiled. "Marcellus is almost done warming up Pietro. I'm going to round up your helpers." With a wink, he patted my shoulder and left me alone.

I exhaled and sat back down. *I can't do this alone*, I repeated.

THE UNDERGROUND

I watched as PH quietly argued with Marcellus. When they reached an impasse, Marcellus stood up and left, returning to the room with me. He slipped off his trenchcoat and wiped his brow. "Just as stubborn as always."

"We'll break him," a voice said behind me. I turned to see Lucy cracking her knuckles.

All my sisters were there: Margaret (Peggy), Lucy, Carol-Ann, Rebecca, Agnes, Rachel. Their beautiful eyes filled with care. They wanted to help their big sister. They'd do whatever it takes.

This time, I'd let them.

Our father winked. "Go get him, girls."

The seven of us stormed into PH's cell. He was startled at the sight of us all. Jumping to his feet, he reached for his sword which was no longer in its sheath.

With a smile, I greeted, "Hello, Pietro."

"HIIII Pietro!" Agnes yelled. She was thirteen, but as obnoxious as a five-year-old.

PH's heterochromatic eyes darted back and forth. They landed on Rachel, particularly her leg. "You... you," he stammered.

"It's me," Rachel said with a trembling voice. She remembered him all too well. He hurt her. He scared her. "You did this to me. I'm your sister," she croaked. Her eyes welled up with tears.

"N-no you're not," he decided. "None of you are."

"Yes, we are, Pietro," Lucy retorted. "Maybe I can knock some sense into you."

"Hold up, Luce," Peggy said. She reached into her pocket and pulled out the first Hollinger family photo: a young couple with their first born son. A photo Shane salvaged after our parents were abducted. Peggy held it out to PH.

His eyes fell upon it and he scoffed. "Who is this supposed to be?"

"You," Peggy said sweetly. "Our big brother."

He snatched it from her and examined it. A photo of our parents holding our big brother: a round faced little boy with curly hair and freckles. His toothless smile was wide and his happy eyes were unforgettable.

He traced it with his fingers, but shook his head in denial. "Any kid with curly 'air looks like this."

"The eyes," Peggy said.

PH held it so close it touched his freckled nose. His eyes widened as if someone pricked him with a pin. Running to the window, he looked at his reflection. He stared at his appearance, then looked back at the picture. He held up the photo by his round face, comparing the two.

The toddler in the image had the same heterochromatic eyes. The green eye shone with valor while the blue eye was filled with sadness. The two were beautiful, mysterious, unforgettable. Both pairs of eyes told the same story.

Pietro Hollinger's story.

PH couldn't believe it. His arm hung limp at his side and he rested his forehead against the glass. The photo floated to the ground like the last leaf falling in autumn. He took a shaky breath. His entire world was untangling like the Moirai's strings.

PH took a deep breath. "*Codladh, mo ghra*," he sang. His voice was melodic and peaceful like the sea.

"*Tá Lá ag deireadh*," the seven of us sang in unison.

A single tear drop fell to the floor. The cell was silent until PH finally croaked, "What do you want?"

"More than answers," I replied. I put a hand on his shoulder. I thought my stomach would churn, but it didn't.

I was ready to give him a second chance.

"We want our brother back," I finished.

Turning his head, he looked me in the eyes. He scanned my face. He and I looked the most alike. The blue of our irises, the way our curls fell around our faces, our height, our stature. All the same.

In his face, I saw he *wanted* to believe me. His heart longed for a family, but didn't expect it to be like this.

Shaking off the feeling, he spat, "What answers do ya want?"

I sighed and held up Marlene's sheep shears. "The Moirai Atropos took these from a little boy, making them his Token of Memories. If they're returned, it might kill him. What do we do to prevent that?"

He thought. "Memories aren't gone; they're locked away. Sometimes it requires two keys. If Atropos is *inside* the boy, the keys could prove fatal." He leaned in and whispered, "His situation is unique. The boy is the Moirai's vessel. They do as they please. If 'e doesn't remember fully before 'is thread is cut, 'is heart will cease to beat."

Cut. Heart. Cut. Heart. Those words flooded back to me. I was running out of time and wanted to do all I could to save Donnie despite PH's doubts.

One thing at a time.

Switching topics, I asked, "Next, are you aware that the location of the Order of Xenophon is Chernobyl, Pripyat?"

The word struck PH and he did a double take. "Are you certain?" he gasped.

"Do you doubt?"

"No, no, it makes sense," he began, walking away from the wall. "Even Titans were forbidden from knowing the location. Not only did they not trust us, they didn't want us to leave."

"Do you think the place still hurts people?" Rebecca asked.

"If you mean radioactive, then absolutely," PH replied. "The Order conducted more tests before the Cleanse. Claimed to have done more damage than the Chernobyl accident."

"How were you not exposed?" I asked.

"We're probably underground, but I can't be sure," PH said. "Wherever it is, it 'as to be spacious and 'ave access to a lot of power. That city 'as not 'ad electricity for decades."

"There's no time to waste. We'll need your help pinpointing the location before we go storming the city," I explained.

"Why not use Pietro for bait?" Carol-Ann suggested. "Wouldn't they tell him where to go?"

"Bait is not the best word, C.A.," Rebecca scoffed, rolling her eyes.

"Tackle?" Agnes asked innocently.

"Fish," Rachel put in.

"A decoy," Lucy butt in impatiently.

"Nah, fish is more fun," Rachel protested.

They bickered about nonsense. PH couldn't help but chuckle. "Does this 'appen a lot?"

"More than I can admit," I smiled. When they stopped, I asked, "PH, would you be willing to help us?"

He paused, thinking about everything. His heterochromatic eyes met each of ours, noticing my sisters' features. Their freckles, eyes, hair, all of it. Subconsciously, he rubbed his freckled cheeks and slowly said, "For now. My curious mind isn't satisfied. If I went back to the Order now, I'd never get the answers I desire. "

I smiled. "Thank you. Note, we're still going to keep an eye on you."

"I expect nothin' less." Then, he followed the rest of our sisters out to meet with Michaelson.

I looked through the window to see my father and Marcellus smiling at me. They mouthed if I was going to join them, but I shook my head.

A little boy needed saving first.

I'm going to have Yared take over from here. Even though I'm the one who returned the shears, I think Yared should explain what happened next.

He more accurately describes the lingering pain of Sting's actions.

Godspeed and goodwill,

Shannon Hollinger

Shannon Hollinger
Royal Strategist of RRPR

LETTER 38 (PART 2)

Yared: X

Joshua,

I'm not telling you this to feel absolutely horrible about yourself, man. I'm telling you this because killing Sting was the right choice. You prevented her from doing more damage.

"I understand your thinking, but tell me why once more?" I asked through gritted teeth. I argued with Mark and the gang in the lounge area for almost an hour. RRPR denied Ethan an immediate burial.

"I'm sorry Yared," Mark repeated for the twentieth time. "It's best if we wait and send Ethan's remains to the Isles to be buried alongside Zita and Harold. We'll build him a monument like the rest of the fallen."

"What if we don't get that chance?" I asked.

"You will," he stated.

"You don't know that!" I cried. My best friend *died* saving me. I can't give him anything but a proper goodbye. Mark wasn't giving me that chance.

"Yared, please," Alison put in. "Ethan knows you care, but I think it's best to wait. Let him rest alongside his Isle members. He'd want that more than anything." Her voice shook. The pain of Ethan's death was evident on her face.

In fact, it was evident on all their faces—Mark's, too. I was blinded by my pain that I couldn't see my friends suffering with me.

"We need to stay focused, mate," Lucas added. His wings twitched anxiously as he spoke. "If I go to a funeral now, the pain'll sink in and I'll go bonkers. Let's take the time to avenge him first."

"He's been avenged," I argued. "Joshua did it a little too late."

A hush fell over the room.

"Sting's dead?" Aaron whispered.

"Yes," I spat. Glaring at Mark, I crossed the room and sat on the couch. I exhaled and put my head in my hands. "Why couldn't he have done it sooner?"

"Everything happens for a reason," Mark said gently. "Ethan's death will not be in vain. I promise you that."

Before I could argue again, Shannon entered, gripping Donnie's shears. "Where's the boy?" she asked, but bit her lip when she saw the anguish on our faces. "I'm sorry; I didn't mean to interrupt." Pain covered Shannon's face, too. Ethan was a member of the team and became part of the RRPR family.

We *all* suffered from Ethan's death.

"It's okay," Mark reassured, putting an arm around her. She let him embrace her. "Are we ready to save Donnie?"

"Almost. We need to figure out one more thing." Shannon turned the shears over in her hand. "Pietro said memories have multiple locks. What's Donnie's second key?"

"Do we have time to find out?" I snapped, getting to my feet. "Joshua said Donnie's thread is running short."

"But does it mean what we think it means?" Aaron asked.

"I believe so," Mark said solemnly. "Shannon, what were the words you thought about for the Token of Memories?"

"Cut and heart," she replied. Her mind was in a trance. She tried to decipher the words, but came up dry.

"We know that 'cut' is the shears, right?" Alison said. "What's heart then?"

We discussed possibilities when there was a ringing. Mark went over to the kitchenette counter to answer its phone. He put the receiver to his ear and said hello. His face fell and he turned to us. "We need to get to confinement, now," he ordered as he dropped the phone and ran out the door. Quickly, we followed.

We met Johanna in Donnie's room. She cradled the boy. Sami sat in the corner sobbing hysterically. The Asset was in a straight jacket and screaming bloody murder. His sandy blond hair was caked in blood from a cut on his forehead. Johanna had a mirrored wound. When he saw us enter, he snarled and growled.

"Donnie, please calm down!" Alison shouted, standing beside Johanna. "What's wrong?"

"Y'ALL DID THIS TO ME!" he bellowed. He thrashed and yelled until he grew tired. "It hurts… it hurts," he panted.

"Shannon, we have to try now, please," Mark begged.

She knelt down next to the boy. "Johanna, unlatch him." Donnie's arms were set free, but he didn't swing. He sat up in Johanna's lap and locked eyes with Alison, ignoring Shannon's presence.

"Alison, he's only going to listen to you," Shannon whispered. She took the Bionic's metal hand and placed the shears in it.

Alison knelt down in front of him. "Donald 'Donnie' McArthur," she began. With her organic hand, she stroked his dirty freckled face. "You do *not* belong to the Moirai," she stated. "You are an Asset of the Isles. You had two best friends, Ava and Marlene." She lifted the sheep shears. "These belonged to Marlene. She was your Top Banana." Alison choked back tears as she spoke.

Donnie's gray eyes locked on the shears. He lifted a shaky hand and touched the rusted metal. He gasped as if it sent a shock to his brain. "Whose is this?" he asked.

"Yours now," Alison told him. "Marlene saved your life. Ava, saved your life." She gently pressed his little fingers around the weapon. "It's your turn to save your own."

He lifted the shears and looked at them caringly. He was remembering, but not enough. Sweat dripped down his face and his body trembled.

Atropos didn't want him freed.

"She left you something else, didn't she?" Shannon put in.

The boy nodded.

Shannon's face lit up. She remembered what it was. "Marlene was the little sister to a good friend of ours." Lifting her hand, she gently put it in the pocket of Donnie's overalls. He didn't object. Shannon slowly pulled out the Best Family heirloom: the pocket watch. It wasn't ticking. Shannon held it in her palm and lifted it towards Donnie.

Donnie's expression went blank. His eyes became distant. "I… remember," he said slowly.

He started to smile, but it quickly turned into a frown. Not out of anger or sadness but pain. His mouth opened and blood curdling screams escaped. Dropping the shears, he lifted his wrist and gripped it. "IT BURNS! IT BURNS!" Donnie screamed. He fell on his back and writhed.

"What's wrong with him?!" Alison cried.

Shannon tore his hand away and looked at his wrist. Blood pooled from the three slits. "Atropos did this when she took his memories away," she said. "She must've—"

Donnie screamed and started convulsing. His arm turned purple and his veins bulged. "GET OUT! GET OUT!" he screeched.

I didn't know what to do. None of us did. We stared at our poor friend as he screamed and shook in agony. I felt helpless.

The Moirai were cutting their puppet's strings.

"Go get Janelle!" Johanna yelled as she cradled him.

Abruptly, Donnie's screaming ceased. His shaking body stopped and he lay still. "Don't..." he croaked. "It's okay, Johanna." Foam bubbled in his mouth as if waves crashed out of his throat. "They're... gone." He winced and took several deep breaths. "They left... they left something..." He twitched and rambled off random numbers which Aaron scribbled into a notebook.

When Donnie finished, a smile spread across his face. "It was... meant to be." He laughed, spitting foam everywhere. He looked up, staring into the bright lights. "It is finished," he gasped. "I'm gonna... see Marlene and Ava." Blood and tears streamed from his eyes. "We're... gonna play... on the farm every day now. It's so beautiful. Mr. Calvin is there... and and," his gray eyes widened like he saw the most beautiful flower, "He's there too. He'll take me home now." He closed his eyes, clutching the shears to his chest. "Thank y'all... you... saved... me..." he exhaled a final time and his body fell limp in Johanna's arms. A peace upon his face like I've never seen.

Donnie was called home.

I couldn't believe it. Donnie was gone. I dropped to my knees; all was silent.

We lost another.

"They've won," Sami cried. She dug her nails into her head of black hair. Her cat tail tapped frantically against the ground. "They've won... they've won."

"No, they didn't, Sami," Aaron replied, holding back his tears. He needed to be strong for his sisters. He wrapped his arm around his twin. "They've failed. Donnie is at peace."

I couldn't take it. Ethan was gone. Donnie was gone. *Who is next?*

My fists clenched; the veins in my neck bulged. "We went through all that pain and suffering for them to take him from us?!" I screamed. *First Ethan. Now Donnie. Probably Axel. Who is next?* "What goodness comes from death? What is suffering? Why does this happen?" My chest heaved and I knelt next to the boy I fought beside. I first met Donnie when he was my team for the Isles Challenge. I was his leader, but he was braver than me.

At the end, he still was.

I stroked his cold bloody arm. My fingers felt the slits Atropos gave him. The boy's blood burned at the touch.

The Moirai must die, I thought.

I don't care if I die in the process. They need to pay for their crimes.

Still holding Sami, Aaron announced, "I loved Donnie. We all did. But like Mark says, everything happens for a reason. Even now, I believe him."

Mark was silent; his blue eyes locked on the small boy's lifeless body. Pain encompassed him. Donnie was like a son to Mark as are we all.

Helplessly, he watched another child die.

I needed to hear his encouragement. He always knows what to say, but Mark was motionless. Nothing escaped his lips.

Aaron cleared his throat and shook his notepad. "Everything happens for a reason," he repeated. "Donnie gave us coordinates."

"To where?" I spat.

"The base in Chernobyl," Shannon whispered.

Aaron nodded.

I sat on the floor. I couldn't believe it. This little boy sacrificed his life to get us what we've been searching for. The Moirai were in his head for months, but he never gave up.

He fought to the end.

"Guys," Shannon gasped, looking down at her hand. She held the Best Family pocket watch. Lifting it to her ear, her eyes widened. "It's…" she choked, "ticking again." She smiled as a tear rolled down her cheek. "Donnie is home. Donnie is safe now."

I have nothing more to say.

Bravery and fidelity,

Yared Prinz

Yared Prinz
Seer Commander

THE UNDERGROUND

Letter 39

Joshua: XX

Yared and Shannon,

I am sorry for your loss. It seems both of our suffering is grave. I wish I could've gotten the shears to you sooner. Don't let Donnie's sacrifice be in vain. Plan to attack Chernobyl as soon as possible.

Something happened here that I didn't expect.

I broke the sorrowful news to Axel. He sat in his chair, tears dripping from his gray mechanical eyes. "I should've been there," he cried through gritted teeth. "I wasn't there for Ethan and now Donnie. God forbid… oh Alison." He rubbed his hands through his white curly hair. He mumbled to himself, letting all his feelings out.

I half listened. My mind was distant. Sting's blood was on my hands. The hands I used to hold her, caress her, love her. Those same hands gripped the blade that was driven through her, taking her life. The last words she heard were from that of a traitor. I betrayed PH, I betrayed Sting…

No, Joshua. You didn't, a voice inside me said. *Stay strong. You're almost there.*

After almost eight years, I wasn't sure anymore.

"Joshua?" Axel said aloud.

I hadn't heard my name spoken by another in a long time. It frightened me. Did it still belong to me? "Don't say that," I scolded.

"Sorry." Axel stepped out of his chair. "How are you holding up?" He quickly dried his damp cheeks. "I mean with your own pain."

I paused. I didn't want to tell him that I regretted killing a murderous villain.

THE UNDERGROUND

"I know you loved her," Axel said, reading my thoughts. Despite his own unbearable grief, he worried about me. "The justification of killing is difficult to identify, but you prevented more sins from being committed."

I nodded and got to my feet. "Remember, you're free to roam," I instructed, ignoring his comments. "Survey the area. They had REM in the Entrance Ritual chambers, but now I'm not sure. Do whatever you can to find him and report back."

Axel's eyes widened. "Are you saying what I think you're saying?"

I nodded. "We're getting out of here."

Saying nothing else, I left Axel to grieve alone.

Time for my leadership training.

I walked with my eyes forward but my mind elsewhere. I didn't notice Diego climb onto my back until he slapped me in the face. I was startled. "Where did you come from?"

He squeaked, pulling on my combat jacket collar. He wanted me to turn around and go somewhere.

"Not right now, I need to meet with Zeus. You know this is important."

He leapt off my shoulder and stood in my way; his arms out.

"I don't have time for your games, Diego!" I was annoyed. I wasn't going to be bossed around by a little monkey. "In the name of Xenophon, I order you to heed."

The monkey snarled. Despite being an animal, his mind responded to the order his Master obeyed. He stepped out of the way and hissed. Our eyes locked. For a moment, I saw Solomon in the brown eyes of the creature. He was in there and trying to tell me something.

But I didn't listen.

I went through New Greece and up to the Temple of Zeus where the god-like man sat on the steps. In his hand was an electronic clipboard with a case the same color red as his suit.

He stood up. "Welcome, Wolf. Are you ready?"

"As ready as I'll ever be, sir," I replied.

He smiled. "Let us begin."

He led me through the temple and down the damp corridor to where the Mutants were kept in cages. They snarled, growled, and rattled the rusty iron bars. Some were excited to see us, others terrified.

We walked to the center and Zeus lit the fires. Standing outside of their cages were three Mutants I feared to face: Dylan the Bear, Adeline the Fruit Bat, and Clive the Fox.

I thought my heart would pound at the sight of them, but today I had no fear. Well, Wolf had no fear.

I didn't know where Joshua was.

Zeus locked eyes with the beasts. He raised his arm with his palm facing outward. He folded his fingers and pointed. With a click of his tongue, he twisted his wrist, his finger pointing towards himself.

With a grunt, the Mutants lumbered forward. Dylan Cheatle the Bear sat down before Zeus, looking up at him like a dog waiting for food.

"Not yet, *arkoúda*," Zeus whispered, ruffling the Bear-boy's hairy head. It grunted and exhaled through its snout. "Many say harsh commands and whips," Zeus began as he scratched Dylan's chin, "are the only ways to get through to beasts." He whispered a command in Greek and Dylan obeyed, rising to his feet.

I peered into the dark eyes of the towering Mutant and saw the memories of the chubby boy I once knew. Inside was the timid young Umbrella who'd bake cookies with the Hollinger girls. Now, he's a circus bear for a sinister ring leader.

"I beg to differ," Zeus continued; he keenly watched Dylan. "Their minds are already fragile. It doesn't take much to sway them one way or the other."

"How do you do it?"

He pulled up his red suit sleeves. Around his wrists were slim metal bracelets. "The Children of Hades respond to movement more than commands." He raised both hands high above his head. All the creatures silenced. They stood at attention; their chins in the air. Waiting.

"They feel my heartbeat." Zeus closed his eyes and inhaled. "They respond to my breathing." He held his breath and pulled his leg back. With no warning, he drove it forward into the side of the fire pit.

The Mutants went insane as Zeus winced at the pain. The creatures were frozen in place, but screamed at their Master's affliction. They suffered with him. Dylan the Bear roared and growled before us, but didn't step forward even though he wanted to.

Zeus let out a deep breath and shook his throbbing foot. As his heartbeat calmed, so did the Mutants'. "You see, Wolf, it's more than raising your hands like a preacher. It's about controlling your emotions, your feelings, your thoughts." Lowering his arms, he turned to me. "They respond to *you*."

I nodded. Normally, I would've been terrified. I would've been afraid that the Mutants would feel who I really was. They'd know I was a traitor.

Today, *I* didn't know who I was

"How do you control one individually?" I asked.

"They know whom you wish to speak to." He looked over and lifted his chin. With a whistle and a flick of the wrist, Adeline the Fruit Bat leapt into the sky, flapping the wings that were sewn to her arms. "Just as you feel a person staring at you from across the room, or you know when someone means to say something. The Children of Hades detect that." He snapped and

Adeline descended; the rest of the beasts became at ease.

Zeus slid the metal bracelets off his wrist and held them out. "Titan Wolf of the Russian Pandemonium," he began. His booming voice bounced off the cave walls. "I'm entrusting the Children of Hades to you. You'll learn to be their leader, their commander, their father." I lifted my hands, and Zeus slid the bracelets over my wrists. A stinging surge of energy shot along my arms and to my head. When the pain dissipated, the Mutants silenced and shifted in their cells. Their glowing eyes watched me.

"They're waiting for you," Zeus whispered.

"What are the commands, sir?"

Zeus smiled. "You'll know." He patted my back and turned to take his leave. "Practice all you wish. Report to me tomorrow." He looked over his shoulder. "I know you won't disappoint me, Titan Wolf." His footsteps faded until the room was silent once again.

I let out a deep breath, looking at the metal bands around my wrist. I turned to the *arkoúda*, *nychterída*, and *alepoú*. Their familiar eyes watched me carefully. I looked back at Dylan, whispering "*arkoúda*" under my breath. With confidence, I raised my hand, causing him to look to the sky. Slowly, I brought it back down and the Mutant-Bear copied until he was gently laying at my feet. I stepped aside, leaving the pathway open. I opened my palm and Dylan got on all fours. With a whistle and a flick of the wrist, the Bear-Boy bolted. He barreled down the path, grunting and roaring.

He wasn't going to stop until I told him to.

Before he crashed into the wall, I whistled and swung my arm the other way. Dylan skidded to a stop, turned around, and ran back towards me. I lifted my hand, palm facing outward. Dylan slowed his pace until he stopped at my feet. With a growl he lay down to rest.

"Good job, *arkoúda*," I said with a smile.

"You know his name," a voice growled.

My heart leapt and the Mutants felt it. There was a ruckus. The beasts in their cages screeched and howled. I turned to see a face of orange and white fur staring at me with wide eyes.

Clive Foxwood the *alepoú*.

"I beg your pardon?" I scowled.

He snarled, showing his perfect sharp teeth. "Don't play games, Umbrella. You know who he is. Who we are." He stepped forward; his bushy fox tail swayed behind him. With a whisper, he threatened, "We know who *you* are, Joshua."

My heart raced. The sound of my name made my stomach churn. The Mutants grew rowdy and anxious. They banged against the iron bars, trying to bust out. I needed to take control.

I was the leader, not Clive.

JOSHUA: XX

My surprise turned into fury. My brow furrowed and I gritted my teeth. Taking a deep breath, I steadied my heartbeat and thrust my hands into the air. A silence fell upon the hall like rain ceasing after a storm. The Mutants calmed and listened intently.

"Clive," I started. "From what I heard, you were the only one to remain sane." I bent over and rubbed Dylan's head. He didn't protest. "With a conscious mind, you chose your side."

"I like who I *am* now," he spat. "I don't like *where* I am. I chose to be with the psychotic hippie scientist." He cast his eyes downward. "He betrayed us."

"That surprises you?"

Clive growled. "I was naive, all right? Five years is a long time. I've matured since then."

"Prove it," I challenged.

His yellow eyes glowed. "None of us want to be here," he said in a low voice. "We're wild animals. We deserve to be free. We're not the Order's circus act." He stepped forward. His hot foul breath blew on my face, but I didn't budge. "Are you going to get us out of here, Joshua?"

I didn't want him to say my name. I didn't want anyone to say it. I didn't want to hear it. "I will try," I quietly promised.

But did I mean it?

I lifted a hand and gestured for the Mutants to return to their cages. Clive gave me a side eye and went back.

Once they were secure, I turned and left them with an empty promise.

I marched out of the Temple of Zeus, fiddling with the bracelets on my wrist. As I walked, there was an ear piercing noise in my head and a voice. It was Emel. *Wolf... Children of Moirai... now.*

Obeying, I ran out of New Greece and towards the kitchen. As I raced, I heard the patter of little feet and a screeching behind me. Diego tried to catch up with me, wanting to tell me something.

I still didn't listen.

I ran into the kitchen and headed towards the fridge. Diego hopped up onto the counter, grabbed a vegetable, and threw it at me. It bounced off my temple. It didn't hurt, but I was agitated. I turned to the monkey and glared. "I am not in the mood, Diego," I growled.

The creature screeched and smacked its face.

"No, I'm not being ridiculous."

Diego hissed.

"Think what you want. Emel needs me." I turned and went down to the Children of Moirai. I wasn't fast enough shutting the door, so Diego followed.

"Wolf, there you are," Emel called. Dark circles were under her eyes.

She looked fatigued and anxious. "I have some dreadful news."

I already knew. "What's wrong?" I asked calmly. I ran down the stairs and met her by the computers.

"Do you want the bad news or the heart breaking news?"

I took a deep breath. "Give them both to me quickly."

She exhaled through her nose. Her lips tightened to form a straight line. After a pause, she said simply, "Sting is dead and the treacherous traitor is loose in our base."

My eyes widened. "You don't mean—"

"Goliath," she finished. "He murdered Sting. I'm sure of it."

"Have you found the body?"

She shook her head. "Sting wouldn't disappear without mention. Besides," she took a knife that rested on the computer monitor, "the Children of Anemoi found this when they transported some of my Children." It was Sting's venomous dagger.

My face expressed horror and sorrow while my mind was elsewhere. *Children of Anemoi*, I thought. I never heard that name before. *They must be the ones taking us to the missions and back.*

"I'm sorry, Wolf," Emel whispered sympathetically. "She was a lucky girl and your respect for her was admirable. Out of line, but admirable."

I pretended to swallow a lump in my throat. "What are we to do about the traitor?" I said in a low voice.

"Find him," Emel spat. She covered Sting's dagger with a cloth and handed it to me. "And kill him with the blade he used to murder your lover."

I took the knife and gripped it. "I will."

She smirked. "I know you'll succeed. Prove to us all you're worthy to lead. Avenge. You have until your next departure."

"Which is?"

She turned and tapped the computer screen. The blue hologram in the center of the room changed from maps to an image of a man wired up to various machinery. It was Blake. He lay flat on an uncomfortable cot. He wore pajamas of all red and a breathing mask over his face. His white hair was so dirty it looked black. I watched him breathe in and out. The noise of ticking and a scribbling occurred every time his chest rose.

He was dreaming.

"They're interpreting it as we speak," Emel whispered as if Blake were going to hear us and stir. "From what we gather, the enemy gained vital intel and are planning an attack." She turned to me. Her dark eyes filled with... worry. Something I'd never seen in Emel. "We think they know where we are."

This time, my fear and worry was real. My face paled.

"We have to prepare for the worst, Wolf," she stated. She tapped the computer, changing the hologram back. She let out a deep breath. "An end is coming."

"Whose end is it?"

She looked up and smirked. "Time to find out."

After dismissing me, Emel rejoined her sisters to plan for the upcoming attack. I overheard Atropos call about the shears missing from her desk, but I didn't have time to eavesdrop. I hope she assumed it was the "traitor".

Running up the metal stairs, I found Diego waiting for me by the door. He was silent and made no noise. I let him jump on my shoulder, but we didn't speak.

As I was returning to my quarters, I got a message from Axel: "*I found Blake.*"

"A little too late, unfortunately," I said aloud in reply.

"*Sorry, man. This place is bigger than I realized. I also can't get him right now. It's dangerous until we have a new plan.*"

"Is he in New Greece?"

"*Nah, man. They keep him in a hidden room next to the torture chambers. I wouldn't have found it without the help of my new friends.*"

I stopped in my tracks. "What friends?"

"*Goliath and his fellow Interpreters.*"

Demand an explanation from Virginia Michaelson. What is the meaning of her sending her troops here? Why is Goliath one of them and I had no idea? Do you think I am not good enough to succeed?

Pass along this message as well:

The Order of Xenophon knows you're coming.

With safety and secrecy,

Joshua Wolfrum

Joshua Wolfrum
Titan of the Russian Pandemonium

THE UNDERGROUND

Letter 40

Shannon: XI

Joshua,

While appearing contradictory, everything has a reason.

I sat in the conference room with my fiancé, waiting for our fathers and my brother to join us. It initially was only Marcellus, my dad, PH, and me finalizing the plans. However, stubborn Shane refused to leave my side.

"I'm all right, I promise," I told him as I scribbled notes.

He took my hand and held it. "I'm sorry about the boy," he whispered.

I pinched my eyes shut. *He's home... he's home... he's home.* It still hurt. It still stung. I know he's happy now, but the pain of loss lingered. For the first time in a long time, I went in for Shane's embrace. I let him hold me. I felt his arms wrap around me. I closed my eyes and imagined Donnie free, skipping through bright fields and holding hands with Ava and Marlene.

Shane stroked my head, nestling his chin in my hair. "It's okay."

"I didn't know him as well as the Isle members," I choked, "but I fought beside him. I watched his pain. I watched him suffer."

"And you watched him be set free. You helped save him." Shane kissed my forehead. "We have to let him go."

I knew that. I needed to remember it.

My father and Marcellus entered. They both smiled when they saw me in Shane's arms. My dad was pleased to see me opening up. He blessed our engagement from the beginning... before the two of us even knew.

"You all right, darling?" my dad asked, sitting down.

I gently pulled away from Shane, rubbing my eyes. I nodded.

"Good, because we need you," Marcellus put in. He laid out maps of

Chernobyl on the table.

As we weighed down the crinkling paper, PH walked in. He looked different in our RRPR uniform. His freckled face was no longer covered by his green scarf. He was open. Exposed. His brown hair curled nicely on his head. Coloring returned to his freckled cheeks. The long double edge sword returned to its rightful place on his back. Each eye showed a different emotion: green, determined and blue, doubt.

Half of him doesn't know what he's doing here, I thought.

"There you are, Pietro," our dad greeted with a smile. "How are you?"

"As well as I can be, Leprechaun," PH replied. He refused to acknowledge Leprechaun/Quinn as his father. He was warming up to my sisters and me when he agreed to help us. *I hope it's not a ruse…*

"Let's dive right into it, shall we?" Marcellus began. "Thanks to Donald McArthur," he paused out of respect, "we know their base is here," he tapped the map, "where the power plant was in 1986."

"Is it still radioactive?" Shane asked.

Marcellus and Leprechaun/Quinn looked at each other then to PH. "I would assume so, yes," the young Hermes Titan said.

"You mean we want to send in all our troops to a place that could kill us?" Shane said matter of factly.

"You make a good point, son," Marcellus replied. "But I see no other choice."

"What about the Interpreters?" Shane asked. "Can't they assess that first?"

"Unfortunately, there is no time," I chimed in. "OX knows we're coming."

Shane slumped back in his chair, but he wasn't defeated yet. "What about Joshua and his new friends?"

"That's what we must figure out," my dad put in. "But let's decide the real plan."

"Do we really want to go that route?" I asked.

My dad looked to Marcellus and PH who both nodded. "I think it's the best option," my dad went on. "The frequency was tested and confirmed. It proved success the day that," he paused, "we lost a good Savior."

We were silent for a moment. As we were quiet, Yared and Michaelson stepped in. "Hello everyone," the Interpreter Director greeted. We rose. "Please, be at ease," she raised her hand and we sat. "Yared tells me there is some concern with my soldiers."

"Yes, ma'am," I cleared my throat. "Were you aware of Interpreters living within the enemies' walls?"

"Yes, I did," she stated.

Confusion crossed my face. "Why didn't you say anything? Is the monster Goliath one of yours?"

"He's a recent addition," Michaelson confessed. "My Interpreters aren't front men. They go into a situation, assess it, and report back. That's why I refrained from saying anything. I didn't want to interfere with Joshua's mission."

PH's face fell. He must've thought about Goliath. He was one of PH's soldiers within the English Pandemonium. *He must feel more betrayed every day...*

"So you knew what was happening within the walls the entire time?" I asked sharply.

Michaelson shook her head. "Never. I will be honest, I was unsure how many were still alive. We haven't been able to communicate since Marcellus left."

Shane and I looked at him. "You were an Interpreter?" Shane asked; his mouth agape.

Marcellus chuckled. "Not officially. It was more of an honorary position."

PH glared at his former superior but said nothing.

"Hate to interrupt the exposition," Yared snapped, "but can we please get back to the task at hand? I need to prepare."

"Of course," Michaelson apologized. "If the fact that I never told you was your only concern, let's move past that. Tell me your plan."

I took a deep breath. "We plan to use your Interpreters around the globe to establish the frequency at the temples where the Annex has taken full effect." I tapped the locations on the map. "They will go down simultaneously, offering freedom to millions at once. Your Interpreters will remain with them, providing explanation and assistance."

"And if the survivors rebel?" Michaelson asked, folding her hands. "What if they prefer their lucid state and wish to return?"

"I've considered that and I'll say," I paused, "we pray for the best. We won't have the best outcome, but people choosing to be horrible on their own is better than zombies doing nothing." I looked at my dad and Marcellus. "What do you say?"

"Free them first, worry later." Marcellus smiled. "Then they can't turn on us with the flick of a switch from the Children of Moirai."

"Good point," Michaelson said. "Now, the rest."

"Regardless whether Chernobyl is radioactive or not," I continued, "the remaining soldiers will bomb the Order's headquarters. If that fails, we'll besiege, trapping them inside until it's safe to storm and take the base by force."

"And our men inside?" Michaelson added.

"Hopefully, they'll assist us," I said, stifling a sigh.

My father noticed the detail. "You doubt?" he asked, slightly worried.

I bit my tongue. I shouldn't have swayed with my response. "It's a minor concern."

"It's still a concern," my father challenged. "Joshua regretting his decision?"

I hesitated.

"Oh dear," my dad sat back in his chair. "If he doesn't pull through, we may never get down there."

"He will," Yared chimed in. "If he doesn't, Axel will. I'm sure of it." Deciding he heard enough, Yared headed for the door. "I'll prepare my members for the first wave."

"Can you handle it?" I asked.

He paused. "We're hanging on to hope," he said quietly. His strength was failing. He didn't know how much longer he could hold on. Standing up straight, the Seer left.

Shane tapped his face, utterly confused. "Where are they going?"

"To Chernobyl first as a diversion," Marcellus explained. "If the Order of Xenophon thinks they're the only troops, they won't prepare as much."

"Assuming they're not complete idiots?" Shane quipped.

"Our men can handle it," I reassured. That's what I wanted to believe anyway.

My dad leaned over the table and grabbed my hand. "They'll be fine. I'm sure Joshua has a plan. He's with the Interpreters now."

Michaelson nodded. "They'll put him on the right track."

Shane blew out an exhale and shook his head. "I hope Yared hangs tight until that happens."

"Don't worry, I have someone to catch him," Michaelson added. Satisfaction gleamed in her light eyes.

She's hiding something else, I thought, but didn't say anything.

All the while, PH was silent. In his blue eye, I saw fear. Was it fear for the Order or fear for us?

Were we walking into a trap?

I'll let Yared take over from here. The others and I discussed logistics. You know the basics, now hear what's on its way.

Godspeed and goodwill,

Shannon Hollinger

Shannon Hollinger
Royal Strategist of RRPR

LETTER 40 (PART 2)

Yared: XI

Yo Joshua,

If you don't get your head in the game, I'm gonna whip your *ERROR. CENSORED*. Correction: *we're* gonna whip your *CENSORED*.

I apologize for the language. Well, I guess I don't have to apologize because this *CENSORED* tablet blocks it out. Just like my personal log...

The reason for the harsh words is because the way I saw my team today made me furious. The fact that you even *doubt* your loyalty makes me sick.

I left the meeting room with my head hung low. I didn't want to think, but I had to. I didn't want to act, but I had to. My mind was so preoccupied that I didn't look where I was going until I bumped into Prince.

"Sorry, sir," he apologized, helping me stand upright.

Oh no, not this character again, I thought with a groan. I know most of the other members had wonderful family reunions, but if this guy actually was my dad, I didn't want to know. "Forget it," I said abruptly. I didn't know why I was rude.

Wait. That's how I always am. Nevermind. I'm getting too self aware writing these letters and it's annoying.

I was walking away when he called out to me. "Yared Prinz?" I turned. I saw a familiar smile. "You'll keep them safe," Prince stated with sincerity.

That small comment coming from a kind face gave me encouragement. Father or not, he gave me strength. I thanked him and went on my way. We had a mutual understanding and connection that I vowed to leave unspoken.

I entered the lounge area to find Mark alone. He rested his elbows on the counter and held his head in his hands. I knocked on the side of the fridge. Startled, he turned to face me. "Sorry, Yared," he apologized. His eyes were red. "Lost in thought."

I wanted to comfort him, but I couldn't. Seeing Mark suffer brought me more anguish. My own pain prevented me from relieving his. "Are you ready?" I asked.

He let out a sigh. "Are you?"

"As ready as I'll ever be," I shrugged.

He nodded slowly. "How are the others?"

I tried to think of the right word. I couldn't put a finger on it.

"Disheartened," a female voice said behind me. I turned to see Alison walking through the doorway. She was decked out in her Bionic armor. She was the only one ready to go. Gray mechanical eyes stared out from beneath her white bangs. Worry aged her pale face. She was no longer a teenager looking for a fight. She was a woman ready to end one. "Mark, you need to give them another pep talk. I have nothing to say."

Mark nodded. I hoped he'd come up with words of encouragement. He always did. *Now, I'm not so sure.*

Silently, we grabbed our packs and headed to the hangar to meet the remaining Isle members: Aaron, Lucas, and Sami. Just the six of us now out of seventeen. We hoped to rescue Axel and make it seven again.

Lucas took his goggles off, watching us. In his freaky compound eyes, you could see the reflection of our sad faces. Hidden behind them was his own sorrowful soul. "Hey, mates," he started, "I know it's going to be hard and dangerous. But honestly," he shrugged his shoulders, "what have we got to lose?"

"Whatever we've got left," Sami choked. Her green cat eyes welled up with tears. Her lip quivered around her fangs. Alison went over to comfort her younger sister. When Donnie passed, she snapped out of her hysterics. It was like she felt Atropos leaving the boy's body. While her soul is more at rest, her heart still aches and mourns.

We stood in silence while Sami steadied her breathing. Mark lifted his eyes up. He met each of our faces individually. "It's because of those we have left that we have to go," he began. His mind and heart were inspired. "We made a promise, didn't we? We wouldn't take the life of anyone we loved for granted." He reached into his jacket and pulled out the pocket watch. "This heirloom doesn't just represent the Best family; it represents all those we've lost," he gripped it tighter, "Ursula, Zita, Harold, Becca, Cecil, Ava, Marlene, Jeremy, Ethan, Donnie, and all those I've lost from RRPR." He shook his fist. "This watch went through hell and back just like us. But in the end," he held the heirloom up to his ear, "it's still ticking." Extending his arm out, he opened his palm; the watch face up. "Despite our sorrows, we're still going. We're still ticking. Time stops for no one; our friends knew that. They accepted it, but that doesn't mean they wasted it. They don't want us to waste it either. Let's not fail them." His blue eyes scanned us again. They weren't demeaning. They were the eyes of a father who cared for his children.

That's what Mark was to us. He was more than a friend.

He was the father we orphans never had.

I reached out and laid my hand on his. I felt the tick of the watch beneath my calloused palm. "For my Seers and everyone else," I stated.

One by one, the others did the same until we were all touching. I felt the warm comforting presence of my friends…

No. My family.

I felt my family close to me. We suffered together. We hurt together. If we had to die together, so be it. But we wouldn't make it easy.

Our clock was still ticking and we were determined to keep it that way.

As we pulled away, Mark smiled. "Now, let's go put an end to all of this and save Axel and Blake."

Everyone boarded ahead of Mark and me. We stayed behind to make sure everything was set with the other pilots. They were to land in a neighboring country and stay on call if something went wrong.

We were about to board when a high voice called from behind. "Mark! We're coming, too." I turned to see Aymie, Johanna, and Nic rushing up to the plane.

"Girls, it's not safe. Not to mention you were *shot*, Aymie," Mark stated. "Nic, you were also injured, you shouldn't be coming either."

"Like we care, stupid," Johanna retorted. "You need us."

"No. The Interpreters at the Temples need you," Mark corrected.

Nic chuckled and put his massive hand on Mark's shoulder. "You're going to need more if you want to take down Zeus and his monsters. Besides, *I'm* a Mutant," he winked, "I recover quickly."

Mark growled. He didn't like the idea of endangering more people, but Nic had a point. "If you say so then Nic, *you* are welcome to join. I have no authority to stop you since you're Stanley Wyght's Co-Director."

"Which means you have no authority to get rid of us," Johanna stated. Without letting Mark say another word, she boarded the plane with her fiancé.

Mark's hand shot out to pull Johanna back, but he stopped himself. With a sigh, he turned to his sister. He was about to say something, but she put her hand up.

"Mark, I don't care what you say." She glared at him with her gray eyes. "I am fine; my leg healed. I can't stand by and watch anymore." She gripped the straps of her backpack. "My boyfriend is imprisoned and being tortured by the Xenophonians. I want to get him out."

Mark exhaled through his nose. He didn't want to endanger his sister, too. She suffered enough. It pained him to agree. Even if he wanted to, he couldn't stop her. Aymie was dressed for battle from her headwrap to her boots. Her mind was ready and her heart turned to stone. In silence, she pushed her way past us.

Mark whispered to me, "Can you get an answer from Joshua about the Interpreters and Axel helping us out?"

I nodded. "I'll work on it once we're in the air."

And here I am. Like I said before, Joshua, if you even think about betraying us, you're going to be wanted on both sides. It won't end well for you.

Finish what you started.
Bravery and fidelity,

Yared Prinz

Yared Prinz
Seer Commander

Letter 41

Joshua: XXI

Yared. Shannon.

Stop accusing me. I'm sick of it. You think I don't know what the mission is? You think I'm not loyal? For your information, I'll be causing a lot of chaos for *you*.

After sending that last letter, I waited to retrieve Blake. He was alive, and that's what mattered.

I put off finding Goliath and his Interpreters. Emel told me to do it immediately, but I needed time. I wanted to make sure I was capable of replacing Zeus if—I mean *when* the time comes. I knew the moment I met with Goliath everything would go downhill from there.

Zeus left me alone to train the Children of Hades. My leg almost fully healed; I was ready to fight. I prepared to lead the Mutants in case something went wrong. After an hour of command drills, I dismissed them.

As they returned to their cells, Clive the Fox looked over his shoulder and whispered, "When are we making a move?"

"You'll know," I replied simply.

He scoffed. "But will you?"

I saw through his yellow eyes. I knew he doubted me, too.

"Just get back into your cage," I growled.

The Fox put his hands up and walked backwards. "Yes, my lord." With a sinister smile, he stepped inside his cell and shut the door himself.

With a glare, I went back upstairs. I stalled long enough. I received your reply the night prior.

Time to find Goliath.

I was exiting New Greece when I sent the first message to Axel. "Where should I go?"

"*Hangar where PH's tank used to be.*"

"Used to be?"

"*Yeah, his tank is gone. It was in pretty bad shape so they got rid of it when he was captured.*"

I stepped through the hangar door and to the back where a new fighter plane sat in the place of PH's beloved Challenger. Strangely enough, my heart ached to see its replacement. Another reminder of someone I lost.

"I'm here," I announced. My voice bounced off the massive metal weapons. "Now what?"

"*Go towards the front of the plane and stand next to its landing gear.*"

I did as he said.

"*Now kick the wheel.*"

An odd request, but I smacked the side of my foot against the rubber.

"*Harder.*"

I was annoyed. Out of pure frustration, I drove my foot into the tire. Before I had time to pull my leg back, I lost control. I was free falling. I kept my feet first, but my body wanted to spin. I plummeted hard and fast down a pitch black tunnel. I couldn't see the bottom. I felt my glasses slipping off my face so I grabbed them and slid them into my pocket.

"Hold your breath!" a voice shouted.

I obeyed. I crossed my arms and kept my legs straight, hoping I'd hit what I was anticipating. I shot through brisk water. Air tried to escape my lungs. Once my body stopped its dive, I frantically swam upwards. My limbs grew tired and I felt lightheaded.

Breaching the surface, I gasped in the dank air. I looked around and saw a figure with blue lights spread across his body. It was the Bionic.

Axel stood on a ledge, waving towards me. I swam over and he pulled me out of the water. I lay on my back, panting.

The Bionic leaned over and smiled. "You're all right, *amigo*. Now, put your glasses on and let's finish what you've started."

I pulled the spectacles out of my pocket and placed them on my face. They survived the fall. Axel offered a hand. I took it and he hoisted me to my feet.

Silently, he led the way down the dark corridor. His armor lights illuminated the path, encompassing us in a blue hue.

As we marched, I felt a stinging sensation on my bare neck followed by my stomach aching, my eyes burning, and my throat catching fire. I wrapped my arms around myself, trying to keep it together. I felt... weird.

Axel shot a side glance, but said nothing. He didn't appear affected. *Lucky Bionic body...* Then again, I shouldn't be jealous of having no legs.

We reached what appeared to be a dead end. Placing his hand on the grimy wall, Axel traced his finger along its grooves. The door slid open with an electronic *swish* and we stepped inside. I stifled a gasp.

The area stretched almost as far as the base was long. It was dimly lit and smelled of rotting flesh and vomit. I gagged and covered my mouth with my shirt. Walking through, I saw men and women sleeping shoulder to shoulder on rusted cots all around us. There was no room for them to walk or simply be. Along the walls were niches with toilets and an occasional shower and sink. These poor people lived in filth.

And I didn't know they existed.

"Does this surprise you, Wolf?" Axel said aloud. "These are the Children of Anemoi. They were chosen to bring the Xenophonians to missions and back." He waved to the further end of the encampment. "Past those curtains is where the Eros Division resides." I peered into the distance to see a small wall of thin sheets. I didn't dare imagine what happened on the other side.

"Why are the Children of Anemoi treated so unjustly?" I asked, looking at the dirty sleeping bodies.

"The Order of Xenophon *just*?" Axel scoffed. "I hope Zeus isn't getting inside your head. You know the cruelty of the Order. Look around. What's different about these individuals?"

I peered at one of the members. A man lay on a cot, staring at the ceiling and breathing heavily. At first glance, he appeared tired. Then, he rolled over. He only had one leg and his arms were missing patches of skin.

"They're imperfect in the eyes of the Order of Xenophon," Axel explained quietly. "Whether it's from birth or during life, all these individuals are considered defective. The most impure."

I looked around and met eyes with many of the members. It broke my heart. Some had birth disabilities, others were impaired from the Cleanse (the Accident). Many of them were covered in burns, blood, and missed patches of skin.

Axel caught me staring at a man whose ear was burned off. "You do know where we are, right?"

"Chernobyl," I mumbled.

"More particularly," he paused and tapped his metal foot, "we're standing on top of one of the nuclear reactors."

I froze, staring at him with wide eyes. "You don't mean?"

Axel tightened his lips and looked around. "You felt it in the hall. These people are surrounded by nuclear radiation every moment. " He gestured towards the people. "The Order doesn't care that it's radioactive. They put their least important members down here. Ones who are still impure, but can prove useful. They're still slaves to the Order, but suffer a long, cruel sentence." His gray eyes narrowed and he shook his head. "They're sent here to die."

It broke my heart. These people were ripped from their homes, and taken from their children. These are the parents, grandparents, aunts, uncles, cousins, and family of our Resistance.

They were abducted and left here to rot.

Axel patted my back, snapping me out of my depressing thoughts. "*Vamonos*, Wolf." He nudged me to the center of the encampment where several cleaner members sat around a small artificial fire. One looked over at us and stood up.

It was Goliath.

He didn't seem like his terrifying, brute self. He was a strong soldier. A spy in an Ares uniform. Around his waist was a blue utility belt.

"So you *are* an Interpreter," I marveled.

Goliath smiled. "Indeed I am, Wolf. As are we all." He gestured behind him. Several members stood up from their places. I only recognized three.

Solomon, Diego the Monkey, and the woman whom I ordered to dispose of Sting's body.

Subconsciously, I rubbed the poisonous dagger on my belt.

The woman stepped forward. Getting a better look, I noticed something familiar about her. She was a solid woman with beautiful curly brown hair. Her dark eyes were kind and her persona motherly. She reached out and touched my arm. "*Mi dispiace per il tuo dolore.*"

My glasses translated her Italian. She was sorry for my pain.

"It's all right," I replied. "I brought the suffering upon myself. I'm sorry you had to endure it with me."

She nodded and stepped back.

"Vero has been an Interpreter with her husband since the beginning," Goliath explained. "She used to speak English, but her memory was affected when Emel chose her for the Children of Moirai."

"Does she remember anything of her past?" I asked.

Goliath nodded. "She knows her husband and that she has eight children." He looked at me. "All of whom you know."

My eyes widened. "Mrs. Hollinger?"

A smile spread across her face. "*Sì. So che parli con mia figlia e sei amico di mio marito e mio figlio.*"

"Yes, I talk with Shannon every day," I smiled. "And Leprechaun and PH—" I paused, trying to recall their Mortal names, "I mean Quinn and Pietro grew close to me over the past year."

"Quinn was the one to start *this* clan of Interpreters," Goliath put in, sitting back down. "Marcellus' Interpreters perished years ago, unfortunately." He gestured to a seat across from him.

I sat, staring through the flames at his powerful face. His double edged sword tattoo glowed in the firelight.

"Now, Wolf," he began, "the time has come. You're in the favor of Zeus and the Moirai. With you at our side, we cannot fail. We are at your command."

"But first, might I ask how you and Solomon got into this mix?" I demanded.

The corner of Goliath's mouth rose and fell. His mind was flooded with a sorrowful memory. "I've been searching for a way out my whole life. When my brother abandoned me to aid a traitor, I've never been the same." He let out a deep breath. "I've feared death and he was the one to protect me. Without him, I was exposed and desperately looking for a way to have an advantage against the Order."

He fears death. That phrase was familiar…

"Solomon here," he continued, gesturing to the old man to my right. "wanted a way out after what they did to him." The wrinkled Child of Moirai stared into the flames. Diego perched on his staff and gently stroked his master's head.

"In the end, we all fear something. We all hate something. We all *believe* in something." Goliath looked to the faces of the other members. "Quinn said that's what united us. He started this clan and we became Interpreters secretly working for Director Virginia Michaelson and Thomas Hodgins aka Marcellus."

My mind tried to understand it all. "I get you're called Interpreters, but what does that imply? I thought it was just a weird name for Michaelson's soldiers."

"Interpreters handle intelligence. Most of Michaelson's reporters are trained to be scouts and to infiltrate enemy encampments. They intercept and interpret the codes the Order sends out. That's what we," he made a circular motion with his arm, "were meant to do. Unfortunately, it's never that easy. The Children of Moirai challenge us in skill and number. We've tried many times to sabotage their computers but have failed. As you can see, our numbers are small. We used to be greater."

There was a moment of silence.

Finally, I spoke up, "So you think since I'm here, you can finally sabotage the Children of Moirai?"

Goliath nodded. "Between you, the attack on Chernobyl, and us, we'll be able to take down the Order of Xenophon from the inside. Someone has to get to the computers and corrupt the virtual data. Just because you destroy a base doesn't mean you get rid of an army."

I understood. If we wanted to defeat the Order, we needed to pull out all the stops. No stone left unturned. Destroy them physically, mentally, virtually. All of it.

But something didn't feel right.

"It's not that easy, is it?" I asked.

Goliath shook his head. "While the RRPR and the outside Interpreters have the base's location, they can't just swoop in and bomb the base. We need to get all these people out of here. They're innocent; they need a chance at life."

"How do we do that?" I inquired.

"The Mutants," Axel chimed in. "You can control them to come down here and remove all the Children of Anemoi from the premises. Everyone else is on their own."

"Zeus will be in charge of the Children of Hades," I explained. "They won't be able to."

"They have to," Goliath ordered. "Find a way. That's *your* mission."

I growled. It made things more complicated, but nothing was supposed to be easy. "Fine. What else is there?"

"We'll need to break out REM in the chaos," Goliath explained. "We can't get him now. There would be no hope for any of us to survive."

"That's where I come in," Axel said, smacking his metal chest. "I'll bust through those walls and fly out with Blake. Nothing to it."

Sure. Nothing to it. "So, let me see if I understand this right," I held up my hand. "Zeus, me, and the Mutants are outside battling RRPR. Axel breaks out REM and then you guys cause chaos."

Goliath chuckled. "You have it a little backwards. Chaos comes first, always."

"*Caffè prima del caos,*" Vero argued, referring to Emel's morning slogan.

I cocked my head to the side. "So, when *is* first?"

A high pitched noise rang in my head and a woman shouted, *WOLF! Moirai... now!* It was so loud and sharp that I winced from the pain.

A smirk spread across Goliath's face. "Right now."

I jumped up. "Axel, take me back to the surface," I ordered.

He nodded and turned to leave. I was about to follow when I felt a hand on my arm.

I turned to see Solomon's wrinkled face smiling at me. Kindly, he said, "*When there is moral rot within a nation, its government topples easily. But wise and knowledgeable leaders bring stability.*"

I nodded. "I won't let you down."

"We know you won't," Goliath replied. "Now, go end this eternal suffering, Joshua Wolfrum."

My eyes widened. Hearing my name from any man was strange. But Goliath? Nothing made sense anymore.

I thanked them, wished them luck, and ran out behind Axel.

Things have gotten heated and I'm being pressed left and right. They don't know what's going on, but something is causing a ruckus among the members up here. The Moirai don't know what it is and frankly, neither do I. Lachesis/Emel asked if I killed Goliath, wondering if it's his doing. I wanted to lie but couldn't. They know he's still alive and think he's the one causing all the discord. To my surprise, Lachesis/Emel is not as upset with me as I thought she'd be. I am relieved, but Wolf feels uneasy. If Goliath is the one causing conflict, I hope he'll stay hidden so I'm not pressured to go after him again.

Axel and I are waiting with the Children of Moirai, watching the three sisters bicker. Slyly, I wrote you this letter.

They've finished arguing. They came to an agreement. They're coming over now; I wonder what they'll say.

But I know what *I* have to say:

Good luck, everyone. Stay strong.

With safety and secrecy,

Joshua Wolfrum

Joshua Wolfrum
Titan of the Russian Pandemonium

THE UNDERGROUND

LETTER 42

Yared: XII

Joshua,

That craziness? That was us.

Yared here, shedding light on our side.

We arrived at Chernobyl before dawn broke. Clothed in darkness, we hid on the outskirts of the city. The air was untrustworthy, so we wore oxygen masks and were fully covered. I peered around the building that guarded us, looking for signs of life.

The land was vacant. No humans, animals, or Mutants crawled the streets. Everything was dark, cold, and lonely.

"I wonder what this place was like," Sami whispered, playing with her tail nervously.

"No one quite remembers," Mark put in. He calculated something on his clipboard. "It was destroyed so long ago."

"And you think it's still radioactive?" Alison asked.

I cocked my gun. "Joshua and PH claim that it is," I stated, "so we can't take any chances."

She nodded and turned her attention back to the cold facility in the distance. "Is Axel all right?"

I chuckled. "Last I checked, he's gonna unleash hell inside and save Blake."

"For my sister's sake, he better," Mark added. He slid his finger across the screen and looked up. "The others are in position: here and around the globe. The frequencies will be sent out momentarily."

"Which blokes are coming to our aid once it's active?" Lucas asked, snacking on crackers before the fight. He pulled down his mask just enough to eat. The Dragonfly didn't care about radioactivity. He needed his snacks.

"The rest of the RRPR Officers, Marcellus, Leprechaun, and PH with whatever troops can be spared," Mark informed. "Hopefully, there's enough of them." Mark clicked the side of his BoMF.

The countdown began.

Gripping my gun, I ran ahead, leading my friends through the concrete city. Everything remained in shambles; no attempts at restoration were made.

"Five minutes," Mark called.

I ran faster.

"Three minutes."

My heart pounded.

"One minute."

My grip tightened around my weapon. I counted:

Three. Two. One.

In the distance, you could hear a faint sound. It was quiet to the ear, but you could feel it in the earth beneath us.

"Do you hear that horrible noise?" Sami shouted as we ran.

"I can only hear my heavy breathing!" Aaron yelled back, trying to take in gulps of air through mask.

"How can you not hear it?" she cried. I looked over my shoulder to see her wincing. "It's so loud!"

"Your cat ears must hear their alarms," Mark guessed. He darted to the side and we followed. We dove behind a nearby building to catch our bearings. The facility wasn't far.

"You think it worked?" Lucas asked. He fluttered his wings to clean them of fallen dust.

"I know it worked," Mark declared. "The world is in shambles as we speak."

"We'll have Shannon attest to that," I told him. A smirk spread across my face. "Now, let's have some fun."

Mark nodded and spoke quietly into his BoMF. We covered our ears.

The first round of bombs went off. My teeth chattered as the explosions shook our bodies. The impact cracked the earth, creating chasms before the facility. The second followed. The power plant shook. Dust flew off as if a breath of wind swept it away. Then, the final round of explosives. The building trembled. The roof caved and one side of the facility crumbled to the ground.

After the final explosion, we ran forward, reaching the powerplant without a struggle.

"Where are the soldiers?" Aaron asked.

Mark hopped up onto a pile of rubble. "Hopefully distracted by the frequencies cutting ties with the survivors." He, Lucas, and I tore away rocks that blocked an entrance into the facility. When there was room, we crawled through.

We ran through the main lobby of the plant; guns aimed and ready. All was quiet. We made our way through cold overgrown corridors, searching in every room. No one was there.

Reaching the control room, Mark went up to the main panels. "Strange to think the downfall of Chernobyl happened by the men in this room." He rubbed his fingers along the dusty console. "Selfish, careless men."

"Do you think the Chernobyl accident was actually an attack by the Order of Xenophon?" Sami asked.

"Quite possibly," Mark replied. He scanned the controls. "Now, how do we find the entrance to the base?"

"Joshua said the Children of Anemoi and Moirai are beneath their first floor," I thought aloud. "Either the base is directly below us or," my eyes darted to each corner of the room, "right around us."

"Alison, scan the area for thermal readings," Mark ordered.

Alison stood in the center of the control room and slowly turned in a circle with her eyes straight ahead. "There is something, but it's faint," she said after a few rotations. She raised her metal hand and pointed. "Behind that wall."

Covering the front wall was a large hexagonal panel with small spheres that made a pattern like a mosaic.

"That's a display of the reactor," Aaron marveled, adjusting his glasses.

"Kinda makes the entrance obvious, don't you think?" Lucas mocked.

Mark went over and tapped a few buttons in front of it. "Well, no one is supposed to come here, let alone know it's the base of OX." Nothing worked.

"Let's do this fast, shall we?" Alison motioned for Mark to get out of the way. He stepped to the side, and Alison lifted her arm with her palm down. Missile launchers raised from their hiding place and into position. She tightened her grip and fired, blasting the panel. Dust and debris shot to the sides. The display was now a gaping hole.

"Let's go," Mark ordered. He jumped over the console and into the opening. We followed.

We raced down the long dark corridor. Sami said she heard footsteps coming from all directions. Alison saw bodies converging in different rooms to our right and left. OX was ready to attack.

"Dumb question," Aaron yelled as we ran, "but why didn't we wait for backup?"

"We need to get Blake and Axel before anything happens," Alison snapped. I watched as she stared ahead of her—almost lost in thought. She tried to communicate with Axel.

THE UNDERGROUND

Mark stopped short and waved us against the wall. We reached a fork. I held my breath and gripped my weapon. I couldn't wait for the firefight to begin.

Sadly, the Xenophonians marched by without noticing us.

We continued with Alison leading the way. She knew where to find Axel. We raced down corridors for what felt like hours, but must've been a few minutes. No one noticed us which was peculiar.

Alison led us to a hallway of glass that overlooked pristine white rooms filled with chairs and torture equipment. The chambers for the Tolerance Tests.

"This is where they had Blake last," Alison explained. "But where is Axel?"

"I hear him," Sami whispered aloud. Her cat ears perked up. "He is getting Blake now."

"Is there a struggle?" Mark asked.

She nodded slowly. "We should get out of here."

Before I could ask, there was an explosion and the catwalk shook. The pristine room below billowed with dust and smoke. The glass wall cracked like lightning across the sky. In the screen of white I saw lines of blue: Axel's armor.

I heard muffled shouting. Before I could process it, there was a shatter of glass. I raised my arm, protecting my face from flying shards. I peered out to see Axel hovering with a sleeping Blake in his arms. They both were hurt. Axel's armor sparked and Blake was covered in bruises.

"Don't just stand there!" Axel shouted, pushing through us. He flew out and we raced close behind.

The troops finally noticed us. Loud alarms blared throughout the compound. Lights flashed blue and red, bathing us in a purple glow.

"We don't have much time!" Axel yelled.

Angry Xenophonians screamed and shouted behind us. Moments later, shots fired. They had poor aim, thank goodness. I looked over my shoulder to see the angry faces of mindless chaotic Xenophonians. I reached into my jacket pocket and pulled out a gravity bomb (specialty of Isle V). Pulling the pin with my teeth, I tossed it over my shoulder.

The Xenophonians didn't stop. It exploded after the first wave passed over it, taking down twelve. The next wave climbed over the bodies and raced after us.

Lucas stopped mid flight and raced in the other direction, passing over my head. I tried to call after him but it was too late. He took on the first line by himself.

"Alison!" I shouted. "Help Lucas!"

Looking over her shoulder, she gasped and flew back.

The two of them can handle it. I decided to run forward and take up the front with the others.

Shouting echoed down the hall ahead of us. We skidded to a stop and tried to turn right, but soldiers marched that way too. No use going left either.

We were trapped.

Mark took on the men in front of us, throwing grenades and keeping them at a distance. Aaron and Sami fired at the men to our left who backed off also. I gripped my weapon and opened fire to our right. Some went down, but the rest kept coming. These men and women weren't as afraid. I shot, and they shot back. They would've killed me if Axel hadn't swooped in. He turned his back towards them, taking the heat of the bullets. They bounced off his armor like they were BBs.

But he couldn't take them all.

He ordered Mark and me to hold Blake. Once REM was secure, the Bionic clenched his fists and leapt into the wall above us, busting a hole through the top. He returned and took Blake into his arms again. One by one, we leapt up into a new, dark part of the facility.

"The Interpreters and the Children of Anemoi can take it from here," Axel explained. "Let's get out of here." We followed him out as he broke through the walls of the facility.

We escaped. We raced back through the city to our meeting spot.

No one followed us.

Nic, Johanna, and Aymie waited in the encampment and communicated with the other members who were on their way. Aymie looked up to see Blake in Axel's arms. A scream escaped her lips. She tore off her headset, jumped to her feet, and ran to him. Tears dripped down her cheeks as she stroked her boyfriend's white hair and kissed his bruised and bleeding face.

Blake's light eyes fluttered open. He looked at her sweetly. He weakly clasped her face with his hand. "Aymie…"

"Shh, shh, don't speak," she whispered through tears.

He shook his head. Fear filled his light eyes. "You… shouldn't… have… come," Blake panted.

Aymie's lip quivered and she kissed his hand. "I had to. I couldn't leave you."

Blake looked up at Axel who was still holding him. "I'm… sorry."

"Guys?" Aaron called. "Where are Alison and Lucas?"

I looked around. "I thought they were behind us."

Sami stood quietly listening. "I don't hear them… in fact," her face paled. "I don't hear anything."

"Are they not fighting back?" Mark asked.

Blake let out a shaky breath. "Yared… write… Joshua… letter."

I obeyed, and here we are.

THE UNDERGROUND

Where are Alison and Lucas?
Bravery and fidelity,

Yared Prinz

Yared Prinz
Seer Commander

LETTER 43

Joshua: XXII

Yared and Shannon,

Alison and Lucas are alive for now.

If you couldn't tell, there's a sudden silence. OX isn't coming after you yet. We suffered major losses. The Interpreters destroyed many sections of the main base in Chernobyl, the Reborn Xenophonians are running amok, and we have no control over the survivors who are at the Temples of the Annex.

Zeus regrouped with the remaining Titans and Moirai. We needed a better plan.

It was several hours after the attack. I sat on my throne, watching the events play over in our holographic flames. I watched as Shannon and Shane ran about in their black uniforms, corralling the confused survivors at one of our Temples. They calmed many down while the rest of the team explained the situation. I watched another clip as Myles and Sonny armed many of the civilians who were ready to fight back. Thankfully, no clips of PH were shown, but one thing was certain:

The Resistance was winning.

On the outside, Zeus remained calm and collected. Inside, a storm brewed and lightning was ready to strike.

"Sir, what is our next move?" one of the Titans asked with fear in her voice. There were now three empty thrones: PH's, Sting's, and Munazam's. My fellow Titans started losing hope.

Zeus rubbed a hand over his face, watching the flames intently. "We must plan carefully. One wrong move will cost us."

"But we outnumber them, my lord, don't we?" she replied.

"In number, yes," Lachesis/Emel put in. "In brains? Nope. The only smart ones we have are in this room."

"Besides, we haven't killed Goliath and the other traitors," Atropos/Morana stated. "They're still causing panic and destruction within our walls."

I needed to think of something to steer the plan according to my liking. "We do have several advantages," I said aloud. All eyes fell on me. "Not only do we have the Children of Hades, but we have two enemies in custody." I raised my hand and the flame changed to Alison and Lucas.

The two Isle members were huddled in the corner of a room. The cruel Xenophonians tortured them. Spat on them, beat them, and called them harsh names. Alison's blue lights flickered; her left arm sparked from a gash. Blood dripped down Lucas' forehead and his membranous wings were bent.

My heart broke at their condition, but I kept a stone expression. "Let's use them to draw away the attack of the Resistance," I continued. "They appear too attached to their own to endanger them."

"What proof have you to make such claims?" Atropos/Morana sneered. "You know nothing of the enemy. The traitors in our grasp must be killed to teach the Resistance a lesson."

Lachesis/Emel came to my defense. "The boy has been out in the field more than you have, Morana. I trust Wolf's discretion."

Atropos/Morana wasn't a fan of her sister's opinion. The two argued. Then, their third sister joined in. Harsh and hurtful language was used. No remorse. These women battled stronger with words than weapons. *Emel always said they fought...*

Zeus heard enough. He slammed his fist onto the stone throne he sat in. The Moirai's lips shut. "Wolf and I will lead the attack on the surface, utilizing the captives as a distraction," he declared. "The rest of you, take control of the base."

"Are you certain you want to put yourself out there?" Clotho/Arata asked, concerned.

"No questions," he snapped. He rose and straightened his jacket. "Wolf. Come."

All eyes were on me as I stood. The Moirai and Titans were tense, uneasy.

They doubted their god.

I followed Zeus beneath the statues to where the Mutants were kept.

Standing before the cages, he pulled out two pairs of metal bracelets. "I'll lead the Children of Hades primarily." He slid them onto his wrists. "You will be my watchful eye and second command."

I nodded and put on the bracelets. The pain shot from my wrists to my head, but I didn't wince.

Zeus looked downcast. "If anything is to happen to me up there," he said softly, "promise me this." His dark eyes met mine. I saw something that I didn't expect to see:

A worried mortal man.

"Promise me," he continued, "that you *will* take the name of Zeus. My lightning emblem will become yours. You will lead the Order to its triumph. As long as we still stand, nothing will stop us."

"I promised you before, and I intend to keep it," I declared, tracing the scar on my palm. I said it so passionately and truthfully that… I almost believed it myself.

A smile spread across Zeus' face. "Good. Now, I will bring the Children of Hades to the surface. You go retrieve the Woman of Metal and the Insect. I will send you a message when we are ready."

I nodded and turned to take my leave. As I walked away, I heard the slamming of gates and the cries of the Mutants.

Entering the room with Alison and Lucas, I ordered all the Xenophonians to leave. They were to get to their stations and prepare to defend the base. Once they were gone, I went over to the two.

Alison looked at me with despair. She was in pain and knew in her heart things weren't going to end well. Lucas was hunched over; his head on the floor. With his compound eyes, I couldn't tell if he was tired or knocked out. He was breathing, and that's what mattered.

"Are you all right?" I whispered.

Alison nodded weakly.

I pulled a canteen from my belt. I was about to hand it to her when something held me back.

Wolf didn't want to help any enemy of the Order.

They're not the enemy, I reminded myself and let her drink.

Graciously, Alison gulped down half of it. She poured water into the cap and brought it to Lucas' lips. He groaned and didn't move. He was too weak to even drink.

A few moments later, a group of Xenophonians in all white came to retrieve Alison. She didn't object. She stroked Lucas' face and whispered something into his ear. He moaned but couldn't speak. Weakly, Alison stood to her feet and let the technicians put cuffs on her. Her mechanical eyes filled with sorrow. Her metal body creaked and shook with every step.

Alison was afraid.

I gave the Xenophonians a nod and they took her away.

I wasn't sure what would follow.

There was nothing I could do. In silence, I sat with Lucas and wrote this letter.

A message from the Order just came in.

THE UNDERGROUND

I received word from Zeus.
Time to begin.
With safety and secrecy,

Joshua Wolfrum

Joshua Wolfrum
Titan of the Russian Pandemonium

LETTER 44

Shannon: XII

Joshua,

I was too late. My observation skills failed, and my family paid the price.

The moment we received word about Alison and Lucas' capture, we boarded a plan to Chernobyl. On the way, your letter came through. I clutched the straps of my seat tight. I wasn't sure how we'd fare against what Zeus had in mind. Not only were our numbers small, I feared what he'd do to our friends.

My fiancé slipped his fingers in mine. By my expression, he knew what I was thinking. "Shannon, it'll be all right," he whispered. "We can do this."

"You know me, Shane," I replied. "Always thinking too hard."

"You're a Hollinger, darling," my father said. He sat across from me. A smile spread across his face. "You're also a Capello. Your mum's a fighter and never gave up. Neither will you."

My heart ached thinking about her. You said she was alive. Unfortunately, I had a hard time accepting it without any proof.

My gaze fell on my brother, PH. He was quiet; his heterochromatic eyes cast downward. He was about to go and destroy everything he'd ever known. Everything he'd ever fought for. His entire life was turned around in less than a month. *I hope he's still with us*, I thought.

"Shannon," Marcellus said. His gray eyes looked at me kindly. "Remember, you're never alone."

I squeezed Shane's hand tighter. I finally accepted that not everything fell on my shoulders. The burden could be shared.

THE UNDERGROUND

Though I wished it never had to be.

The warning light flashed overhead and the bay door slowly opened. Standing up, I zipped up my jacket and pulled my breathing apparatus out of my pocket.

Shane leaned over and kissed my cheek before the metal mask expanded over my face. "Love you, Detective," he whispered. With a wink, he jumped out the back of the plane.

He didn't give me a chance to say it back.

No. We'll survive this, I scolded myself. *We'll all have that second chance.* Taking a deep breath, I took three steps and leapt into the open air.

I ejected my parachute when I caught sight of the meeting point. Down below I could make out Nic and Johanna waiting for us. The Mutant Gorilla waved his hairy arms. At first I thought he was trying to signal where to land.

No. It was a warning.

Guns rang out around us. Bullets whizzed past my head. I pulled my knees to my chest and curled myself into a ball, reducing the chance of being struck. I felt I was falling faster than I should have. I glanced up to see my white silk chute had as many holes as a cheese grater. I unclipped myself and braced for a tough landing.

I thought I was going to hit hard when I heard a loud hum of an engine. Before I knew it, something metal struck me and I was carried to the ground. Axel saved my fall. He brought me down to a new meeting point where the others were. No major injuries, thank goodness. My father and Myles had near misses with the bullets, but nothing fatal. Aymie and Johanna bandaged them.

"They're closing in on us," Nic said as he peered around the side of a building.

I listened closely and heard feet marching from all directions.

"They're Ares," Sonny informed, pulling his gas mask over his head. "They're big, dumb, and slow."

"But they're strong and 'ave great aim," PH added. "And I wouldn't say *you're* very big, Mars," he mocked.

"What would you know of big, PH?" Sonny replied sarcastically.

PH had it coming, but he wasn't in the mood. He slid a gun into its holster and eyed Sonny.

"If they're so good, why'd they miss us?" Shane joked.

"More fun killing us face to face," Sonny replied seriously, and PH nodded in agreement. Shane shut up.

"We need to get past them and to Zeus," Marcellus reminded. "He's our primary target. Let's take him out and the Mutants under his control."

"If we can somehow get his metal bracelets," Myles put in, tapping his electronic clipboard. "Then, we can use the Mutants against the Ares."

"Joshua was supposed to use the Mutants to save the Children of Anemoi," Yared put in. "Besides, we don't have the firepower. We're spread thin. Our soldiers here can't handle it."

"We *will* save the Children of Anemoi without the Mutants," Nic reassured. "Michaelson is sending us a gift." He smirked, but explained nothing more.

"The plan was to surround and besiege," I recalled. "Can we still make that happen?"

"Yes, but we'll need to take more dangerous measures," Marcellus explained.

In minutes, we reworked our plan to meet our current situation. We concluded and prepared for battle. Before I ran to my post, my eyes caught sight of Blake who rested behind Aymie. His pale face had a look of sorrow. I watched as tears streamed down his cheeks. He looked at Yared who told him everything would be okay. After Yared left, Blake's eyes met mine. I stopped and returned the stare.

"Shannon, let's go," Mark called. He looked at me and then at Blake. "Sami, Aaron, and Myles are staying to take care of him," he whispered, grabbing my arm. "We have to move."

My gaze remained locked on Blake. Wide eyes begged me not to go. Though he made no sound, his face screamed something was wrong.

I wish I listened.

I nodded to the twins and Myles and ran out with Mark, leaving Blake in mental agony.

My objective was to help a small team get to Zeus and propose a trade: PH for Alison and Lucas. I stuck with Axel, Yared, and Mark while the others went the opposite way. PH aided our team in the shadows. We'd retrieve him when we met up with Zeus.

Behind us, Sonny and Marcellus challenged the remaining Titans that led the Ares members. They all recognized the former Xenophonians and were petrified.

Aymie, Johanna, and my dad remained hidden on the rooftops; ready to ambush when our reinforcements arrived.

We ran around the outskirts of the facility. When we were halfway there, Myles' weapons were ready. Mark sent back the word and Myles and Aaron controlled them from the meeting point.

Explosions went off. Drones flew in from all directions, attacking the men below. Screams and cries reached my ringing ears.

To my horror, they weren't only Xenophonian. The Titans led a ruthless army that withstood the attacks. When one soldier fell, more appeared to take his place.

The ground rumbled, causing me to lose balance. While my legs kept running, my heart stopped when I saw the earth open up and hundreds of Xenophonian armored vehicles emerged.

The tanks fired, tearing a hole in our defenses. I skidded to a stop and watched the slaughter. Our soldiers were dying and there was nothing I could do. As the Strategist, keeping our fighters alive was the priority. This new plan made them expendable.

Mark noticed I stopped and ran back to me. "Detective, we have to go!" A group of Xenophonians noticed our team heading towards the base. Turning on their heels, they trekked towards us with their weapons raised.

I was frozen. *Move, body, move.* But I couldn't. Our soldiers were screaming. I felt their blood beneath my feet.

And there was *nothing* I could do.

"DETECTIVE!" Mark screamed as the first Xenophonian put his finger on the trigger and—

A streak of black whizzed past my ear and struck the Xenophonian. He staggered backwards before he and his comrades went up in flames.

"Detective, I thought you were more observant," a familiar voice scolded.

Mark looked behind me and laughed. "You sure do your name justice!"

I turned to see a man with chocolate skin in a black combat uniform. His familiar eyes looked out beneath a mask.

"Justin Thyme," I gasped.

The RV Combatant chuckled. "Told you I'd be back. I hope you didn't forget!"

There was a beep in my earpiece. *No one could forget about the new Director of WHYP,* a husky voice said.

Hope and confidence rushed from my head to my toes. "Mr. Wyght," I cried.

Do you really think we'd abandon you now? Director Wyght said.

There was a *woosh* overhead and I saw planes rushing to the scene. Bombs dropped on the enemy, causing their vehicles to go up in balls of fire. I turned in circles to see the perimeter of Chernobyl surrounded by soldiers: young and old alike. They marched inward, starting the besiege.

"Who are they?" I asked.

"Interpreters, survivors," Thyme smirked, "and Isle members."

We have more Bionics, Saviors, Geeks, Assets, Seers, and Mutants to fight alongside us, Director Wyght said. *Led by three Keepers: Allaway, Agro, and Mallory.*

Mark's face lit up. His second family heeded his call. "Let's end this so we can have a joyful reunion," he declared.

Agreed. Go get em, kiddos! Director Wyght concluded.

Our reinforcements charged. Aircraft struck from above. Trucks traversed through the destroyed city. Thousands of Isle members and WHYP soldiers rushed into the heat of the battle. They had their positions and the element of surprise.

The Order of Xenophon was thrown into an unorganized chaos.

My confidence was restored. I was ready to *win* the fight.

I met up with the team at the perimeter of the power plant. Their faces beamed. They knew who came to our aid.

Peering out from behind debris, I saw no sign of the Children of Hades. Our path was clear, but it worried me.

"Do you think the Interpreters inside the base will succeed?" Yared asked.

"They better," Mark replied. "If not, we'll fight the old fashion way rather than watching them drop like flies."

"Well, thanks to Thyme, Wyght, and the Keepers, we're doing well," Yared smirked. "I've no doubt, but I'd prefer not to lose anyone else."

"The Interpreters inside *will* succeed," Axel promised. He turned his jets back on. "I know they will." With a nod, he flew out into the open and we followed.

As we closed in on the base, I gazed into the gaping hole of the facility. Only blackness.

Then, two small lights penetrated the void. Thousands of other pairs followed suit.

I realized they weren't lights.

Grunts, cries, screams, growls, howls poured out of the blackness. Swarming out like wasps were the Children of Hades: Zeus' Mutants. They snarled and sneered, ready for blood.

"GO!" Axel bellowed. He flew over to the first line of defense while we ran. Axel hovered between us and the enemy. He aimed and fired. Most Mutants focused their attention on him, but others were smarter and chased us.

Yared turned and opened fire, taking down several inhuman beasts. Mark did the same. He tossed grenades far into the cluster of monsters, taking out over a dozen.

But they kept coming.

The plan was to scale the side of the power plant, and hopefully find Zeus on the rooftop. I knew he needed to be close to and see the Mutants to control them. It was my best bet, so we went with it. I gave my second choice to the other team.

Hope we find him first, I thought.

Reaching the side of the building, we found the rusted ladder depicted in the old blueprints. Most of the rungs had broken off and the screws were loose.

"We have to try," Yared ordered, jumping onto the first step. We followed and attempted our ascent.

Below us swarmed hundreds of beasts. Their fangs bared as they yanked at the ladder. I clutched tightly as it shook beneath my weight. I tried not to look down at the drooling mouths ready to consume me.

I looked above to see Yared yelling into his BoMF. In the blink of an eye he was gone. Then Mark. Suddenly, Axel's hot metal arms encompassed my body, and I was flown to the roof only to be greeted by enemies.

As my feet touched concrete, I whipped out my pistol, aiming at the three Mutant figures before me. My finger was on the trigger, ready to pull, but my heart stopped me.

My eyes saw three old friends: Dylan Cheatle the Bear, Adeline Zarra the Fruit Bat, and Clive Foxwood the Fox.

I shook it off and aimed my weapon again. *This has to be a trap. They're being controlled,* I thought, but with little conviction.

The three of them stood between us and a figure in a red combat outfit and black hat. But that's all they did. Stood. The Mutants made no notion of attacking. They stared.

Mark locked eyes with the Fox. "Are you?" he whispered.

Clive nodded and pressed a hairy finger to his lips. He jerked over his shoulder to the man on the ledge who led the Mutants.

"We've got him," Yared whispered. He aimed his gun; the head of the man in red locked in his sights. The man's arms were raised, as if he was conducting, but appeared frozen in time. The three Mutants shook their heads frantically. They didn't want Yared to shoot. The Seer didn't listen.

He fired.

Somehow, the man in red sensed it and dropped to the floor. The bullet grazed his upper back. He screamed and cried in bitter agony. It was familiar. The man turned and faced us. He was wearing goggles… large, round goggles.

Lucas.

Yared exhaled sharply and dropped to his knees. "No…" he whispered.

Lucas shook and weakly peeled off the red jacket that was wet with blood. The bullet had missed the base of his neck, but did something I never would've imagined.

It tore off his wings.

The membranous wings were stuck inside the jacket that was thrown to the ground. Lucas staggered and almost toppled off the building, but Axel swooped in and grabbed him. He laid him face down. Red and green blood pooled around him. Lucas moaned in agony and breathed heavily. The pain was excruciating.

Yared sat in shock. Mark ran to help, but Dylan swatted at him. Mark skidded across the ground, but quickly jumped to his feet.

"We have no choice," Clive explained. "We're holding off as much as we can, but can't control it much longer."

They're fighting Zeus…

"Stop him." Clive's yellow eyes darted to his left. I turned to see another building in the distance. My second choice. I watched our other team rush towards it. Two red figures stood on the roof.

Dylan growled and swung again. The three of us jumped back.

"Go, NOW!" Clive ordered as he twitched. He got down on all fours and snarled.

His sanity left. The Children of Hades were in control.

Mark whistled and Axel scooped me up first. He flew me over to the other building.

A smile spread across Zeus' face when he saw me. The element of surprise was gone.

No, he doesn't know we brought PH with us, I reminded myself.

Just before Axel put me down, my earpiece beeped and a young voice said: *We have a problem.*

My heart dropped at the message, but I couldn't reply. My feet touched the roof, and I looked upon the face of the one I despised. A shadow of a figure that finally took shape.

Zeus' hands raised over the Mutants below us. He smiled when I took a step forward. His arms lowered. The grunts, cries, and shouts of the Mutants slowly died down like waves calming after a storm. The beasts stood still. Their glowing eyes locked on their master.

The fighting of the other Xenophonians continued to rage. Bullets fired, swords and axes swung, and our trucks tore through. We were winning, but Zeus wasn't admitting defeat.

"What do you think, Detective?" Zeus asked. "A glorious sight, is it not?"

I wanted to shoot him, but I needed time. Alison was still in his possession. I kept my gun pointed at Zeus' acquaintance who kept their hands up.

Axel returned with Mark. When he landed, the Hodgins tore off his mask, revealing his identity to the enemy.

Zeus gasped and surprise spread across his face. His dark eyes widened when he recognized my friend. "*You* are the son of Marcellus?" he marveled. He never saw the children in person. "You were on my side. Mark, right?"

"Yes, but that was before I realized what side I was actually on, *Mr. Devin Page*," Mark growled, dropping into a stance.

Zeus blinked. He almost didn't recognize his Mortal name. "Where are your siblings?" he asked, still in shock. "PH and Sting were after them, but failed miserably."

"Sting actually captured my brother, but never told you," Mark said smugly. He wanted to taint her image. "She kept him as a trophy. She hid things from you, sir. She was as much of a traitor as my father."

Zeus was unimpressed. "Is he with you?"

We didn't answer which told him all he needed to know. Zeus nodded and looked back at the Mutants below him. He wanted them to attack.

"We want to make a trade," I exclaimed before he could lift his hands.

Zeus' arms jerked, but he kept them lowered. "What could you possibly offer me? I have no need for the Children of Marcellus anymore. They were to just draw the traitor out so we could kill him. Now that he's here, there's no sense."

"We have one of your loyal Titans in custody," I explained.

I saw the other figure shift nervously out of the corner of my eye. They said nothing and kept their arms in the air as I held them at gunpoint. Their fingers twitched nervously. A mask was drawn over their face; I couldn't get a positive I.D., but I had a feeling...

"You'd return Hermes Titan PH to me," Zeus started, "in exchange for what?"

"Safe return of our soldiers," Mark spat, aiming his weapon. "Where's the Bionic?"

Zeus chuckled. "I assume you found the Insect." His eyes looked towards the roof where Yared shot his friend. "Where is the proof that you have my Titan?"

I spoke into my communicator, ordering Axel to retrieve PH.

Detective, we have a problem, a voice said again. I didn't have time to answer. I put my communicator on vibrate.

Axel's rocket thrusters hummed. Out of the corner of my eye I saw the Bionic speeding ahead with PH dangling in his arms.

Zeus smirked when Axel hovered before him with the Hermes Titan in his grasp. He stayed a good distance away. One wrong move and PH would fall to the hard concrete a hundred feet below.

"Man of Metal," Zeus announced. "Thank you for returning my loyal Titan to me."

Axel jerked back, clutching PH like he was a toy he didn't want his father taking away. "Not until you let our soldiers go."

Zeus clicked his tongue. "Never can make anything easy, can you? Your brain couldn't even conform to the Order properly."

I felt my communicator vibrate with a *bzzz*. I ignored it.

"We aren't the easy going type," Axel retorted. "Now where is she?"

Bzzz.

Zeus rolled his eyes. "Fine, as you wish." He lifted his left hand high into the air gently, almost gracefully. However, I noticed his opposite hand twitch.

Bzzz. Bzzz. Bzzz.

The corner of Zeus' mouth turned upward.

My heart sank. *Oh no...*

In a flash, there was a clash of metal against metal. PH was free falling. Zeus jumped.

The commotion of the Mutants below started up again. Adeline the Fruit Bat swooped down from the rooftops, snatching Zeus and PH. The figure in red on the roof ran to the edge to see what was going on.

I looked into the sky and my heart tore in two.

Alison fought Axel. Punches, kicks, screams, and cries fell to my ears. I looked closely to see Alison's armor lights had turned from blue to white. All connected to her heart.

She was a ticking time bomb.

Mark's jaw clenched and his knees bent. He turned on his heel and charged the second figure in red. Clashing, Mark shoved him into the ground and aimed his gun. "What have they done to her?!" he bellowed.

The figure in red peeled the black mask off his face and replaced his glasses.

It was you, Joshua.

Mark and I said nothing and stared at you. Shane and Nic clambered onto the roof until the five of us hovered over you.

"What's going on?" Nic demanded.

Bzzz. Bzzz. My communicator kept going off.

You said nothing, but kept your hands in the air. Your eyes darted toward your wrists. Wrapped tightly around them were metal bracelets.

Grabbing your hands, I tore them off. There was an electronic surge as I ripped them and you winced at the pain. The metal bracelets turned white hot and singed my fingertips. I hissed and dropped them.

For some reason, you were about to snatch them. Out of instinct, Shane swung the butt of his rifle, hitting your head with a crack. You fell unconscious. Shane was about to pick them up when a pale hand shoved him out of the way. Pushing through was someone who never should've come.

Blake.

"What are you doing here?!" I cried.

Blake didn't answer. He snatched the burning bracelets off the ground and slid his hands through. He hissed as steam emanated from his wrists. "Please," he croaked, "go help the others."

"What's going on?" Nic demanded again.

Tears streaked down our friend's face. "This is the only way," Blake whispered. His wrists got redder and redder. The bands got hotter and hotter.

He took a deep breath and stepped towards the ledge.

Bzzz. Bzzz. Bzzz. There was a faint shouting.

I looked to the right to see Aymie running forward as fast as she could, holding her communicator to her face. Her headband had flown off, and her bald head was exposed. She was chased by Mutants. Fear contorted her beautiful face. Her gray eyes found Blake. Her jaw unhinged as she screamed and pumped her long legs harder. The Mutants were closing in.

"Kong, let's go," Shane ordered.

"Right behind you, Zippy," Nic replied. Together they slid down the ladder to go rescue Aymie.

I watched Blake who stood at the ledge, shaking. His eyes were locked on the two Bionics fighting in the sky. Sparks flew, Axel was screaming, but it was no use. Alison wasn't going to give up. She was no longer herself…

She was a puppet of Zeus.

I looked in the distance to see Zeus standing on a ledge. PH was on the ground with Adeline Zarra watching over him. Zeus' arms gracefully yet fiercely flew through the air while the fight was ensuing.

"He's controlling Alison," I said aloud.

"So Joshua controlled the Mutants?" Mark baffled.

"Y-yes," Blake stammered. Blood dripped from his burning wrists. The bracelets wanted to return to their master, but he wouldn't set them free.

Blake turned to see the Mutants closing in on Aymie. The couple's eyes locked. A peaceful smile spread across Blake's face as he looked at the woman he loved more than anything in the world. He would've given anything for her. In fact, he always did. Since they were children at the Quartermane mansion. Since they watched their families burn to ash. Blake knew Aymie didn't always trust him. He knew she resented his gift at times. But in the end, she pulled through. She believed his gift was from God and he had to serve a greater purpose.

Blake believed that, too.

Blake raised his arms into the air. The Mutants below jerked their heads to look at their new master. The Officer's light blue eyes shut and lips tightened. He reached his pale fingers to the sky. He exhaled. His hands swung down to their respective sides and the sea of Mutants parted. Half rushed back towards the power plant, scrambling inside like frightened rabbits. The other half rushed into the heat of battle, attacking the Xenophonians from behind.

Mark and I stared amazed as Blake used the Mutants against the enemy. I looked at Zeus, trying to gauge his reaction.

He was too focused on the Bionics. When he finally realized, his face became cross. He fumed as he sliced the air with his arms. Alison jerked and flew towards our troops. He wanted her to take out our men in one fell swoop.

Behind me I heard a faint groan and a harsh whisper.

It finally happened. What we were waiting for.

The Xenophonians in the field froze where they stood. Their bodies trembled. Sweat dripped down their faces. They dropped to their knees. I thought they would convulse, but the Order had a stronger hold. Blood pooled from their ears and noses. Agonizing screams escaped their lips.

The Strange Voices of Xenophon ceased to speak to them.

The Xenophonians ran frantically while the Mutants and our soldiers slaughtered them. We had no choice. The Children of Moirai would try to regain control.

The volunteer Xenophonians screamed and fought harder than ever. But they couldn't win.

Blake cracked open an eyelid and saw the commotion. He threw his left arm across his body, pointing to the nuclear power plant. The Mutants rushed inside, returning to the hive.

Blake kept his arms out, gently flicking his wrist from time to time. God only knows what he had the Mutants doing inside.

Mark and I stood there, dumbfounded. We didn't know what to do. We didn't know what to say. The Xenophonians were falling, the Mutants were gone, and the base was destroying itself from the inside out.

Had we won?

Bzzz. Bzzz. Bzzz.

Not yet. Finally, I took out my communicator to read the message. My heart fell into my boots. My breathing quickened and I cursed myself. If only I read it seconds sooner:

DON'T LET BLAKE CLAP HIS HANDS.

I looked over to watch that split second before palm met palm. Time slowed down, and I watched Blake's pale raw bleeding hands clash with a quiet clap. I reached forward to grab him, but it was too late.

A shot rang out.

On the building across from us, I saw Zeus with a smoking rifle in his hand.

Blake's white hair splattered with red. His eyes fluttered and he teetered back and forth. Mark ran to grab him, but wasn't fast enough. Blake toppled forward over the ledge. A second later, we heard a thud.

I heard Aymie's blood curdling scream. She bawled and cried for Blake. There were the sounds of body blows and then another *crack*. She was knocked out, too. I watched as Nic carried her to safety, trying not to get caught in the heat of the battle.

Alison flew back out of hiding. Zeus must've ordered her to take cover while he killed REM. She cut through the sky, smashing into the lines of our reinforcements below. In her rage, she slaughtered many Isle members.

The horror on their faces was unbearable. The last thing they saw was their beloved Bionic before she crashed through them.

As Alison was about to attack again, Axel grabbed her and chucked her with a scream back towards the power plant. She flipped in the air and struck the building. A dust cloud encompassed her body.

Zeus decided he had enough. He held his arms out. His turn to clap his hands.

Alison was going to explode.

I couldn't take it. I screamed into my communicator, hoping someone was nearby. Zeus' arms pulled back. He smiled and thrust them together.

But they never met.

Three shots rang out. Zeus staggered backwards. His eyes raised towards the roof of the powerplant.

Yared leaned over the edge with his rifle propped on its stand.

Zeus dropped to his knees and Alison fell down to the earth. Axel swooped in and caught her. They lay on the ground together. Neither moved.

Zeus' eyes met mine in the distance. I saw a faint smirk as he fell forward on his face.

My heart raced and my head pounded. *Is it finally over?*

Of course, nothing is ever easy. Mark shouted, and I turned to see Joshua was gone. I looked back to notice Zeus, PH, and Adeline were gone, too. All in the blink of an eye.

"Where'd they go?!" I screamed.

"I don't know," Mark replied. He grabbed my arm and pulled me toward the ledge. "We have to go, now!"

I looked down to see Axel clutching Alison. I screamed to the Bionic that we had to move, but it was no use. His arms wrapped tightly around Alison. Tears dripped down his dusty cheeks and he rested his lips against her forehead. He wasn't going to leave his girlfriend.

Alison's armored lights were a blinding white. Her eyes met mine for a second and then went back to Axel. Weakly, she lifted her hand and stroked his pale face. I watched her try and push him away. He wouldn't budge. He cupped the back of her head and firmly pressed his lips to hers. Alison's cheeks dampened with both of their tears.

She pressed her hand on his shoulder and shoved him off her. "It's okay," she comforted. "I'm going to see Jeremy. Go save yourself."

He wouldn't obey. His arms wrapped tighter around her blinding white body.

Screaming and shouting echoed out of the powerplant. They weren't Mutant; they were human. A large group of men and women raced to the surface. They yelled for us to get away. I listened and we ran.

Behind me, I heard cries and metal clanging. I looked over my shoulder and gasped. Five other Bionics with crestfallen faces dragged Axel away from Alison. They knew their Commander was beyond hope. All their eyes watered as they flew off with their thrashing Second-in-Command. Axel's voice could be heard throughout the city as he screamed her name.

I couldn't bear to hear the pain. To see the suffering. My stomach churned and my lungs burned at what we did.

We left her to die.

As I ran, I pulled my communicator out and ordered a retreat. Thankfully, the work was finished. In a flash, the soldiers of RRPR, WHYP, and the Isles jumped onto trucks, planes, tanks and traversed away from Chernobyl.

I felt the poison in my chest stir. The breathing mask wasn't doing as well as it should. My legs were turning to jelly and my vision was fading. Debris caught my foot and I felt myself tumble forward. Feet stomped around me, heading for cover. Strong arms scooped me up. It was Shane. I wrapped my arms around his neck. The poison got the better of me and I passed out.

In what felt like a dream, I heard a distant explosion, followed by blood curdling screams and cries.

I awoke in the infirmary and immediately wrote this letter to you, Joshua, to demand one thing:

What happened?

-

Shannon Hollinger

Shannon Hollinger
Royal Strategist of RRPR

THE UNDERGROUND

LETTER 44 (PART 2)
Yared: XIII

Joshua,

I watched Shannon write her letter as tears streamed down her face. She tries to be strong, but her pain is grave.

So is mine.

I took her letter before she sent it. I have my own questions, but I'd like to tell you what happened here after the fact.

We took shelter in an old school building acting as the Russian Interpreters' basecamp. My mind couldn't wrap around the battle. All hope was lost until Thyme, Wyght, and the Keepers showed up with reinforcements. I was inspired. Confident. But that was ripped from me like everything else I clung to.

I sat in a classroom where our wounded Officers lay on cots: Shannon, Aymie, Myles, two of Shannon's sisters, and Lucas. I listened to their quiet breathing and sleeping whimpers.

My insides churned watching Lucas as he lay on his stomach, struggling to breathe. Blond hair draped over his dragonfly eyes. Mr. Mallory tended to his wounds. As sick as the hippie scientist was, the pain in his face was apparent. His heart ached for Lucas. The Keeper wrapped the back of the Dragonfly in medical gauze, but blood seeped through. Quietly, Mallory tied off the bandage. He stroked the sleeping boy's face and turned to take his leave. As the Keeper left, he shot me a side glance, but said nothing.

He knew it was my fault.

Looking at Lucas' horrible wound made me sick. I dug my nails into my knees and hung my head low. The love I had for the fight. The adrenaline

I felt in battle. All of it disappeared in an instant of foolishness. Of course it wasn't Zeus. Why couldn't my brain detect that?

Lucas bore the scars of my mistake.

After I shot him, I couldn't go on. I sat on the rooftop, wallowing in self pity. The three Mutants left me and I remained. Then because of *my* hesitation, we lost more. I watched it happen. I didn't shoot. I didn't stop. I watched.

Blake.

Alison.

I felt both of their deaths. My soul trembled at their pain. My chest felt Blake's body hit the road. My limbs ached as Alison exploded. My heart connected to both of them.

And I did *nothing* to save them.

There was a rapping at the door, followed by a kind voice. "Yared, are you all right?"

I turned to see Virginia Michaelson in the doorway. I got to my feet. "Fine, ma'am," I said matter-of-factly. "Watching over them."

"As a woman, I know 'fine' means something else." She sat down and gestured to my chair. "I know I may not be Papa E or Counselor Watterson, but I'm a good listener."

I sat down. "What is there to say?" I stated. "How could I be all right?"

"I don't expect you to, but your heart is heavy." Her soft light eyes met my hardened soul. "We won this fight, but we suffered losses."

"Casualties of war," I corrected. My Seer nature tried to classify them as such, but my heart couldn't bear it.

"But that doesn't mean we shouldn't grieve." Michaelson reached out and gently touched my hands. She lifted the fingers that I dug into my skin. "It also doesn't mean we should blame ourselves." She massaged my palms, trying to ease my tension and prevent me from hurting myself. "We sometimes make grave mistakes," she continued. "I won't lie; we'll be haunted. I lie awake at night, thinking about what happened under my watch. How many Interpreters I've lost… " she bit her lip. She suffered, too. "Despite these faults—these sorrows and pains—we cannot beat ourselves up. We must repent, make penance, and continue forward."

"Does that mean forget?" I croaked. I gripped her hands tighter.

"*Never*," she stated. "Let go of your burdens, but remember those you lost. Then," she shook my hands, "continue to fight. Harder than before. You're strong, Commander Yared Prinz. This world needs you." Slipping her hands away, she reached behind her and unclipped the blue utility belt she proudly wore. She held it out. "The Interpreters and I need you. Your friends need you."

I took it from her. "What do you need me to do, ma'am?"

"Continue the fight," she stated. "Fight alongside us. Fight alongside me."

I couldn't believe it. *Join the Interpreters?* My mouth went dry. To be an Interpreter means the fight won't stop. Ever. *That's my purpose, isn't it? To fight?*

Lucas' whimpers brought me back to reality. His incapacitation was my doing. A pang of guilt struck me. *How could I leave them now after all we've been through?*

Concern painted my face, and she added, "I won't press you. Family first *always*. Just think about it." She stood and left me in the infirmary.

I exhaled and slumped back in my chair, holding the heavy utility belt in my hands. It was worn and saw many battles. *Just like me.* It'd be an honor to work alongside such an esteemed general. It's what I was made for. And yet, I made a promise to my comrades. *Why must I make this choice?*

"Yared," a voice groaned. I turned to see Peggy—one of Shannon's sisters—sitting upright in her bed. "Where are we?"

"Safe." I handed her a bottle of water from the bedside table and instructed her to lie down.

She sipped, but couldn't swallow. The liquid choked her as the memories of the battle flooded back. She spat the water all over herself. "B-blake," she stammered. "Is he really?"

I held my breath. I didn't want to be the one to break the news to her. This Hollinger always followed Blake around back at WHYP, teaching her photography. She was his best little friend.

All he left her were empty cameras.

My expression said it all. Peggy burst into tears. Her sobs were so loud and hysterical that she woke the other patients and Shane and Mark ran in.

Shannon sat up in her cot, breathing heavily. "Peggy… what's… wrong?" she panted. The lights in her electronic mask glitched.

Aymie slid out of the bed, teetering from dizziness. A welt formed on her bald head where Nic knocked her out. She staggered to Peggy and sat down, wrapping her arms around her. "It's okay, you're safe now." She rocked her back and forth.

Peggy shook her head and nuzzled it against Aymie's chest. "B-b-b," she blabbered.

Aymie froze. Her arms went limp around Peggy's waist. The Hodgins sister's face paled. Her gray eyes shook. "No… it was just a dream." She gently pushed Peggy away, stood up, and stepped towards her brothers. "It was just a dream. It was just a dream."

Shane's and Mark's lips were tight. Aymie stared at them. She didn't want to believe it. The brothers didn't know what to say.

Shane placed his hand on her shoulder. "I'm sorry, Aymie."

THE UNDERGROUND

The world crumbled beneath her. Her legs trembled, her arms shook, and her lip quivered. Pinching her eyes shut, Aymie dug her fingernails into her bruised scalp.

Shane tried pulling them away, but Aymie swung her elbow and struck his wrist.

"NO!" she screamed. "NO, NO, NO!" She spun but wasn't sure where to go. She tried shoving past her brothers to run outside, but they held her back. Her screams were unbearable. "He can't be, he can't be, he can't be..." Her words repeated until she had no breath to speak. She collapsed to the ground, trembling. Her eyes raised and saw Shannon. The Strategist's gaze turned a dial in Aymie's mind. Her body tensed, her jaw clenched. She turned red with rage. "*You*," Aymie spat through gritted teeth. With a growl, she lunged.

Shannon's blue eyes widened and her guard raised as Aymie fell on her. Enraged, Aymie swung hard and fast at Shannon's face, screaming uncontrollably. Weakened, Shannon suffered the blows.

Mark grabbed his sister and yanked her back. Shane stood between the two, taking Aymie's hits.

"THIS IS YOUR FAULT!" Aymie screeched. "BLAKE IS DEAD. IT'S YOUR FAULT!" She thrashed, trying to get back at Shannon. Shane and Mark lifted their sister and rushed her out of the room. Her blood curdling screams trailing away.

Shannon lay on her bed, panting and crying. She pulled her mask off and rubbed her face. Aymie struck the mask several times and it dug into her skin. Shannons freckled cheeks were bruised and cut. Blood and tears stained the bed sheets.

Shannon's sisters Peggy and Lucy sobbed. They couldn't bear to see any more fighting. Their eyes were red, their lips quivered, and their bodies shook. Shannon couldn't bear the sight. Sliding off her bed, she gimped to hold Peggy. Myles jumped up and tried to comfort Lucy, but it was no use. The rains of sorrow washed over them.

I called for Quinn Hollinger on my BoMF. Seconds later, he and the missus barreled in. The Hollinger girls' reaction to their mother's return entwined with their sorrowful sobs. Their hysterics increased, and they couldn't speak.

"*Sono qui, ragazze mie,*" Mrs. Hollinger choked, wrapping her arms around the three girls. She brought them to their feet and she, Mr. Hollinger, and Myles ushered them out of the infirmary.

Lucas and I were left. I turned to see the Dragonfly sitting up in his bed. We looked at each other, but said nothing. I wanted to apologize, but a lump caught in my throat when I saw the blood that outlined his figure on the white sheet. My eyes burned. *It's my fault.* I shoved my palms into my eye sockets, trying to shove the tears back down.

I felt a warm touch on my shoulder. Lucas stood before me. I saw my reflection in his compound eyes. I was haggard and worn. I was *weak*. He had every right to punch me. To tear at my back with a knife.

But he didn't.

He clasped his hand tighter around my shoulder. "It's all right, mate," he croaked. His voice was hoarse. "I know you're sorry."

I was too weak to say it. "Lucas, I—"

I was interrupted when Sami and Aaron entered. The twins' eyes were bloodshot, their faces pale, and their bodies weak. I couldn't believe they could stand after what they endured. First, they lost their little brother Jeremy in the Battle of the Isles.

Now, they lost their big sister.

Sami looked at Lucas. Her green cat eyes watered and she cried for probably the hundredth time. Lucas stood up straight and extended his arms. Sami ran to them, and he embraced her. Together they wept.

While they had their moment, I went to Aaron. His spiky blond hair was unkempt. Behind his glasses were distant blue eyes that wanted to be lost forever.

I opened my mouth and shut it again. *What do I say?* My Seer instincts battled with my human nature. My friend was breaking and I wanted to help. However, the Seer part of me won and I asked, "What's our next move?"

Aaron choked back tears. My question was rude, but he answered it anyway: "Th-they say the war is won."

Those six words. They should've been spoken over a loudspeaker with trumpets blasting and parades through the streets. We should've been drinking champagne and cheering. Those six words should've brought joy.

But they brought pain.

My body went numb recalling the suffering, but my Seer instincts continued, "Are we going to rebuild?"

Aaron nodded frantically. He removed his black glasses and cleaned them anxiously. A tear dropped onto the lens.

That drop caused a wave in my inner ocean, crashing into my Seer instincts and sending them off to sea. My heart raced and I felt human. Aaron watched his twin slip into insanity. This teen lost two siblings in only a year. The four Alexuses were now only two. Jeremy was gone. Alison was gone.

How *dare* I ask him for mission details?

I swallowed the lump in my throat and did something I never would've thought a heartless Seer like me would do. I tapped his arms and pulled him in for a hug.

Aaron didn't object. He rested his head on my shoulder and dampened my jacket with his tears. I felt his chest heave as he held my body close to his.

As I listened to him and his sister cry, it finally hit me.

We Isle members were orphans. We could only hold onto each other. But we never held on tight enough.

Zita, Harold, Cecil, Marlene, Ava, Ursula, Becca, Jeremy, Ethan, Donnie, Alison. The family members that slipped through our grasp.

The Seventeen was now only six.

The memories flooded back. Zita and Harold: our healers. Marlene and Ava: our joy. Cecil and Becca: Aaron's and Sami's best friends. Ursula and Jeremy: my two subordinates. The ones who believed in me. The ones who stuck by me even when I was a pain. They were gone.

Now, little Donnie was gone. My best friend, Ethan, was gone. Now, Alison, our motherly leader was gone.

I couldn't hold back anymore. Tears slid down my cheeks. I clutched Aaron tighter. Taking a shaky breath, I pinched my eyes shut. I tried to swallow the fiery lump in my throat. I never felt so frail in my entire life.

A lean hand pressed against my back. Another pair of arms wrapped around Aaron and me. It was Mark. Silently, he comforted us. I was encompassed by the two tall Geeks, but I didn't care. I reached out from the center and pulled in Sami and Lucas. Mark embraced them also like a father does to comfort his children.

As we pulled away, a mechanical figure emerged through the doorway. Axel wore full battle armor. Allaway and the Drones patched it up. His body looked as good as new, but his face aged one hundred years. Mark stepped forward to comfort him, but stopped when he noticed the look in Axel's mechanical eyes.

Fury.

"Axel," I started, wiping my nose with the back of my hand.

"What was Joshua thinking?" he spat. Despair and hatred in his voice.

Shocked, I asked, "What're you talking about?"

"Joshua had a hand in this," he growled through gritted teeth. He tried staying angry, but he held back tears. "He *knew* of the plan. He *knew* Alison was wired to blow. He *knew* she was going to die. He *knew* Blake was going to die." His face reddened and the rage returned. "Why didn't he SAY SOMETHING?!" he screamed as he swung his fist to his left, smashing a hole in the door frame. The blue lights in his armor flickered like lightning.

We stood there, dumbfounded. We didn't know how to respond.

"What makes you so sure he knew?" Mark asked, trying to hide the distress in his voice.

Axel's shoulders heaved. Tears trickled to the floor. "Blake," he croaked. "Blake foresaw the whole thing." He gestured to the twins. "Sami and Aaron know. They heard it."

"Blake said 'the applause happens at the end'," Aaron explained. "He was sad, but peaceful. He knew what he had to do." Aaron bit his lip. "He also warned that another would be lost," he finished softly.

"H-he also said," Sami stuttered, "t-that OX would n-never d-die."

"'Our victory only temporary'," Aaron added. "We'll be betrayed once again."

"So tell me, Yared," Axel snarled. "Who betrayed us?"

I was speechless. I believed every word. I looked to Mark for help, but he wanted to hear what I had to say. My brain tried to think of an explanation. I came up with two: "Either PH is still the evil menace we first encountered or," I threw my hands down in exasperation, "Joshua wants OX to succeed."

"Find out," Axel demanded.

They watched me write this, Joshua, and will be awaiting your response.

Shannon's question: What happened?

Our question: *Why* did it happen?

-

Yared Prinz

Yared Prinz
Seer Commander

LETTER 45

Joshua: XXIII

Yared. Shannon.

I'm through with you both. The accusations. The demands. The pressure. For almost eight years I've suffered. Eight years I've been ostracized. Eight years all you've cared about is answers and delivery. Eight years I've been paranoid that I'd be killed by the Xenophonians.

Not anymore.

I woke up days later in an old brick fortress in Babruysk, Belarus. I lay on a cot alone in a dark and eerie room. My soft pillow could not comfort my throbbing head. I clasped the bruise caused by the butt of Shane's rifle. I was sore, achey, and tired. Sitting up, I looked out a small window to see a sea of black. The night was still and starless.

The first thing I did was read your letters. I felt no sorrow. I felt no pity. I threw the tablet to the other side of the room and slipped out from beneath heavy red covers. I took my cracked glasses off the nightstand and wandered the halls. Everything was quiet. Nothing was familiar.

I rubbed my calloused fingers along the brick. I felt familiar grooves beneath my fingertips. Peering closer, I noticed the OX symbol was carved repeatedly into the red. *This must be a safe haven,* I thought.

"Ah, you're awake," a familiar voice said. A voice I almost forgot.

I turned to see PH standing in the doorway. Something about him was… different. Without his scarf, I made out his full physique. Even at 5'4", he looked tall and intimidating. His freckled face aged and his heterochromatic eyes were warm and friendly.

For some reason, it made me sick.

"What are you doing here?" I snorted.

PH made a face. "That's not somethin' I'd expect from a mate."

Don't call me that... I bit my tongue. I felt cross towards him. He wasn't the diehard Xenophonian anymore. Something about him changed. "How did you escape from RRPR?" I asked, keeping my act going.

PH cocked his head to the side, surprised. He thought I'd know everything. "I didn't escape."

"They let you go?"

"I was supposed to be bait. They didn't intend on me returnin' to the Order. And now," he raised his arms and then dropped them back at his sides, "'ere we are."

"Do you want to be back here?" I asked, genuinely.

PH hesitated. He was unsure. His face was crestfallen. His mind was confused. His heart was torn.

I felt no pity towards him.

"If you don't know for sure," I walked over and whispered in his ear, "then you don't belong here." I left to find the Moirai.

As I marched, I heard a squeaking and footfall. I turned to see Goliath, Solomon, and Diego following me. They were bruised and burned, but still walking.

"What are you doing here?" I asked. I thought their plan was to escape with Mrs. Hollinger and the other Interpreters. They were traitors to the Order. The Moirai wanted them dead.

Goliath managed a smile. "Don't worry, no one knows we're here," he explained. "We couldn't leave you on your own. The faithful Children of Anemoi took you before we could rescue you."

Solomon nodded and Diego chirped. The monkey leapt from his master's staff and clung to my shoulder. I was repulsed. I didn't want the filthy creature treating me like his personal transportation anymore. I'm tired of being used. With disgust, I threw the monkey off my shoulder. Diego struck the ground, hitting his head a little too hard. He cried in pain and rubbed his bruise.

I looked to Solomon who staggered backwards and placed his hand on his own head.

Goliath's eyes widened and his lips parted. "Wolf, is everything all right?"

I looked at the little creature and back at the old man. I felt no remorse. "I don't want him having a free ride today," I spat. "What is it you want?"

"The mission is not fulfilled," Goliath whispered. "Zeus is alive."

My heart raced. From your letters, I assumed he was dead. The purpose of my undercover assignment tried to surface, but I shoved it into the recesses of my mind. Joshua wanted to fulfill his duties, but Wolf did too.

Wolf wanted to help Zeus create a new world. A better world.

But with no army and no base, I wasn't sure how that'd happen.

Maybe we still have the Mutants, I thought. I looked at my hands. The metal bracelets were gone; still wrapped tightly around the wrists of Blake's corpse.

"I'll see that the mission gets completed," I replied. I sensed my comrades' doubt as I turned and stomped away.

I walked through the halls of the base, glancing occasionally into the rooms. There were no low ranking Xenophonians outside a few Children of Anemoi. No mindless Children of Moirai, Eros, Ares, or Hermes. I supposed Blake set the rest free when he took control of the Mutants. The survivors were Supervisors—the volunteer Xenophonians. No Titans survived. PH and I were the last ones.

I found the three Moirai sitting in old chairs beside a small fireplace; its flames died slowly. The women stared at one another, not saying a word. They wore fighting uniforms with their respective emblems on their arms.

I rapped on the door and the three jumped, aiming weapons. I threw my hands up. "Forgive me."

They sighed in relief and lowered their guard. "Hades, Wolf," Emel chuckled. "You sure are light on your feet."

I shrugged. "I'm a Hermes."

Arata nodded and sank back into her chair, letting out a long exhale. Her almond eyes were sad and her porcelain skin was cracked with cuts. "This was not the path we started out on."

Morana leaned against the fireplace. Her square jaw was firm and her eyes were fixed on the flame. "This is not the end I would've chosen."

"Of course not, Morana," Emel retorted. "This was never part of my—I mean our plan. Something happened that was beyond our control. Unexpected. Unseen." Emel plopped her round body onto a wooden chair that creaked beneath her weight. She grunted and asked, "Wolf, how're you holding up? You've quite the welt and your glasses look like they've seen hell."

I rubbed my bruised forehead. "I'm all right. Just more confused as to what happened."

"Zeus was caught off guard and it cost us," Emel spat. "He was so blind with revenge and being a showoff that he didn't just blow everyone up with the girl like he was supposed to." She rubbed her cheeks. "If he just sent her to self-destruct in the enemy camp, none of this would've happened."

"What are we to do now?" I asked.

The three women sighed simultaneously. "We have a risky move to get us out of check," Emel explained. "They haven't checkmated us yet."

"We need your help, Wolf," Arata added. "Zeus is unreliable now. He failed us."

"His time has come," Morana declared, taking her hand off the fireplace mantel. The orange glow illuminated her bitter angular face. "We need a new leader." She motioned for me to come closer and lift my hand. I did so, and she gently turned it over, placing two silver rings on my palm. Looking closely, I realized there was something different about them. Lightning bolts were etched on the inside.

They belonged to Zeus.

"Titan Wolf of the Russian Pandemonium," Morana continued. Emel and Arata stood from their chairs. "Do you accept the burden of becoming the god of the Order of Xenophon?"

My heart should've been racing, but it wasn't. I was calm. I was at ease. I was thrilled. I worked tirelessly and painfully for eight years. I deserved this.

Taking a deep breath, I made eye contact with each one of them. "In the name of Xenophon, I accept," I declared.

Sinister smiles spread across the faces of the three women. Arata and Emel stood beside Morana. They placed their hands on mine. Together, they folded my fingers over the metal rings. Taking a step back, they bowed.

Arata went over to her chair and lifted up what looked like a thick spool of thread. She turned it around on her palm. With her free hand, she let its thread fall to the floor.

Clotho.

Emel lifted it, rubbing it between her pudgy fingers. She gently tugged it from Arata, measuring out what they needed.

Lachesis.

Morana took the slack and draped it along her strong shoulders. When Emel stopped feeding it to her, she pulled a sharp pair of scissors off her belt. She snipped, cutting the thread from the rest of the spool.

Atropos.

The three Moirai handed me the thick string. It wasn't long and Morana's snip left its edges frayed as if the cut was sudden and unexpected.

Then, I realized what I had to do.

"This is for Zeus, isn't it?" I asked quietly.

The three nodded. "He was born into the Order a long time ago," Arata began.

"He lived his life as he should've. I say he fulfilled his purpose," Emel continued.

"Now, it is time to cut his thread," Morana finished. "Time for the new Zeus to rise."

I tucked the string into my pocket. I slid the bracelets on my wrists, welcoming their electric shock. I knew my mission and gladly accepted it.

But for some reason, I felt pain.

"Understood, ma'ams. Your will be done." I bowed.

They returned the gesture and instructed me on where to go. With obedience, I left them to fulfill my duties.

I found Zeus alone in a room at the end of the hall. He lay in a hospital bed set in a sitting position. Blood seeped through the bandages on his torso where he'd been shot. Nothing fatal, but they were disabling. Yared's aim was shaky.

He stared at the ceiling as if it'd open up and take him away. My light steps were like a march in the stillness. Zeus' eyes slowly found their way towards me. "Wolf," he croaked, managing a smile. "I'm glad to see you're all right." He coughed harshly, covering his mouth with the back of his hand.

I was afraid to say something. I wanted to get it done quickly.

Confusion fell upon Zeus' face. "You're all right, aren't you?" The way he asked made my stomach churn. It was like he was actually concerned.

He feels nothing, I told myself. *He's a coward with a lust for power.*

"I'm fine, sir," I replied as I walked to his bedside. "How are you holding up?"

He chuckled weakly. "I've been worse. The Anemoi got there just in time. Don't know why they were so delayed."

I nodded meaninglessly. I didn't want to continue the conversation. I knew my mission. I walked around his cot, pretending to explore the room. "Is this one of our safe havens?"

"Indeed it is. One of the first ones we built."

"Why not build one in Ancient Greece where the ancestors of the Order lived?"

"We have one there, but it hasn't been occupied in a long time." He sighed. "We were forced to flee after we were attacked by the enemy during the time of Marcellus' betrayal. That's why we built New Greece beneath Chernobyl. No one would dare enter there. We were safe." His explanation was cut short by a coughing fit, and he requested the oxygen mask.

I went behind his bed and turned on the machine, but left the oxygen mask dangling from the I.V. poll. "Safe," I said softly. I lifted the string out of my pocket, rubbing the thick red thread between my fingers. "Are we ever actually safe?"

There was a pause. "I like to believe the lie," he whispered. His voice sounded weak and cracked. It almost made me pity him. "Even with the Order, there is no one you can trust. Everything is lies and it's each man for himself. That's why I've led from the shadows for so many years." He rubbed his fingers along his bandaged torso. "Despite the wounds, it was nice to step into the light. To see that people aren't all bad." He tried to look over his shoulder to see me. "It's a pleasure to mentor you, Wolf. I can't remember the last time I trusted someone or enjoyed the presence of another." He turned forward, closed his eyes, and took a raspy breath. "Thank you."

I didn't want him to say those things. Words like that made me hesitate. I grabbed each end of the string and pulled it taut. "Sir, I don't know what to say," I replied honestly.

He coughed again and waved behind him, wanting the oxygen mask. "No need to say anything. I mean every word. I hope someday you'll bear my name and lead the Order."

Lead. That snapped me back to the moment. I wanted—no, *needed* to lead. I deserved it. I earned it. No longer would I serve. People would serve *me.*

"It may be sooner than you think," I whispered.

Zeus gasped.

I threw my arms over his bed. I wrapped the string around his neck and pulled it tight. With all his might Zeus thrashed and clawed at it, but it was no use. I yanked him back towards the bed frame. I stretched my arms out as far as I could go, tightening the cord. I watched his feet kick. Short gags escaped his throat as he tried to breathe. His actions became weaker and weaker.

He stopped.

His body went limp and he moved no more.

My breath escaped in a sharp exhale and I let go of the thread, sinking to the ground. I didn't dare look at his dead face.

I... can't... believe it, I thought. *After eight years, I finally won.*

A smile crept across my face. My hands burned, and my chest shook. I laughed.

It started as a soft chuckle but became uncontrollable and loud. A testament of insanity.

Am I admitting I'm going insane? Maybe.

I ran my fingers through my curly hair and sat on the cold floor. I embraced the icy concrete beneath me. "It's over, it's over, it's over," I repeated.

No, it's not, a voice inside reminded me.

I stopped laughing and listened. I couldn't tell whose voice it was.

Was it Joshua's?

Was it Wolf's?

I wasn't certain, but I didn't care.

My mind returned to the present. I realized what I did and what it brought me. Standing to my feet, I headed towards the door. I exited and shut it behind me with a metal thud. I didn't look back. I didn't need to.

Everything I worked for was ahead of me. Zeus is gone. The Order of Xenophon is in shambles.

But I'm still standing.

I'm still strong.
I'm still powerful.
And *I'm* in charge. I'll do anything to keep it that way.
See you in a few days.
In the name of Xenophon,

Zeus
The God of the Order of Xenophon

THE UNDERGROUND

LETTER 46

Shannon: XIII

Joshua,

You are a *fool*.

I write to you with hope that the love you had for us may be rekindled.

The moment I received your letter, I sent out a message to our teams. We needed to prepare for battle. You've clearly lost your mind and need to be stopped.

I finished preparing for the dreaded encounter when my father summoned me. I met him, my sisters, and my mother outside our Russian safe haven. The chilly air nipped my bare skin as I stood on the frosted ground.

I embraced the cold because it meant I was alive.

I stood before my family, admiring their brave faces. Even though I had a proper reunion with my mother, I still couldn't believe she was there. I reached for her hand, hoping I wouldn't pass through it like a hologram. She smiled and took it. Her touch warmed my shivering body.

She was real.

Age increased my mother's beauty. Her eyes sparkled and her will was strong. My three youngest sisters—Agnes, Rebecca, and Rachel—flung their arms around her. I didn't want her to let go, but my sisters needed her more. Peggy, Lucy, and Carol-Ann stood close at my father's side. My mother sang the Gaelic lullaby, soothing their worried spirits.

I missed her voice so much. I missed her more than I realized. The moment her song touched my ears, my heart was moved. I pinched back tears. I needed to be strong.

When my mother finished, my father said, "Shannon, darling, what are you doing in uniform?"

"Preparing for battle," I stated. "The preparations are set. I'm ready to stop Joshua."

"No, you are remaining behind," my father ordered. "You're in no condition to fight. Nor are you in your right mind."

I growled. I was the Royal Strategist. I made the calls. "Father, I disagree—"

"Quit acting the maggot," he snapped. "My family was finally put back together. We lost one again. I am *not* going to lose you, too."

I bit my lip. He was right. My mother was back. My father was back. My sisters were still alive. We had PH in our grasp then he slipped through our fingers. "If you let me go, I'll get him back."

He shook his head. "You won't be able to. You'll be blinded."

"By what?" I spat.

"The anger of injustice," he stated. "Joshua *hurt* you. He hurt all of us. We trusted him, and now he is lost. Darkness consumed him. Sorrow is within your heart and confronting him will make it worse." My father stepped forward and put a hand on my shoulder. "We need you alive."

I let out a deep breath that burned my chest. My father believed I'd die during the mission. My episodes were worsening. My lungs were shot and the poison would consume me at any moment. He also believed my feelings would absorb me and I'd lose sight of what mattered.

He was right.

Tears escaped my eyes. "I can't let them do this without me," I croaked. "It's my fault we lost so much. Let me make it better."

My father brushed his thumb across my freckled face. "You've done enough good." He cupped my cheeks and shook me gently. "Let go, Shannon."

My pride didn't want to listen. Years of sacrifice, strategizing, and suffering led to this moment. I worked so hard. I lost so much. I wanted to see it through.

Thinking about how much I'd done made me anxious. My breathing became heavier. My lungs burned and my throat tightened. The poison stirred inside me.

That's when my pride finally submitted to my heart.

I let out a few deep breaths, and the poison subsided. *I will surely die on the next mission.* I looked into my father's eyes. They were desperate. They were caring. They were love. *How selfish could I be?* I wasn't going to put my family through more suffering.

My eyes watered. "I'll let go. For you, Dad," I sobbed.

My father pulled me in for a hug, gripping me tighter. I felt my curly hair dampen with his tears. "Thank you, my dear," he whispered.

After we pulled away, I stood and spoke with my family for a long time. My mother's stories made my heart ache, making me want to destroy the last bit of the Order of Xenophon myself.

But I'd be an obedient daughter.

An hour passed before my communicator beeped. I left my family and went to meet the team.

I met Shane along the way. He stood tall in his combat uniform as he spoke with Mr. Wyght. My heart wanted to rejoice at the Director's and Thyme's return, but I was too sorrowful. The two saw me and waved.

"My dear, Shannon," Director Wyght greeted. "It's been some time. How are you?"

"Alive." That was the truest reply I could give.

The white-haired man chuckled. "Good thing, too. No one else could strategize this plan as well as you." He frowned and his wrinkles deepened. "The fact that we have to go through with this upsets me." Sadness pooled behind his eyes. He suffered. The loss of Blake, Alison, and our other soldiers cut him deep.

Your betrayal sliced him in two.

Shane clasped a hand on the Director's arm. "We'll get through this. We always do."

Wyght managed a smile. "You always were optimistic, S. Hodgins. Lazy and a troublemaker, but optimistic." He patted Shane's strong face, tousled my curly hair, and left us.

"He isn't doing well," I whispered to my fiancé.

Shane shook his head. "None of us are. Between our losses and this situation, how can we?"

I slid my hand in his. "We can't, but we shouldn't let our pain consume us. Our friends mustn't have died in vain."

"They won't. I'll see to it." As he squeezed my palm, I sensed his anger and desire to fight. "I haven't felt like this since Masdit and Gerrior slaughtered my family, the Royal Circus, and everyone else in between," he continued. "But in my heart, I know I've avenged them. This time, I'm not fighting for myself. I'm fighting for the Isle members and all they've been through. I'm fighting for Blake and all he believed in." His green eyes met mine. "I'm fighting for you too, Shannon."

Despite the despair, my heart couldn't have been happier with his words. My fiancé was back and he was better than I could've imagined. His pride was gone, his fear dwindled, and his love overflowing. I stood on my tiptoes and pressed my lips against his. Warmth spread through my body as he held me like he'd never be able to again.

I prayed that wouldn't be the case.

He pulled away and rested his forehead against mine. "Shannon, I don't want you to come with me," he stated.

I chuckled softly. "I've been grounded. You get to run away from *me* this time."

He flashed his handsome smile. "Your dad is the best." He pecked my forehead with his lips. "I'll be back before you know it. Pray for us, okay?"

"Always."

He gave my shoulders a squeeze and ran to board the plane.

I walked down the runway to wish the rest of the team luck. First, I encountered Yared. This teen and his friends went through hell and back in one year. The curious and innocent minds that first came to the Underground were now filled with pain and nightmares. His dark brown face was worn and scarred. His sunken eyes were tired and red from tears. His mouth formed a permanent scowl.

"Yared, I—"

"There's nothing to say, Shannon," he interrupted. His voice wasn't rude. It was broken. "We'll do what we must. Lucas is remaining behind with Keeper Mallory, but the others are coming." His knuckles turned white as they gripped his rifle. "We joined RRPR to fight. To stop this war. We knew the consequences. *Alison* knew the consequences." He choked on his words. "She convinced us to keep fighting. Now, Joshua took her away along with Ethan and Donnie."

He was right. There was nothing to say. I held out my hand and he took it. I rubbed his calloused palm. The hands that fought even when he wasn't sure of the cause. A faithful soldier. A loyal Seer.

A teen who suffered.

Yared needed encouragement, but I found none. He needed something to keep him going. But I could only make out two words: "Avenge them."

They weren't uplifting. They became an order.

Just what the Seer Commander needed.

The corner of his lip turned upward. Clicking his heels, he saluted me and nodded. "Yes, ma'am." In silence, he left to meet his Isle members on the plane.

After I wished luck to a few Officers, Aymie approached me. Her face was stained with tears, and cuts and bruises spread across her bald head. I expected to see anger and rage in her face, but I only saw sadness.

"Shannon," she said in a low voice. "I need to ask you something." I nodded and she took a deep breath. Her gray eyes shook as she whispered, "Can you forgive me?"

I was taken aback. "What for?"

She bit her lip. "It's not your fault," she confessed. "It's never been your fault."

SHANNON: XIII

I swallowed a lump in my throat. "Aymie, I don't know what to say…"

"I'm sorry," she croaked. "I needed someone to blame, but you're always the one making the hard decisions while the rest of us criticize. In the end, it's our own actions that cause our fall." Her eyes cast upwards. She searched the sky. "I realize now that Blake did everything of his own accord. He did it to save us. As did Shane, the Isle members, and all of the rest. " She rubbed her eyes with the back of her hands. "I love you as a sister, Shannon," she sobbed. "I never told you that, but I've never been more grateful."

My lip quivered and my limbs shook as I pulled her in for a hug, trying not to squeeze where she'd been shot. She was taller than me, but I did my best to hold her as she sobbed. "Of course I forgive you, Aymie," I croaked. "There was *never* a time when you weren't forgiven."

She bawled. Her loud cries were filled with pain. My gut wrenched as my heart shared in her despair. This young woman watched her foster family burn to the ground, stood helpless as her best friend sacrificed herself, felt responsible for Zander's betrayal and the fall of WHYP, experienced the loss of *both* of her brothers, and now mourned the man she desired to spend her life with.

Despite her unspeakable sorrow and internal suffering, she was the motherly face of RRPR. The soldiers woke each morning to the sound of her soothing voice. They sought her in a crowd. She made them feel safe.

On top of all of that, she saved my life. She stitched me up when I was shot by the poisonous arrow years ago. Thanks to her, my heart beats.

I should've apologized.

"Aymie," my voice cracked, "I am sorry, too. Your suffering is incomparable, and I wasn't there for you. I promise I'll make it up to you." I prayed I'd get the chance.

Together, we wept.

After several minutes, she pulled away. Even after crying hysterically, her face was still radiant. I hoped she knew how beautiful she was.

"Thank you, Shannon," she sniffled. "I pray you and Shane are always happy." I wanted to say something else, but without another word, she turned and ran to the plane.

Mark greeted her and helped her up the steps. He looked back at me. His mysterious blue eyes asked if I was coming.

I shook my head and patted my chest.

A smile spread across Mark's face. He knew I'd be safe. He winked and boarded the plane with several Officers and Isle members: Nic, Shane, Sonny, Aymie, Sami, Aaron, Axel, and Yared. Even our prisoners went in my stead. Theo the Shrew, Jordan the Slowloris, Gerrior of Ares, and Brand of Fallout joined the fight as a chance to repay their debt. Meeting them on the field would be Thyme, Wyght, two Keepers, and their soldiers.

Marcellus, my family, Lucas, Johanna, Myles, and I were left behind.

I spun on my heel and walked away. A bad feeling churned in the pit of my stomach.

I knew some wouldn't return.

Yared will tell you why you are a fool. Why you are a coward.

-

Shannon Hollinger
Royal Strategist of RRPR

LETTER 46 (PART 2)

Yared: XIV

Joshua,

No one wanted this.

I sat in the truck beside my fellow officers with my gun locked and loaded. I was ready. Ready to end it all. I failed before. I wouldn't fail again.

Mark sat across from me. His blue eyes were serious as he mulled over the plan. It was apparent he didn't like it. We were meeting the enemy halfway between Belarus and our safe haven. Our only order: fight hard and win.

We were quiet as the truck jerked back and forth over the bumpy terrain. No encouragement was shared. No final words. Just utter silence.

A silence that masked rage.

The vehicle jerked to a stop. One by one we climbed out and dove for cover. I lay beside Aaron and Mark. "What's going on, guys?" I asked.

The Geeks were propped up on their elbows, tapping their electronic devices. "The mines are laid thanks to the Interpreters and Myles'—I mean Einstein's—drones are in place," Mark answered. "Now we wait."

"Are we sure they're coming this way?" I asked.

"Positive," Aaron replied, fixing his glasses. "The Interpreters reported the enemy is on route."

Mark cocked his gun. "They also said to show no mercy."

After several minutes of agony, I heard it. The clamor of trucks and the scream of Mutants. I looked into the distance of the flat land to see a mob of glowing eyes. Behind the sea of monsters were trucks and three military tanks. There weren't many, but enough to destroy our Russian encampment.

THE UNDERGROUND

"Here we go." Mark exhaled and slid his finger across his electronic clipboard.

The first line of mines went off with a deafening explosion. The blast threw the Children of Hades in all directions. Those struck fell dead. The ones behind clambered over and pressed forward. Mark set off each row, striking more Mutants each time. Whoever was controlling them didn't care if they lived or died. He sent them to their deaths.

The final row of mines exploded, and we weakened their line of defense once again. The Mutants decreased in number, but hundreds of soldiers rushed forward.

It was our turn.

Clutching my rifle, I looked down its scope and fired as the rest of our defense did the same. Each bullet found their mark. One by one Mutants and Xenophonians fell. I watched as the trucks and tanks traversed closer. On top of the middle t64 Russian tank was a young man in a red combat uniform. His curly hair was shaved at the base and dark eyes glared through black rimmed glasses. Around the wrists he held aloft were metal bracelets.

"Joshua," I growled.

The tank trekked closer and closer. It wasn't going to stop. It didn't fire, but it kept coming. The man atop wanted the sadistic pleasure of crushing us beneath its tracks.

We had no choice but to get out of the way. I rolled to the side and leapt up. Pain shot through my shoulder and thigh. I hissed at the sensation. My wounds from Sting hadn't fully healed, but I refused to tell anyone. If Aymie and Nic could fight with recovering bullet wounds, so could I.

We'd go through with the mission no matter what.

On my feet, I realized there was no high ground. Everything was flat. It was dangerous to run out into the open.

But we had no choice.

I gripped my rifle and let out a warrior's cry. The rest did the same. Full of adrenaline and rage, we raced out into the battlefield, fighting head on. Bullets, claws, and blood flew through the air. The waves of soldiers crashed into each other, creating a tsunami of death.

Somehow, the new Zeus was able to avoid every bullet. Standing atop his tank, he was an easy target, but nothing struck him. It wasn't a miracle. It was an act of the devil... or science. Whichever came first.

There was a *woosh* and I watched Director Wyght's and the Keepers' aircraft fly overhead. Bombs whistled as they dove to the earth, finding their mark amidst the Xenophonians. My ears rang as I watched the targets and dirt fly through the air. The next round of bombs aimed for one of the tanks.

Then, I realized why PH and Zeus loved standing atop.

The bomb slid off the hull like a bead of water on a flower petal. It met earth and destroyed a line of Xenophonians and RRPR soldiers. The tank was untouched.

It had a sort of forcefield.

I cursed aloud as I slew a Mutant Honey Badger. *Bombs and bullets may not get through, but* I *can.* My eyes narrowed at the man in red. It was my mission to end him. I planned to do it.

I looked at Sonny and Nic for support. They caught my gaze and nodded. Nic dug his feet into the ground and took in a deep breath. Then, he roared. The veins in his neck bulged as the inhuman sound caught the Xenophonians off guard. The Children of Hades looked at him, Sami, Theo, Jordan, and the Keepers' Mutants with wide eyes. They recognized that they were battling their own kind. With a savage fury, Nic tore through lines of the Mutants. Sami and the others aided.

Then, three more Mutants added to the confusion: Clive the Fox, Adeline the Fruit Bat, and Dylan the Bear. They attacked their own men. While the Xenophonians stood in shock, Sonny led the other soldiers against them.

I had an opening. I wove through the crowds and whistled to Shane and Axel. The two dashed to my side. Together, we fought our way to Zeus' tank.

Almost there.

A bullet whizzed by my face. It just missed my nose. Enraged, my attacker charged. I sidestepped and fired my weapon but this brute of a Xenophonian was too quick. Shane was about to fire his pistol but was charged by a Mutant Buffalo. The Hodgins brother flipped over the creature and took it on. I looked to Axel for help, but he was preoccupied saving Aaron from a swarm of Children of Hades.

It was me and the Ares Xenophonian.

I'm running out of time, I thought. Once our numbers decreased, the tank would fire. We were too close. It would wipe us out. From what I could see, that was their plan. The Children of Hades formed a circle around us, pushing us inward. They didn't care if they survived. They'd die trying.

I locked eyes with the Ares and aimed my rifle. I shot repeatedly, but he dove out of the way. He pulled out his pistol and returned fire. I ducked behind a staggering Mutant who took the hit. Using the creature as a shield, I leaned around it and fired back. The enemy rolled across the dirt and hid beside one of the trucks. He was trying to get the high ground. While he was distracted, I ran towards the tank.

I heard a distant gun blast, and I felt like a spiked metal hand punched me in the leg.

I looked down to see I was shot. I was so careless. Reckless. The bullet tore through my left thigh. I hissed at the pain and clutched my leg. I was already weak from my previous bullet wound.

THE UNDERGROUND

No… no… I can't stop. Not now.

I looked up to see the ugly smirk of the Ares Xenophonian. With his gun aimed, he was about to fire again when something latched onto his face. He yelped and staggered backwards. A wooden stick swung through the air and hit his gut with a *thwack*. He fell backwards off the truck. Peering over was the face of an old man. A monkey leapt up on the hood.

They both waved for me to keep going.

I mentally thanked Solomon and hobbled forward. I leaned against the tracks of the tank. No one saw me yet. I clawed at the metal, trying to hoist myself up. The pain was unbearable. I sank back down and clutched my bleeding leg. My body wanted to surrender.

"SEER!" a female voice shouted. Running over to me was Aymie Hodgins. Her jacket was missing a sleeve. In a flash, she grabbed my thigh and quickly fastened a tourniquet with a torn piece of material: her jacket sleeve. "You need to get out of here."

"No," I scolded. "I am ending this *now*." My thigh throbbed, but my adrenaline pumped harder. I was going to see it to the end.

Her lips pursed, but she nodded and hoisted me to my feet. Pointing to the top of the tank, she cupped her hands. I placed my foot in them and she hoisted me up.

When I pulled myself onto the hull, my body felt like it submerged in water. The cries and grunts of battle sounded muffled. Bullets meant for my head bounced away like they struck rubber.

I was right; Zeus was protected.

I gripped my pistol and aimed it at the back of the Xenophonian. His curly hair was in my sights.

Zeus sensed I was there. With one hand still raised, the other whipped around, gripping a handgun. I dropped and it fired. The bullet ricocheted off the metal. I rolled beside the turret then crawled around the back, but Zeus saw everything with those Optic Transmitter glasses. For a moment, he let his other hand down. I watched as the Mutants stood helpless. Our troops saw what was happening and took the advantage.

I rolled over my good shoulder and stood on the other side of the turret. I was face to face with the enemy. I looked into those brown eyes. I saw them once before. They were secretive, paranoid, but kind. Today they were deadly, hateful, and ruthless.

Joshua was dead. Wolf took over and became Zeus.

A sinister smile spread across Zeus' face. He aimed his gun and fired again. I ducked for cover, but he jumped up and tried to find me. We fought in circles around the top of the tank. I grew weary and my leg throbbed. He was toying with me.

I grabbed my pistol and fired, but Zeus was quicker. He ducked and shot back. Screaming in pain, I clutched my arm. Blood pooled through my fingers.

I can't die.

My eyes narrowed and I gritted my teeth. I had it. With a yell, I ran around the turret and tackled Zeus, throwing him off guard. I pressed my arm across his neck, pushing all my weight down. Zeus turned blue and thrashed beneath me.

I thought I had him when an excruciating sensation shot up my thigh. He dug his fingers into my bullet wound. I recoiled at the pain and Zeus put his feet on my stomach and pushed me off. I fell on my back; the wind knocked out of me. Out of the corner of my eye, I saw my pistol. I needed to reach it.

I tried to wriggle my way over, but Zeus hovered over me. Evil glowed in his eyes. One hand gripped Sting's dagger. The sight of it burned my insides as the painful memories it caused rushed back. Zeus twisted its hilt; the black venom dripped down the blade. He raised his hand above his head and—

There was a scream and Zeus was shoved to the side. He fell, striking his head against the metal. I looked up to see Aymie standing tall with her fists clenched around her gun. Our eyes met and she nodded.

Her attention returned to Zeus. "How *could* you?!" she bellowed. Anger in her voice. "You were our friend!"

Zeus said nothing and staggered to his feet. He forgot about me and looked into Aymie's eyes. The girl for whom he saved Blake back at WHYP. A triplet he'd sworn to protect.

Now, he wanted her dead.

He said nothing and gritted his teeth. He raised his gun, but there were no bullets left. Aymie saw an opening, put her finger on the trigger, and fired.

But she wasn't fast enough. Zeus attacked first.

It happened so fast. I did a double take. Zeus' arm was extended. His hand pointed towards Aymie. Her bullet missed. I turned to Aymie and gasped. Lodged in her abdomen was Sting's dagger. Red blood and black venom dripped from the blade. She staggered backwards, clutching at it. She didn't cry. She tore it out of her stomach with a *squelch*.

Enraged, I leapt up and grabbed Zeus from behind. Aymie screamed and ran forward, attacking Zeus with the blade. The blade that caused so much pain.

Zeus let out a quick breath as the dagger was plunged into his side.

"This... is for... Blake," Aymie spat with whatever strength she could muster.

Even with the blade inside him, Zeus wouldn't admit defeat. He elbowed my chest and headbutted Aymie. He wriggled out of my grasp and hobbled to the hatch, leaving behind a trail of blood. It swung open and he disappeared below.

I was about to go after him when I heard the creaking of the turret. We needed to get off the hull.

The tank was going to fire.

I shouted to Aymie through the noise, but it was no use. She was fading fast. I got to my feet and limped over to her. She was still standing, but not for much longer. Looking into her gray eyes, I pressed my bloody hand to her pale cheek. "No, no, Aymie, stay with me," I pleaded.

Slowly, she shook her head. "It's all right, Yared," she coughed. Blood dripped from the sides of her mouth. Her bald head was bruised. Tears cut through the dirt on her beautiful face. "My soul is at rest," she continued weakly. "I received forgiveness. I fulfilled God's plan. Blake said it would be so." Her eyes raised to heaven. "It's my turn to go home. To be... with those we lost." She dropped hard to her knees and lay against the turret. Trembling, she pulled her dogtag out of her shirt. She rubbed her red fingers gingerly across the *H* emblem, covering it in blood. "My brothers," she whispered. "I love you both and wish you the best in the world." She took Blake's silver ring that was also on the chain and kissed it, staining it red. She slid it onto her finger with the dog tag beads lodged between. "My turn to be at peace with the one I love." Shutting her eyes, she exhaled for the last time. A peaceful smile on her face.

The pain in my wrist and my thigh receded as I looked upon the face of my dead friend. I wanted to scream. I wanted to cry. The one we thought was on our side turned on us. The one who helped this woman in the past. The one this woman and the rest of us trusted.

He betrayed her. He betrayed all of us.

I grew dizzy and wanted to collapse. I staggered backwards. I had no strength to stand. My chest heaved and I teetered backward off the tank.

My body left the forcefield and the noises encompassed me. I was ready to welcome the hard ground and firefight, but I felt hot metal beneath my arms. Axel grabbed me and we flew away from the scene. He saw Aymie's body, but said nothing. The pain in his eyes was loud enough. There was nothing he could do.

"Where... are we... going?" I asked as I struggled to breathe.

"Solomon, Goliath, and PH are taking it from here," he replied.

Below, I saw our soldiers retreat purposefully. I watched as the two remaining tanks turned inward. Their turrets aimed at the one in the center. The one Zeus cowered in.

When our troops were a safe distance away, the tanks fired. I watched the balls of fire as the missiles struck their target. The center tank went up in flames, then the second, and finally the third. The Mutants surrounding the base of the tanks were blown away. The surviving creatures were thrown into utter chaos and confusion. They scurried in different directions like frightened mice.

I watched the tank with Zeus inside go up in flames.

And I smiled.

Joshua, you deserved everything. You better not reply. If you do, that means our mission failed and you're still out there.

Otherwise, sleep well in hell.

-

Yared Prinz

Yared Prinz
Seer Commander

THE UNDERGROUND

LETTER 47

Joshua: XXIV

Shannon. Yared.

I didn't recognize the consequences of my actions until it was too late.

I dropped to the floor of the tank, heaving from the pain. I pulled the dagger out of my side. No venom secreted from it. That was in Aymie's body. *I can survive this,* I thought, cleaning my wound.

PH stood by the gunner in the tank. Seeing the gash, he asked, "What 'appened?"

I wrapped myself in bandages and commanded, "Order the men to fire."

PH's heterochromatic eyes widened. He looked at the men and shouted in Greek.

It wasn't what I wanted.

"I told you to fire," I spat through gritted teeth.

PH scowled. Without warning, he left hooked me across my face. I spun and fell to my knees. I felt a crack on the back of my head and I went black.

I woke up shivering in a field lit by hundreds of torches. I looked around to see hundreds of tents surrounding blazing campfires. I watched as people with burns, wounds, and disabilities gleefully prepared to settle down for the night.

I was in the Children of Anemoi's encampment.

I sat up, wincing at the pain in my side. I touched my wound and felt stitches. Four figures hovered over me: PH, Goliath, Solomon, and Diego the Monkey. I struggled to my feet. No one offered to help me up.

"What are you staring at?" I growled.

Solomon snarled. He gripped his staff and swung it across his body, hitting me in the face. Staggering back, I held my bleeding nose with my hand.

Diego leapt off his master's shoulder and clung to my head, tearing at my hair. I yelped and swatted at the creature. He ripped the glasses off my face and jumped to the ground. Screeching, he danced and snapped them in half.

Enraged, I bellowed, "What is *WRONG* with you?!"

Goliath crossed his burly arms and sighed. "Not us, Wolf. *You.*"

"Ya know what you did, right?" PH asked. He tried to sound sympathetic as if I was unaware of what was happening.

I held my forefinger and thumb a half inch apart. "I was *this* close to defeating the Resistance. *That's* what I did. You prevented my success."

Sadness swept over PH's face. I never saw that before. It caught me off guard, but I didn't loosen up.

"Wolf, I'm sorry," PH whispered. "You show no remorse. We can no longer trust you."

I couldn't believe what I was hearing. After all we went through.

PH was my best friend. We endured everything together.

How dare he betray me? His friend? His god? I thought, bitterly.

"What are you saying?" I asked.

"We're freeing the Children of Anemoi and leaving the Order," Goliath stated. "Solomon, Diego, and I are joining the Resistance. The two can live in peace, and I won't fear death by the hands of Xenophon any longer. I'll be reunited with my brother."

Gerrior... The one who was after the triplets for so many years. He was present at the battle, fighting for his freedom. I pieced two and two together. The two Ares brutes feared death.

"In time, I'll return to my family as well," PH confessed with a soft smile.

My blood boiled at their statements. They were liars.

Traitors.

"You're all going to leave me?" I snarled.

They shook their heads. "We never left you, Wolf," Goliath explained. "You left us. You betrayed us."

"This is your own doin'," PH added.

"*Whoever conceals his transgressions will not prosper, but he who confesses and forsakes them will obtain mercy,*" Solomon said firmly.

I gritted my teeth. Their accusations weren't angry. They were sad. It infuriated me.

They *pitied* me.

"I don't need to ask for forgiveness," I spat. "I do what I am ordered to. I never once thought for myself. I always did what people asked. You're going to leave me for *that*?"

PH sighed. His freckled face was crestfallen. "Wolf, mate. You were on a difficult path for a long while. But please, look and see what you've done. If you surrender now, maybe you'll receive forgiveness. Maybe RRPR will take you back. Maybe they'll give you a second chance."

My face burned and my fists shook. "'*Maybe*'?" I bellowed. "After eight years, all I get is a 'maybe'? Well, how about this." I rose to my feet, ignoring the excruciating pain in my side. I stepped forward and stared at my subordinates. "I'll keep 'spying' on the Moirai and the Order. If I feel like it, I'll return. I don't need permission. And I don't need their forgiveness." My eyes narrowed. "I will *never* ask for it."

The three looked at one another. Despair filled their faces. I was enraged. I didn't know what was so wrong. I always did what I was told. I always delivered. I never asked for anything. I didn't understand their feelings.

I was blind to the fact that I became the very thing I sought to destroy.

A tear trailed down PH's freckled cheek. Shock and surprise filled me again.

I betrayed him a second time.

"You'll never ask for forgiveness?" PH choked.

His sorrow made Wolf infuriated. "Never," I snarled. "No matter what anyone says or does. I am in no need of forgiveness."

PH pinched his eyes shut. "Then, you've chosen your fate."

Before I knew it, Goliath's fist cracked against my jaw and I crashed to the ground, unconscious.

I woke up half naked and staring at the sky. Stars glistened from the heavens, but they didn't shine for me. I lay across cold stone, surrounded by tall Greek pillars. They weren't as pristine as the ones in New Greece. They were ancient. I noticed that all the structures were. Then, I recognized where I was:

Olympia, Greece.

Rolling over, I hissed at the pain in my side and tried to sit up. I struggled but realized it was no use.

I was tied up by thick red thread.

My heart pounded and a lump caught in my throat. I was a spider in a web. *What is happening?*

I felt heavy footsteps shake the ground. I watched Emel approach with a smug look on her face. Tucked under her arm was an electronic tablet.

The one I use to send these letters.

My face paled as she knelt down and gently stroked my bruised cheeks. "You're all banged up, Wolf," she clicked her tongue, "such a shame. You know what else is a shame?" She pulled out the tablet. "This right here."

"What is that?" I asked as calmly as I could. My act failed me. Wolf faded and Joshua returned. The ruthless Zeus within me disappeared like the shadows of night leave with the sunrise. Only this time, the sun was not warm. It was red hot and burning my—Joshua's—insides.

She scoffed. "Wolf, you know very well what it is. As do I." She placed it down next to me. Her dark gaze stabbed my heart like a million knives as she snarled, "I've always known, *Joshua Wolfrum.*"

My name coming from her lips punched my face. My eyes burned and my throat tightened. "No…" I gasped.

"Oh yes. Not much happens without me knowing. You think your secret frequencies could hide your letters from *me*?" Violently, she yanked me up. " I chose to protect you instead of killing you."

I tried to ask why, but no words escaped my dry lips.

"You know my sisters and I fight. Like everyone, they know I am the most powerful. I am the one who should be in control." Emel leaned in and whispered, "I needed someone to take the fall. I needed someone to break down the Order so that *I* may build it up again as I please. You did that perfectly, but now you're useless. No need to hoard trash. I plan to do things *my* way now."

I choked on her words.

She used me… I was a pawn…

She loosened my bonds enough so my hands could grip the tablet. "I want you to send one final message before your thread is cut," she ordered. "Tell them 'this war is far from over. Lachesis has a new plan for the world'." A sinister smile spread across her face when she said, "'The Order of Xenophon will never die.'"

Before I could type anything, she hoisted me up and carried me over her shoulder like a child carrying its rag doll. I winced as my stitches ripped and red pooled out. Emel didn't care.

My blood spilling meant her triumph.

She brought me to the center of the archaeological site of Olympia. Flaming torches encircled a giant crater-like hole. It was so deep and the bottom was pitch black.

Emel put me down so I stood on the edge. One wrong move and I'd slip. On the other side of the pit stood PH dressed in his OX combat uniform. His green scarf covered his mouth and nose, but his heterochromatic eyes glistened in the firelight.

They were red with tears.

Out of the corner of my eye I saw the other two Moirai. They came over and joined their sister. I felt their icy fingers against my bare back. Their

nails dug into the Wolf tattoo that marked me. I winced as they etched an
O and *X* in my skin. Blood dripped down my spine. Then, they each took a
piece of the coarse string that entangled me and pulled it backwards. I felt
them tugging tightly, causing me to stagger.

Three hands shoved against my bleeding back. Gravity grabbed me and
yanked me forward, but it didn't pull me down… yet. The ropes cut against
my bare skin.

I glanced over my shoulder to see the Moirai pulling me backward. I
was leaning over the edge, but not falling. I couldn't stand myself upright. I
had no way of regaining my balance. I peered down into the pit. I watched
rocks bang violently against the sides and disappear into the blackness. I
didn't hear them hit the bottom.

I clutched the tablet in my hand as tears slid down my cheeks.

The three Moirai tied their ropes to a pillar to keep me from falling.
They came and stood at my side.

"Titan Wolf, Zeus of the Order," Arata began, "in the name of
Xenophon, we hereby sentence you to death on account of treason."

Emel leaned closer. I felt her hot putrid breath on my cold face. "Write,
you lying scum," she snarled.

The three watched me as I wrote this letter. Tears trickled down onto
the tablet, cleaning it of dust. When I saw my reflection in the shiny glass,
I recognized the monster I became. My dark eyes were filled with lies. My
scarred face lost its innocence. My heart ached as I thought about what I'd
done.

I betrayed you all.

I didn't help stop the suffering. I encouraged it.

I write this letter to you with utter sorrow. For eight years I worked in
fear of failing you all at Resist, Rescue, Protect, Retake. I only wanted good
to triumph. I only wanted to make you proud. I wanted us to live in peace.

I now undid everything I worked towards.

You gave me three chances to say sorry, but I turned down every single
one.

I've never been so regretful in my entire life.

The Moirai have disappeared behind me.

My time has come.

"I, Clotho, sentence you to death."

GAH! I'm falling forward. They're cutting my thread. I don't have
much time.

Shannon, Yared, everyone at RRPR and all the Isle members. I am so
sorry.

"I, Lachesis, sentence you to death."

I failed every one of you. I hope that the sacrifices you endured will bring peace for years to come. I hope that something good will come out of my death.

"I, Atropos, sentence you to death."

I pray that one day, you can forgive me.

With sorrow,

Joshua Wolf

Joshua Wolf—

...

TRANSCRIPTION PAUSED. AUTO-SEND TO BASE.

...

SENT.

EPILOGUE

Shannon: XIV

The following letters are written for those who found these testimonies after the fact.

Joshua Wolfrum—better known as Wolf—perished due to his own faults. However, the work he conducted before his demise is noteworthy. Before temptation and torture overtook him, Joshua was a good man. He aided project Resist Rescue Protect Retake and the Interpreters in fulfilling their purpose: destroying the Order of Xenophon and bringing peace to the world.

It's been three years since we received Joshua Wolfrum's final transmission. That last battle left holes in all of our hearts. My fiancé Shane, his brother Mark, their father Marcellus, and all of us grieved the death of our dear Aymie. I lamented with the Hodginses. My dearest sister-in-law. She loved so much and wanted the best for all. At least she is at peace with the man she loved the most: Blake Bain. Our secret Weapon. The man with a gift from God.

The one who saved us all.

My soul aches at the fact that we couldn't give them a proper farewell. But I know that Aymie and Blake see what's in our hearts. I believe they're watching us from heaven, holding hands and happily reunited.

The five remaining Isle members—Aaron, Sami, Lucas, Axel, and Yared—suffered gravely. They lost much when they dedicated themselves to RRPR.

But none of it was in vain.

Earth started anew. A world without the chaos of the Order of

Xenophon. Virginia Michaelson and her Interpreters across all continents are aiding the released survivors. Together, they are rebuilding society.

As for Thomas "Marcellus" Hodgins, he made it his duty to travel from country to country helping where is needed and reporting back the progress. This is no different than what he did in hiding. Now, he does it freely and communicates with his sons every day. His family was broken enough. Every day he thinks of his beloved daughter and wife. He continues his work in remembrance of them and to keep the world safe for his boys. From his most recent report to Shane, the rebuilding has been going well during these three years.

My father, mother, and siblings returned to our old home in the United States to live without fear. They visit the other Officers and myself frequently. Despite them being home, their work isn't finished. As a family, they dedicated their lives to rebuilding the USA alongside the Interpreters.

As for the remaining eight Officers of RRPR, we chose to go separate ways. We're still in contact, but it was about time that we built normal lives for ourselves. Although we'd never known normalcy. It'd be another adventure.

Myles Powell Junior reunited with his family and now runs Powell Enterprises alongside his father. The blond boy genius is in charge of the largest technological company in the world. At 22 years of age, he handles inventing and distributing equipment to Interpreters all over, aiding in rebuilding.

Sonny Wilcox left RRPR a week after receiving Joshua's final transmission. He knows the Order of Xenophon still lives even if the numbers are only 3. He's determined to track the Moirai down and fight them alongside his best friend, my brother Pietro Hollinger. I hope one day the two of them can return.

Nicolas Eerkens and Johanna Watterson—my best friend—married and settled down in North Dakota where the first RRPR base once stood. To honor Aymie and Blake, they've renamed the location Base Quartermane: the home where Aymie and Blake's love first kindled. Alongside RV Combatant Justin Thyme, the base has been rebuilt and new recruits are being trained. Aiding them in their mission are Goliath, Solomon, and Diego the Monkey. Goliath reunited with his brother Gerrior who was our captive. In fact, Gerrior, Jordan the Slowloris, Theo the Shrew, Brand, *and* Zander (believe it or not) turned their lives around to serve the new RRPR cause. They agree with Sonny that as long as the Moirai are alive, OX still stands. They refuse to take any chances. To be honest, I thank them all for carrying the torch.

Mark Hodgins will forever be a nomad. He spent five years with the Isle members. They've become his family now. He is a father to the five remaining orphans. Wherever they go, he goes. My platonic love for Mark runs deep and I pray one day he will find peace and happiness.

As for Shane and me, we finally settled down. We had a beautiful wedding in a newly built chapel on the Isles. Our hearts were heavy at the sight of many empty seats, but we refused to remain sorrowful. It was thanks to all of those lives that we could finish ours together. It was thanks to their sacrifices that I was able to look at Shane and say, "I do."

To those who gave all, I thank you from the bottom of my heart.

Before I seal these letters, I would like to pass the pen to Yared. He has a few things to share with you as well.

Godspeed and Goodwill,

Shannon Hodgins

Shannon Hodgins

THE UNDERGROUND

EPILOGUE (PART 2)

Yared: XV

Hello to all,

I'll be honest, I didn't think I'd get this far. Shannon passed me the tablet pen, and now I don't know what to say.

Shannon depicted our emotion and trauma after the battle pretty well. However, nothing can attest to the actual pain we experienced.

After the battle, the remaining Isle members, Keepers, and RRPR Officers went to the Isles to do something we've desired to do for a while:

Bury our friends.

My heart breaks at the fact that we could only bury two bodies out of the three. We stood amidst the tall memorials with the faces of our recently fallen friends etched in the stone: Ethan Shaw, Donald "Donnie" McArthur, and Alison Alexus.

The memorial service was when the pain sank in. We realized how much we had lost. The flowers laid across the graves were to remind us of their lives, but our sorrowful souls only remembered their deaths.

I forced myself to watch little Donnie's body return to the earth he loved so much. He was used, abused, but yet he proved his love and loyalty until the end. Donnie fought the Moirai with everything he had. Now, he is running amidst glorious fields with Marlene and Ava.

My eyes pinched shut as they lowered Ethan's body into his grave. My gut wrenched and my limbs quaked. He saved my life. My best friend. We were a dynamic duo in the field and back at base. Even though I never voiced it, I wanted our friendship to last forever. I hoped we'd each find a woman and start families. Our kids would grow up together. My children would learn to fight while his would continue to heal. I would have a Prinz army of Seers with a little army of Savior Shaws at their side.

But the Shaw name ended with Ethan.

Finally, Alison. The eldest of the Alexuses. The one whose success launched the Isles. She was our leader, our friend. Her motherly nature kept us going. She was always there for us. She inspired us to keep fighting. Alison vowed to never stop no matter the cost.

She paid the price and kept her promise.

Sami and Aaron held each other before her memorial stone. Their wails overpowered the crashing waves of the Isles. The four Alexuses were now only two. Alison left her twin siblings to keep their baby brother Jeremy and parents company until it was time to be reunited once again.

Axel the Bionic was beside himself. He cared for Alison. Ever since they were eight years old; he finally confessed when we reached the Underground. Bionics had a hard time expressing emotion, but Axel knew with every circuit of his being that he loved Alison. He wanted to make her happy. He wanted to make her whole again. He wanted to protect her.

In the end, Alison showed her love by protecting him.

Our sorrowful souls couldn't bear the sight of the memorials. Out of the Seventeen that started on the Isles, only six remained: Aaron and Sami Alexus, Lucas White, Axel Ramirez, Mark Hodgins, and myself—Yared Prinz.

After the burial, the RRPR members returned to the Mainland while we remained on the Isles for a few months. Mark stayed with us. We spent most of the time catching up with our Keepers and Director Stanley Wyght.

Our beloved Isles serve a greater purpose. Isle VI of Genetic Testing is a safe haven for *all* Mutants: Isle, Fallout, and Children of Hades. Those that survived the Order of Xenophon were brought by Clive Foxwood the Fox. He wanted nothing more than to reconcile for his sins. Together, he and Mr. Carl Mallory are working on a way to give sanity back to the Mutants starting with Dylan Cheatle the Bear and Adeline Zarra the Fruit Bat.

Dr. Damian Agro turned Isle II into the world's largest medical center. RRPR representatives Janelle Arends and Prince (who turned out to *definitely* be my dad, but I won't get into that) frequent the Isle for supplies and aid. The Keeper goes above and beyond. He does it all in honor of his fallen Savior students: Ethan Shaw, Zita Raneri, and Harold Spears. He even named the medical facility "SRS Center" after the three Saviors who gave everything to save others.

Mr. Cameron Allaway's heart broke at the time of Alison's death. He was at the battle. He watched her explode, and there was nothing he could do. He loved her like a daughter, but never got the chance to tell her. In her honor, he promised to never take *any* life for granted. He dedicated himself to aiding the disabled Children of Anemoi who shall live the remainder of their lives happily on the Isles.

One thing Shannon forgot to mention is where she is living now. She and Shane are living peacefully on Isle IV: Assets. The Isle where Marlene Best, Ava Conner, and Donald "Donnie" McArthur resided. The place where Marian Best—Shane's old supervisor—would have dreamed of living.

Together, the newlyweds became the Keepers of Assets. They run the farms, sew the clothes, and package the supplies with the help of the remaining Assets members. They ship goods to the Mainland and back again. She says they've settled down, but that doesn't mean they've stopped helping. Together, they work joyfully every day to honor the ones they loved and to give to those who need it.

As for Aaron, Sami, Axel, Lucas, Mark, and me, we were inseparable. We never wanted to be away from one another. We didn't dare try to start normal lives or find someone to settle down with. Our souls were too distraught for anything of the kind.

Although after burying our friends, we weren't sure what to do.

I remember sitting in the Library of the Isle III facility, thinking of what to do next. Normally, Mark had all the answers. This time, he didn't. Well, he acted like he didn't.

He wanted us to choose for ourselves.

Aaron and Sami were too full of sorrow to decide. Without their brother and sister, they had nowhere to go. Lucas became indifferent. He lost his wings and was now an earthbound man. He didn't know what a "bug-freak" like him could do now. Axel's heart was broken. He imagined a life with Alison. Now, he didn't know what to do.

I looked at each of their faces. They aged well beyond their years. We were teenagers with the experiences of old military veterans. We had the memories, the sorrow, the gusto, all of it.

All eyes looked at me. They wanted me to choose. I was the Seer. I was the General. I was the leader (excluding Mark, of course. He's Dad now.).

It was a difficult choice. I couldn't think for them, so I thought for myself. I had two options. I could live a cushy life on Isle V, leading a new army of Seers to work alongside the new RRPR. Or I could run back into danger as Virginia Michaelson's top Interpreter.

I chose the latter.

I never wanted to stop fighting. I told them that. I told them that our friends sacrificed so much. I felt like I didn't deserve to live a cushy life. Not with the Moirai still out there. Not with the possibility that everything might be undone.

I told them I chose Virginia Michaelson. I pulled the blue utility belt out of my backpack and put it on.

THE UNDERGROUND

The expressions on their faces were not surprised. They were not angry. They were not disappointed.

They agreed to join me.

It's three years later. I'm 21-years-old and a top Interpreter for Virginia Michaelson, fighting alongside Aaron, Sami, Axel, Lucas, and Mark. We travel across the world. We gather intel, we examine situations, and we report back. We've met with Sonny on occasions. He says he has gotten close and PH is leaving clues just as Marcellus once did.

PH wants to be found. The hunt is on.

Shannon and I have these final words for you. We know our lives will never be the same, but we have accepted it. Everything is in the hands of God. Even if evil remains, as long as there is good to fight it, there is still hope.

We are the lights of the world. No darkness will snuff us out.

Our stories live forever: Alison's, Sami's, Aaron's, Shane's, Aymie's, Mark's, Joshua's, Shannon's, and Yared's. Each of these members—all of our members—have unique stories to tell. Each has its own lesson, its own history, its own purpose.

Our testimonies are for the world to hear, so now we release them to you.

What will you do with them?

Bravery and Fidelity,

Yared Prinz

Yared Prinz
Top Interpreter | Isles Sector

THE END OF BOOK 3 OF
THE TERRA TESTIMONIES

Isle VI

Isle III

Isle I

"Left Lane Only"

Mark hates Math

Agricolae

Princess Playing Piano

WHYP

The Mainland

Time stops for no one.
Pictures help me keep those memories forever.
I never want a moment to pass by unappreciated.
— Blake Aleksander Bain

2 / 7 Hollingers

Shores of Isle III

View from NJ Base

During The Cleanse

The Underground

The Annex

The Resistance

Our Broken World

A Self-Portrait

My Gift to You

Photography by Blake

THE UNDERGROUND

Joshua's Reference Sheet

Hello Terran,

In case you didn't know, you are the Terran. You're a person of earth. That's our general greeting for Mutants, Humans, Bionics, and Xenophonian-psychos alike.

If you're an alien, I'm sorry. Don't be offended.

With Shannon and Yared's help, I (Joshua Wolfrum) compiled a list of terms, things, and people to know while reading our letters. This was mostly for my benefit since I've been out of the loop for a while, but Shannon said to send it to her with a greeting for a "Terran". I'm not sure what she's planning on doing with this, but I trust her judgement.

The next few pages were at the end of the first letter I sent. I hope you find the lists helpful, whoever you are.

With safety and secrecy,

Joshua Wolfrum

Joshua Wolfrum

TERMS

Accident, The - the first phase of the Invaders' (Order of Xenophon's) plan which included the destruction of the world and the slaughter and abduction of millions (also known as The Cleanse)

Agricola(e) - the farming/survival Branch of WHYP

Asset - the farming/survival sector of the Isles

Bionic - a human with enhanced biomechatronic prosthetics

BoMF - Bracelet of Many Functions (the Isle members wear these)

Cleanse, The - the first phase of the Order of Xenophon's plan which included the destruction of the world and the slaughter and abduction of millions (also known as The Accident)

Combatant(s) - military Branch of WHYP

Drone(s) - the weapons and invention Branch of WHYP

Godly Name - the name given by the Moirai to a Survivor turned Xenophonian

Interpreters - soldiers that focus on reconnaissance who are overseen by Virginia Michaelson

Invaders - what the Isle members call the Order of Xenophon (OX)

Isle members - the group of teenage survivors who left the Isles to aid RRPR

Isles - six islands founded by ex-Titans Nikita Patya and Walter "Wally" Jarvis who desired to raise armies to overthrow both the Resistance and the Order of Xenophon

Keepers - the men who are in charge of the Isles

Moirai - the three fates represented by three figureheads within OX

Mortal Name - a Terran's birth name

Mutant - a human Spliced with animal genes due to the experimentation of Carl Mallory

Nerd(s) - the hacking, computer, techie Branch of WHYP

OX - the Order of Xenophon

Pandemonium - normally preceded by a language (ex. English Pandemonium) and identifies a vast group of Xenophonians of all Divisions who speak that language

Polymath(s) - a Branch of WHYP that encompasses all the others and oversees their students

RRPR - operation Resist Rescue Protect Retake; a major resistance movement

Reborn - Survivors whose wills have been altered by OX

Resistance - general name OX has for their enemies

Royal Veteran (RV) - a high ranking member of WHYP or RRPR

Savior - a doctor from the Isles

Seer - a soldier from the Isles

Terran - a person of Earth

Titan - a General of OX

Umbrella(s) - the Branch of WHYP for those who have not found their talents or focus on helping the youth and betterment of others

WHYP - Wyght's Home for Young People

Divisions within OX

Ares - the military and assassins

Eros - chosen for selective reproduction and toys for high ranking Xenophonians. Nasty folk.

Children of Moirai - I don't know too much about them yet. Sonny said they control the signals and messages sent to the minds of the OX members

Hermes - members who scout, deliver supplies, train newbies, and bring messages to Xenophonians across the world

Sorry if some of these are vague or if I missed any. I'm still learning.

PEOPLE TO KNOW
9 RRPR Officers

Aymie Hodgins - Royal Veteran Polymath with a photographic memory, sister of Shane and Mark, and girlfriend of Blake Bain (CODENAME: PRINCESS)

Blake Bain - the Weapon that aids the strategies of RRPR with his precognitive dreams, boyfriend of Aymie Hodgins (CODENAME: REM)

Johanna Watterson - Royal Veteran and psychologist/counselor for the soldiers of the Resistance (CODENAME: DOC)

Mark Hodgins - Royal Veteran Nerd, R&D Isles Commander, master hacker, ex-Fallout (criminal gang) member, and "dad" to the Isle members (CODENAME: BANDIT)

Myles Powell Junior - Royal Veteran Drone, a child prodigy who excels in inventing, coding, and anything technical (CODENAME: EINSTEIN)

Nicolas Eerkens - Royal Veteran Combatant, Co-Director of RRPR, and Mutant Gorilla (CODENAME: KONG)

Shane Hodgins - Royal Veteran Agricola and an incredibly fast runner, skilled acrobat, talented musician/singer, and fiancé of Shannon Hollinger (CODENAME: ZIPPY)

Shannon Hollinger - Royal Strategist, eldest Hollinger daughter, and fiancée of Shane Hodgins (CODENAME: DETECTIVE)

Sonny Wilcox - Royal Fighter and ex-Order of Xenophon member aka Erik Patya (CODENAME: MARS)

8 Isle Members (excluding Mark)

Aaron Alexus - Research & Development (Isle III) Second-in-Command, Overlord, all around nerd, and twin to Sami the Cat

Alison Alexus - Bionic, Biomechatronic Testing (Isle I) Commander, eldest Alexus sibling, and girlfriend of Axel

Axel Ramirez - Bionic, Biomechatronic Testing (Isle I) Second-in-Command, boyfriend of Alison, and Argentinian sweetheart

Donald "Donnie" McArthur - Asset (Isle IV) Commander, youngest of the Seventeen

Ethan Shaw - Saviors (Isle II) Commander, a skilled doctor

Lucas White - Mutant Dragonfly, Genetic Testing (Isle VI) Second-in-Command, and proud Aussie

Sami Alexus - Mutant House Cat, Genetic Testing (Isle VI) Commander, and twin to Aaron the Overlord

Yared Prinz - Seer (Isle V) Commander, focused soldier, and the Isle member to write letters to me

Xenophonians

Goliath - Ares Member who I threw a rock at when he attacked Rachel

Leprechaun - Hermes Member, bartender at Lucky's

PH - Titan of the English Pandemonium (my superior) and the one to blow up RRPR's base

Solomon - elderly Hermes Member who has a monkey named Diego

I don't know any other Titans or Xenophonians at this point. I'm sorry; I wish I did.

Other Resistance Members

Agnes - sixth Hollinger daughter

Carol-Ann - fourth Hollinger daughter

Guy Vandewater - Royal Veteran Nerd of WHYP, blind as a bat, good friend of Mark and Thyme

Janelle Arends - Aymie's childhood friend and medic of the Underground

Justin Thyme - Royal Veteran Combatant of WHYP and Director Michaelson's right-hand man

Lucy - third Hollinger daughter

Peggy (Margaret) - second Hollinger daughter

Prince - Survivor of The Accident (aka the Cleanse) and PA to Janelle and Michaelson

Rachel - seventh Hollinger daughter

Rebecca - fifth Hollinger daughter

Stanley Wyght - Director of WHYP

Virgina Michaelson - ex-Royal Veteran Umbrella and now the Interpreter Director overseeing the Underground. Mostly referred to as solely "Michaelson"

These are the only ones I remember. To my RRPR and WHYP acquaintances, I apologize if I forgot you. It's been a while; please don't hate me.

Shannon said she shared a timeline with you. Hopefully that helped jog your memory. It definitely assisted me. I'm very grateful for her organization.

ACKNOWLEDGEMENTS

Fifteen-year-old me never would've guessed where "The Isles" would be today. I had no idea where I was going, no concept of book writing, and yet, I pursued it. I took the idea and ran with it, unsure if I'd hit a tree or something. It's been a crazy seven years, but now I can finally say it. "The Terra Testimonies" trilogy is "complete", but the story will never stop there. As long as there is a message to be shared, my hands will write.

However, none of this would be possible without the ones who've been there for me through thick and thin.

I want to first thank my inspirations for the Hollingers—my family: **Mom**—Thanks for literally everything. You've been my manager, editor, comforter, and guide. You've always picked me up when I was down, encouraged me, and helped me become better. I can never thank you enough. **Dad**—You've always supported me and been there to back me up. You've helped me carry my heavy loads at book fairs, manned my stations, and been my videographer. **Mary Grace**—I thank you for helping me with whatever hair-brained scheme I have and sharing my stories with your friends. **Therese**—Thank you for listening to my rants, being honest when I ask for help, and assisting me when you can. **Catherine**—My go-to-helper, my reading buddy, my IG photographer, my cashier, and everything in between. You're always willing to help and I thank you for everything.

Next, my betas: **Samantha**—My go-to-girl. The one who helped me start it all. Thank you for always being there for me no matter what time of the night it is. You're the one I can count on for support and help. Love you girl, and thank you for letting me throw a wig on you and make you my real-life Sami the Cat. **Ashleigh**—Axel's second-favorite girl (Alison beats you). Thank you for all of your love and support. Your enthusiasm encourages me to keep going and helps make my stories come to life. And your fanart of my babies will forever be one of my favorite things.

To my supporters on social media. There are too many to name. However, I want to shout out my #TerranTribe Street Team: **Ashleigh, Han, Carolina, Katie, Melody, Raquel,** and **Ashley**. You girls are rock. Also, thanks to **Adelaide Thorne**; my fellow Catholic Sci-Fi writer and the one to come up with the wonderful ship name #Shannark (Shannon x Mark) when reading book 1. (I'm thinking about #Shannannon for Shane x Shannon, but I think it needs work. Too many "annannannons.")

Also, to my cousin **Lauren**: Sorry for torturing you with the suspense of killing off a certain couple. I can't wait to see your reaction when you read the book (and this acknowledgement). I'm not sure if you're going to read this first, so I won't say any spoilers.

All those part of the #TerranTribe. My Terrans, you're all amazing. Your love and support keeps me going. And ladies, I promise. Mark will have more stories, and who knows? Maybe a nice girl will be involved.

And of course, to my **King**. The One who gave me life, love, and purpose. I pray that my books and their messages have made You proud.

I hope that my stories are more than words on a page. I pray you're inspired to always *Seek Truth*, *Have Hope*, and to *Stay Strong* no matter what life throws at you. You cannot fathom your own worth and importance. *"One person and their story is enough to change the course of history"*.

Together, let's change the world.

With truth, hope, and strength,

Sara Francis

Sara Francis

ABOUT THE AUTHOR
Sara Francis

Ever since she could remember, Sara Francis was always a storyteller. At first, she told them through music as a songwriter. In her early teenage years, Sara Francis felt called to tell stories through work as a writer and media communicator for an online magazine.

From there, everything fell into place.

Now, Sara Francis has a Bachelor of Science in Media Communications and a Master of Science in Instructional Design & Technology, is the author of several books, and is a speaker/presenter. Throughout it all, there is always a story she is trying to convey. Whether she tells them through her writings, art, or music, her stories always have a deep, truth-filled meaning behind them.

Every word she writes, everything she designs, every song she performs means something more and connects with the world we live in today. Through her work, she hopes to inspire people and encourage them to seek what is true.

Sara Francis is determined to light a torch in the darkness with the desire that people will do the same and make the world bright again.

Check out her website:
www.Sara-Francis.com
Follow her on Instagram @SaraFrancis_Author

Visit Sara's website and sign up for her newsletter to receive exclusive updates, resources, and short stories within "The Terra Testimonies" universe!

More Information

The story will never be over. Sara Francis has already started to write more short stories and novellas for "The Terra Testimonies" universe. She also is working on other publications. Be sure to stay in touch!

» Visit Sara Francis' website for her other books, updates, services, study guides, character art, and more: **www.sara-francis.com**
» Want to read more? Visit Sara Francis' blog for writing advice, author interviews, and short stories of the characters in The Terra Testimonies: **www.sara-francis.com/blog**
» Follow Sara Francis on social media:
  » Facebook:@sarafrancisauthor
  » Twitter: @sfrancis_author
  » Instagram: @sarafrancis_author
  » Visit the author's site to subscribe to her YouTube channel!
» Any questions or would like to book Sara Francis for an event or workshop? Contact us at **info@sara-francis.com**

Author Request: If you enjoyed the book, please be sure to tell your friends, share on social media, and/or leave a review on Amazon, Goodreads, or any book review site!

CPSIA information can be obtained
at www.ICGtesting.com
Printed in the USA
FSHW011719180920
73855FS